ISBN 978-1-333-68508-9
PIBN 10535515

1 MONTH OF
FREE
READING

at
www.ForgottenBooks.com

By purchasing this book you are eligible for one month membership to ForgottenBooks.com, giving you unlimited access to our entire collection of over 1,000,000 titles via our web site and mobile apps.

To claim your free month visit:
www.forgottenbooks.com/free535515

English
Français
Deutsche
Italiano
Español
Português

www.forgottenbooks.com

Mythology Photography **Fiction**
Fishing Christianity **Art** Cooking
Essays Buddhism Freemasonry
Medicine **Biology** Music **Ancient
Egypt** Evolution Carpentry Physics
Dance Geology **Mathematics** Fitness
Shakespeare **Folklore** Yoga Marketing
Confidence Immortality Biographies
Poetry **Psychology** Witchcraft
Electronics Chemistry History **Law**
Accounting **Philosophy** Anthropology
Alchemy Drama Quantum Mechanics
Atheism Sexual Health **Ancient History**
Entrepreneurship Languages Sport
Paleontology Needlework Islam
Metaphysics Investment Archaeology
Parenting Statistics Criminology
Motivational

MAN AND NATURE
ON TIDAL WATERS

BY

ARTHUR H. PATTERSON

ASSOCIATE MEMBER OF THE MARINE BIOLOGICAL ASSOCIATION
OF THE UNITED KINGDOM

WITH THIRTY-ONE ILLUSTRATIONS

METHUEN & CO.
36 ESSEX STREET W.C.
LONDON

First Published in 1909

TO

MY WIFE

AND

MY NATIVE TOWN

I DEDICATE THIS BOOK

258465

"I love all waste
And solitary places ; where we taste
The pleasure of believing what we see
Is boundless, as we wish our souls to be :
And such was this wide ocean, and this shore
More barren than its billows : and yet more
Than all, with a remembered friend I love
To 'row and then be rowed' :—for the winds drove
The living spray along the sunny air
Into our faces ; the blue heavens were bare,
Stripped to their depths by the awakening north ;
And, from the waves, sound like delight broke forth,
Harmonising with solitude, and sent
Into our hearts aërial merriment."

SHELLEY

AUTHOR'S NOTE

THE kind reception given to my three previous East Coast books has emboldened me to add another volume to the series. I make no apology for its appearance. My chief reasons for publishing it are that I may interest others in the wild life and unique characters of a delightful corner of East Anglia, and record traits and features that ere long must be greatly altered or wholly lost.

I have added many new incidents and impressions of birds and other creatures, and as far as possible I have dispensed with dates. Many of the characters introduced will be new to my readers, and those whom they may have met with before are accredited with entirely new facts. Alas! since the publication of my other volumes, some of the poor old fellows, whose sayings and doings I have recorded, have been gathered to their fathers or have drifted into obscurity.

ARTHUR H. PATTERSON

IBIS HOUSE,
  GREAT YARMOUTH

CONTENTS

LIST OF ILLUSTRATIONS
IN THE TEXT

xiv MAN & NATURE ON TIDAL WATERS

LIST OF PLATES

THE KEEL (AN OBSOLETE CRAFT)

MAN AND NATURE ON
TIDAL WATERS

CHAPTER I

IN WINTRY DAYS

" Where, from their frozen wins, mute springs
 Pour out their river's gradual tide
Shrilly the skater's iron rings
 And voices fill the woodland side

 . . . . .

And gathered winds, in hoarse accord
 Amid the vocal reeds pipe loud."

LONGFELLOW

PUNT-GUNNING

JANUARY, 1909, went out on the wings of the north wind. The thick rime frosts of several successive days had disappeared, when the westerly wind veered round to the nor'ard, from whence snow-clouds came up and whitened the marshlands, speckled the red-tiled town with blotches of fine dry snow, and then freckled all with a parting sprinkle of hail that stung the face like storm-driven shingle on a stony beach.

B

The boom of punt-guns in the morning announced the arrival of troubled wild-fowl, and the sharper crack of the fowling-pieces told of the harassed cripples and restless shore birds. These sounds were heard at intervals in the afternoon, when I strolled along Breydon Walls. It was no pleasant ramble ; the walls were gluey and slippery after the slight thaw ; the grasses, shaggy and ragged, were bent and soaked with melting snow, and the wind, rushing in with each snow-squall, took the breath away if one attempted to scramble along on the top of the walls.

There is always born in one a vigorous feeling when, wrapped to the ears and fitly clad, one looks out into the wild, with a past squall blackening the southern sky, and another sweeping, streaky, whitey-blue blizzard bearing down from the far north, shutting out the distant, and then the nearer landscape. Like steam it looms up, and then thick, like a fog. Then the blast strikes one with the first thin sprinkling of snow ; the wind roars across the water, creasing the dark, drab, up-rushing flood-tide with white, vicious waves, that break on the walls with a noise as of the sea.

During one of these squalls two amateur punt-gunners were blown on to the lee-walls, coming in broadside, but by great good luck striking against some fish baskets that the gale had blown *over* the flats. The big grey-painted gun, which I recognised as having been through the hands of several old wild-fowlers of my acquaintance, swung in a reckless fashion as the waves broke on the port side, flinging spray in drenching showers over the luckless gunners. When the squall had spent itself, they wisely made for home, as all fine-weather sportsmen should do when Breydon is troubled and angry.

All nature seemed unhappy. As I came on to the walls from the town, chaffinches flitted about the marshes in that fitful way they have in stormy days. A few redwings and fieldfares disconsolately hunted around and among some fresh-cast mole heaps, vainly hoping for some grub the moles had over-looked. Dunlins and a few knots flitted in an unsettled sort of fashion above the half-submerged vegetation on the " rond." Finding no footing there they dashed across Breydon, making for the beach. A few bunches of mallard and wigeon, whose ranks had been thinned in the morning, still kept trying to settle on the flood ; but were repeatedly " put up " by some gun-punt whose strange behaviour before noon might have taught them caution.

Along the walls, close wrapped and vigilant, four or five shore-gunners were spread, eager for snow-squalls which sometimes bring duck, mallard and coots, within range of their guns. One man obtained two ducks this morning and was out again in search of more.

When chatting with aged gunners I have been impressed by their dogged adherence to the belief that the winters of their earlier days were "harder " and more protracted than those experienced now-adays : no amount of arguing will persuade them that long severe spells of snow and frost were the exception and not the rule. Then, too, they forget to take into consideration the absence of a close season at that time gave them opportunities to shoot without restraint into large flocks of wigeon that came, as now, from March to early May. Large bags might be made almost every year, if it were not for a watcher. Let a sharp spell of wintry weather set in for a few days in December or January, and it is astonishing what numbers of fowl—duck, mallard, wigeon, and "hard-fowl," *i.e.* scaups, pochards, tufted ducks, golden eyes—will rush in from the northern seas or from the broads, where even now in open winters great numbers of duck resort.

That distinguished winter visitor, the goosander and his kindred "sawbills" are almost sure to turn up in lesser or greater numbers,—but never numerously, in snow-time. This species is very rare here in full adult plumage, more especially the male. Hardly a winter goes by but one or more is seen suspended with other aquatic birds in our market-place; and in what are known as "goosander-years," several are killed and in most instances thrown away as unfit to eat, one or two immature birds in a collection being considered more than sufficient. In these "goosander-years" small parties fish in company, as many as twelve and fourteen have been observed together; half that number, however, is more frequent, consisting probably of family parties.

A few years ago two punt-gunners, "Pintail" Thomas, and Beckett, went up Breydon, in the former's punt, in search of prey, their especial quest being a party of goosanders, consisting of seven birds. With characteristic obstinacy Thomas's aged weapon refused to explode the cap, misfiring no less than three times, to the huge indignation of Beckett, who had a good supply of adjectives ready for such occasions. The birds were so remarkably tame that they drew together into a more compact bunch, merely turning their heads as if to inquire what was amiss, and then slightly scattered again to fish. At the fourth trial the gun went off, killing two, and wounding three. My informant Quinton, who was in a punt hard by, gave me a lively description of the exciting chase that followed the picking-up of the dead birds. The wounded ones dived and swam under water with the speed and ease of grebes; like fish, they darted here and there, baffled now and again by the shallowness as they neared a flat. One bird Quinton detected swimming under water in his direction. It went under his boat, and then a chance shot from his gun stopped its career, and the poor hunted thing came to the surface where it floated dead.

I confess that to-day I never can hear these stories of slaughter without feeling strong repugnance, interested as I am in hearing of the endurance, cunning, and prowess of the old gunners. In my "unregenerate" days, however, I would inflict the same torture on defenceless creatures as these men did; gloat over a parcel of little bodies lying with feet drawn up and heads and plumage wet and bloody; and knock a wounded bird on the head in order to place it alongside them. I suppose the love of sport is a legacy left to many of us by our stone-age ancestors, who slew to keep themselves alive. The best of us, who still delight in the flesh of once-living animals, excuse ourselves because we do not see the pain and torture inflicted by civilised butchery. Perhaps we try not to think of it.

"Old Stork," the father of three other "Breydon Storks," was a calculating gunner. Once when Breydon was frozen over, he broke and kept open a "wake," which became crowded with coots, golden-eyes, tufted ducks, and others. He fired his punt-gun at a hungry, half-tame parcel of two or three hundred, killing and wounding a considerable number. He proceeded to gather up the dead and all the sorely wounded he could get at, and then set off over the ice, pushing his punt ahead of him, after those that fluttered broken-winged and otherwise partially dis-abled. The ingenious old rascal had fitted some small wheels under his punt, and would run her about with the ease and grace of a costermonger's barrow (1) Many of the less-wounded cripples dived under the ice, a few going some hundreds of yards and coming up in the main channel. Some failed to get clear of it and were drowned, while others became attached to it. When the thaw caused a break-up, and the tides carried down the floes, dead birds were found floating among them or fastened by their feathers to the ice.

Only one or two of the old punt-gunners who knew "Squire" Booth survive; "Short'un" Page, Gibbs, and Jimmy Hurr are still living, but are aged and decayed. "Pero" Pestell used to delight in relating his reminiscences of the great collector.

PUNT-GUNNER LYING AT FOWL

PUNT-GUNNER PICKING UP FOWL

" He used to hire me or Gibbs, or—well, he gave us all a turn, and paid us well: but he allers insisted on being put on to birds, and for any birds what he got as he wanted badly, he'd think nothin' of chuckin' down a good English sovereign as a sort of—what-you-call-it?—thank offerin'.

" 'Pestell,' says he, one day, 'I'm wanting a good grey plover.' And we was all on the look-out for one. We never made much more 'an a shilling of a really good black-breasted one to the stuffers, and hardly that off the game-dealer.

" 'There's one,' I says to him one morning, ' a splendid black 'un over there,' I says, pointing him where it was running on a flat. And off he goes. I see him kill the bird through my glasses. I see him no more for several days, and had all but forgotten it ; but one day he comes rowin' by.

" 'Hallo! Pestell,' says he, 'I got that plover ; but I haven't seen you since to pay you for it. Hev a drink!' and he actually hulls a sovereign into my punt. He *was* a good 'un ; and though he wouldn't give a thank for the rarest bird you might take him, he'd pay up like a banker if you put him on to it if it was ever so common."

Personally, I am not enraptured with the ponderous death-dealing punt-gun. There may be excitement attendant on it, and there may be profit, but there is little sport, unless butchery be the essence of it. I have never been in a punt to see one fired ; but I have seen big guns fired many a time ; and to see a " lane " cut through a flock of birds has produced in me feelings quite the reverse of those which must possess the user of so atrocious a weapon. As recently as the last day in January, 1909, I watched through my binoculars a big-gun approaching a parcel of five duck and mallard, on the other side of Breydon, a full mile away. Foot by foot the punt, sculled by a gunner lying almost prone on the bottom-boards, drew up to within striking distance ; the fowl, alert and restless, bunched and swam ahead. Moment by moment death seemed creeping nearer to them, when, fairly alarmed, up and away flew all five of them, the gun immediately after belching forth fire and a coil of white powder-smoke. What that man and his companion (for another man had been crouching in the punt) said, I can only conjecture. Had they read my thoughts, and known how my pity for the birds was greater than my hopes for their success, I fear they would have exhausted their vocabulary of East Norfolk expletives.

I remember how, one bright September afternoon, a flock of thirty odd curlews, some of them fine old females with long mandibles, alighted on a flat a few score yards above me as I lay moored against the decaying timber of the old *Agnes* in the ship channel. I was watching their playing antics as they turned the *zostera* over with the tips of their mandibles, seeking hiding shorecrabs. Now and again one straightened a wing, and stuck out a leg in stretching ; now and then one yawned. They piped in a low comfortable key to each other, and gossiped as they trotted to and fro. It was altogether a bonnie sight—these seven and thirty quaint, grey-feathered, blue-legged birds of the moor and mudflat.

The thought of danger never entered the heads of the happy things.

A gun-punt glided past me, its occupant lying low, with his right hand mechanically working the scull thrust out astern and his eye glancing along the barrel of his gun. Presently he drew in his hand, placed his forefinger upon the trigger, and elevated the muzzle to the deadly level.

"*Boom !* " roared the fowling piece, and a "lane" was cut through that flock of curlews, shot cutting through neck and wing, body and leg, while stray ones flung up mud beside them. Away went about two-thirds of the birds, screaming and terrified, one or two dropping as they crossed the flat. Nearer lay some nine of them killed outright; three or four, with smashed wings and broken legs, looking mere bunches of mud-bedaubed rags, struggled on their sides, or ran, with wings hanging, across the flat.

The gunner might have thought me a madman had I commented adversely upon his "great good luck"; but who gave him the right to slay those beautiful birds? And had I not as much right to lie there watching their happiness as he had to spoil theirs and mine?

Quite recently I watched a punt-gunner from an opposite point of view. I had been to my old house-boat, to fetch home the blankets and cushions before the winter frosts made the cabin ceiling trickle with moisture. I had had half an hour's mushrooming, and had crept up the walls to get into my punt. Peering over the walls I saw a parcel of grey plovers, about a dozen in all, feeding on the edge of a mud-flat some hundred yards away. Two were washing their already clean plumage in the shallow water—bathing for the very fun of it. Beyond them, three hundred yards or more away, a gun-punt was being slowly sculled up to within gun-shot. I squatted in the grass, my forehead and glasses only being above the level. Now, I had never been in front of a big gun before at firing time, and for once I decided to risk it. It was foolish, no doubt. Presently I saw that the gun was within range, and the gunner preparing to fire, the muzzle pointing, I thought, a little bit to the left of me.

"*Boom !*" rang out the gun, as it vomited forth nearly a pound of double-B shot, smiting six of the little migrants, which fell dead without a struggle. One shot hit my punt, and fell into the well. Two or three swished through the grass beside me, and one or two whisked overhead.

I felt sorry for those poor little things ! A few minutes later forty others flew in from sea, and I fear they also fared badly, for they were, I have no doubt, mostly young birds of the year, the earliest flocks of their species travelling southwards on the easterly winds that begin blowing in September.

DECOYING

Since the advent of close seasons, sportsmen of the humbler sort, who are now debarred from harassing wigeon that drop in upon local waters in March, and who are not allowed to prowl around in search of flappers in July, have felt much aggrieved with those wild-fowlers whose longer purses give them facilities for shooting on the protected broads.

" It's like this," remarked one man, with emphasis and anger, "there's one law for the rich and another for the poor. These 'ere gentlemen hire a bit of shootin' on the edge of a broad, and are unmuzzled by your blessed Protection Acts. The fowl what breed there are knocked over afore they've got their full flights, and nobody outside have half a chance.

" Even the fowl what come over from abroad at the beginning of winter drop in there, and there they pops at 'em unless a very sharp frost shuts up the broads; *then* perhaps a few flocks come to Breydon, and give us a chance. Even then them gentlemen's keepers row about the broads and keep the wakes open, and there we are again.

" Then them decoys, I wish they'd freeze up to the bloomin' sky ! There the fowl drop in in hundreds, and there they meet with bloomin' butchers. We ain't got half a chance."

These are the feelings and the attitude of shore and punt-gunners; and when I have dared to hint that, in the days when decoys were more generally worked, and fowl were harboured more abundantly through being fed there, there were greater numbers of fowl for other sportsmen, they pooh-poohed the idea. Nevertheless such was the case however remarkable it may seem. Mr. Christopher Davies[1] states that, when the Ranworth decoy was worked, fowl were much more plentiful in that neighbourhood. Since then it appears to have been commonly accepted by the local flight-shooters that the giving up of the decoy "was a bad job" for them. So silently and skilfully were the decoys worked, that while a few score birds were being inveigled into the nets, and others were having their necks wrung, hundreds would be sitting on the water within a stone's throw, entirely ignorant of what was going on.

This was exactly the condition of affairs when, early in January, 1909, I accepted an invitation from the owner of Fritton decoy, to run over and see the decoyman exercising his unique calling. There had been a sharp frost for days, and the lake had become frozen over, save here and there where a "wake" or clear space in front of the pipes had been kept open by the keeper.

"I fear you've come too late for this frost," said the sturdy young decoyman as I walked up to the lodge door. "If you'd been here a day or so ago, before the thaw came, you'd have seen me capturing two or three hundred in a day! However, we'll have a walk round now you've come if you feel disposed ; but I'm about sure the fowl won't work."

The decoyman loosened from its kennel the brown retriever that acted as a decoy. He then

---

[1] *Norfolk Broads and Rivers*, pp. 160–161. See also Davies, *Experiences of Decoying*, pp. 160–173.

picked up a piece of dry peat from a heap in a shed, and went into the house to light it, for it was deemed essential that the human scent, so quickly detected by the wary fowl, should be overcome by fumes that did not appeal to their imagination and instincts. In a rat-proof shed into which I peered, I saw a live drake tufted fowl which was destined to adorn a northern park, in company with any other " tufts " and wigeon or rarer waterfowl that might be taken.

The dog slunk in our tracks like a shadow. He had visions of chunks of bread, with which he always associated this trot round to the nets. Only the cry of a spotted woodpecker, the jarring notes of a jay, and the distant squabbling of rooks broke the silence, save the far-away crow of some startled pheasant and the softer pipings of the fowl on the lake. Coming to the labyrinth of wide trenches cut deeply into the soil, we walked in a stooping position, careful not to stamp on any twig. The ducks quacked in gossipy tones to each other, and occasionally we heard the whistling of wigeon.

" Look you through there! " whispered the keeper, pushing a thin wedge into a screen of reeds, turning it, and making a convenient hole. Through this crevice a goodly company of duck, mallard, and wigeon, could be seen, many paddling in the black water of the "wake" that wound away between the ice from the decoy-pipe into the broad. Pairs and small bunches sat preening themselves on the ice-edges ; while processions of coots beyond strolled across the ice in Indian file, searching for likelier feeding places.

Peering through another screen we saw half a dozen fowl feeding beneath the great arches at the front of the pipe. Then we passed through more trenches, walking softly on the pine-needle carpet covering the sandy soil. The third pipe showed odd birds feeding on the Indian corn strewn within upon the bottom, under water; others had settled comfortably on the ice or in the wake for a short afternoon nap.

"Look you!" said the decoyman, "they've winded us." And slowly, but with more than one suspicious turn of the head, a duck and a mallard paddled out into open water. I noticed that the turf was no longer smouldering. "They won't work, I'm afraid," he added; "but I'll see if we can't get those that are *in* the pipes."

I noticed that the decoy-pipe was very much like the half of a funnel cut longitudinally. A series of hoops ran in from the mouth of an artificial creek cut slightly on the curve. The mouth of the pipe was about sixteen or eighteen feet wide, succeeding hoops running smaller until the last one was only just big enough for a man to creep through. The hoops were covered with large-meshed wire-netting. At the small end a "tunnel net" was fixed; this was made of hoops covered with cord-netting very much like an angler's keep-net laid on its side. The first hoop was fixed to the end of the decoy-pipe, the extreme end being tied to a stake. Screens of reeds, placed obliquely, ran from the "cod-end" of the net, halfway down the outer sides of the decoy pipe. These screens were high enough to render unpleasant

ENTRANCE TO DECOY PIPE

stooping unnecessary, and they were connected with lower screens over which the dog jumped. All the openings between the screens looked *up* the pipe. In a small wire enclosure a lively decoy duck was kept.

From behind my peep-hole in the reeds I could see without being seen. I saw that the dog was exceedingly eager—for a bit of bread ; and no sooner had he jumped one barrier, and come back over the next, than he opened his jaws ready for the thrown morsel. He scampered over one barrier after another ; but the ducks, although turning their heads, refused to be decoyed.

Ducks usually betray much curiosity over the decoy dogs' manœuvres, and with outstretched necks they follow him eagerly ; but to-day they were obdurate. We did little on this occasion ; the dog and decoyman did badly—I did worse ! for being overcome by curiosity, I peered behind the screen looking *up* the pipe, forgetting that there were scores of fowl *outside* it. With a roar of wings and many a frightened quack ! up flew fifty or sixty fowl alarmed at such an apparition.

"Did you show yourself?" asked the decoyman, who was wringing the necks of three or four mallard, which had been feeding well up the pipe, and which had been driven into the tunnel net.

"I think I must have done so!" I replied, smiling.

At the next pipe we did a little better, but even then the fowl would not work. The dog was tried, but without avail ; and nothing remained but for the decoyman to show himself to a few duck and mallard that were feeding well into the pipe, and frighten them into the fatal cod-end. I managed better this time, and let only one scared mallard pass me at a rare rate of speed. Once he struck the net above, and fell nearly into the water, but he saw his opportunity, and dashed out. The decoyman had by this time lifted the first sections of the tunnel net and turned it over, shutting in the wild struggling birds. The hoops he pressed inwardly, as one shuts up a concertina, and bird after bird, as fast as he could lay hold of them, came out in his hand, to be quickly slain and thrown in a heap on the turf.

I tried my hand at a "kill," placing my thumb against the vertebra, and my fingers above the bill as he did; but my first attempt was a failure, and must have been painful to the poor doomed bird.

"No," I said, "you do the rest, for I shall only bungle."

And he "did" the rest neatly and quickly, as only a trained hand can.

Directly each one's neck was wrung it was thrown on the turf, to struggle, without pain or feeling, while the blood was centreing itself in the fracture; and then it stiffened out and died. It was a weird sight to see the broken fowl jump and squirm for a while with the head hanging like a broken reed-tuft.

We tried the succeeding pipes, until all four had been cleared of the ducks caught feeding in them, for not a solitary bird "worked" in from the broad. Our total capture was thirty-one duck and mallard, rather more males than females, and one male tufted duck, which I carried away alive, to become a companion to the little prisoner in the cage behind the keeper's house.

The keeper tied all the ducks into one large bunch and slung them over his back—a fairly good weight by the time we reached home. When we arrived at the well-ventilated "dead-house," he smoothed each poor dead thing, tucking its head under the right wing, and laid them side by side, duck and mallard alternately—rows upon rows, unruffled, beautiful as in life, not a drop of blood upon their perfect plumage.

The excitement that must attend a "good" day's working, when hundreds of fowl are captured, I can only imagine. It was my first acquaintance with decoying, and a novel experience. It was superlatively *interesting*.

WHERRIES AND WHERRYMEN

Without a Norfolk wherry upon the canvas, no picture of peaceful Broadland would be complete. It is at once the most picturesque sailing craft in use for trade purposes, the most graceful in lines and general contour, not to say the swiftest and most manageable vessel to be seen on inland waters. The white-winged sailing yacht—the butterfly of the waterways—does not look half so much in keeping with the green marshlands as the gaily-painted wherry, with its huge, high-peaked, tanned sail. It thrills one when skimming along upstream in a little punt to see her bowling ahead on the shimmering river, the cloven waters bubbling and hissing on either side of her clean-cut bows, her huge brown wing bellying before the wind, and having such a spread and a "way" on her that she seems to sweep everything before her. Even in baffling winds she makes headway slowly but surely, as she creeps along by the weather shore, her sheet close hauled, slipping ahead through "scanty reaches" to save an awkward tack; or, may be, tack she must, and then how petulantly that great wing flutters and flaps until she feels the wind again. Should the wind prove altogether contrary or fail her, the skipper plunges the toe of his long pliant quant into the bank or the mud, and clapping his shoulder to the head of it, presses her forward, walking the length of the plank-way with bent back and straining muscle until he nears the end. Then with a quick pluck the quant comes to the surface, and trailing it behind him, he repeats the vicious dig, and once more pushes the wherry on her way. It is slow, toilsome work, sometimes continued for hours together, the wherryman at every stride watching his vane to see if he may throw the quant along the hatches to rush to his sheet and tiller.

Old B——, a characteristic son of the marshes, towy-headed and bushy bearded, stood in the well or stern sheets of his dingy old wherry, toying with his stumpy clay pipe. His craft was empty, and he awaited the return of the flood tide.

"What are you after now?" I asked him.

"Bricks," he replied.

"You haven't used the paint-pot lately," I ventured to say.

"No," said the old man, shaking his head. "She's like me, she's seen her best days. Time was when I was a triflin' bit sprucer and more kedgy,[1] but it's like us as with hosses, we gets old and foky,[2] and wore-out. So's the old *Stokesby Trader;* but I dare say she'll last my time out. And things is that harnsey-gutted,[3] in the wherryin' line, they 'ont stand tu't. Lor' when I was a younger feller she wor the smartest craft on the three rivers; I was allers paintin' and warnishin', and fussickin,[4] and fiddlin' around her.

"You might as well come into the cabin as keep jifflin[5] about on that moorin' stump. The missus is knockin' up a cup o' tea.

"Give him a cup, old woman," he added, as I followed him into the cabin.

"Now then, *what* is it you want to know about this old wherry? How old is she? Well, she wasn't a young 'un when I bowt her : she may be sixty years, she may be more—or less, though that ain't likely. She's done me a sight of work, and some hundreds of times hev I bin up and down river in her. I used to be a good deal in the corn-shiftin' line, and done a lot of other freightage—flour, coals, jineral cargoin' and all that ; but you see the railways hev cut us up so, and now them steam barges: look at 'em! You see N——'s steam wherry, loaden herself, and towing four and sometimes five great iron hulkin'

---

[1] Active.   [2] Unsound.   [3] Lean and poor.
[4] Pottering.   [5] Fidgetting.

barges, reg'lar ugly, biler-like tubs, too, they are, neither shape nor make, but holdin' twice as much as a ornery wherry. Then they can go aginst wind and tide. Drat 'em! They're spiling wherryin'!

"I wor tellin' you," he went on, "the *Stokesby Trader* wor once the smartest craft for miles around. I wor main proud on her. I've had no ind of painters, and these ere likeness takers, paintin' her or snappin' her in my time, and I allers fared to raise myself inches taller when I see her beautiful lines and curves drored in to the very life, as it might be, with me in the stern sheets with my old red tammy-shanter on. Lor, sir, what *can* lick a Norfolk wherry either for lines or the way she lays afore the wind stroming[1] along. Nothin' can touch her. They do say theer ain't her likes on any waters barrin' ours. She's *the* bird o' the broadlands, sure-*ly*!

"They do say our wherry is built on the very same lines as wor the old Danish ships what inwaded this country years afore Oliver Crumble's time—let's see, it was afore King Alfred, wasn't it? They called 'em the sea-kings, but perhaps you've read more 'an I hev; though I've heerd our parson trot out suffin about 'em. But I heerd as they hed lug-sails, or suffin like that.

"My old craft is fifty fut long, with a beam of twelve. She draws under three fut o' water, and more she ha'n't need, for the rivers well up—the Bure, anyway—are no pertickler credit to them as has the management of 'em. But still, we know pritty well in the dark where the shoals are. She's capable of carryin' about thirty tons. I once know'd

[1] Striding or pacing it.

a huge old tub, leastwise she was then a new 'un, as was built for eighty tons. They called her the *Wonder;* and so she was. We all used ter wonder how they managed her, and it worn't long afore we wondered what hed become of her!

"You know, of course, the hull of a wherry is one long hold; and this here cabin is a kind of junk of it partitioned off. It's cosy, anyway, specially when the doors is shet, and a bit o' steam coal is glowerin' in the grate. And you see the settles are comfortable enough for sleepin' purposes; you don't need fear rollin' out. The covering of the hold—the hatches—are very handy, and neat fittin'; you can lay the whole of the hold open by stackin' one hatch on top the tother.

" The hull is tremenjussly strong-built; all English oak, the ribs bein' solid and closely put together. She'd need be, too, seein' the whoppin' great tough pine mast, stepped well forrid, and the huge sail she's got to carry, while on the heel of the mast more 'an a ton of lead is bolted. And ain't it wonderful how easy that big bulkin' lump of timber is balanced on the tabernacle; why, with one fut I can rock it up and down, and one chap can easily raise it or lower it. We sometimes sail up close to a bridge afore we let go the sail, what has to be raised by the windlass swung in front of the tabernacle. I'd like to bust up some of them dratted little stone bridges through which you go scrapin' sometimes when the tide's up, till you gets a puff of brick-dust in your eye and use langwidge! We ain't hardly wherry's length out of the archway, afore up goes the mast again, the jaws of the gaff go slidin' up of it, the forestay is made fast, and things is all taut again.

"On a strong tide with a fair wind, seven or eight miles an hour the old *Trader* thinks nothin' of, and then don't make half the fuss a four-tonner yacht, or one of them pesky little motor launches do. And I suppose you know a loaden wherry sails better 'an an empty craft.

"Get upsets? not often, bless yer, and more we hadn't need. I've heerd of one goin' over and drownin' a score frolickers (which no doubt they *was!*), but that was afore my time. I've bin sunk once through bein' stove in on a stump on Breydon, and the Commissioners, who oughtn't to hev allowed it, had to haul me out agin, and make up for lost time and cargo. Of course, we carry a big sail, but we reef it accordin'-ly; and though we haint any partic'lar keel we go stiff enough, and there ain't no fear with ornery care. We don't hev but one sail, though we clap a *bonnet* on the old gal now and agin'—that's a strip we lace on below, to biggen it—and the sail goin' a bit higher makes it as good as addin' a tops'l.

"The life hard? Well, not more 'an you'd expect. We have a decent time in the finer months, though it's rafty at times, and uncomfortable in bad weather, and not over cheerful in snow-time. Anglers call us hard names at times, but the fules orter know moorin' in awkward places ain't to their own cumfit no more 'an ours. And when the rivers is laid, ice *is* a nuisance, because it can't be turned into money like it used ter be.

"I remember in days gone by what good old times we—well, I speak for myself—used ter have with the gun, for it was nothin' oncommon in autumn and winter for ducks to 'light in the river; and a nice plump mallard worn't to be sneezed at when dinner was on the way. I've shot a goose or two in my time, and goosanders. Once I copt an avocet; and 'tworn't many year ago when old G—— shot that glossy ibis, up there by Acle, as it stalked about on the mud at the riverside."

"Netting?" I ventured.

"O yes," he frankly admitted, "I've done a bit of it; for, like the birds, I could allers get rid of half a ton of fresh-water beauties, and more if I could get 'em. They wasn't so particular *them* days; but you mustn't tow a boat astern nowadays or the bailifts is wantin' to know what it was built for and that; and now nettin' is a missdemeaner, a feller can't afford to risk his credit for a risky quid. Old Colby can tell more about that little game than I can. Wherryin's enough for me nowadays, without spicin' it with a bit o' sport, though wherryin,' as I said afore, ain't what it wor. Still, I suppose it'll be a long time afore we're altogether run off the road, so to speak; and a fleet of wherries waitin' against the quayside on the west of the river, nor'ard of the haven bridge, is a sight that still delights yer eye; and there is sights nowadays, with all your fancy shows, as 'oant come up to a fleet of 'em startin' on the early flood. Aye! and ain't it a stirrin' one to see 'em careening afore the wind cuttin' acrost old Breydon?

"Well, if you must go, you must, and I think as

how I might be under weigh myself, for I see the
tide's a-makin'."

.   .   .   .   .

When the trawling industry flourished in Yarmouth, and hundreds of smacks went in and out
the harbour, to and from the North Sea, much ice
was a necessary part of their paraphernalia, both for
accompanying the freshly-taken catches into the ice-
room, and for the better preservation of it when
taken out of the cutter and hurried into trucks at the
quayside for the inland markets. Ice-houses were
then an institution, but they are now obsolete. Quite
a brisk competition existed amongst local wherrymen, whose eager crews, with ice-picks and pole-
nets (dydles), toiled up the rivers by night and day,
filling their holds with the clattering cargo, or quanting
energetically down stream to the ice-merchants ; for
from ten to fifteen shillings a ton as remuneration was
not to be trifled with.   The busy scene at the quayside
as sturdy lumpers ran up the steep ladders to the ice-
house door, laden with baskets of ice, or as nimbly
ran down, sliding their empties on the railing, was a
sight to be remembered.
   " I remember some years ago," said " Short 'un "
Page, " gettin' into a nice scrape up at South
Walsham.   There was 'Lucky Bob,' old John
Edmonds, ' Spunyarn' Thomas, and a couple of
others.   We went up with two wherries arter ice, and
as a stall-off,[1] a few fathom o' reeds.   When it got
duskish, t'others got out a net, and we all went ashore.

1 Excuse or blind.

I was innocent enough, thinkin' they'd got leave, and of course, jined 'em. We didn't get much, but, howsomever, somebody was a spyin' on us, though we didn't know it. Well, we'd hed a smoke and a yarn round, made up the fires, and turned in, bein' nice and warm, and as cosy as you wanted to be.

"Presently there was a knockin' on the hatches, and a scrapin' of feet along the plankways.

"'Hallo! there!' somebody shouted.

"'Hallo! what's up?' hollered 'Lucky Bob,' rubbin' his eyes and hullin' the door back. A bull's-eye was turned on us. We all pretended, of course, to be asleep and snorin'.

"'Come out on it,' says the superintendent of police. 'Come ashore here,' he says, 'we've come to arrest you for night-poachin',' he says.

"He'd got ten or eleven keepers and chaps with him to help him, and we see the game was up, and hadn't a chance, not half a chance even. Then they slips the snips (handcuffs) on us; but we declared we wasn't going to walk, they might carry us if they liked. So they gets a carrier's cart, and up we clomb, I handin' back my snips, sayin' as how they worn't no use to me, my wrists and hands bein' so small. They laughed, in course, knowin' *I* couldn't do much without help, let alone with it. We laid in Acle lock-up all night, passin' the time on larfin' and yarnin' and that.

"In the mornin' they got a magistrate in Blofield, and took us afore him, givin' us another ride for our trouble.

"'Well,' he axes, pretendin' to be sympathetic,

'what have you got to say for yourselves?' after all the rest had swore this, that, and the other.

"'I'm innocent,' I says, 'so far, thinkin' my pals had got leave. That's all, yer honner.'

"Then one and another told *their* tales; one had had no work for weeks; another had jist come off a sick bed; and one had got fourteen little children.

"'What have you to say in extennywashon?' he axes 'Lucky Bob.'

"'Well, your honner,' he says, 'I'm very sorry. I thought a few common fish mightn't be such a great loss to the rivers and broads, seein' how many a angler catches more 'an we got with his one line alone, hullin' 'em on the banks to rot and be a nuisance. A few fish would have fed my little 'uns.' And he gets out his handkerchief, and begins to blubber that natural—well, bor, I a'most felt like cryin' alongside him. The magistrate blowed his nose, and hardened his heart.

"'What fam'ly have *you*?' he axes, eyein' Bob up and down.

"'The missus is jist laid up with the twenty-fourth!' says he, moppin' his eyes again. 'I'm werry sorry, sir; for their sakes it shorn't occur again. We hopes as you'll overlook it.'"

"Of course he did?" I jibed in.

"Not he," said Short'un. "No such good luck. He must ha' thought Bob was lyin'. So he claps on a £5 fine—*each!* mind you, but gave us time to pay it in."

In the "good times" of the wherryman, not so very long ago, there were various ways of earning "little extras" in addition to the freightage on stuff brought down or taken up the local rivers. Cargoes of ice, in the sixties and seventies, proved remunerative, and made up for losses of freights when the rivers were hard frozen. Those wherries which got ice-bound up the river, had nothing to do but wait for a thaw that might or might not be weeks in coming.

Old Colby, my cripple shrimper friend, in his younger days, besides going trawling and drifting, had his spells a-wherrying.

"Oh yes," said the old chap, when I introduced the subject, "ice worn't to be sneezed at when there worn't nothin' else to be had.

"I once went icing 'long with Hicks (he's bin dade this ten year). Ice was rather scarce on the river, but the broads was laid. We got up as far as Ranworth Decoy.

"'Look here,' I says, 'here's our chance.' So he shoves the wherry jist into the broad, and starts scoopin' it in. Presently up comes the keeper and axes what we was adoin' of.

"'Tryin' to earn a honest shillin',' I says. 'Things is mighty slow—the missus and kids a'most starvin' for a bit of brade, the poor missus bein' very onwell.'

"'You must get leave from the house,' he says, bein' half persuaded. So to the house we went, where two old maids was living. Knowin' Hicks had got an oilier tongue than I had, I says to him, 'You'll do the talkin'.' But afore we went, we jist slipt into the nearest pub and axed the landlord to set us up with a small bit of blue ribbon. He gave us a bit without much axing, being good costumers, and I pinned it on his coat, to look as if we was at least decent chaps. The only thing I feared that he'd be like enough to do was to let out a blaggard sort of word onawares, or onbeknown, becos it came so natural to him. He wor a pretty promiscuss talker.

"They has us in, and we makes our bow, bein' as solemn as if we was goin' to a execution.

"'Beg pardon, ladies,' he says, 'but we're two respectable men, summat hard up, b—bloom—blessed hard up, too.' (I thought he was goin' to make a thunderin' hash on it, and I 'h'ms,' and nudges him.) 'You know, ladies,' he says, 'God sent the ice,' says he, rollin' his eyes, but not too much, 'for our good. They couldn't use it, didn't want, perhaps, an' all the better for them. Sure-ly they wouldn't stand in the way of two poor strugglin' men, anxious to do right, with fam'lies dependin' on 'em.'

"That told on 'em like soap. They gave us permission prompt as anything, tellin' us that we might come agin perwidin' we allers axed leave. You may be sure we kept up our dignity-like, and thanked 'em tremenjuss. And we pritty sune had a wherry-load of ice on the way for Yarmouth. We jinerally made from five to ten shillin's a ton at the ice-house. Of course, that depended on supply and quality and that.

"Once we runned a wherry-load to Oulton Broad, and got through with it to the smacks 'lyin' in Lowestoft harbour. We sold two or three tons at

fifteen shillin's a ton, when up comes the ice company's bloke, havin' found us out. He went to the
smacks and told the skippers that if they persisted
in takin' it off us, they'd have no ice in summer, not
from them, when they most wanted it. So we had
to back out with more than half a load still in the
wherry. Them beggarin' ice companies with their
new-fangled ammonia-carbine-made stuff—what have
they done? Why, simply messed up poor men,
though I suppose if I was one of the company I
should sing a different tune. Lor, bor, we used ter
reg'lar look to earn, in them old hard winters, suffin
like twenty-five pounds and up'ards. But we don't
fare to get the winters now as we used ter, even if
ice-loadin' was a payin' game.

   " *Times!* ah! we *had* some rollickin' old times
up the river in them days. I remember when I was
a boy 'long with my father on the old *Enterprise*
wherry, trading to Wroxham, and up that way, in
1855, we had the master-piece of a frost you ever
know'd in your life—leastwise, I suppose you wasn't
born jist then. Winter set in in the second week of
January, what you call properly. It snew, and blew,
as it do sometimes after a great flood, for we had
a rum 'un in the first week in January. Why, the tide
broke through Breydon walls and carried away
hundreds of yards of railway metals—reg'lar scoured
'em out of their bed. Well, we got froze in this side
of South Walsham, and the ice got that thick, people
come skatin' up from Yarmouth and Norwich. A
thaw didn't set in till the last day in February, and
it was the fifth of March afore we got down and

moored at the quay-side, agin what's now Colman's wharf. They got froze in up at Reedham jist the same.

"I remember bein' froze up also in January—I think it was in 1871. I remember, too, seein' a orter (otter) killed on a rond by a feller shootin', jist previous to which another chap what was a skatin' copt hold of it by the tail, the duzzy fule, and, of course, the brute turned on him, and tore all his wrist with its teeth. The thing was over four foot long, and I made a guess as it weighed over two stone. You see, it got hard up for wittles, and had to turn its hand, so to speak, for suffin' else for a livin', and got to duck stealin'.

"I had some rare times with old Barber[1]—he's a rum pup, ain't he? a deep 'un. Folks has got to get up early in the mornin' to get the right side of him. One night, up the Norwich river, he got pounced on by a river watcher, who seized his nets aboard his wherry. His nets were drippin wet, and looked snydey, of course, though he'd washed the scales all off. The keeper demanded to see thc inside of the wherry, so Barber shifts two or three of the hatches. He'd been artful enough to fill her up with half a cargo of ice, which he'd covered all over a heap of fishes at the bottom of the hold.

"'Theer you are!' says Barber, 'why couldn't you believe what I told you?'

"Anyway, the keeper collared the nets, and took 'em with him, keepin' 'em a fortnight; but he'd still got his master to deal with. He couldn't bring a

[1] Barber died in April, 1909.

conviction aginst Barber, so he'd no right to collar his nets. Barber, cunning as a mouse-hunter, put in a claim for damaged nets, for they'd sweated and rotted! The artful old bounder!

"One rainy and blowy night I went with old Hicks (we was both younger then), got ahead of Barber's wherry, and fished all the best reaches, takin' the bulk of the fishes, to his awful annoyance, when he finds it out, you may be sure.

"One night me and old Bugles had made such a haul that we couldn't get the net out for fear of breakin' it; so we ladled as much as we could of 'em in with a hamper. We filled between twenty and thirty peds,[1] gettin' several fine carp and pike amongst the roach and bream. We sold the roach at eightpence a ped, and got a shillin' a ped for 'prime,' that is to say, the perch, carp, and pike. We got good prices in Lent, and as sure as you're alive, and can believe me, we've earnt as much as £3 and £4 a night."

"Where did they go to?" I inquired.

"Ah! now you want to know," said Colby. "Old 'Dilly' Smith[2] bought 'em, but where they went to, I don't know. We used ter watch the river bailiff into his house, see him go upstairs to bed with his candle, and then we'd actually net round the house. Another watchman who succeeded him wouldn't

---

[1] A ped is a hamper; a round basket with a lid to it.

[2] "Dilly" Smith was a noted waterside publican, who aided and abetted everything that savoured of poaching either by land or water. See *Wild Life on a Norfolk Estuary* pp. 329–330. The Jews in inland cities were the chief buyers of these fresh-water fishes which they ate on fast days.

peach on us. Why? Why because he worn't above sharin' in the bunce!

"Once when we was loadin' ice near Langley dyke we'd got fifty or sixty peds of fish in the wherry. We got a sound that the watcher was comin', and hurriedly filled her up with ice. When he boarded us there was too much ice stored for him even to suspect anything below it. But there they wor—fish. and nets, both under the ice, if he'd got eyes enough to see 'em or wits enough to suspect 'em. But he hadn't, and all the better for us."

.   .   .   .   .

Any one coming in contact with wherrymen for the first time would imagine them dull, obtuse, and positively boorish; but a closer acquaintance soon dispels this impression, and whilst a few may be uncouth and doltish, the majority will be found to be men possessing keen powers of observation, genial, if they think they can trust you, capable of looking after themselves either in a scrimmage or in matters of business, and ever ready to "do a hand's turn" for the yachtsman, or for each other, "if dacently civil" in return.

So recently as a quarter of a century ago quite two hundred wherries navigated these east coast tidal waters, and freights were plentiful enough. Then, as now, the towzle-headed, solemn-visaged wherryman delighted to decorate with bright blues, vermilions, yellows, and other striking colours, his hatches, mast-head, cabin-ends, and fore-peak. Gilt even added to the brightness of "Jenny Morgan," who held the narrow flag upon the vane. It was

D

only when grown old himself, like his wherry, that garishness faded, and when general cargoes, corn, billet, timber, and other clean loads gave way to coal and dirtier burdens. In the more leisurely days the voyage up or down stream was not so rushed as in these days of steam and struggle. Towards evening quite a fleet would moor beside some riverside staithe, near a public-house, where a boisterous night was often spent; and far too often a knavish landlord made it temporarily worth while for a wherryman to leave a ton of coal, or some deals behind him. The boards would be reported as fallen overboard *en route,* and other subterfuges invented to account for other losses.

Other "lapses from grace" were not unknown; but I have known honourable wherrymen who scorned to do a shady action. I was chatting recently with such an one who, after fifty years of faithful service, at seventy was thrown adrift penniless, although still hale and a better man than many in the prime of life.

"The steam done me, sir!" said he, with bitterness. "Them 'ere steam barges, with their lighters, some of 'em carryin' 120 tons, are doing the work of several wherries. Look go there (pointing to a steam wherry towing four heavily-laden iron lighters), them's as good as sixteen ordinary wherries knocked clean out!"

Noah Nicholls is one of the drollest wherrymen I ever met—a quiet enough fellow but full of dry humour and yarns of other days. His present avocation is that of a peripatetic book-seller; his books

and magazines, of every conceivable order and condition, are purchased at auction sales and by private
barter. Rarely a really good volume gets mixed in
with the mass of refuse literature spread upon his
barrow-board. The mispronounced names and the
subject matter described are often extremely funny,
for Noah is illiterate, goes much upon covers, and
often tells a would-be purchaser to feel "just the
weight on it!" However, he picks up an honest, if
often a very slow, penny; book-buyers laugh at his
queer descriptions, and charitably overhaul his wares.

For many years Noah pursued the wherryman's
calling; and he knows to this day every hole and
corner, every reach, every set of the tide of the whole
of the Norfolk and Suffolk waterways. He knows
each wherry by name and by its peculiarities ; he has
reeled off to me many of their quaint names. There
was in his younger time a *Pill-box*, a *Snipe, Rifle, Hit
or Miss, Beer-tub, Ginger*, and *Rat-cage*. The smallest
he ever knew was the *Cabbage* wherry, a tiny craft
built to carry four tons, whose owner always "worked
on the cross," and seldom carried an honestly bought
load. Griffin was the skipper ; a donkey supplied
the motive power when the winds were foul, and
often towed her along miles beside sedgy ronds.
Noah tells me that the earlier wherries were short
and broad, and drifted somewhat to leeward in
awkward reaches : they had not, as some have now,
a false keel that could be shifted or fixed. Wherries
to-day stand a lot of bad weather, and his favourite
old craft, a huge wherry (in those days) of eighty
tons, could be handled with great ease through her

improved build.   He once took in a lot of water that broke over her bows at the Narrows, near Berney Arms, and unfortunately his cargo consisted of bricks, which "sucked up" the water so that the pump was of no use.   To save her he had to throw a number of bricks overboard.

I tried to get out of Noah a few incidents relative to the morals of the wherrymen, but like most of the Norfolk watermen he was careful of committing himself.

He had incidentally told me of some most abominable frauds perpetrated on him by one of his owners—the then proprietor of the *Wonder*—who kept a public house, with the wherry as a supplemental venture.   It would seem that while he could trust Noah, he was ever on the look-out to cheat the skipper.   On one occasion, when Noah had taken in a cargo of some sixty tons of ice, while lying frozen-in at Oulton Broad, S—— (the owner) wheedled him ashore, and put his son aboard to navigate the wherry home, which he did ; and then clandestinely disposed of the cargo.   Now, as ice then fetched about twelve shillings a ton, and Noah was entitled to a third, it came hard on him to lose some ten or twelve pounds, and to take the four pounds offered him.   But Nicholls knew his man, as he did another man who sat drinking on a settle.

"What would have happened?" I asked Nicholls.

"That chap was a bully," replied Noah, "and I know'd S—— had knuckle-dusters ; in fact, I see 'em on the chap's fingers—he'd lent them to him. And he'd ha' used 'em if I'd turned up nasty; I wasn't takin' any, so I took the four pounds and chucked him."

It can hardly be wondered at that men who served under hard taskmasters should occasionally "get a little of their own back." But Noah, according to his own showing, was always a model of propriety.

"I remember one night," he went on, "I was layin' moored at Reedham, waitin' for tide and the mornin'. I had just turned in. My mate was asleep on the opposite settle, when I hears a gentle tap against the side of the cabin. Then some one rapped again.

"Openin' the cabin door, I makes out some one slippin' down into the stern sheets.

"'Any one 'long with yer?' he axes, in a low voice; then I know'd the voice. It was a chap pritty middlin' well off, who'd got a wherry of his own, but done a lot on the cross (dishonest dealing).

"'Only my mate, Ted. Why?'

"'Is he all right?' he axes, slippin' in, and lookin' to see if Ted wor asleep.

"'Go on,' I says. '*What?*'

"'Look 'ere,' he says, 'I can do with three ton. I'll put you right over it. S—— owes me quite that.'

"Now, I'd got a load of rattlin' good gas coal for Norwich what I took out of a barque lyin' at Yarmouth, and was the last wherry loaded that day, and consequently the hindermost.

"'My wherry lie a mile or two higher up,' says he; 'we can do it all right. I'll be there.'

"I didn't say nothin' to Ted, but a little later on

I gets the sail up, and, though it was dark, made ready to go. Then I wakes him up, much to his dislike.

"'What 'cher mean?' he axes. 'Why can't 'cher lay till mornin'?'

"'Help me round the next reach or two, till I get fair way on, and you may turn in,' I says.

"I know'd every inch of the river by daylight or dark. Just as I got abreast of the Cockatrice Inn, and was close to the shore, some one jumps aboard out of the dark, and I know'd it wor that fellow. Ted had gone below, and lay grizzlin' about the flappin' of the sail keepin' him awake. Now, I'd hoped to give the blaggard the slip. I didn't want to get mixed up in no dark deeds.

"'When are you goin' to stop?' he axes.

"'Not at all,' says I.

"'O ain't you?' he says, blurtin' out an oath.

"'Dare you touch the sail,' I says. 'If you do I'll hull you overboard,' I says, 'and go overboard with you, if I hev to,' for I could swim then like a duck; and I puts the helm over, and just touches the bank.

"'You're a —— fool!' he snorts, as he jumps ashore. And I wor glad enough to get shot of him. You never know who's eyes are about, even in the dark.

"I got to Norwich by the mornin', in front of some of the wherries what had started afore me. I'd got clear when one of the others comes up.

"A chap on one of the other wherries says to me, 'It's a rummen about "Scratch" B——,' he says, 'and that chap K——.'

"' What's that ?' I axes, kinder tumblin' to suffin'.

"' Why,' says he, ' K—— lighted on the *Royal Oak* (wherry) with a smelt-boat, and was takin' in coals, when a country policeman catches 'em both. He could hear the rattlin' of the coals into the boat.'

"I said nothin', but I thinks the more. Suppose it had been me instead of ' Scratch ' B——?"

"What did he get?" I asked.

"K—— got six months, ' Scratch ' got nine!"

Noah Nicholls, according to his own account, had no taste for river-poachers, although he, like others, probably, had come into close contact with them. I suggested this to him.

"Well, you see," said he, "I never cared for theer company because they're generally so fly; you may get copt, if you're a wherryman, and they get free. They'll lie through thick and thin that the fish in your hold was not their takin'; and unless they were actually seen, how's the police goin' to prove it?

"When I worked L——'s tar-wherry up and down from Norwich, he got kinder [rather] cross with me becos' I wouldn't give W——[1] (a noted poacher) a tow down, now and again. My tar-wherry you know, wor a steamer; and W—— used ter take my master a nice perch or tench now and again, or a basket of smelts. So he fared kinder friendly with him. I gave W—— the slip whenever I'd a chance, and he used ter tell L——, who stopped

---

[1] For reasons best known to myself I have suppressed the real name of this river poacher.

me earning a extry bob or two by pluckin' a yacht now and agin downstream, all through it.

"I worn't afraid of W—— though most of the wherry chaps was. I once lost a nice new quant, and suspicioned W—— as havin' snook it. I went round to his back yard and found it there. So I took it. He arterwards wanted to fight me agin the White Swan. I took him on and gave him the poulticin' he wanted—and more.

"Well, he once done me. I'd got a cargo of chalk (this was in another wherry). While I wor ashore for an hour at night, he got aboard, slipped the middle hatches off, and dropped pretty nigh half a ton of bream and roach into the middle of the chalk where it was hollow, you know, amidships. He axed for a tow down next mornin' lower downstream ; and seein' no fish in his boat, nor nets, I let him hang on. When we got down to the Bowlin' Green he ups and tells me what he'd done, and axes me to put in at the Green. Well, I was glad enough to do so to be shot of 'em, and as there was peds and boxes alriddy waitin' there, we soon got rid of 'em.

"He once rowed up to me at Cantley with two other chaps, and I tried hard to get shot of them. Somebody told the bailiff at Buckenham W—— was on the job ; and he got on the scent.

"The wind was easterly, and I sailed on to Coldham Hall. W—— followed me up, and told me he wanted to get on to Surlingham. He'd been fule enough to show hisself at a pub, and that's how the police got to hear of him. Well, I gave him

the slip again at Surlingham and got on to Norwich.
I'd hardly got my moorin's fast afore a policeman
and the bailiff comes aboard, and told me they
intended searchin' for fish or nets. They ordered
me to show them the hold, which I did ; they looked
down the fore peak.

"'Oh,' I says, pretendin' to be very innocent,
'there's some nets,' showin' them some ice-dydles.

"'Rubbidge,' says the policeman, 'you can't
poach with them.'

"'Then I've got nothin' else to poach with,' I
says.

"'Oh!' says they.

"'Now,' says I, 'if you'd know'd your business,
you'd have searched W——'s craft and not
mine!'" ...

Noah navigated a condemned fishing boat which
had been converted into a tar-boat, the whole hold
being used as a receptacle for tar-water, which
was brought down from Norwich to some chemical
works on the Bure. For some years he had a black
man, named Sambo, to assist him. The tarry colour
that clung to everything did not affect Sambo so much
as it did Noah, who, when the summer's sun bore
down with great heat upon him, suffered considerably.
Nicholls used to grope up some mud from the ooze,
and plaster his face with it to neutralise the burning
effects of sun and tar : this answered until the heat
cracked the mud. All the victuals as well as their
clothes reeked of tar ; the bread turned yellow : everything they ate was seasoned by it. But it was a
fairly well-paid job. One day Sambo lay down

on the hatches to sleep, and on waking found he was unable to rise, for his wool had become "glued" to the wood by the melted tar. Noah was in dire straits, for he had no means of freeing his mate from his unpleasant predicament. It was at length agreed that he (Noah) should put the craft to the shore, and then run to the nearest farmhouse for a pair of scissors. This farm was a mile away; and until Nicholls' return poor Sambo had to lie there patiently. It was the matter of a few minutes to clip Sambo from his awkward imprisonment . . .

As I have hinted, the wherryman's life is not all pleasure. There are adverse winds, tedious spells of towing or quanting, sharp frosts, gales, and drenching rains. Time and tide wait not for him, and he has to take advantage of both, no matter what the weather may be like. Rheumatics and asthma are not rare amongst our watermen; and they grow old early from hard work and exposure. Nor is the life without its dangers. A quant may break when pushing in deep waters, and unless the wherryman be a good swimmer, he may have no easy task in getting out again, especially if he be working alone. Frosty weather may make the plank-ways slippery, and death may result from a fall into the cold, sullen stream. "Death by drowning" is by no means a rare verdict in the coroner's court; and alas! only too often it has come out in the evidence that the poor fellow had been indulging too freely in what does not tend to the well-being of man in any walk of life.

But there is not a finer waterman then the wherryman. Long may he remain an "institution" with
us, for his gallant craft is an ornament to our
sluggish inland tidal waters.

RUFFS

LAPWINGS

CHAPTER II

ON GUNS AND GUNNERS

"He rises early, and he late takes rest,
   And sails intrepid o'er the wat'ry waste;
   Waits the return of shot-seal (flight-time) on the lake,
   And listens to the wild-fowl's distant quack;
   At dusk steers homeward with a plenteous freight."
                                   Life of a Fenman 1771.

GUNNERS IN GENERAL

CERTAINLY no person can be more fanciful in his choice of a plaything than a gunner; no one, unless he be sufficiently well-to-do to have a really good fowling-piece built to his especial liking, fit, and weight, ever appears really satisfied; and the chopping and changing which are known amongst gunners of my acquaintance to-day, seem to me really ridiculous. And then the awful weapons I have known! the very recollection of them makes my heart beat faster.[1]

I cannot say that I inherited a love of slaughter, for my father could never pluck up heart to kill a chicken; and those we kept usually died of old age, unless I undertook to be executioner unknown to him. My great-grandfather, a Highlander, carried his flint musket, under Wolfe, all through a long campaign, doing some killing, but getting not a solitary scratch in return. And my grandfather, in Napoleonic times, had been drafted into the militia. My father has related to me with gusto some of the adventures of his father, who loved not soldiering. At an inspection one day his flint lock refused to fire a blank charge, and before he could explode it command was given to load again. A second time it obstinately disobeyed the trigger, and yet a third time he added a full charge, on top of the two still in the barrel. On pulling the trigger at his triple loading, the flint ignited the powder. My grandfather was the only man who fell that day, but he was speedily helped upon his feet by sympathetic comrades, with a very sore shoulder and a bad headache.

My first weapon was a cross-bow, made at my urgent request by my ailing brother, a few months

[1] See *Wild Life on a Norfolk Estuary*, pp. 57–62; and *Nature in Eastern Norfolk*, p. 36.

before he died.   In imagination I slew more game and wildfowl with its weak projectiles than I ever did afterwards with deadlier weapons.

I have a distinct recollection of one day getting afloat in a Breydoner's punt which lay moored to the quay side.   The Breydoner's small son accompanied me.   The owner of the punt had foolishly pushed his loaded gun under the fore peak—not an unusual thing in those days—in readiness for use when he next visited the mudflats.   As we drifted upstream we were surrounded by large gulls ; and by a stroke of bad luck I discovered the gun.   It was a huge and ancient 8-bore, heavily charged; and without a thought of the consequences I lifted it to my shoulder. It exploded the charge with scarcely a touch of the finger, the gun knocking me all but senseless on the floor of the punt, from which I arose bruised and sore enough, glad to find my limbs and collar-bone unbroken.   We pushed the gun back to its hiding-- place, and said nothing about it.   But next day I got into hot water with the Breydoner, who had at- tempted to fire at two wigeon he had sculled on to after long manœuvring to get within shot of them.

My first gun, purchased after months of secret saving, was a noted weapon which had belonged to one Manthorpe, a great killer of woodcocks.   I kept it until I could afford a breech-loader, but added to my stock other old and more dangerous weapons. A great bright-barrelled 10-bore, purchased for a few shillings, and the muzzle of which was worn so thin that I could trim my nails with it, I dared not venture to use, until, having trebly loaded it, and tied it to a post, I marched to the rear some hundred and fifty yards, and exploded it by pulling a cord attached to the trigger. The report, magnified by surrounding walls, must have almost wakened the dead, for it was near the cemetery. It echoed and reverberated like the going-off of a howitzer. The only damage my great charge did to the gun was to wrench off the guard, which I replaced.

"Talkin' about guns," said old Billy Sampson, on Christmas Day, 1907, when I visited him as he lay almost helpless in his comfortless bed. "Talkin' about guns, I've seen a many of 'em used as wasn't only good enough for the scrap-heap. I can remember flint-guns, plug-breeches, and patent-breeches—and I'd done with guns soon after pin-fires come up. You remember *old* Jimmy Crowther ; he was an overlooker in the factory, and as a sort of hobby dabbled in guns. He reg'lar tinkered 'em up, and spoilt even bad 'uns. I had a big old Dutch piece, a plug-breech—a reg'lar hard hitter. All the gunners of my time knew it as 'old Closh,' for many of the old guns had names they was known by. The plug once blew out, and I took it to Crowther to make a new 'un. He made one, but split the barrel a-screwin' of it in : the screw was too big. He cut a piece off, and tried ag'in ; and split it with another ! The third attempt was successful, but he'd reduced the barrel by that time from thirty-six to thirty inches. And he'd spiled it ; for you couldn't shoot yourself with it—it wouldn't kill at all.

"Ah ! the guns I've know'd ! Well, you see, guns was dear in them old days afore breech-loaders comes up and knocks 'em out.   And there was feelin's of pride as there is now: gentlemen almost hulled muzzle-loaders away as bein' out of date.   It's just with poor men now as it was then, they'll get things as good as they can afford ; and guns that cost thirty or forty pounds to build got into their hands for a mere song.   But till then they'd swear by old 'Brown Besses' and Spanish muskets ; and rant about flints, and Joe Mantons, and rifled barrels, and pistol-stocks, and all that.   Now, of course, they want conwerted rifles and cheap Brummagem breech-loaders, as ain't a bit better than the old cast-iron gas-pipes of my young time.   Some of 'em had rare characters though, and got quite a reputation for their killin' powers.   It may be they wasn't so good after all, and possibly fowl was tamer ; they certainly was plentifuller in them days, and you could get right in among 'em.   Maybe fowl have grow'd artful.   One chap now comes to mind who was a crack goose-shooter.   He had a long old gun with a shank that weak and rickety he had to hold barrel and stock together with his left hand, while he pulled the trigger with his right.   He used ter work the Langley meshes (marshes) where geese used ter come, walkin' an old dickey and cart for a stalkin' horse.

"But there ain't anybody hardly nowadays around here as is anything more than hedge-poppin' amateurs ; nothin' only boys, what don't orter be trusted with guns any more than you could trust 'em with a next-door neighbour's cradle with twins in it.

"Some of them gunsmiths, as they called theirselves, wasn't worth a tinker's cuss ; they spoiled guns, and nothin' more. The only man worth callin' hisself a gunsmith was Hickling, on Fuller's Hill. He could make an old gun almost into a new 'un. Short'un Page's father (Page hisself is gettin' an old man now) had a flint-lock what shot three-quarters a pound of shot, what he (Hicklin') converted into a 'crack-patch.' She was a clinkin' little punt-gun. I remember one day old Thomas (Pintail's father)— 'No. 2' we used ter call him—got his gun so wet that it wouldn't go off; so he comes back and borrows Page's, tellin' him there was a bird or two on the Lumps—the last place, you know, to get covered. It was, in fact, crowded with birds, and Thomas went back and shot three maunds-ful (bushel-size) of godwits, knots, grey plovers, and sitera, all in proper colours—bein' May. She *was* a clinkin' little gun.

"Old Serjent Barnes—'patent-breech Barnes' they used to call him, was a proper gun-spoiler, and a tricky old villain into the bargain. He used ter doctor and do up plug-breech guns, filing a circle at the proper distance from the breech-end to imitate the juncture where the screw should be, then he'd sell 'em to muggs as patent-breeches, the old rascal!

"Accidents? Oh yes! I've know'd a many, such a rough lot of guns was sure to play hanky-panky now and again. 'Locket' Nudd—him as shot the first Pallas's sand-grouse—once loaded his cart with shingle on the beach, and then laid his gun on the top, for he generally took it on the beach with him. He'd got a brand new coat on. Just as he was going off, a fowl came by, and he snatched up the gun, which was down on

E

the hammer, and jarred it. The consequence was
it went off, blowin' a piece clean out of his collar,
the charge goin' within an inch of his neck. As it
was he'd a stiff neck from the powder-burns for a
whole blessed week!

"Tom Smith was out rowing one day on the
North river, with his gun under the thwarts, when
a hare comes up of the bank and sits lookin' at
him. He reached over for it, jarrin' the silly thing,
when off it goes, blowin' out the bows of the
boat. He'd a narrow squeak, too, of gettin' ashore.

"You knew 'Deaf' Hunt?" he asked.

I assured him that I did.

"Well, old 'Deaf' Hunt had a rattlin' good
breech-loader, and whenever he was hard up he
pawned it at M——'s. He must have been hard up
pretty often, for the gun was mostly at uncle's, who,
for a number of times, pulled it out of its case,
looked over it, and planked down the money asked
for it. He got so used to it, in fact, that at length
he'd take it, and hand over the money, without
examining it. One day it occurred to him that the
gun had been unusually long without bein' redeemed;
and the ticket had all but run out. So he takes
it down, and looks at it. Greatly to his surprise
he finds only a wore-out old muzzle-loader, what
was worth only as many shillin's as the other was
worth pounds!"

"Billy" himself was, in his younger days, no
mean sportsman, his favourite beat being the allot-
ments, or Bure-side marshes, whither he repaired
night after night for ducks at flighting time. His

practice was to take a bundle of straw with him for a "carpet," upon which he knelt or stood all through the bitterest nights, often coming home in the morning wet through and weary, but happy beneath a bunch of mallard, teal, and occasionally pintails or other ducks. His dogs, skilled in all the arts of fowling and chicanery—he trained dog after dog as the years went by—were of rare assistance to him,[1] retrieving the birds dropped on the marsh (for flighters often killed by firing at fowl whose positions they judged by sound alone); now and again adding to their master's gains the victims of others' guns. The intelligent animals would hear the thump of a stricken fowl as it struck the earth, and quietly slip round and retrieve it. How much training, and how much inherent love of wrong-doing had to do with this perfection of impropriety, I cannot venture to say.

This aged fellow has much interested me. There seemed something so superior in him, and so altogether different from the uncouth illiteracy of the class of men he had to mix with. He has had the respect of all, yet he has to an extent held himself aloof from them save in "business" hours. His nights, since he relinquished babbing and picking for eel-buying, have been spent in reading—a lone man ashore and afloat.

His father seems to have been a farmer in a big way, a gentleman-farmer in fact, who was reduced by an unfortunate law suit; indeed he lost everything. The family removed to Yarmouth when

[1] Vide *Notes of an East Coast Naturalist*, pp. 254-58.

Billy was five years of age, his father becoming a cattle herdsman. At that age "Billy" began to work, helping his father, and educating himself because he had no chance of going to school. He laughed and said he was a second David, who kept his father's flocks from straying off the common.

He had his first gun when he was twelve; he had learned to shoot with his father's before he could comfortably hold it straight. One day a man, who was much interested in the youthful "sport," saw a woodcock alight near a "low" (marshy swamp).

"Billy," said he, "go take your nets (bird-nets) home, and bring your father's gun. I'll show you where it is."

Off went the boy to his home, presently returning with the gun. The bird was flushed, but the boy missed it. Again he put it up, this time killing it.

"Good on you, boy!" said his admirer, "I'll take that cock; and I'll make you a pair of shoes in exchange for it." He thereupon measured Billy, and was as good as his word.

"They were," said Billy to me, "the first pair of shoes I ever earned, leastwise, with a gun!"

.   .   .   .   .   .

Where all the decayed guns come from, when a rush of snipe enlivens our marshes, or an unusual number of ducks are driven hither by heavy snowfalls and continuous frosts, it is difficult to surmise. I saw some remarkable weapons brought into use only as recently as September, 1908. The following "notes" which I sent to the *Zoologist* will bear me out in this respect :—

Incursion of Godwits. Not for at least eighteen years have so many bar-tailed Godwits (*Limosa lapponica*) put in an appearance on our Breydon mudflats as were observed during the earlier days of September. It was generally on the spring migration that this species was commonly looked for in the earlier half of the last century, when the "12th of May—Godwit day," was hailed by local gunners with considerable excitement. I have recorded (*Nature in Eastern Norfolk*, p. 237), where Gibbs, an aged punt-gunner, still living, saw in the early seventies, during an easterly gale, "hundreds of thousands" constantly coming from the south-west (inland direction). I have known many a May pass without any number, and sometimes without an individual being seen. The past May was remarkable for their scarcity. The prevalent winds were, I believe, southerly or thereabouts, and of no abnormal velocity, and what accounted for the incursion I am at a loss to suggest. I saw a large flock on September 7th, amounting to three hundred birds, feeding leisurely on a mud-flat, in spite of the incessant firing in various other directions, where smaller flocks were on the move —knots, redshanks, and whimbrel—to which at dusk an immense flight of terns were to be added, making Breydon exceptionally lively. Every lout who knew one end of a gun from the other obtained his quota of chicken-tame birds, which were mostly young and exceptionally fat. On the morning of the 7th, I accosted a shoeblack, who owns one of those "murderous" weapons—a converted rifle—whose face was bandaged with hospital wrappings——

"What have you done?" I asked.

"Oh!" said he, "the cartridge bust, and went off at the wrong ind of the gun; *but I'd got eight godwicks afore I done it.*"

There was no sale for the victims, the taste for shore-birds having become practically extinct in Yarmouth, where not even a game stall other than for *bonâ fide* game birds now remains since the death of Durrant, of some reputation as a wildfowler himself. Gunners mostly cooked their own birds.

.   .   .   .   .   .

In a certain small public-house, the Horse and Groom, much frequented by gunners, there met one night thirteen or fourteen of the fraternity to chat over past exploits. A bagatelle match was decided upon, and they retired to the warm little parlour at the back; some to play, others to criticise and to make merry. Presently in came a poacher-like ne'er-do-well, one Jessop, surnamed "Chair-bottom," from his more civilised calling as a mender of cane-seated chairs. We also knew him as "Jibro."

He had been out on the marshes with his gun, but with no success, and had dropped in for a drink and a warm-up, carrying his short-barrelled muzzle-loading gun in halves in the recesses of his pockets, a practice beloved of those who gun piratically.

Suddenly the barrel slipped through the worn lining of his coat, striking the floor, and a terrific explosion occurred, the cap having been struck in the fall. One end of the barrel hit the fender and rebounded to the other side of the place, to the consternation of the crowd in the room. When they began to collect their senses, to count heads and compare notes, they were immensely relieved to find that the charge of shot had gone clear of all the fourteen pairs of legs under the table and around it, and buried itself in the wall opposite to the fireplace.

"Dighton" Smith possessed a favourite fowling-piece that boasted no trigger; the hammer was always more than willing to smite the nipple of the gun, and always returned to it immediately it was released. So "Dighton" fastened a piece of cord to the top of the hammer, with a loop in one end, into which he hitched his thumb. When a bird had been sighted the thumb was withdrawn from the loop with a jerk, and the gun went off.

"Brusher" Broom had a big shoulder gun, for which he contrived a knee and swivel in his punt. He had taken great pains to design this combination. One day he laid at a brent goose in one of the drains, and fired.

"Good night!" he told me, "the gun went off, and I was pretty nigh blinded; and what do you think with?"

"No?"

"Well, with *powder* from the stock of the gun, which being so worm-eaten, had blown all to smithereens! only the barrel being left."

"Get your goose?"

"Oh, yes! as soon as I'd cleared my eyes of the dust, I see the goose lying dead on the water."

Broom, when working in a village a mile or so up the Bure, borrowed his employer's gun.

"I see the old gun," said he, "on one of the rafters, and asked the loan of it."

"Oh yes," said the owner, "but there's no hammer on it."

"We'll manage," said Broom, who, with a companion, went to a likely spot for a brace of partridges. Lying behind a hedge, they agreed to work together.

"We took a small hammer with us," narrated Broom, "and I says to my chum, 'When I say strike —*strike!*' I was to aim, while he was to hold the hammer in readiness. We managed in that way to kill four, by his *hammering* on the cap I'd stuck on the nipple."

The owner of the gun was puzzled as to how they managed, but as Broom said, "we'd got the partridges to show we *did* manage."

There lived in the town one Phillips, a pawnbroker. The old gentleman, when first I knew him, was past the prime of life. He had been fond of a gun, and a small window utilized for a display of weapons of all sorts and conditions, was filled with them just before the end of the close season. Some really good guns were seen there side by side with some really bad ones. If a man found a fowling-piece in an unhealthy condition, he would touch it up to the best advantage, take it to Phillips, tell him some plausible tale, and allow him to examine it—a proceeding which gave him unbounded pleasure, for he prided himself on his armourer's instincts. Tom Burton, a gunner, purchased a double-barrelled gun off him one night, and went up Breydon walls next day and shot at a curlew. The barrels and stock blew into fragments, cutting the old man's face in a shocking manner.

Very few accidents with large punt-guns have been recorded. I know of one instance, however, of a wildfowler discharging a punt-gun, when the recoil so jarred a shoulder-gun lying under the forepeak, that it flew backwards, struck the stock on a rib of the boat, and discharged its contents at the same time. Fortunately, the whole of the charge entered the rolled up sail, doing no damage whatever to the boat. In another case, a gun went off from a similar cause, the charge of shot on this occasion going through the side of the boat, an entirely new streak having to be put in.

A certain shooter possessed a double gun of very uncertain temper; the sere and one or two other internal parts of the lock had become worn and very capricious in action. The gun was an extraordinary killer, but after going for several days in a straightforward and becoming manner, it would suddenly refuse to do its duty, and on several occasions, even after its refusal had been accepted, it would, entirely on its own initiative, explode the charge in most unexpected positions. The barrel and worn stock did not work in perfect harmony, and a long strip of cloth had to be placed between them to save jarring. On one occasion Q——, the owner, fired at a large bunch of snow buntings, when off went both barrels together, knocking him upon his back in a dazed condition, with a great gash in his cheek. After that he sold the gun. " Jibro " Jessop was its next owner, and for three or four days got on nicely enough with it. He praised its killing qualities—in fact, "he'd never before had such a killer!"

"All right! Go you on and you'll find out yet!" said its late owner to himself.

Next time he met Jessop he saw him with his arm in a sling! So "Jibro" got rid of it, and it passed into the hands of a gunsmith, who provided it with some new fittings, and a zinc band round barrel and stock, which added to its safety if not to its appearance.

Two instances, equally alarming, in connection with these ancient fowling-pieces, occurred in smithies. In both cases the blacksmith, before undertaking to unscrew the breech, had been assured that there was no charge in the gun. It was the custom, in order to avoid the risk of injuring such highly tempered metal, to make the breech-end hot, and then screw it into a vice and carefully turn the barrel. With a deafening roar both of these guns exploded charges of powder while still in the fire; in one case the charge narrowly escaped going through an onlooker's body, the shots expending themselves on an adjacent public highway; in the other a wall was struck, and a brick broken, to be pointed at in future as a solemn warning.

Q—— had a curious knack of getting into close fellowship with bad guns and careless shooters. Once he went up Breydon with a "swell" gunner who was a remarkably clumsy person. He was continually "jiffling"[1] about in the boat, and persisted in sitting

[1] Fidgetting.

with the gun between his knees, to the great alarm of the rower. Q—— at length became so apprehensive, that he rowed to the shore and peremptorily ordered the man out of the boat, telling him that " If he wor game for payin' him for a day's *outin'*, it didn't come into the contract to blow his innerds out ! "

Another indifferent gunner, while in a market garden, took up a loaded gun, which had a very loose-fitting screw holding the trigger to the lock, the spring also being defective. Carelessly laying the gun on a radish-tying board, he essayed to screw the trigger tight by means of a flat-pointed clout nail.

" Good Gord ! " said Q——, " see where you're p'inting that barrel ! If that had gone off you'd have drilled a hole through me." He immediately sprang aside to a safe position, but not a moment too soon, for with a roar the gun went off, the shots going out at the door. Both men were greatly scared, and the offender would not handle a gun again for years.

It was Colonel Hawker, I think, who went into raptures over the flint-lock weapon of his time, and made an elaborate appeal on its behalf when he found detonating guns coming into the field. The same thing applied to the percussion gun ; there were those who upheld its killing powers as being infinitely superior to the breech-loader's. Personally, I liked the old muzzle-loader better than the newer weapon, and a single gun at that : there seemed to me to be more sport in giving a bird the chance of a miss. When I rose to the dignity of ownership of a double-barrelled muzzle-loader, and then of a double-breech, I very seldom fired the second barrel

if I missed with the first, for I felt that the bird
deserved to escape. Of course, it was a matter of
mere sentiment, and I frankly admit that I enjoyed
the excitement of loading a single-gun when there
was a possibility of a fowl coming within range in
the meantime. And although I exchanged the gun
for a pair of binoculars years ago, I still have respect
for the former, for did it not, in my younger days,
lure me out to study bird-life when otherwise there
might have been less enticement. I always went out
eager to meet with a duck, and while engaged in the
quest, I learned to *watch* the doings of many other
birds. I soon learned to look upon killing even a
duck as a regrettable if necessary incident. Like
Richard Jefferies, " I liked the power to shoot, even
though I did not use it." I confess to relishing the feel
of the beautiful laminated barrels in my hand, and
the consciousness of power a shapely, well-made
weapon under my arm gave me ; it was not merely
the killing that was alluring. But bird-watching
without a gun may become in time as attractive, and
it is a far less dangerous pursuit. But I should
write an untruth if I did not own to possessing a
liking for men with true sporting instincts, for many
gunners are capable observers, often with a stock of
interesting nature reminiscences.

The old flint-guns must have been exceedingly
trying, more particularly on stormy days, which are
often the most suitable for wildfowling. There lived
in the 'thirties a wildfowler who swore by his anti-
quated flint-lock. On one snowy, boisterous day, he
pushed his boat into deadly proximity to a vast

concourse of wild fowl—golden eyes, pochards, wigeon, mallard, and what not, which had gathered in a wake in the ice, tame and hungry, and indifferent to their own safety, as they will become when long frozen out. He saw visions of at least a bushel of fowl as he pulled the trigger. But there came no explosion, the flint was bad or the powder damp. The birds drew together and wondered. He pulled again, but the gun did not fire ; a third time he levelled his piece, with the same result. The birds, however, had had enough of it, and with a great rattle of wings they left him to his own devices. Chagrined enough, he turned the boat round and began to row home. At that moment he espied two fowl making towards him ; and as if by instinct, he raised his gun and pulled the trigger. This time it went off with a roar, and when the smoke had cleared, he saw one bird floating dead in the water.

There would seem to be no end to my reminis-cences of the local gunners of my youthful days. There was *old* Jex, father to " Saltfish " Jex,[1] who impressed me by his dirty, lazy, iron-constitutioned person, with his face all wrinkled, its lines being accentuated by the ingrained ooze that filled them. " Saltfish " pursued wildfowl while the nineteenth century was still in its teens. He possessed a flint punt-gun carrying a half-pound of shot ; it was so thin, worn, and frail from old age, that a rib had been brazed to the underside the whole length of

---

[1] Refer to " local gunners," *Wild Life on a Norfolk Estuary* p. 48.

it, as a precaution against possible bending by an accidental blow.

Jex always provided himself with a handful of dry cinders, which were carefully kept in a convenient and dry position in the punt. Should the pan or pan-cover get damp, he would chafe the metal with a dry cinder, until all dampness had been removed by the friction.

An acquaintance of mine, some years my senior, who was a noted *habitué* of Breydon, took his first lessons in wildfowling at the feet of this eccentric tutor. The gun was fixed to a knee that ran like an arch across the boat, which was like a Dutchman's scow, and more conducive to comfort than speed. The gun had no sights.

"Pint her *above* the heads of the fowl," Jex would say to his pupil, "and lose sight of 'em; she'll find 'em!"

My friend was by no means enamoured of this precocious weapon, which needed constant probing, to keep the powder inside the barrel in touch with the fresh supplies constantly dropped into the pan. He finally resigned his position as mate in this venture, when, after a shot at a couple of shoveler ducks (which he missed), he observed smoke issuing through a flaw—a "rust bite," near the end of the barrel.

"Silky" Watson,[1] whose prowess as a wildfowler survives to this day—he was an old man when I first knew him—had no equal as a gunner, if only half be true that has been related of him. He had a

1 Vide *Wild Life on a Norfolk Estuary*, pp. 61 and 99.

favourite and aged "Brown Bess" on which he set great store, preferring it to an ordinary swivel-gun. It stood six feet in height, some inches taller than himself; and he had perforce to stand tip-toe in the boat to load it. It was rammed with a steel rod, which announced its business by the bell-like clanging it made as it hit the barrel on either side. His contemporaries named it the "marsh rail."

He was observed one July day by a rival gunner, who was watching him through a pair of binoculars, to leave the shelter of the wall and push off after five young "flappers" that were feeding on the "grass." He had shoved for some distance with a "set" pole when the boat got fast in the grass. With a spider-like movement out went one foot, and he pushed ahead; but the water shallowed again, and out went his claw-like hands, on either side the punt, with which he once more sped her onwards, pulling at the *zostera*, and scooping at the mud. So squat had he laid, and so stealthy was his every movement, that he got within range and killed three out of the five fowl.

"Sell her!" the old fellow would say, "*not* me! No, not for a £5 note!" Such a killer she was, that he took no end of pains to preserve her. He had so anointed her with boiled linseed oil, that no rust could work from the outside through the numerous successive coatings. And far from despising her for her many frailties, he patiently unscrewed the lock with a small tool he always carried with him, after each time of firing, in order to replace the mainspring which tumbled out of place at each discharge

Watson's punt, like several at that time, was painted buff-colour in order to resemble, as much as possible, the Breydon mud-flats. She was narrow and exceedingly low-built, and she laid to the water like a frightened pintail-duck. To-day the favourite hue is lead-colour ; and instead of the cumbersome "beam"-knee, fastened with chocks, an iron structure, of a neat and improved pattern, is fitted to the few shaplier punts.

A long departed hero of the mud-flats was one "Granny" Reed, the progenitor of a race of wildfowlers, represented at present by a great-grandson—who, by the way, turns out the handsomest and most seaworthy gun-punts ever built. "Granny" followed Breydon until long past "the allotted span," in a buffcoloured punt with a bell-mouthed punt-gun, that had been converted into a plug-breech from a flint pattern. In his old age he sallied forth only on fine days, when young flappers had not yet learnt to be cautious, and of course long ere close seasons had been instituted. He always carried a whalebone gamp, probably as ancient as himself. This he opened to favourable winds, and moved leisurely to and fro, and shot from under it. Crowther had one day taken up his position [1] near a rond, when "Granny" came sailing up, and staked his boat out in the open, to the disadvantage of the other. An exchange of courtesies began :

" Come ashore, please, Mr. Reed, if you have no objection," said Crowther.

The old man grunted.

[1] Vide *Wild Life on a Norfolk Estuary*, p. 49.

"If you do not," went on Crowther, "I shall be under the painful necessity of *towing* you in."

Still no acquiescence.

"As you persist in your obstinacy," said the now ruffled man, "I shall most decidedly undertake to teach you manners." Whereupon Crowther pushed out, tied the old man's punt to his own, and rowed him back to the rond, the patriarch wildly gesticulating, like a Red Indian, his vocabulary having failed him. "Were you a younger gentleman," Crowther assured Reed, "I should feel myself justified in taking the law into my own hands."

He thereupon pushed the boat hard into the rond and staked it there, daring Reed to shift it.

One other departed worthy was Squire Berney, whose name survives in the tiny hamlet and the public house at the far end of Breydon, known as Berney Arms, a wild, desolate place in the heart of marshland.

Squire Berney sailed about Breydon in a strange flat-bottom craft, with a foremast and mizen, adding to her spread two jibsails. It was a sort of hybrid canoe-yacht. He had built for him an enormous swivel-gun, that belched forth two pounds of shot at a time. I cannot gather that he did much execution with this ponderous weapon, except that wood-pigeons found it "a holy terror." To use the gun on the land, he had a carriage built for it, so that it much resembled one of the long-range quick-firers one sees on board a man-of-war. He had a screen put up to resemble a hedge; an aperture was made in it, and the gun planted behind it. For days at

F

a time the ground in front would be baited for wood-
pigeons; and at favourable intervals, this "Long Tom"
would send forth its message of destruction through
their ranks.

THE SNIPE-SHOOTERS

Several of the old school of gunners of my
acquaintance, who were men above the average
hedge-popping order, pursued with ardour some pet
kind of shooting, or exhibited a keenness for some
particular species of bird. For instance, "Pintail"
Thomas,[1] the punt-gunner, was ever on the alert to
distinguish Kentish plovers, and eagerly scanned
each scattered flock of small waders for these handsome little fellows, which, he declared, "ran like
mice on their little black feet." Police-sergeant
Barnes, after his discovery of Richard's pipit on the
North Denes, in 1866,[2] haunted that locality for
years in hopes of procuring another. He was never
tired of telling of its points, behaviour, and the
manner in which he slew it. He was equally bent
on the slaughter of the shorelark, which used the
shingle patches above high-water mark, occasionally
in company with snow-buntings. Quinton[3] one day
had killed three or four shorelarks, when Barnes,
who had been breathlessly endeavouring to forestall
him, came up with him, and demanded to know what
he had shot. Quinton refused to tell him what he

---

[1] See *Nature in Eastern Norfolk*, p. 41.
[2] *Ibid.*, p. 126.
[3] See *Nature in Eastern Norfolk*, plate, and p. 77.

had in his pocket, and Barnes flew into an uncontrollable passion.

"Good heavens!" said Quinton, in narrating this incident to me, "I thought he'd gone off his dot (head); and when he shot hisself within a week after that, I congratulated myself on his not havin' shot me!"

Durrant, the game-dealer, during the latter years of his life, went to the seashore with a heavy fowling-piece, when strong easterly gales were blowing, anxious to secure his favourite prey, the brent goose. Then there was big Milligan, in his blue slop, who had spent years at sea, catching fish, and years ashore in selling the same useful commodity. He also ranged the foreshore on rough days, watching the passing flocks of gulls, desirous of finding among them stray skuas, or "molberrys" as he called them, which were, in the old days of ferrying fish ashore, much more in evidence than they are now.

One Bostock, a local tradesman, was devotedly attached to ringed plovers; he pursued them at all seasons of the year, slaying without mercy every bird that came within range of his gun. He would boast of the numbers he had slain, and of the care with which he "hung" them until fit for the pot.

"Never let a ring-dotterel go by!" he would say to me. "*I don't*—if I can help it."

I knew three or four men whose ambition lay in the direction of woodcocks; they put themselves to no end of labour, tramping over sand-dunes, upon the furzy common-land, and in and around the market gardens in search of them. They prided

themselves on the number of axilliary feathers—one
from each bird slaughtered—bedecking the bands of
their hats. I will not vouch for the truthfulness of
their tallies, for vanity is not unknown among
sportsmen.

Others, again, desired snipe above all else. Captain
Burch was a mighty hunter of this species, and spent
days patrolling the Burgh marshes, a large bed of
reeds, half-way to Burgh Castle, being one of his
favourite haunts. Barnes, also, went eagerly after
the snipe, and tramped the New Road marshes for
hours in search of them. He once secured some
twenty-two brace of common snipe there, and was
seen gloating over them at his shop, in a back street,
where he displayed for sale a few second-hand pieces
of furniture and sundry guns, the cleaning and
oiling of which were a positive delight to him. We
always looked on him as more than half insane ; and
he proved to be wholly so one day, when, in a fit
of despondency, he placed the muzzle of one of them
to his mouth and blew out his own brains.

John Leach, mariner, fisherman, gamekeeper
(when he could settle down for a while to a country
life), recluse, and prowling gunner by turns, when I
first knew him, in the prime of life, was a square-built,
shaggy-bearded fellow, whose brown corduroy jacket,
big woollen Tam o' Shanter, rolling gait, and in-
variable habit of walking with his left hand in his
coat pocket, made him easily distinguishable a long
way off. He was a man of few words, even when in
his cups, which were not many ; and when in a public
house he heard everything and made few comments.

After a good day's snipe-shooting, he would tell you he had bagged only "a few old sparrows." He was the keenest snipe-man of my acquaintance; and when others saw few birds, he often had some in his left pocket. His greatest pride was in dropping a snipe before it had fairly topped the reeds; and he seldom missed.

I had lost traces of him for three or four years, and had all but forgotten him, when it occurred to me to make inquiries about him, and with the assistance of one or two friends I succeeded in tracing him to the workhouse. On a cold afternoon in February (1908) I saw him in the Union boiler-house, where he acted as a sort of handy man, and very soon we were discussing old times over a blazing fire in the office. He was still a fine fellow, with flowing white beard; his left hand instinctively disappeared in the pocket of his white "jumper," and when he "called me to mind" a tear came into the corner of his eye.

"It's come to this!" said he, with the musical voice I so well remembered.

"You're not the only one of the old school who is finishing up here," I remarked, slipping a packet of tobacco into his hand. He poked the fire, and for a while said nothing.

"Those were good old times," I went on, "when you and I used to meet on Breydon Walls near the reed-bed."

"They were!" he emphasised; "and there *were* snipe in them days!"

"I remember my first snipe," he continued, "I

was out with my father, when up jumped one within a few feet of us. I up gun and killed it.

"'All right, sonny,' said my father, 'you've about deafened me (the gun going off against his ear); if you'd a-missed it, I'd have given you the biggest hiding you ever had in your life.'"

John lit his pipe, and pulled slowly at it, enjoying the unexpected treat, and "putting on his considering cap," as he expressed it.

"Snipe! ah! there's nothin' to beat 'em, not to my way of thinkin'. The worst shot I ever made was one day when near that old reed-patch, where Burch and I used to shoot a lot. I put up two snipes from a puddle of water right agin my feet, and missed 'em both with a right and left, when up jumps a duck from the very same spot; and my gun was empty. Its colours were so like the broken sedges and rough stuff around, that hadn't it moved, I should have the next step walked on it.

"I once see a snipe—it was snowin' heavily at the time—agin a small puddle. My gun-cap had got wet by the snow melting round it. Six times I snapped that cap, but the bird kept a-feedin'—it must have been pretty hungry—and on the seventh time of pullin' the trigger, the charge exploded and 'Longbill' fell. Get many? Ah! in those days snipes was as common as stints, but everywhere is so drained nowadays. It's only for a day or two at most, when a cold snap sets in, that you see any numbers. I never let a snipe get above the reeds, except I missed it, which wasn't often.

"I've been pretty lucky, you know, Mr. Pattson

One year, old Sergeant Barnes and me got two dark-coloured snipe—Sabine's we heard afterwards they was. He got five shillin's for his ; I made four of mine.[1] Where they went to after they got into Watson's hands,[2] goodness only knows, for I don't, or what he made of 'em. Anyway, I was satisfied.

" I once," he went on, " put up a wisp of snipe, and noticing one much larger than the others, fired at and killed it : it was what they call a solitary snipe (great snipe, *Gallinago major*); you don't often see that snipe in company with others, nor yet in wet places, anyway around here.

"Ah! them were good old days! I'm seventy-two now, and like the shootin', good for nothin'; but I often sit in the biler-house and think of 'em over and over again. How I enjoyed 'em! Oh, of course, I got a few other birds now and again ; my landlady used to make nice pies for me of starlings, peewits, knots, and such-like. I used to follow the herring voyage, and if I'd done well, eked out the rest of the year on my savings with what I picked up with the gun ; for you could shoot all the year round in my younger time. Now and again I'd ship as sailor in a ketch what took malt from Gorleston to London, and I never went without my gun. Now and then we shot ducks in fine weather, and lowered the boat and retrieved 'em ; and sometimes the mate and me slipped ashore on the Essex marshes, and toppled

[1] Sabine's snipe is now generally admitted to be only a dark-coloured variety of *Gallinago cælestis*. What became of the two birds Leach refers to I have not been able to trace.

[2] See *Nature in Eastern Norfolk*, pp. 73-75.

over an old hare or two. We once got set on by two horsemen, and had a breakneck race over ditches and stiles, and only just shoved the boat off the beach as they reached the shore."

Old John's yarn was not so consecutive as the printing of it may suggest. He seemed lost now and again, and between sentences pulled slowly at his pipe. As I have said, he was no great talker; and this gossip by the workhouse fire was longer in duration than all the conversations that had ever passed between us before. And it is possible that years of workhouse life had prematurely aged him and made him dull. He was not very reminiscent. He expressed more surprise at the protective colora-tion of birds than at any other phase of bird-life. He referred to the "stillness" of birds helping to protect them and make them escape observation. Snipes, in colour, were very like the broken reeds they haunted. A mallard's bright eye once caught his attention as the bird lay perfectly motionless beside a grassy tussock, until he actually touched it with the muzzle-end of the gun he was endeavouring to plant upon its back in order to hold it down until he could seize it by the hand. The moment he touched it, up it flew.

He also remembered seeing a hawk and a pigeon together on the bough of a tree, the former banging the woodpigeon with its wing, endeavouring to get it to fly. At last the pigeon suddenly darted forward, plunging into a thick hazel clump and so escaping its disappointed pursuer.

Leach assured me that he once shot a woodcock

as it stood probing at a soft spot in the snow in full daylight, a most unusual procedure for this night-feeding species.

" My recollection ain't good," he said, " you see you get kinder dormant *here;* you fare to have gone out of your life ; things is mechanical, and you seem to live on because you must.   But I just now called to mind a funny little bit what occurred off the Essex coast when I was sailin' in the old ketch. Me and the mate had got out the small boat, and was dodging a black duck—a scoter, you call it— and I was just about to pull at it when a gun went off on shore and killed it.   We hadn't noticed the gunner, who jumped up and ordered his dog to fetch it.   But the beast wouldn't, either by fair request or foul persuasion : so we put in after it.   Law ! how the fellow took on !   He levelled his gun and threatened to let fly if we didn't bring it ashore.   If he'd axed civilly we shouldn't have minded obliging him ; but as he didn't I levelled my gun at him, and showed him I was as prepared as he was to fight it out.   Meantime, the mate pulled quickly out of range, and we got safe aboard—duck an' all.   The skipper's wife cooked it, with two other birds— pokers (pochards)—and we had 'em for dinner. Some folks say they don't like scoter, but sailor-men ain't so nice as all that."

The greatest snipe winter in my recollection was that of 1899–1900.   To my knowledge, Durrant had nearly six hundred brought to him in the course of a few days.[1] A heavy fall of snow had thoroughly demoralised these birds, which flew about day and night in search of likely feeding places. Flocks of from ten to twenty birds were met with by a gunner going up Breydon walls; he mistook them for dunlins. Coming home empty handed he fired at a bunch, and to his surprise picked up four snipes in very fair condition. This induced him to go back for a mile or two, when in the course of his wanderings he secured twenty in all. Coming to Banham's farm, he saw that Banham and a friend had killed enough to fill a bushel " skep " (hamper).

MARSHLAND HARES

Since " poor puss " has lost caste and is no longer dignified by the title of "game," her lot has not been in any way ameliorated; for wherever she may stray from strictly preserved lands the prowling gunner feels perfectly justified in attempting her life, and only too proudly does he spread broadcast the news of his " great good luck " should he be fortunate enough to stop her career with a charge of shot.

It is not long since the hare was strictly preserved, and he was accounted a rascally poacher who dared, outside certain privileged circles, point gun at a vagrant animal. Preservers were not slow nor loth to give him all that the law would allow them to, and probably, at times, they ventured to give him even a trifle more.

It was during the last few years of the hare's

[1] See *Notes of an East Coast Naturalist*, pp. 144-49.

legal importance that some of my old "companions in arms," more daring than I, who was still but a youth, would go out night after night in the late autumn and early spring months, to return in the morning, having had more or less success in the wide-spreading "levels" of marshland bordering on the River Bure. Some of them, knowing the habits of the keepers, and working in couples, after the manner of greyhounds, would either walk the "walls" or make use of their punts ; and I never knew them to be captured red-handed. Others were unfortunate. One rash fellow, known as "Trotter" Lodge, was constantly in trouble, due more to an excess of bravado and bad temper, than to any want of cunning.

Old Blake and "Scarboro Jack," to whom I shall make further reference, were daring, but were never "nabbed," although occasionally they came very near to it. They revelled in the risk ; it spiced their sport ; and only in the presence of trusted and appreciative listeners, would they launch out into a narration of their exciting adventures. The zest with which, in terse quaint sentences, they told them, was an earnest of the enjoyment they had experienced.

All the low-lying levels north and west of the Caister marshes—extending to Mautby, Runham, Stokesby, and far beyond, dotted here and there by alder- and osier-carrs, and bordered by scrub and wooded uplands—swarmed with hares right up to the 'eighties. I have seen "puss" leisurely trotting along the "walls" within a mile of the town; and in winter snows I have traced her footprints on the sand-dunes near the sea. Even to this day she is common enough on the marshes; but gunners are strictly debarred from making use of either the river or the walls; guns are only used by privileged persons who have "rights" of shooting. A casual observer might go miles without seeing one, for "puss" lies low when not pursued, trusting to her protective colouring for concealment and safety. Some men seem to possess a faculty for finding a hare. Old Blake would spot them as if by instinct, when an experienced gunner out with him would see nothing. He protested that he could smell them! In my younger days, coursing with greyhounds was an exceedingly fashionable sport with a certain section of the sporting element, and indulged in with peculiar zest; indeed, it was the premier diversion of this foxless corner of the country. Kennels of greyhounds were kept in town and country; and it was quite the fashion for young sports to be followed about by a leash of hounds. Of later years, however, coursing has gone out of favour, although an occasional meet takes place. In my youthful days, people rode out on horseback from town or the neighbouring villages, whilst carts of every kind were requisitioned: the home-coming reminding one of a miniature return from the Derby.

The poor hares, maddened by pursuit and terror, scattered in all directions. I remember how one came across country to the seashore, plunged into the sea, swam some considerable distance, only to return and be knocked on the head by one of the crowd that had collected to see the "fun." Another came along the beach, turned into the town and raced through the principal streets, a pack of mongrel hounds of every known and unknown description wolfing at its heels, with a surging throng in their wake bearing sticks and cudgels. It was at length cornered in a slaughter-house, and dispatched by a butcher. It was a common occurrence for hardly-pressed hares to make for the "walls," boldly plunge into the river, and swim to the opposite side, much to the chagrin of their whining pursuers. Not in-frequently a hunted hare would put to flight another that had been cowering in her form, when the already heated hounds would turn aside to pursue the fresher animal whose scent would be stronger. In the end they would be worsted and both hares would escape. In doubling on her tracks "puss" would do her hardest to reach the river, or maybe, a convenient willow-carr, where, once she was within it, pursuit by the dogs would be impossible.

It goes without saying that owners of fowling-pieces were on the alert at safe distances in the hope of securing pot-shots. One of my acquaintances knocked over a hare when its capture was esteemed certain by its pursuers. Fortunately for him a wherry was tacking at a convenient reach : he hailed the wherryman in the nick of time, and the craft came a few feet closer before paying off on the next tack. H—— jumped on board, and before the indignant coursers had reached the " walls," he had hidden him-self and his quarry in the wherry's cabin.

Those who loafed in boats, hopeful of securing any hare that might take to the water, went greatly in fear of any watcher, who, provided with field-glasses, might be stationed in the top of the nearest drainage mill.

One coursing day "Short'un" Page [1] was eel-picking in the river when he espied a hare breaking from the hounds.

"Well, bor," said he, "she plumped right into the river, and started swimmin' athort. I measured her up, and got ashore on the rond afore she did. She was makin', I could see, for a broken sort of gap in the rond, and I got there fust, and jist as she was climbin' up, as wet as a boat-mop, I planted my fut on her neck, keepin' her down. Of course, she worn't long a drown'din', you may be sure. Jist then two fellers cum up an' axed if I'd seen the hare. I told 'em 'Yes! she's gone along under the wall,' and off they goes. All the time I was muddlin' about, pretendin' to wash the mud off my water-butes. Thinks I, 'I'm in luck's way for once.'

"Not long arter, another old hare makes for the river; and I wasn't long in pullin' up to her; I stuns her with the oar, and nabs her quick enuf. Bein' afraid there might be people comin' up to see, I whipped out a bit o' trawl-twine, tied it round her neck, and drawed her under the boat, tyin' each end of the cord to a thole-pin; then I rowed away with her ondernean the middle of it. Me and old 'Bugles' lived on hares for the rest of the week, and right nice they wor."

.   .   .   .   .   .

I suppose we may designate hare-coursing a classical sport, for it was followed by the ancient

Vide *Wild Life on a Norfolk Estuary*, p. 96.

Greeks and Romans. It is said by those who become enamoured of it, to be a glorious recreation on a fine sharp frosty morning. It is a sport that can be entered into by horsemen and pedestrians alike : the turnings are to be seen in the open country, where " puss " has little chance of escape. But I should say the elements of sport are more manifest in a wild heathy country, studded with furze, fern, and brambles, for there she would have at least a chance or two in her doublings. Blaine [1] would have us believe that "there is even a philanthropic character about coursing almost unknown to other huntings. It may be said (he writes) to offer a kind of refuge for the sporting destitute, for it holds out innocent recreation to those whose means or whose prudence will not allow them to risk either their neck after a fox, or their wealth after a racer.

The dog lover certainly can look with pleasure on a brace of handsome greyhounds ; speed is suggested in every limb and muscle ; no antelope could be lighter of foot or more graceful ; no racer so beautifully built for running. With forelegs straight as arrows, with loins bent like a bow, with neck elastic as that of a swan, with ears long, soft, and silken, chests broad and deep, and eyes lustrous and bold, what is more graceful than a greyhound's swift race over the turf ?

> " Remember'st thou, my greyhounds true?
> O'er holt or hill there never flew,
> From leash or slip there never sprang,
> More fleet of foot or sure of fang."

---

[1] *Rural Sports*, p 552.

A hare has been put up from her form ; the finder shouts " *So ho !* " Easily the animal steals away as if by no means greatly alarmed. The judge has an eye upon her : " Steady there, my beauties ! "—how the dogs strain at the leash, quivering with excitement, and yearning to be off.

"Steady ! " let the hare have her four score yards of grace. " *Go !* " Away they go, nose to nose, shoulder to shoulder. Puss pricks up her ears, and awakes to the fact that mischief is brewing ; she shows uneasiness. See! how the hounds are gaining upon her : now one has overshot himself, and she doubles. That was a near one ! Had the other dog been nearer he must have driven the hare into its mouth. Now the hare is making back to the covert from whence she started—the hinder dog notices this and turns quickly, gaining a point on its rival, and now taking the lead in the chase. Again the hare turns, and the other dog, which is the stouter and stronger of the two, once more has the advantage. Over a ditch springs the hunted animal, the dogs going over neck and neck not far behind it. " Puss " doubles yet again, the dogs missing her by a yard, and again overshooting themselves ; she still shows game, and bounding across the marsh, reaches a ligger, and scurries over at a bound. The dogs are just behind her and spring simultaneously ; one misses its footing and falls short, but scarce stopping, scrambles out of the water, dripping and chilled, and evidently discomfitted. The hare in her turnings has not pursued that circular course characteristic of the species. Ah ! the dog all but had her then. See ! she is trying her

POOR " PUSS'S " LAST DOUBLE

G

hardest to reach the river "walls"; if she only manages to reach the tops the greyhound will stand but little chance, for running along the grassy slopes is by no means so easy a matter to the dog as for "puss" to bound along the top. Too late, however, has she rounded that way: for when within a stone's throw of the ditch that borders the walls, the greyhound has her by the neck. . . . There she lies, poor thing! how the red stream trickles from her furry nostrils, staining the turf where the blown hound has dropped her.

.　　.　　.　　.　　.　　.

A marsh hare, I should imagine, would be a far more vigorous and fleet animal than one found in the cultivated uplands. "Scarboro Jack" would have me believe so, and that hares, foreseeing a change of weather, change their forms accordingly for purposes of shelter. They are not very fond of a stiff breeze.

Poor old "Scarboro!" Bent like an aged man ten years his senior, "Jack," at seventy years of age, still fairly robust, acts as night watchman for the water-works company when they are road-breaking. At other times he lives "from hand to mouth," content if he can only pay for his room and satisfy his appetite. When I was a lad he carted for a dealer in flour, and the heavy burdens bent his broad back. Cheery and full of dry humour, he treats life as more or less of a joke, and the twinkle of a merry eye bespeaks the spirit behind it.

"*Hares!*" said the old man, stirring his coke fire. "Hares!" he chuckled, "ah, bor, many and many an old 'Sally' have come to my share. There was nothing I liked better than getting on an old 'Sally's' track; and mind ye, when I did get on it, it was a bad night's work for *her*. I studied 'em, yer know, and meant having of 'em when I gave up a night's rest to study 'em. Oh yes, I could do my bit over in the day, and add a little fun and an extra shillin' to it when the likes of you wor asleep. The meshes (marshes) was my night-school; and I attended pretty reg'lar—at times, of course." He chuckled again.

"Life's pretty hum-drum at this sort of game— seeing to lamps, and tryin' to keep awake all the long cold night. Not as I need to be cold," he added, throwing some fresh fuel on to the watch-fire; "but then I ha' had my day, and think myself lucky in gettin' a night job. You get plenty of time for thinkin'; and I often sit here, or wherever I may be, and think o' them nights among the old hares."

" What of the pheasants ? "

" '*Long-tails?*' " said the quaint fellow, smiling. " Ah ! bor, I know something about them—too much in fact. But that was when I was livin' at Norwich. I once lived pretty nigh a week burrowed inside a straw stack what stood near our house. The missus handed me my grub through a back window, and I heerd the police sniffin' about inside the house, searching for me, with a warrant for—well, poachin', if you will have it so."

" Come, now," I said, " tell me the story complete." For I had long known that " Scarboro " had, at one time, made Norwich too hot to hold him.

" Well," he went on, " as long as I've paid for it,

I suppose confession 'ont make things any the wuss.
I was livin' in St. Faith's, in Norwich, at the time. I
used to slip out for a country ramble—I allers was
fond of the country, and, of course, I was pretty well
known, and watched, too, for a matter of that. I
made it a bit too hot this pertickler time, and the
police got on my track: I smelt a rat and hooked it.
I tramped to Yarmouth and got a job, they were
biggenin the Drive; but I got the 'down' and didn't
stop for my last week's wages. I tramped to Wells,
and after a time to Scarborough, sometimes fishin'
out of there, and brickmakin' at others; I dug clay
for the bricks of the biggest hotel there. But I
hankered after Norwich, and, lettin' my beard grow,
I turned up agin at St. Faith's, and even treated the
policeman to a drink what was on the look out for
me. He wasn't sure I was myself, but I suspected
him. I shaved myself and soon after met him agin
in the very same pub, and then he didn't know me,
for he even got discussin' about 'Scarboro Jack' hisself; and I done him once more. It was then that
I hit on the straw stack for a lodgin'; there was only
a tall hedge between it and my back window. I
used to slip out at night, tellin' the old woman I was
hankerin' for an old hare, or a 'long-tail,' and not to
expect me back afore early in the mornin'. Then I
got a job of navvyin' on the line; and if I seed a
gentleman with a top-hat on, and suspicioned him,
I used to be took suddenly ill, and leave my pick,
and go and hide in a sort of cave I'd dug in a bank.
But it got tiresome, and when I'd got a pound or two
in my pocket, I went back to the old 'Crown,' and

handed myself up to the first policeman I see. I got fined £2 and costs, or a month, and paid it; it was easy worth it, to get that fear of the slops off my mind.

"But I allers liked the river-meshes best; for with a little care you might bag an old 'sally' or two, and the sport was worth the risk—more or less. I used to hide my hares in one side of a stack, and my gun in the other, if I suspicioned anything, puttin' 'em high out of the reach of vermin. I'd call for 'em when the coast was clear.

"One night I hid three in a stack near Acle, and gettin' up early next mornin' I killed three more. 'Now then,' thinks I, 'I've got to get 'em home.' So I washes out my eel-trunk, locks it up with them safe inside, winds the chain round it, and plants it on the stern of the punt—you know that's a bit on the round. 'Now,' thinks I, 'if any fule comes athort me as is too inquisitive, a joggle of the boat shoots that trunk of hares into the river, and they'll know nothin' unless I see fit to tell 'em. When I got to Stokesby I did a little bit of babbin'—I'd got an old bab (bunch of threaded worms) in the boat, but I caught only a few little eels. So I cums home. Not a soul interferes with me downstream, but, by gums! when I reaches the Suspension Quay who should be there but Police Constable Gill."

"The Runham Vauxhall policeman, who was down on such as you!" I remarked.

"The very man!" said "Scarboro," poking at the fire, as if to brighten his memory in the brighter glow, "the very man."

"'Hallo! old man,' said P.-c. Gill, 'how many eels have you got?'

"'About three or four stone,' says I.

"'Where did you get 'em?' he axes.

"'South Walsham Broad,' I says. And all the time I was moppin' the boat, and slushin' the eel-trunk to freshen it.

"'You ain't got 'em all out,' he says.

"'No,' says I, 'they'll do for the cat—or you, if you like,' I adds.

"I hitches up the trunk and plants it on the quay, layin' the gun alongside it, grumblin' about fowl bein' scarce, and done it natural enough; but said as how I was glad as eels wasn't pertickler so.

"'You might just give us a lift up on to my back!' I says. And he, innocent-like, helps me to shoulder my hares. I hurries off to my shanty in Laughing Image Corner, not a stone's hull (throw) from the river, and goin' through to the back, I hangs the six old 'sallys' up on the loves (rafters) of my little bit of a fish-house. My missus and me, between us, made two and sixpence a-piece of the lot; we generally know'd where to plant 'em.

"'If I'd known there was hares in that eel-trunk,' swore Gill, when he heard afterwards as there was, 'I'd have about killed you afore you got clear off like that.'"

"Did Watson, the game-dealer, take hares off you?" I queried.

"No!" said Jack, "he was too well in with the game preservers; and it didn't do him no harm to

split on small sportsmen like myself.[1] I once took
him a fresh-killed hare.

"'Where did you get it?' he axes, eyeing me
suspicious-like.

"'Picked it up right warm, near the Denes (I
says), and brought it straight to you.'

"Watson simply remarked he would be out jist
for a minute or so—would I wait?

"It was my turn to suspicion him—he'd likely
enough gone out to fetch a policeman. So I whips
up 'Sally' and bolted, and crossin' Fuller's Hill was
soon home.

"'Look 'ere, missus,' I says, puttin' the hare into
some clean hay in a frail basket, 'spin Watson a
yarn about your bein' the daughter of a gamekeeper,
and didn't want two—one's enough for yar small
family, and the money'd be more use.'

"'Where did you get that?' thundered Watson.

"'It wor sent me by my father, a gamekeeper at
Horsey,' says she, lying as neat as truth, and
forcibler.

"Watson axed no more questions, but slung the
hare on a peg, hulled down harf a dollar, and out she
comes."

"Scarboro" lit his short bit of pipe, and began to
pull at it vigorously. He mechanically stuck the
piece of iron he used as a poker into the glowing fire.
It was a clear, frosty night, and the full moon looked
down on whitening house-roofs.

"It's a bit chilly," he remarked, planting his

---

[1] For similar behaviour over a snipe transaction, see *Notes
of an East Coast Naturalist*, pp. 147-48.

tea-can on the burning coke. Then he pulled hard again at his beloved pipe.

"I once went to do a bit of mesh-mowin' at Stracy Arms, and noticin' one marsh overgrown with thistles, thought it a likely place for a hare to hide in. It grew more thistles than it ever could corn. I advised the farmer to plant it with osiers, and told him he'd never want for an old hare to make use of. He done as I told him, and the hares, finding it out, came there ; they'd swim the river on their own accord to enjoy its snuggery. *He didn't get all the hares what was killed there !*

"Dogs? Ah, bor, my old Snap was a famous dog in his day, and he know'd as much about hares as I did. Mongrel? Well, he wor that, but his breedin' was as carefully selected as if he had the best of pedigrees. He'd got a cross or two in him ; and his sort allers took me three years to get properly focussed. 'Long Jimmy' George had a well-bred Smithfield sheep-dog—a bitch. 'Dilly' Smith had a male lurcher—half a retriever, half a greyhound. I got a bitch pup from this pair, and crossed her with a thorough-bred greyhound belonging to Sufflin'. I know'd the keeper, and for a shillin' and a pint he allowed me the use of him. That's old Snap's pedigree, and for wind, speed, nose, and stayin'-power he'd beat all the greyhounds in the country. I used to take my net now and agin to the meshes with Snap at my heels as close and silent as my shadow ; in fact, he lived in it. When I'd stretched my net athort a likely gate, I'd only got to pint my finger, and over the gate he'd go, and round up a hare like winkin'. He'd find 'em if there was any to be found, but he never pretended to put a tooth into 'em, though it must have been a temptation to him at times. They might try to double or dodge, but he know'd his work, and to the gate old 'sally' had to come. I've know'd him to round up a hare so that it was in the net, its neck broke, and in my pocket in seventeen seconds!

"If things looked suspicious, I'd but to whisper 'home!' and Snap would slip away through the mist like a spirit, though I never see one ; and even if he had to cross the river to do it, he'd give folks a wide berth, and would be glad enough to welcome me home, waggin' his tail in a quiet sort of way, as much as if to say, 'we'll get copt one of these times ; but then it's fine fun, ain't it ?'"

.   .   .   .   .

I caught old "Scarboro Jack" a night or two after, still by his watch fire. He was warming his can of coffee, having just hung out his lamps, which were scarcely needed owing to the bright moonlight.

"You kinder catched me on the hop the 'tother night," he remarked, "or I might ha' told you a lot more of my short-comin's, and long-comin's, too, for a matter o' that. I never told you, did I, how I once saw a funny bit of conversation between a hornpie (lapwing) and a old 'sally'? Oh yes, they can tell one another what's o'clock as well as you can tell me. I was up the North River one spring mornin' in the seventies, afore there was sich things as close seasons, and I see an old hare sittin' crouched on a rond. I pulled ashore to get a shot at her, but that there old hornpie (perhaps she'd got some eggs close by, but never mind that), she must act as a kind of watcher for the hare, and keeps on goin' around her and me too, squakin' for all she was worth. She reglar brushed agin the hare, and roused her up, and so put the scare into 'pussy,' that she gathered herself togither and off she bolted, runnin' over the bank, and disappeared.

"'All right,' says I, 'as long as you've gone and spiled my shot, I'll do what I worn't intending to do—I'll have you!' And I shot Mrs. Hornpie there and then."

"And you didn't feel conscience-smitten?" I queried.

"I don't know exactly what that is, but I didn't feel pertickler pleased. No, Mr. Pattson, I ain't bilt that way. I allers like to get my own back, come what may...."

"Cadger" Brown was one of the most successful hare poachers I ever knew, and he was equally fortunate in evading pursuit and capture, although he bore a very bad name for being an audacious pilferer of tame ducks, geese, and even rabbits. It was a curious error he made that turned the anger of a marsh-farmer friend of mine, who came down early one morning to find a rabbit missing from its hutch, and the door buttoned behind it. He knew the rabbit neither turned nor refastened its button. He knew equally well that "Cadger" was the delinquent; but the stupidity or absence of mind that was exhibited so tickled him that he forgave him.

Old Blake was a magnificently-built man when in his prime, and at times followed the sea as a smack's master. The moment he could get clear of his vessel he would bolt home, slip on a long white jumper, shoulder his gun, and set out for a neighbouring warren. By dusk he would be ensconced in a snug hiding-place, where he would stay for hours. There was a deep sandhole, now part of the golf-links, much resorted to by hares at certain seasons.

"I allers let two old hares, even if I had to wait hours for 'em to do it, cross like so (passing one hand before the other), and then topple 'em over together. My old eight-bore never played me false."

Blake was a good hand at spinning a yarn; but, unfortunately, I was seldom in his company. He would relate with zest how, on one occasion, when he was at sea, a glaucous gull persistently kept company with the vessel, tempting him to load his gun to shoot it.

"I'd loaded," said he, "and felt around for a patch (cap), but no patch was to be found. Not a solitary one hid in my waistcoat pockets; in fact, though I'd got plenty of powder and shot, I'd forgot to bring any patches. So I ups and tells the mate to go and heat the poker. He brought it up red-hot.

"'Now, when I get a sight,' says I, 'and say "*now*," touch the nipple.' But the fule was that nervous he couldn't focus the poker, till it was pretty nigh cold. I orders him to heat it again, and the second time he cums up with it.

"I gets a sight on the bird and shouts, 'Now!'

and as luck would have it, he touched the spot, and I kills my bird!"

In the latter part of his life he took part in the autumnal herring fishing, and spent the remainder of the year out with his gun, living on his "share" of the boat's "dole," and on what his gun brought in. He was known to mark down a hare in her form, and deliberately seize her, ere she had made up her mind to bolt. He was never caught red-handed, and few keepers would have dared to handle so lusty an old fellow. He died full of years: he was braiding a poaching net at his death, which hung half-finished at his bedside.

Dulcior est fructus post multa pericula ductus.

THE GULL-SLAYER

Thumping and stitching, making or mending boots, new and old, in a tiny workshop in one of the back streets, sits all day long, and often far into the night, a shoemaker named Whiley, who is one of the most original and interesting characters with whom I am acquainted. A keen observer of nature and man, there drop in at his cabin men of various orders—politicians, bird-fanciers, gunners, and others —to all of whom he is a sort of oracle, and in terse, broad Norfolk, he airs his opinions on many things, while he has a goodly store of reminiscences with which to illustrate his arguments.

Whiley has just passed the meridian of life; and from long years of close sitting, he now needs a larger waistcoat than many more active men would care to wear. He is, however, an early riser, and with the big, old, hard-hitting, double muzzle-loader (that usually stands loaded up one corner) on his arm, patrols the south beach foreshore from before daylight until breakfast-time. He is known as " a holy terror " to the gulls, which, in considerable flocks, haunt that part of the beach during the fishing season, where they feast on the dead herrings thrown about in the breakers, or cast up at the tide mark. Gulls of every species and of all ages are his particular prey. His usual procedure is to collect some baskets and " swills " (herring-baskets), and pile them into a sort of fortress, over which sea-tangle and weeds are thrown, lay in hiding behind them, and fire at the gulls as they pass to and fro. He carries in his bag a ball of twine to which is attached a long piece of cork, trimmed cigar-shape. Having picked up a herring, he opens it by running a knife along the back, and having emptied the abdomen, inserts the cork, and roughly fastens the divided back together again. Attaching a second piece of string to this so-called " hake," with a small piece of lead to moor it, he throws the bait as far into the sea as possible, his desire being that passing gulls shall stop to pick it up, and in so doing give him a good chance to slay them.

"Don't you think it a rather unfair advantage to take of the wretched birds ? " I asked.

"All's fair in love and war—and gull-shootin'," he replied. " What's the differs in a pheasant-shoot, where the birds are driven right on to you ? "

It was no use arguing that pheasants were bred to kill, and gulls were wild creatures, and——

" And what ? " he snapped. " I want the gulls, and mean bavin' 'em ! "

The numbers of gulls, mostly the immature of the herring and greater black-backed species, with common and black-heads, that I have seen hanging on the rows of nails in his workshop have astonished me. On October 13th, 1906, I counted ten ; on the 5th of November no less than twenty-four ; and he has been seen coming home from one of his expeditions with as many gulls strung in two bunches across his shoulder as he could well carry. After the day's snobbing, he takes his scissors and industriously clips off all their feathers close to the skin, and shreds off the webs from the larger feathers : these are packed in paper bags for drying, and when sufficient are prepared, the neighbours around purchase them for making into pillows, and even beds.

Whiley's annual toll of the gulls he reckons at " a gross all told." In the winter of 1907, he secured 143 victims. " There would have been over the gross," he told me, " hadn't some of the wounded got away, what Rose (the dog) couldn't lay hold of."

It goes without saying, that various wild fowl, including mallard, wigeon, pochards, and different shorebirds, fall to his gun ; and he is keen on diving birds, seldom missing any stray red-throated diver that may wander inshore.

One afternoon I turned into Whiley's workshop to escape a heavy downpour of rain. He was oiling his favourite seven-bore.

" As good a gun as ever any man carried," he remarked, enthusiastically. " You remember Mr.

Adams, the grosher; well, she belonged to him—
that's nigh forty year ago. Adams was a clinker
for the hares, and many an old 'sally' did he get
up on the Breydon marshes in the old days, *when
there was suffin' about!* He'd crouch in the end of a
deek (ditch) up to his knees pritty nigh—that's what
brought on his rheumatics—and as 'sally' comes
trotting along the bank, over she'd go. He know'd
her ways as well as she did herself. He used to
wear a sort of drab fustian coat. One day he'd killed
an old hare—blowed her head to pieces with this
very old gun—and popped her into his pocket.
Though hares was game then, nobody ever thought
of stopping *him*, or dreamt of *his* poaching.

"'You've got her this morning!' says a policeman
he met as he was coming home.

"'I have,' says he, winking, all unconscious that
the blood had soaked right through his coat, and a
big patch of it showed as plain as a pike-staff that
there was suffin' pretty suspicious close at hand.
Somebody else told him of it afore he got home,
when he kinder congratulated himself on the density
of that policeman's intellect!"

Whiley went on to relate how "he once frightened
a bullock pretty nearly into fits by using it as a
'stalking horse,' from behind which he fired into a
flock of lapwings on a marsh."

Whiley had stowed his gun up a corner, and
began to work upon a big piece of cork for a cork-
soled boot.

"I took up the gun again, as you know," he continued, "a year or so back, because of my health. I

fare (feel) as if I must get out more into the open, and I've felt altogether different since I started again. When did I first go shooting? Why, over forty year ago, aye, and afore that. I always was fond of birds, and keepin' live things. My father and mother were country people, and was always used to being among game and live stock, and that. My father settled in Row 93 ; he did the shoemakin', and mother did the closin' of the uppers. I lived 'long with them till I got a big chap, and used to carry a gun. I remember one day shooting at a big blue hawk— a peregrine they called it—and wing-tipping it. I off with my coat and hulled over it, as it lay back strikin' out with its long clawed feet ; and after a bit of manipulating got it into my handkerchief and took it home. I got it on a perch very like a parrot-stand, after mother had thrown a cloth over it, and father had put a leather ring round its leg, which he eyeleted on, with a chain and a split ring attached to it. It became a great pet with my mother, who could do any mortal thing with it. Once when she was sadly, Dr. Moxon comes to attend her, and finds her by the fireside with the bird at her elbow.

"'How I'd like to stroke it as you do!' he said to her.

"'If you do, you do it to your own peril,' said mother, beggin' him not to attempt it.

"Howsoever, he did try it on, and in a moment the bird turned on him, striking him with its left foot, tearing his finger from hand to end right down to the bone. He put the best face he could on the matter, bathed his finger and bound it up, leaving the house a wiser if a sadder man. We kept that peregrine a couple of years, feeding it on lights, mice, and birds; it used to throw up pellets of fur, feathers, and bones.

"Then we had a jackdaw—the masterpiece devil of a mischief; and we used to let it potter in and out of the house. 'Jack' was a terrible prig. Every bright button, pins, nails, and even scissors, that he could pinch on the sly, he snapped up and bolted out with into the backyard. There was a hole in the lid of the rainwater cistern, through which he'd put these things; whether he tried to fill it up, or what, I don't know. Anyway, when we had the cistern cleaned out we got quite a pailful of articles what had once been bright, amongst them scissors, and fifteen tea-spoons.

"Jack died, like most pets, by accident. Father had been hammering leather on his lapstone, which he goes to drop on the floor as usual, beside him; but it so happened that at that moment Jack was snatching at a hobnail he had spied on the floor. The stone landed on his head, splitting it. Everything was done to patch him up, but to no purpose. Jack pegged out."

Whiley firmly believes in the immigration of French partridges in spring,[1] a possibility I at one time sincerely believed in. I am assured that the woodcock, when tired, does occasionally rest on the water; and I once saw a crow, lifting on the crest of a wave, get upon the wing again. I told Whiley so.

"Crows swimming!" he broke in, "why, I've seen

[1] *Notes of an East Coast Naturalist*, pp. 55-56.

H

'em do it, and what's more, French partridges, what come over in the latter part of April and early in May, can swim too, buoyantly enough; but their short wings are incapable of raising 'em agin, and in time they're sure to drown.

"Forty year ago, when the denes *was* denes (sand-dunes), and covered with furze, partridges came there more 'an they do now. I've several times seen 'em drop in the sea, and sent my old dog in after 'em." Then he laughed. Something funny had occurred to him.

"One day," he went on, "I'd wounded a French partridge, which fell into the sea, and old Cooper, the birdcatcher, who was 'at work' against the marams, left his nets, ran down to the beach, throwin' off his clothes as he went; then out he swam and retrieved it. I didn't happen to have the dog with me just then.

"'You can drop that bird,' I said to him.

"'No, thanks,' he says, '*you* should have swum arter it. I'm keepin' it for my trouble.'

"Now, I didn't see no particular fun in comin' to blows about a paltry partridge, so Mason (who was with me) and me stationed ourselves not far off his nets, and every time a bunch of linnets or red-polls came near we fired at 'em, and played that game with him so he never got no more that morning."

As a marksman, my old gull-shooter excelled, and in the sixties and seventies was a crack-shot in the volunteer corps. One morning, when at the butts, he espied a cormorant sitting on a stump of the old *Hannah Pattersen*,[1] which was showing up at low water. This happened to be one of two birds kept by the landlord of the Standard hotel on the Marine Parade.

"I got within about two hundred yards range of it, and fired, my rifle being loaded with ball, toppling it over as dead as a herrin'. Up comes Captain Cubitt.

"'Don't you know,' says he, 'that that there bird was a tame one belonging to so-and-so?'—makin' use of his name. 'I've a good mind to inform of you, for there's a £2 reward offered for any one informing of another shootin' either of these birds.'

"However, it blowed over, for our Captain Cubitt dearly loved a good shot. But a few days after, when we was again at the butts, we see a porpoise tumblin' about around the old wreck, for there was sea-anemones and fish around her broken timbers. Cubitt sees it, and coming up to me, he says—

"'Now then, Whiley, I'll allow you *are* a good marksman if you shoot *him*!'

"'All right, sir,' I says; and I went athort to the same sandhill from behind which I'd pulled at the cormorant, and watched for the porpoise's snout coming up. I fired at the right moment, and put a ball clean through the back of its eye. It sank, and didn't come up again. Next day some drawnetters hauled the carcase ashore, and there was my bullet-hole through its head.'"

---

[1] The *Hannah Pattersen* was a full-rigged ship, laden with 1500 tons of coal, which came ashore abreast of the workhouse where she became a total wreck. This happened on March 1st, 1869.

ON 'GUN-DOGS'

Of sporting dogs,[1] so far as they have come under my notice, I cannot say much that is noteworthy. The retriever is not nearly so common to-day as when I was a lad, the brown variety in particular being rarely seen. Those who "fancy" a dog divide their affections between the useless and, to my mind, offensive collie (which is more or less a mongrel in this locality) and the grossest of mongrels, which are turned out into the streets at all hours of the day, to become nuisances which disgrace an otherwise pleasant seaside resort.

The sporting dog here has practically had its day; there is, as the saying goes, "no work" for it to do. Since the denes have become the haunt of many golfers, rabbits have become extinct. Men of sporting tendencies no longer prowl around there with greyhounds and lurchers; and the only useless beast at present in favour, is the diminutive, semi-skeleton whippet, for whose delectation *tame* wild rabbits are turned adrift on the outskirts of the town, to end their already half-frightened-out lives.

Of mongrels, every known variety and sub-variety under the sun is to be found; and they breed promiscuously with the freedom of pariahs. Gun-dogs are less common than formerly; here and there a gunner devoted to snipe and woodcock shooting trains a spaniel to rouse about in ditch and cover; and a chance sportsman utilises the services of a dog

[1] See "On dogs" in *Notes of an East Coast Naturalist*, pp. 254–58.

for retrieving a wounded fowl or a slaughtered parcel of dunlins. At times the shouting of orders to such a dog may be heard all over Breydon. I know one sportsman who boasted a fine retriever that could never resist running to every gunner who fired his gun ; it was no uncommon thing to see it tearing a mile up the beach, deaf to the threats and whistling of its master. This particular gunner at length resorted to the practice of tying one end of a rope around the dog's neck, and the other round his own waist. The experiment was not a success, for the dog would spring forward at unfortunate moments, as when its master was pointing his fowling-piece at a passing curlew.

An eccentric man named B—— for many years "followed" Breydon as a hobby in spare time, and during holidays, eel-babbing, shooting, and occasionally bird-catching, on the adjoining marshes. He tried many pursuits, enjoying them all in turn, but never making much ; indeed, generally losing money. Once when a shooting fit was on him he speculated in a dog which was, perhaps, seven-tenths of a retriever, and guaranteed to be an extraordinary gun-dog. B—— boasted a great deal about this animal, representing it as unrivalled in this country or any other. When out shooting with Harwood, another sportsman, on the marshes, he shot a lapwing, and sent the dog after it.

"Now you'll see," said B——, "what he can do ! " To the dog—" *Hie on !* "

Away rushed the dog, jumping the ditch, and securing the bird.

"Good dog!" said B——; "come along."

But the brute, disregarding orders, squatted down with the lapwing between his fore paws, and deliberately ate it, head, legs, and most of the feathers.

"He brought the bird back," said Harwood to me, "*but inside him !*"

"Billy" Sampson's rough mongrel, well-named "Rough,"[1] has ever had a warm corner in the old gunner's heart: he has seldom talked to me of the "old days" without having something new to say about it.

"The rummest bit of reasoning," said Billy, "I ever know'd in a dog, was one day up the North River when I'd shot a golden eye, which dropt on to a bit of floating ice. The little beggar sprung on the main body of the ice, and then on to a big floe, what broke off and was driftin' downstream. There he hung, or rather balanced himself, till the twisting of the tide drew the odd pieces together, when, jumping on to the bit what the fowl was on, he seized the bird, and made over piece after piece till he got safe ashore with nothin' wetter than his feet.

"Once," went on Billy, "there was a sort of half-bred Italian greyhound what suddenly sorter ran wild, and bolted on to the denes, where it lived on what it could catch—rabbits, or anything There was a reward out for it, but nobody could lay hold of it. At last several of us surrounded it and drove it into the sea.

[1] Vide *Notes of an East Coast Naturalist*, pp. 254-58; also *Nature in Eastern Norfolk*, pp. 19-20.

" 'Go on, Rough ; áfter him,' I says ; and off he went, nabbed it by the ear, and swam back to the shore with it.

"Nobody know'd," added Sampson, "what that dog *could* do ; he was the masterpiece I ever had."

Overend, the collector,[1] possessed a fine example of a black retriever, which exhibited extreme intelligence. It was trained to do many interesting tricks. It regularly fetched its master's *Times* from the stationer, and carried it to a small circle of readers in proper rotation ; it purchased its own biscuits, and did other little errands.

A local sportsman of shady character owned a mongrel that waited on his every sign with a devotion and willingness worthy of a better master. It was this man's practice on a Saturday to do the week's marketing, and in going for the beef for his Sunday dinner the dog accompanied him. He seldom went to the same stall twice. His procedure was to glance over the stall with his roving eye, ask the prices, and after placing his finger tips on a certain piece of beef or mutton, walk off, making some excuse for not purchasing it. All this time the dog would be watching by the side of its master, with whom it would depart when he took leave of the butcher. When at a convenient distance the dog was told to "go on!" and the man made himself scarce ; whereupon the animal would skulk back to the stall, and at an opportune moment, when he saw the butcher was busy, it would snatch up the joint and hurry off by devious ways to its master's home.

[1] *Nature in Eastern Norfolk*, p. 78.

"Rose" was a fat and aged retriever. Her first master was an ardent sportsman, as also was her second, his son, at the period I knew her. She waddled out on to the mudflats with all the eagerness of her youth until her eye dimmed, and she became as deaf as a stone. I have seen her tackle a wounded heron with adroitness, seizing it by the neck, not, however, without receiving a nasty pick in the back from the dagger-like bill of the terrified bird. She would gather up three or four dead shorebirds at a time, to save herself extra runs across the ooze. I mention this animal as one instance of a deaf retriever working well. I have known several dogs lose their sense of hearing, a fact probably due to water getting into their ears when they plunged into it or when waves broke over them.

" GOOD DOG "

PINK-FOOTED GEESE

CHAPTER III

'PUBLIC' AFFAIRS

" Kind was his heart, his passions quick and strong,
  Hearty his laugh, and jovial was his song ;
  And if he loved a gun, his father swore,
  'Twas but a trick of youth, would soon be o'er,
  Himself had done the same some thirty years before."
                                            SCOTT.

'AN AFTERNOON SITTING'

BREYDON is noted for its hosts of gulls and the
peculiar tenacity of its mud ; Norwich for the
number of its churches ; Yarmouth for its public-
houses, which are legion. The most popular man is
the brewer, who rules Bench and bar-parlour alike ;
while all sorts and conditions of men do him

homage. I suppose it is so nearly everywhere, more especially beside tidal waters.

On the quays fishermen and waterside labourers may be seen crossing and recrossing at intervals: some to quench their thirst, others to rinse away the dust of loading and the emptying of ships. After the day's labour men draw together, often from uncomfortable homes, to spend the night, until closing time, in emptying tankard after tankard of beer, or in dallying over a pewter mug; some making up for short imbibings by long spells of yarning and argument. Sometimes snatches of song are indulged in, and maybe boisterous horseplay, which occasionally ends in a bout of fisticuffs. The bar-parlour is a rough school, but it affords studies of the queerer side of human nature.

It is a recognised thing that certain public tap-rooms are frequented by particular classes of individuals; one will be the resort of butchers or cabmen; in another wherrymen or fishermen will foregather; while the gunning fraternity have their favourite quarters, where they discuss passing events in bird-land, compare notes on past achievements, "argufy" and over-reach each other, and often outwit one another in downright lying.

There stood, until the nineties, on the North Quay, a small ale-house with high windows. A decayed and blistered signboard hung above the door, announcing its distinctive title, the *Lord* ——, and on its blistered sides the remnants of a cocked hat, and a red nose, with a patch or two of yellow that probably signified braid, could be distinguished.

The small parlour had a brick floor, which was kept well sanded ; an empty barrel or two did duty for tables, whereon three or four pewter pots or earthenware mugs could be stored, still leaving room for using between them a packet of greasy cards.

On one of the rough and pew-like benches sat a couple of Breydoners, arguing a knotty question that called for strong words now and again to clinch points supposed to have been gained. Two or three others, leaning against the counter, loomed up indistinctly through a haze of smoke, like luggers coming up through a sea fog.

" I say he shot *nine !* "

"You're a liar!" protested " Pintail " Thomas, banging his three-fingered fist, with emphasis, on the barrel-head, and upsetting " Cadger ", Brown's beer-pot, "theer wor only tree (three) knocked over."

" Hold 'ard!" roared Brown, "you've knocked over my —— mug. Are you near-sighted ? "

To lose a drop of the precious liquid went sorely against the grain with " Cadger "; so to recoup himself, he snatched up " Pintail's " half-filled tankard, and before the irate and fiery little gunner could stop him he had emptied its contents down his throat.

" We're quits, Master Johnny !" he said, amid a roar of laughter from the company. Thomas had not yet sat long enough to become very irascible, which usually happened after his third tankard.

" I was a-saying," continued " Cadger," " old George Blake shot nine hares that night on Mautby meshes. I see 'em myself."

" Shornt believe it, not if I was kilt," shouted

" Pintail," stalking up to the counter for another pint.
"Nine hairs, *per*haps, grey 'uns at that, p'raps ; but
you 'ont stick it inter me as they wor four-legged
ones. I 'ont believe it!"

"What differs 'll it make if you don't?" asked
"Fiddler" Goodens. "You swore I never took a
stone of eels with four strokes of the pick."

"I never believe nothin' I don't see myself!"
declared the cantankerous Thomas. Then he turned
to "Snicker" Larn, and referred to the company as
a lot of "idgetts as didn't know a Tom Taylor from
a Moll Berry!"[1]

"Talk about molberries," jibed in "Snicker," "I
see one on 'em up Breydon this arternune, chasin' a
parcel of gulls around suffin' terrific. Gord bliss my
sowl and body! he wor up arter 'em like a narrow
from a gun. They hollered and screeked like so
many stuck pigs, but theer wor no gettin' away from
him ; he wor down on 'em, round 'em, and all ways
at onct ; and he gleed along that smuthe—jist as if
his wings wor iled. Presently up gulps one of 'em,
and reg'lar spewed smelts ; and great beauties, too,
they wor—the greatest shame you ever know'd,
robbin' our nets."

"You worn't nettin', you wor a eel-pickin'!"
snorted Thomas.

"Well, who said I *wor* a nettin'?"

"You said as how they wor a robbin' your net!"
snapped Thomas, appealing to the company.

"He mean all on us!" ventured "Cadger"

[1] Tom Taylors, *local* for stormy petrels : Moll Berrys—
skuas.

Brown. "That obstroperous little devil 'll argue you blind. How many smelts; Snicker, did that old mol-berry whip up afore they reached the water?"

"Lemme see," replied Snicker, winking wickedly at "Cadger." "*Seven* I think, out 'er six."

"You ——!" but here Thomas choked.

"You talk about rats!" remarked "Short'un" Page.

"Who said rats?" snapped Thomas.

"No one," said Short'un, "only I was going to say suffin', and you wouldn't let me. I hate 'em, the warmin. While I wor a sleepin' 'tother night in my houseboat up in Acle deek, I feels suffin' squeezin' under my neck, what woke me up.

"'Lor lumme!' I says, 'what the dowst wor that?' I put out my hand, and felt suffin' hairy; and bein' half asleep I nabs hold on it. I didn't want to axe a second time, for my nibbs fangs me by the finger, and made his teeth meet. 'You ——,' I says, 'I wonder what you're arter?' and I tumbles off the settle, and laid hold of a wrigglin' iron, what I use for wormin'. The rat jumps down and round, tryin' to get away, and presently, spyin' a hole in the bottom-boards, under he went. I ups with the boards, and sees the brute scroudgin' up a corner a-trying to smallen hisself——"

"I wonder he didn't eat you up, Short'un," grinned "Pintail," referring to Short'un's diminutive person.

"You ain't much to brag on, Johnny Thomas," retorted Short'un.

"Give it him, Short'un!" from three or four of them.

"Shove *you* in a sack, Master Johnny, and they'd hev to shovel in more rubbidge to help to fill it. But I was a-saying, mates, as theer wor the rat, and theer was I. And I makes a jab at him, runnin' the sharp crowbar clean though him; but as bad luck would hev it, I started the butt-end of a plank, and drove him clean through the boat. In course, she begins to take in water like a sieve, and afore I could dam the hole with a blanket I'd got four or five inches of water in. A bloomin' nice thing with the water freezin' cold, and snowin' and blowin' like blazes."

"What had he bin nibblin' at?" queried Watson.

"I'd fresh iled my hair," said Short'un, "with some pork lard I had in a cup, and I suppose he liked the taste on it. He'd gnawed a lump out of my wig, anyway."

"Rough mornin', boys," said old "Fates" Bowles, opening the door and walking up to the counter.

Reed, the publican, with a nod of recognition, pulled a pint of ale and set it upon the counter. "Fates" gripped the pot, and crossed the parlour to his favourite corner, just vacated by "Cadger" who, without a word of adieu, edged out into the street.

"Rum pup, *him!*" remarked "Fates" to "Pero" Pestell, who had just finished a game of cards and was calling for another half-pint. "He'd rob his own gran'mother's coffin of the lid if he wor hard up for a bit o' firewood."

"He's a —— monkey!" snapped "Pintail," who was getting a bit flushed and quarrelsome.

"You're another!" retorted Pestell, who didn't care a button for the pugnacious little punt-gunner.

"And you looked like one," he went on, "that time what I see you hangin' on a stake, with your punt 'tother side the channel. You *must* ha' been drunk, and not for the first time. Didn't you drink a swell gunner's whisky one day, and he hed to be rowed home in old Jack Gibbs's punt?"

"What if I did?" asked Johnny. "And if I wor as big as you, and wor a milishey-man, I'd kill you—*that I would.*"

"You'd better try it, Johnny," suggested "Fates."

"What a awful smell round about here!" roared Pero. "Why, as I'm a livin' man, your old top-hat's afire!" he shouted, knocking "Fates'" silk top-hat off the bench, and jumping on it with both water-boot encased feet.

Now "Fates" Bowles, who combined the professions of costermongering and eel-picking, had one great weakness, which brought down upon him the anathemas of a number of his friends: he gloried in wearing a top-hat—a battered, and ugly chimney-pot of the tallest order. It had been pelted with mud by men who swore that it frightened all the birds off the flats; and who also maintained that it brought bad luck to the eel-fishermen whenever he showed himself. As for himself, he was a strange fellow, more than fortunate at eel-picking, for he seemed to know, by a sort of instinct, where eels were to be found; but he greatly disliked being overlooked when at work. No matter how good the "ground" he was working, he would snatch up the oars and row away directly any other Breydoner rowed up to him.

"I'd like to know who did that," roared "Fates,"

snatching up the hat, which Pestell had crushed into some resemblance to a concertina. But no one ventured to say *who* had quietly drilled a red-hot poker through that ugly example of the hatter's handiwork. "Fates" was so "done" that his vocabulary failed him. He quietly straightened out his miserable head-gear, pulled it over his ears, and stalked out, looking very much as if a fit of apoplexy was brewing. There was much uproarious laughter at his going. "Fates" Bowles's pride had been fatally injured that night. He never set foot in the *Lord* —— again.

"Well, bor!" said Pestell, who had laughed until he cried, "old 'Fates,' takes the cake. I believe he used that old tile for a eel-pot, and that's how he copt 'em."

Looking over the window-sill at the retreating Bowles, "Pero" added : "Don't it make him look just like a monkey at the end of a chain towed by a barrel organ!"

"Did I ever tell you that yarn about a monkey we once had aboard the old steamship *Nineveh?*" queried an old fellow up in a corner, who all this time had been quietly playing a game of cribbage with two other sailormen.

"No!" replied more than one of the audience. "Tell us it now, matey,"

"Wal," he said, "we was bound for home; this was in the airly days of the canal; and theer wor a lot of them Arab pirates still knockin' about there. A ship as left Calcutta a week afore us had been cut out by 'em, and every blessed man aboard hed his throat cut. But that's neither here nor there. We had a monkey aboard, ' Jim ' we called him, a red-faced little warmin, with hinder quarters of a sim'lar culler, a short tail, and as knowin' a look on him as——

"As Pintail!" jibed in "Pero."

"Begger me!" spluttered Pintail, who was fast passing into a state bordering on homicidal mania, except that he was too helpless to go straight at it. "If I—wal, if you worn't so big as me, I'd—wal, half you with a eel-pick."

"I wor a-sayin' as knowin' as old Harry," went on Sharman. "Well, we'd also got a great white cockatoo; and both on 'em had the run of the ship. The monkey used ter climb the riggin', and play a rare game in the cook-house, perwidin' the cook worn't a-lookin'. The cockatoo used ter fly around some-times and also perk in the riggin'. One day Cocky took his breakfast—a big banana—up into the riggin' thinkin', no doubt, to be all by himself. But no, master Jim liked bananas, and when he sees the bird lighting on the cross-trees, he goes quietly hand over hand up a rope, and afore Cocky could holler for assistance, he hed nabbed the banana, and was chucklin' to himself as he turned to go. But Cocky wor too quick for him, and siezin' the tail of the monkey made her teeth meet!——"

" *Teeth!* " hiccuped Thomas, "you mean her trunk!"

No one heeded this interruption.

" Jim screeched and hollered, dropt the banana on deck, and sat jabberin' at Cocky in a towerin' rage.

Then suffin' must ha' happened. Perhaps the monkey pounced onawares on the bird ; he must ha' copped her round the neck, or why didn't he get bitten? Presently, howsomever, feathers comes droppin' on deck and flyin' past the ship like a snow-storm.

"'It's a rummon!' says the mate, 'I never know'd a snow-storm afore in the Red Sea!'

"Then we sees as it wor feathers ! 'Cocky's on the moult, I reckon,' I says to him, 'and if I ain't mistaken, Jim's helpin' her to moult!'

"'You'd better shin up and see,' says he. On which I goes up. I sees the monkey a-grinning, and he shoots off to the far end of a spar as if he wor guilty.

"'Where are you, Cocky?' I axes, not seein' any cockatoo.

"'In the cook-house!' says Cocky; 'I'm cold!'

"Then I catched sight of her; and *she wor as naked as she wor born !*"

"I thought birds wor *hatched !*" snarled Pero.

"It's all the same thing!" said Sharman.

"I've yet to lern as steamships has cross-trees and spars an' that!" remarked a knowing customer, who had taken no part so far in the discussions.

"They did in them days!" snapped Pestell, who, as a boatbuilder, prided himself on his knowledge of ships.

Just then the door opened, and a shaggy head was thrust in—

"Who're you lookin' for?" queried the landlord.

"My sweet brother," answered "Stevey" Bowles.

"Come in, and we'll tell you," said Pero Pestell, with a mischievous twinkle in his grey eye. "It's

nice and warm in here; we've got another old
mallard a-bilin' on the hob. And well peppered
him too!"[1]

"One's enough on a cold day," snapped Stevey,
"specially if it's well peppered," on which a laugh
went round, for they knew something about Stevey's
dinner, to which a whole box of pepper had been
added.

Pero lit his pipe, and went over to the little
aneroid barometer hanging near the door.

"Don't like the look on it," he remarked, "it's
jumpin' for a nor'erly wind."

"It's frightful raw and nasty outside, by gums!"
chipped in Stevey; "I've just come off Breydon."

"Any fowl dropped in?" asked Pestell.

"*Thousands!*" replied Stevey. "I could ha'
killed with a pop-gun, they wor so tame."

"What wor they?" questioned Pero, with a
cautious look out at the weather. "Sounds *big*."

"Swans!" put in Pintail, "black swans, swans
with two necks."

"Theer wor a few *pintail* ducks among 'em,"
retorted Stevey; "some on 'em wor three parts
drunk!" The shot was at Thomas.

It roused him, and he flew into a towering rage,
squaring up at the burly man, who, with his hands
in his pockets, asked him "if his mother know'd
he wor out?"

Johnny would have pitched into Bowles, whose
great fist had settled many a more powerful
antagonist, but the landlord intervened—

[1] Vide *Wild Life on a Norfolk Estuary*, p. 31.

" No fightin' in here, Johnny," he insisted ; while
Snicker and Bessey forced the irate little man back
into his seat, still growling and glaring.

" Pintail," said Bowles, in a conciliatory tone,
handing him his tobacco pouch, " try that 'bacca."

Thomas looked rather dully at it, hesitated, and
drew the pouch towards him.

" You don't mean real swans ? " asked the little
man, fumbling for his pipe in every pocket, and
finding it inside his empty mug. It did not occur
to him to inquire how it got there.

" You're heard the yarn of my Uncle Parmenter,"
Bowles continued, without answering Thomas's query,
" him as wor a noted wild-fowler on the Lincolnshire
coast, 'tother side the Wash, at a willage close ter
Wainfleet."

" I hev," said Pero ; " I know'd him when I lived
out that way ! I've seen him many a time when
I've bin shore-nettin'.[1] I ha' bought knots, cur-lew,
smee (wigeon), pewits, and all sorts, off him, when
I ha' wanted to make up a hamper of 'em for
Leadenhall Market. He *wor* a good shot, though
he didn't foller the gun reglar. He wor a blacksmith."

" That's right," said Stevey.

" Right ! " snapped Pero. " He ha' made me
picks ; and he used ter do the iron-work for me
when I built a boat. I know'd his old gun."

" ' Pifflin Jenny ' was the name she was know'd

---

[1] Shore-nets are placed vertically on stakes near the sea
in Lincolnshire for snaring wild-fowl, *e.g.* plovers, curlews,
knots, etc.

by," went on Bowles, taking his pipe out of his mouth, and expectorating into the fire."

"She——

"Dry up, Pestell, if you know about her, let the man go on."

"Well, old Dave, that wor my Uncle Parmenter, simply adored this ancient Spanish piece, which wor forty inches on the barrel. She wor a flint-lock, hed a steel ramrod, and a lot less rivets and screws in her fittin's that wor consistent with good behaviour. I wouldn't hev fired her off for a pension. She worn't no credit to a blacksmith ; but he allers said that if he once touched or tinkered her up, or puttied a blissed hole in her stock, her luck would change—— "

"Superstitious!" interjected Snicker.

"Lots of peepel are, though they 'ont own it."

" I ain't," said Snicker ; "though I'll allow I never go under a ladder, 'cept I'm forct to, and then I allers spits through the rungs. And I never had no luck on Breydon if I met a cross-eyed man agoin'. That ain't superstition, that's a Gord's truth. I've seen it many a time, and I've come back agin."

"Superstition or not," put it Stevey, "you're right. Cock-eyed people *are* unlucky. Then there's the evil eye. I've know'd people what hev it. Polly Ribbons had it. Somehow, she thought I oughter hev married her; but I allers felt more afeard on her than not, and young chaps don't jinrally marry gals they ain't a bit gone on. Well, mates, she reglar mock-mawed me—— "

"Bewitched yer!" broke in Pestell.

"Well," said Bowles, with a shrug of the shoulders, "she mock-mawed me; and things was the very devil with me for years; I done rotten with the eels. But one day she meets me and says—

"'Bowles! you'll catch a stone of eels to-day!'

"And so help me, mates, I got right in among 'em; and when I weighed-in the eels at old Bessey's, as true as I'm a livin' man, they pulled the scales down to a lumpin' fourteen pounds. She took the mock-mawrens off me that mornin', and ever arter-wards my luck wor changed."

"Why—a, superstitions," ventured Q——, a gunner, who drew up to the little crowd near the bar, "is all rot, and blamed on-convenient."

"*You're* superstitious," jibed in Pintail.

"How's that?" demanded Q——.

"You wear rubbidgely old eel-skins for garters for rewmatix!" sneered Thomas.

"And they're the best things in the world for 'em too," snapped Q——; "lots of Norfolk people used ter wear 'em more 'an they do now."

"Fates Bowles's hat wor unlucky," said Pestell. "I ha' seen birds git up out of the water a mile away, and wondered what wor a skeerin' of 'em, and turnin' round I ha' seen that tarnation old chimbley-pot loomin' up like a steamer's funnel, p'raps half a mile astern—— "

"My brother," went on Stevey, "ha' got a weak-ness for that hat; he thinks it a kind of link between the harrystocracy and us poor devils. He hopes to die and be buried in it. And why not?"

"It'll save a coffin!" sneered Pintail, amid a burst of laughter.

"Dave Parmenter," continued Stevey, "wouldn't hev no new-fangled notions about guns; he swore that nipple-guns wasn't safe; they didn't hit straight, and all that. 'Give me a flint-lock,' he'd say, 'and none of yer crack-patches.' He used ter load her with a handful of powder, and chance time with real duck-shot; but more often with iron filin's for small birds; and for geese and swans, theer wor nothin' like hoss-shoe nails, and stuff like that. Gord bliss me! he'd load it halfway up the barrel. He only once got me persuaded to go arter geese with him, but never no more.

"You know that every October-end there's great flocks of geese come to the Holkham meshes, round there by Wells; theer's white-fronts and pink-foots, mostly pink-foots, hundreds of 'em. They keep much to the land, and play the devil up with young growin' corn. If it's a bit stormy, they fare to break up into smaller lots and go foragin' further afield. South-easterly winds brought some of 'em to Wainfleet, least-wise, that wor old Dave's notion. Nothin' roused up his sanguinary instinx like geese. 'Theer's pickin' on 'em, my boy,' he'd say, 'and none o' yer pinglin', same as you hev on a teal or a skylark.'

"So on this day—it wor a Friday—he got me to go to the sand-hills, where he know'd there wor a flock of pink-foots—twenty of 'em in all."

"I trembled to see him load. Fust he put a bit of paper on the touch-hole, and lowered the trigger. Then he shot a lot of powder into his hand, and balanced it, to guess the proper weight: this he lowered down the spout, rammin' a big bit of brown paper down on tu it. Well, you'd think he wor hammerin' a hoss-shoe on a anvil, the way he punched into that wad, the swet reglar startin' on his forehid. Then he stood her by the vice, while he scraped up a lot of hoss-shoe nails, a big handful of 'em.

"'Uncle,' I says, 'air you goin' to sink a man-o'-war ship or shoot elephants?'

"'Stow that gab!' he says; 'what 'cher take me for—a fule?' I made no answer.

"Arter he'd primed her, off we goes goose-huntin'. When we got near the sand-hills, he pints to a lot of birds which I could see wor geese. They hadn't yet gone to breakfast. They wor cleanin' theerselves, and one old feller fared to be on sentry go.

"'Lay you agin that hump o' furze,' says Dave, 'I'll try what stalkin' 'em will do.' Theer wor an old dickey moachin' around, feedin' on furze, moss, marams, or anything he could find. No doubt he filled up with sand at a pinch. Dave Parmenter nabbed the moke, and clutchin' it by the short upright mane, nudged it with his elbows into a walk. The dickey fared nervous, and no doubt he'd ha' had a fit if he'd know'd what wor comin'. To cut matters short, Uncle Dave got within range of the geese; but the old sentry—he wor gettin' a bit skeart—holds his hid up and then digs at the next goose with his bill, pluckin' out feathers tu get him tu compare notes on the subjeck. He gives a sort of '_honk!_' when Dave, who wor waitin' for that minute when they all drawed a bit togither for a start, lets fly.

"Well, friends, I've seen a wreck blow'd up by dynamite, and I've seen a ingin bust up; but I never saw anything like that dickey goin' up, and turnin' a complete somersault, and then clearin' out. And the way Uncle, who'd shot under the donkey's belly, shot out back'ards, and comes down flat on his back, wor a sight to last a lifetime.

"I forgot all about the geese, and runs up to Uncle, expectin' he'd bin killed straight out.

"'Uncle,' I says, 'old feller, what's happinged? Do open yer eyes! Air you dade?' That's jist the manner of takin' on as cums first to my mind. I felt skearter 'an ever I'd done in my life. There *lay* Dave, his face black with powder smoke, for it came out of the gun like a fackterry chimbley. And a great bruise wor a-showin' up on his right cheek, evidently wheer the gun had punched him. I felt on him, but finds him sound in bone and limb, though if theer'd bin six ribs and two collar bones broke I shouldn't hev been surprised.

"Then thinks I, if you're dade, I must get you out of this; so I tried to lift him, but he wor plumb dade weight. 'Theer's one thing,' I says to myself, if I go and fetch a hand-cart you 'ont run away, and nobody 'll come nigh nor bye, unless it be the old Kentish crows—*they* might come and investigate, and a jab in the eyes of either.a dade or a live man ain't pleasant to think of. So I offs with my coat, and was jist hullin' it over Uncle's face, when I see his eyelids slowly open.

"'Good lord!' I says, 'Uncle, I thort you was kilt. Here's a nice pickle you put me in!'

" 'Boy,' says he, slow and solemn, 'where am I ? '

" 'Well, Uncle,' I says, 'if your sins wor forgiven, you've bin about as near Hevvin as you ever wor ; but as things has turned out, you're on Wainfleet sand-hills ! '

" 'Help me up ! ' says he, kinder dazed. ' Reach me old Jenny.'

I picks it up and I says, 'Uncle Dave, sure-ly you'll hull that beast on the scrap-heap afore you ever use it agin.' I looks at the gun as I gingerly gets hold of it ; it wor rusty as a hoss-shoe ; theer wor tarry twine carefully coiled round the barrel, holdin' it to the stock, with thin little wedges driv in to tighten it. And theer wor no trigger guard, the stock worm-eaten, and some holes in it wor puttied up.

" 'Boy,' he says, solemn-like, 'jist run and figger out the geese ; I'll wait till you come back.'

" So I hops off and goes to where the geese had been, and picks up three, as dade as nits.¹ One had got the hid blow'd off, another wor ripped up, and the other had a hole through the breast, what I could run my middle finger in.

" 'Dade ? ' hollers the old man.

" 'And pritty nigh resurrected,' I hollers back ; it worn't a fair shot noways ; I reckoned it was more like a 'sassination ! '

" I'd propped the old chap agin a sand-hill, and while I wor retrievin' the game, he'd bin rubbin' his cheek, feelin' all round his heart and limbs, and moppin' blood off his nose with a bit of cotton waste.

¹ A Norfolk figure of speech.

"'Nothin' amiss?' I says.

"'Sound in wind and limb!' he says, smilin', and lookin' lovin'ly at the old weapon. "'How long wor I onconscious?' he axes.

"'Twenty minutes,' I says. 'Why?'

"'Why, becos, boy, she's a real pet of a gun, and hev behaved right magnificent to me this mornin'. Why, I've been nearly a hour a-comin' round afore now; but *it ain't often she misses her goose*, bliss her old sowl."

"That all?" inquired Bessey.

"What more'd you hev?" asked Bowles.

"I'd ha' had Dave kilt," returned Bessey, "because that 'ud ha' been more tragic."

"Tragic be blowed!" retorted Bowles, "you can't allers kill people to order." . . .

"Is my man Johnny there?" queried the sharp voice of a red-faced woman, who, at that moment, thrust her head in at the door.

"Yes, missus," replied Pero Pestell; "pritty nigh tidly, as usurel. He wants lookin' after. Now then, Pintail," he added, turning to Johnny, "here's *the guv'nor*. You've got to go into the garden to pick guseberries."

"Guseberries be ——!" choked Johnny.

"Enough said," broke in Mrs. Thomas, as she strode across the parlour, and caught hold of her smaller half's collar. "You come home along wi' me, you lazy good-for-nothin'." And Johnny, in spite of the laughs of his companions, was obliged to follow his dominant partner; but he seemed to be half-sobered and not a little chagrined by her exposure of his complete subordination to "his old woman."

"I'll make some of you sore for this, you grinning ning-cumpoops!" he gasped, as he went out into the chilly air.

It was well nigh tea-time, and there was then prospect of a fairly fine evening. More than one gunner hinted that there *might* be something come to Breydon since Bowles had come away, and that Mrs. Thomas, having got wind of it, had ordered her man to get afloat and go and see. In the old days fowl were often shot at night when they could not be approached by day. *Old* Bessey was reported to be the doyen of night-hunters. He had a marvellously keen ear, and a quick sure method of calculating distances. He fashioned a sort of hollow chock, screwed it on the fore deck of his punt, and in it he rested the smaller end of his gun-barrel. The chock, upon which he had experimented, was placed at such an elevation that, when the gun rested upon it, and was fired, it was most deadly at sixty yards range. At night, when it was pitch dark, he would paddle up to within the proper distance of a flock of feeding fowl—judging by their cackle and the noise they made in snapping off the grass—and fire into the dark without seeing the slightest sign of a bird. Then he would row round and gather up the spoils, and after calculating the strength and direction of the tides, he would hasten back by daybreak to hunt for the cripples along the walls.

SNIPE. HARD TIMES

A NIGHT SITTING

That night, Thomas, Short'un, Pero Pestell and one or two others were missing from Reed's parlour. Two had gone after fowl: the others had something else to do, for the night proved fairly fine. Next night, however, it came on to blow great guns ; and sleet made the streets bleak and uncomfortable. The red window blinds of the *Lord* —— glowed like danger signals, but failed to warn away those who bent their steps thither at nightfall, as was their wont.

There was a fairly good mustering of the old school, met, as usual, to continue their lessons, arguments, and amusements. Pero,[1] Short'un, and Thomas,[2] as I have said, were absent, but Bessey,[3] Stevey Bowles,[4] "Fiddler" Goodens,[5] "Snicker" Larn,[6] "Scarboro" Jack, Q——, and several others, including a well-known river-poacher, whom I will call F——,[7] had dropped in, and were variously occupied. Some were quietly chatting in twos and threes on the seats around the bar-parlour ; others were leaning on the counter or lounging near the stove.

[1] Pero died in Yarmouth Workhouse, in 1907.
[2] Thomas pre-deceased him by six years.
[3] Dead.
[4] Dead.
[5] To-day is very aged and feeble.
[6] Still hale and robust.
[7] This man, who is still living, has always been exceedingly wary of my attempts at chatting with him : for certain reasons do not think it expedient to name him.

"I wonder how Fates Bowles's hat's gettin' on?" asked Larn. "I lay you a brass fardin its just about soft by his a-weepin' over it. It's stiffinin' it wants to get them kinks out what Pero put in. How's trade, Dinks?"

"Dinks" Cox significantly shook his head.

"Eels—well, there don't fare to be none," he replied. "I got about five pound of little totty things this mornin'; and I got this," holding up a parcel—something wrapped in an old sack.

All faces were turned to Dinks, who shot out on to the counter a tall hat.

"Sure-ly," exclaimed "Fiddler" Goodens— "sure-ly old Fates ain't bin and committed suicide! Let's look at it."

It was handed over to Goodens for identification and then passed round. "It ain't Fates's," he remarked. "It's too respectable." They all concurred.

"I never said 't wor, did I?" asked Dinks. "You chaps fare to me to jump to conclusions. It's brains what cher want—leastwise you've got 'em, most on you, but you don't fare to ile 'em nor make the most on 'em. Is theer a couple of poker-burnt holes in it? Is theer a concertina's wind-bag down on it, what wor invented by Pero? Is it half naked of nap—kinder badly moulted? No! a nice lot of chaps to sware on for special constables *you'd* be."

"Sure-ly you ain't givin' to wear toppers, Dinks?" asked three of them in a breath. "Put it on and let's see how you look." Dinks put it on. It did

not suit him ; on that all were agreed.   Larn thought
it looked "like a nob on top of a pump."   Others
thought "it looked even wusser."

"Well, mateys," he went on, "I bought it for
tuppence off a look-'em-up ;[1] thinkin' perhaps it
might du for poor old Fates.   It 'ud du for everyday
wear, and he might keep the t'other for Sundays."

It was a trifling act, but it revealed Dinks's kindly
nature.

The door opened, and in walked a man whom I
will call H——.

"Hallo, boys!" said he, "anything on Breydon?"

"Very little," replied more than one.

H—— called for something to drink.   He was a
dealer in birds—birds suitable for stuffing purposes,
several collectors being always ready to take rarities
off him.   He also dealt largely in British birds' eggs,
and was reputed to have been the greatest incentive
to ornithological vandalism in the Broadlands.   Ruffs
in their frills, bitterns, bearded tits, their eggs and
nests *in situ*, ospreys, white wagtails, greater shear-
waters, Lapland buntings, tawny pipits, Caspian terns
—all these he had had, and was always eager for
more.   He got them, of course, as cheaply as he
could ; bargained like a Jew, but paid up honestly
and promptly when a bargain had once been struck.

He chatted for a while with most of the company, and then vanished as suddenly as he had
appeared.

"He wor born on springs," ventured Snicker.
"I can't make him out."

---

[1] Marine store dealer.

" *You* ain't no use to him," said " Scarboro " Jack, "he wants bahds ; eels ain't in his line."

" How's the fresh-water fish biz ? " asked Scarboro, turning to F——.

F——'s keen blue eyes wandered swiftly round the room. He wished to feel safe before replying.

" D—— bad," he replied, laconically.

" Ah, bor, them wor the times, afore that blessed Fishery Act comes up and knocks nettin' in the rivers on the head."

" Yes," assented F——.

" You ha' known the time when you and Short'un Page, and Jim Calver, could do three nights' work a week, and live like lords and fightin'-cocks the rest. I once see old Calver and Short'un get the net round such a lot of fish—great old bream, as large round as this barrel-head, roach—beauties, carps, and dowst know what all ;—and they had to bale 'em into the boat with a hamper, for fear of breakin' the net. And when the boat was loaded a'most gunnel deep, they had to lift the leads, and let the remainder go back agin to the river."

" I ha' done that many a time," assented F——, " but not lately."

" No," said Jack, " I did hear you'd gone and jineded the Chirch."

The wink he gave F—— was not returned. At that juncture the door was quickly opened, and " Cadger " Brown leapt in, strode to the counter, and handed something in a bag to the landlord ; who immediately dropped it into an empty barrel that stood behind the counter, and which had a

K

head that was made to open and close in an ingenious manner.

"Cadger's" face at once assumed a look of affable innocence; and it was illumined directly after by a bland smile when he lifted a tankard of foaming ale to his lips. He looked slyly round at the door as if expecting some one.

The door again opened, and in walked P.-c. Gill, who had strong suspicions at all times about the cunning water-cress man, and not without good reason, for he seldom did anything, beyond water-cress gathering, that was not "on the crook." Even his cress, gathered from ditches that bordered hare-frequented marshes, often covered ill-gotten gains.

Gill beckoned to Brown and then went outside, "Cadger" presently following him. What happened there could only be conjectured by the company; but presently Brown stalked in again, and ordered more liquor.

"I done him again that time!" was all he said; and no amount of quizzing could get another remark from him. He was a strange self-contained fellow, and enjoyed his wild escapades. Risk and excitement were to him the spice and flavouring of his law-breaking life. The landlord handed him a silver coin and asked no questions about the sack or its contents. In another moment "Cadger" Brown had vanished.

The next visitor to drop in was the diminutive "Short'un," on whose back was slung a bunch of coots tied by the necks: they were wet with salt water and sprinkled with sleet. From the mouths of two or three were suspended green ribbons of wigeon grass (*Zostera marina.*) The little man had slain some half-score of them. Driven from the broads by the previous week's sharp frosts, they had found their way to the more open waters of Breydon, led probably by individuals who had been there on previous occasions. There they had tasted of the luscious "grass," and had been loath to leave it. Like a flock of sheep they had wandered to and fro, keeping well together, rarely to be caught napping, but occasionally suffering severely when a big gun came within firing distance.

"That all you've got?" asked the landlord.

"Wal, that's all I've brung," replied Short'un. "You may hev a pair of 'em; give us the rafflin'-box."

"Now then, chaps," he went on, turning to the company, "any of you want a brace? Come on, a penny a time."

Pennies were soon forthcoming, the coots quickly changed hands, and the men turned to their cards and yarning. It was the usual thing. Coots were poor men's geese in those days. Short'un assured me that in years gone by—the sixties and seventies [1]—he frequently brought in forty on a Saturday night—"the week's seftings," [2] he termed them. "My old woman," he said, "was a don hand at dressin' 'em. Lots of people used ter bring 'em to her to get 'em ready for cookin'. She seft the feathers. Then she'd powder 'em all over with resin, and rub 'em well: this brought off all the doom (down); and they come up as nice

[1] Vide *Nature in Eastern Norfolk*, p. 211.
[2] Savings.

as a duck. She got a penny a bird for dressin' of
'em."

Then Short'un went over to the counter again ;
he was thirsty. He remarked in going—

" I used ter allers look to coots in the winter to
supply me with bacca and beer."

     .   .   .   .   .

The *Lord* —— no longer exists. It was demolished in 1894, after standing a long time empty.
Its site is now covered by a part of a huge beer-store.
Most of the queer characters who frequented it have
also disappeared ; the few who remain are aged and
decrepit, though one or two of them still pursue their
old callings.   There are still a few small river-side
taverns in which the rough and rugged frequenters of
our waterways congregate, and where the incidents of
their unromantic and toilsome lives are discussed in
language that savours of the salt sea, the flowing
tides, and the wild life amid which they spend their
lives.

THE BREYDON PARLIAMENT

In recent years there stood on Fuller's Hill a
conglomeration of stables and sheds, one of which,
an upstair workshop, was occupied by a cabinet-
maker named Beckett. He was, and is still, one of
the most ingenious of men, and can turn a long solid
cylinder of steel into a beautifully finished breech-
loading punt-gun, or a litter of dilapidated oak
fittings into a fine piece of antique furniture. His
fame as a punt-builder was long ago established.[1]

[1] Vide *Wild Life on a Norfolk Estuary*, p. 82.

One of the strangest things about him was that he never worked so well as when a crowd of gossiping sportsmen filled the greater part of his workshop, filling it with tobacco smoke and a babel of voices. To this day a younger generation of wild-fowlers gathers about him in another shop. In the days to which I refer, when I was an enthusiastic gunner, there assembled around him a host of similar characters—this was in the eighties and nineties. I can remember Harvey[1] the bird-stuffer, Pintail Thomas, Crowther, Quinton the bird catcher, Smith the bird dealer, and a host of others who met together and argued, spun yarns, and debated the news in the world that bordered on tidal waters.

"Go on," said Beckett, "you may all jaw at once, it won't hinder me; the more the merrier!" . . .

It happened one day that a cock linnet, which had been kept in one of Beckett's cages for a decade, died. For some time it had ceased to sing, and having "cage-moulted," it had lost all those beautiful rosy tints which distinguish the bird in its wild state.

"I'll lay you a bet," said one unbelieving individual, "that *ain't* a cock, it's an old hen."

Some disagreed with him; but no one present during the earlier part of the evening was capable of deciding its sex by dissection. Harvey, however, was due to arrive at an early moment; and it was arranged he should be led into a trap and made to reveal his method of solving the question. And so they bided their time.

Later on, up shambled Harvey, as was his wont,

[1] See *Nature in Eastern Norfolk*, p. 79.

in search of any rare or interesting birds, which he was eager to obtain, or even to hear of.

"What luck, boys?" he asked.

"Bad luck!" said Beckett, "as far as I'm concerned."

"What is it?" asked Harvey.

Beckett told him, and boasted what a gallant little cock bird it had been, at the same time telling him that half of the men present had declared it was not a male bird.

"Now, then, you shall be judge, for we can rely on *you*!"

The bird-stuffer was very susceptible to flattery.

"Any one got a pen-knife?" he asked. "*I'll* soon show you what it is!"

A knife was handed to him, and in a few moments the side of the little "subject" had been penetrated, the intestines pressed on one side, and the *testes* proudly exhibited to the now convinced audience. It was on this very occasion that Lowne, the taxidermist, and my chum Ben Dye, first learned to distinguish the sexes of birds by dissection.

"I lighted lucky to-day!" chuckled the wily Harvey. "Done old Durrant (the game dealer) nicely."

"How?" said Dye. "It's no great feat to boast of."

"Well," said Harvey, "I was overhauling the ducks on the stall, and dropt on to a white-eyed pochard, got it for a bob; and he didn't know it from a barn-door fowl."

Harvey, it appeared, was running his eye over a number of hard-fowl—tufted ducks, pochards, scaups, etc.—when his keen glance fell on the distinctive orbs of that locally rare water-fowl, only twenty of which had been obtained in the county.[1] Seeing Durrant busy with a customer, Harvey, in an off-hand manner, threw down upon the stall a tufted duck, a common pochard, and *Nyroca,* as if they were of no particular account.

"How much for the lot, Durrant—these hard fowl?"

"Oh," said Durrant, still busily engaged, "three shillings." Harvey threw down the money, pretended to stow the birds away in his pocket, and walked away. Next day he was still so elated with his prize that he went back to the game-dealer and very unkindly asked him if he knew what he had let him have for a shilling! Durrant was so annoyed that he never forgave him.

"You bird-stuffers are a lot of swindlers," remarked "Admiral" Gooch, a one-time gentleman-gunner who had fallen on evil times.

"How do you make that out?" demanded Harvey.

"Well, I'll tell you," answered the Admiral. "I was on Breydon, in July, 1867, when I saw a small dark bird come gaily tripping along. I thought it was a black tern, for it dipped every few yards at what I took to be insects ; but I could not distinguish a fish in its beak. I soon shot it, and as I had not then started collecting birds, I took it to Carter, who was a good bird-man, but as big a rascal as yourself. I'm giving it you plainly, and you can put it in your pipe and smoke it!"

[1] See *Wild Life on a Norfolk Estuary,* p. 246.

" Hear ! Hear ! " from one or two, and " Draw it mild," from others. Harvey coloured up, and bit his side whiskers—a habit he had when agitated.

"' H'm,' said Carter, when I took it to him ; 'a common stormy petrel : give you a shilling for it if you like—'taint worth more. Besides, it's too greasy for a specimen.'

" I took the shilling, left the bird, and went with a friend into the *Standard,* where we had a port wine each.

" A few weeks afterwards, Silky Watson told me I'd made a fool of myself.

"' Didn't you sell Carter a fork-tailed petrel ?' [1] he asked.

"' I sold him a petrel,' I replied, ' for a shilling.'

"' Well,' said Silky, ' he's been and made three pound of it !'

" So I hold," went on Gooch, " that bird-stuffers are all cast in one mould ; they'd cheat their own grandmothers."

Harvey's patience was becoming sorely tried, but he made no attempt to defend himself.

" Is your cat still alive ? " asked Dye, a smile going round at the question.

" Which one ? " said Harvey.

" Why, the one that ate my turtle dove that I brought you ten years ago to stuff," answered Dye.

" That cat ate more birds than mice," retorted the Admiral. " I know a purple sandpiper and a black-

[1] This is undoubtedly the example referred to in Stevenson's *Birds of Norfolk*, vol. iii. p. 370.

tailed godwit, not to mention a little bittern, which that same cat ate. Pity you didn't use arsenic!"

Harvey looked intensely annoyed, but still said nothing.

"I'm very much mistaken if I haven't seen the *skins* of all three in R——'s collection of local birds. No doubt pussy did eat the birds after you'd skinned them."[1]

"She once ate a glaucous gull, didn't she?" asked Beckett. "I hope she didn't find it fishy!"

At length, Harvey, finding things getting too hot for him, slipped out of the workshop. Conversation now became general.

"Whose swan have you been shooting, Johnny?" asked one.

"No one's," replied Thomas, with emphasis.

"It's a tame one—a cygnet!" replied his interlocutor. "And you orter know better, at your time of life, killing people's property. Why, you'll be shooting cows on a mesh directly."

"That's about all you could hit," retorted Pintail. "Who's to know a tame swan from a wild 'un on the wing, specially in a snow-squall?"

"I reckon if the owner was to see that bird hangin' up at your shop, you'd get locked up!" said another.

"I hold," answered Johnny Thomas, alias Pintail, "that if it hev neither 'nicks' nor other private

---

[1] Harvey was notorious for the excuse that rare birds, left with him to preserve, had been eaten in his absence by the cat ; and there is no doubt that numerous collections in and beyond the county profited, as he himself certainly did, by this trickery.

marks on its bill or legs the owner might swear till he's blue to the back of his neck, and then not convince a judge it's his."

"What is the law on swan-shooting?" queried Crowther.

"The law," replied the Admiral, "as defined forty years ago by one of our magistrates, when dealing with a fellow who shot three of Butterfield's tame ducks, is very complex. Dick Hammond, the magistrate, asked the defendant where he shot the ducks.

"'On the marsh, your worship, where folks from time immemorial have gone "flighting."'

"'Were they flying?' asked the J.P.

"'No, your worship,' said he, honestly enough; 'they were bibbling in the reeds, half a mile away from anywhere.'

"'Queer place to feed,' said Hammond. 'I must fine you just as if you'd shot a straying cow or hen. *Had they been flying* I should have taken a different view of the matter.'"

"The same thing might apply to swans," said Dye, "and I'd shoot a flying swan to-morrow if I had the chance, and for that matter, even if it were bibbling in the mud on Breydon."

"What about parrots, Wigg?" asked a joker.

"Parrots, ah!" replied Wigg.

"What's that about parrots?" questioned the Admiral.

"Oh," said the little shore-gunner, "I was up one day by the big rond, about two miles up Breydon walls, hidden behind a pile of swills (fish baskets). I was laying in wait for some grey plover as were working towards me, when all on a sudden—

"'Hallo!' says somebody.

"'Hallo!' says I, peering round; 'how you startled me!' But I could see no one.

"'It's cold,' said the voice.

"'Good lord, so it is,' I says. 'But where are you?'

"'Go to blazes—and be tarred!' replied *something* or *somebody*; and then I begins to get my dander up.

"'I'll blaze *you* if you ain't a-going, whoever you are,' says I; and then, 'strue as I'm alive! up jumped a green parrot off the top swill behind me!

"'Ha! ha! ha!' laughed the cheeky bird; and before I could check myself I'd let fly, damaging its wing.

"'I'll teach you to cheek a *man!*' I remember saying, for I was sorter annoyed, though I felt a fool after I'd wounded the poor thing. I never found out who it belonged to, and as I wasn't very proud of being fooled, I never made many inquiries."

"I suppose you sent a note about it to the scientific papers as a new species of British bird!" remarked the Admiral.

"No, I didn't," snapped Wigg.

"Like Quinton did," suggested Beckett. "He's a don hand at adding new birds to the list."

"Shaft-tailed Whydah birds," remarked Dye, on which the company laughed, for it was well known that Quinton had on one occasion shot a bird of this species as it flew along the north beach. Feeling sure that no such bird had ever before been obtained on our coasts, he took train to Norwich, and waited upon a leading county naturalist, who very soon satisfied him that no value was attached to this undoubted " escape."

" What's the rummest thing you ever saw on Breydon ? " asked the loquacious Admiral.

" Me ? " asked Wigg.

" *You*, and no other," replied this suave individual.

" Well," he answered, " I believe it was somewhere about thirty years ago,[1] when I was up Breydon walls, that I passed 'Brusher' Broom and ' Putty' Westgate (a well-known painter and gunner at that time) sound asleep on the grassy slope of the walls, when a couple of large, dark-coloured eagles came sailin' around. I passed on, but lookin' back I see one of them circling above them chaps. Thinks I, it's a rummon if they don't swoop down—one on 'em anyway—and I felt half scared, I can tell you, and hollered out. But all on a sudden, up jumps ' Brusher,' and lets fly at the nearest bird, which wheeled round, flew to one of the stakes in the channel, and started pickin' itself as if scratching or biting at where, no doubt, some shot had stung it. They wouldn't be expectin' to meet with anything so large, and so hadn't big enough shot to cripple an eagle."

" I heard of a pair of eagles when I lived at Horsey," volunteered a spare-built man, named

---

[1] I myself saw an eagle pass over from sea towards Breydon one morning in the autumn of 1879 (see *Nature in Eastern Norfolk*, pp. 160–61). Broom himself confirmed the story above related.

Harwood, who had been an intent listener, "they played a rare game with our rabbits." His father had been gamekeeper and warrener there.

"I'm now speakin' of when I was a boy—in '57. My father had shot a stoat and laid it on a rail, and coming back after his rounds, went to pick it up, and it was gone. He swore one of them eagles had carried it away. They never gave him a chance to shoot them, but I believe they were shot afterwards at Winterton or Hemsby, on the warren there."

"Stoats are queer things to tackle alive," remarked the Admiral, turning to Harwood.

"They weren't any too scarce," replied Harwood, "on our warren ; and polecats hadn't all been mopped out. As to tackling them alive, I don't remember much about that. We left the warren before I was ten. I know my father used to trouble very little about either ; and sometimes I had to crawl into the deeper and bigger rabbit holes to nab rabbits by the leg, which I handed out to him. Then father would seize *me* by the legs and pull *me* out.

"I remember once," he went on, "when I was nine, being asked by my mother to get her enough polecats, which were scarce then, to make her a tippet.[1] I dug a hole in the side of a sand-hill, then getting the insides (entrails) of a rabbit on a

---

[1] When this warrener's family removed to Yarmouth, Harwood's father hired a market garden, and Mrs. Harwood "sat" the market with rabbits every Saturday. I distinctly remember the old lady wearing the identical "tippet" round her neck, but whether it was really stoat or polecat fur I do not remember.

stick, I trailed them all round for at least a hundred yards, focussing the "scent" right up to this hole. Then I stuck the giblets with a big skewer into the bank, burying a steel-fall below it, and left it. In a week I got six polecats. We dressed the skins, and mother wore the tippet for years.

"Father wasn't altogether wise, I should say," went on Harwood, "over my rabbit catching: for I once put my arm down a hole to try and reach a wheatear's nest, and laid hold of a viper by mistake."

"I hold," said Beckett, laying down his plane, and putting some pieces of coke upon the fire, "there's a lot too much of that adding of new species, without sufficient evidence." He was harking back to the Whydah episode.

"So say I," remarked Dye; "I don't believe so much in this dividing and sub-dividing of species. No doubt a cole-tit or a starling may differ slightly in wide areas, say half across a continent; but a cole-tit is a cole-tit, even if you call one species a *Parus ater* and another *Parus britannicus.*"

"You're right, Ben," broke in the Admiral, "I don't see that gradual variations, however wide a gap you may make between them, are really and justly entitled to so-called specific distinctions. I suppose every bird-man has an ambition to shine in some way or other, however feeble the twinkle of his star. A few men have greatness thrust upon them, but the majority break their necks, so to speak, in grabbing for the shadow of it, don't they Pintail?" digging his thumb into the ribs of the little punt-gunner.

"So you say," replied Thomas.

At that moment Whiley entered the workshop, and at once made himself at home.

"You know something about swans," said the Admiral, and he repeated the opinions that had been expressed concerning the lawfulness of shooting swans.

"I don't see," said Whiley, "how the law could touch any one, at any rate miles away from where tame swans breed. You know it's generally young ones as wander: the old ones know well enough where grub is always to be had, and they prefer to stop at home. The funny thing about it is that they hardly ever stray except in weather what's bad enough to drive whoopers and Bewicks hereabouts. You've heard the swan song, what they used ter sing?"

"No! no!" came from one and another of the assembly. "Let's hear it, if you know it." And so insistent became the demand, that Whiley yielded. After one or two false starts, he sang the quaint ballad-like verses in a droning voice that was neither a treble nor an alto.

> Come all you young sportsmen,
> Who carry a gun,
> I will have you get home,
> By the light of the sun ;
> Don't you be like young Jamie who was fowling alone
> When he shot his own true love in the room of a swan.
>
> Then home comes young Jamie
> With his dog and gun,
> Saying " Uncle, oh ! uncle,
> Do you know what I've done?
> Consume that old gunsmith that made me this gun,
> I have shot my own true love in the place of a swan."

Then up starts his uncle,
With his locks so grey,
Saying " Jamie, oh ! Jamie,
Do you not run away ;
Don't you leave your own country till your trial come on,
You ne'er shall be hanged for shooting a swan."

When the trial came on
Pretty Polly appeared,
Saying " Uncle, oh ! uncle,
Let my Jamie go clear ;
For my apron was bound round me when he took me
    for a swan,
And his heart now lay bleeding for Polly his own."

" Bravo ! "

ANXIOUS MOMENTS

WHIMBREL

CHAPTER IV

SHALLOW WATERS

"Oh, life is a river, and man is the boat
That over its surface is destined to float;
While joy is a cargo so easily stored,
That he is a fool who takes sorrow aboard."

JEFFREYS

A HOUSE-BOAT 'CONFAB'

YESTERDAY (March 29th, 1908) the wind blew stiffly from the nor'ard, and Breydon fretted itself, flinging spume and choppy waves, thick with silt, against the southern flint-lined wall. During the afternoon black-headed gulls in some numbers had merrily fished the channel for floating food that had been thrown out of the shrimp-boats or carried out of the sewers. Towards sunset there was calm, and the waters became as placid as in midsummer. The temptation to spend a night with Jary in the watch-boat was not to be resisted, so, throwing into the punt a couple of blankets and a basket of eatables, I paddled upstream on the last of the flood-tide.

By this time the blackheads had retired to the flats; the majority of the some two thousand birds were there, preening their feathers and gossiping; those few that seemed still to be hungry were worming at the edge of the flats. How these birds so readily detect a red ragworm in the soft ooze passes my comprehension. Not the slightest movement as of a worm working is to be detected by human eye, although, by looking carefully, you see here and there small round holes, as if bored by a thick needle. It is a rare thing to find the occupant at the surface. At least, that is my experience. Yet with definite thrust the keen-eyed gull, which may possess microscopic powers of sight, grabs at something, and out comes a worm as sure as fate. You may observe the gulls stop suddenly in their flight, drop lightly on to the shallow water, seize a worm, and with a quick, gentle tug, haul it out, in some cases swallowing it inch by inch as it comes out. Some of the ragworms appear to be drawn out to quite four inches in length.

Why these gulls should have been absent from their nesting quarters, or whether they were males off duty from the nest, I cannot say; for the black-headed gull should be "at home" by the second week in March, and eggs are laid by the middle of the month. Their breeding haunts were within an hour's easy flight of Breydon; but they remained with us all night, and had not gone home when I rowed back to Yarmouth in the morning.

There was quite a mustering of redshanks, the male birds "clicking" as if it were already nesting-time, and uttering a variety of calls betokening pleasure, satisfaction, and caution. One large parcel of ringed plovers, among which were a couple of knots, flew around, probably for the pleasure of the exercise. A few scattered herons were faring badly; and I have no doubt that they spent the night hungry; eels as yet were not much in evidence, and flounders were very scarce. At intervals the muscial *smee-ou* of the wigeon mustering on the flats near the "Fleet" water was heard.

Night came on cloudless, and the stars, big and brilliant, were reflected distinctly in the depths of the dark waters. A long glowing line of light hung low over the distant town, and stronger lights twinkled here and there below, some of them being also reflected by the waters of Breydon.

"Seen anything of 'Peg-leg' up here lately?" I asked Jary.

"No," replied he, "I hear his leg's in a bad way—reg'lar worm-eaten, and he can't either get about or get a new 'un," and he laughed heartily, tickled by the joke. I had found him busily engaged in cutting out floats for his new smelt net, using a razor blade lashed on to a stout handle whittled from a bit of firewood. The floats were being fashioned from the derelict floats that drifted up to Breydon during the herring fishery: he had accumulated a sackful in the course of the season.

"Peg-leg" is an old man-o'-war pensioner who had lost a leg. As soon as he could manage to get back to Breydon, he returned to his old-time haunts on river and tide-way, adding to his small regular income a varying additional sum by eel-babbing and picking. He and his small open boat seem part and parcel of each other; I never remember seeing him standing up in it, and it is just possible that had he done so he would have scuttled it with his wooden leg.

The stump of his leg had been inserted in a cup-like structure, with a screw-hole in the end of it. The additional "peg" was renewed from time to time as the old one wore up or was broken by use or accident. "Peg-leg" has his own peculiar methods of embarking and changing his position in the boat; but he prefers to keep them secret. When once afloat, he seldom moves from one position, either to row or to fish.

"You've heard about him settin' fire to his leg once, h'ain't you, Pattson?" asked Jary, smiling.

I pleaded ignorance.

"Well," said he, "he goes home one night after he'd just got his pension, and he sits afore the fire, cogitatin'-like. The fire didn't burn exactly to his likin', so he uses his peg for a poker, as he'd often done afore. It happens he was gettin' drowsy, and also that his toe gets fast between the bars. A smell of burning wakes the old woman; she roused the house up, and comes floppin' downstairs, to find him sound asleep, and the leg smoulderin' well up the stick !"

It was the butt-end now that had gone, Jary said, it had succumbed to the attacks of worms. "Peg-leg" is the most optimistic eel-fisherman I ever knew; I never saw him with a greater catch than seven pounds of eels, but from the way in which he would describe the "whoppers" and "monsters" and "clinkers" that kept biting, you might imagine he was filling his boat. It is quite a usual thing for another fisherman to vary the monotony of a night's fishing by asking the size and weight of the eel he (Peg-leg) had just lost.

"I've got some beauties round about," he would reply, "but they 'ont hang!"

Chatting of wooden legs reminded me of one eccentric character who frequented Breydon until the early seventies. I never knew him by any other name, or nickname, than "The One-legged Stint," from his misfortune of possessing one sound leg only, and another as brittle and rigid as "Peg-leg's." There were other "Stints" little and big in the family who beasted at least a respectable Christian name. "One-legged Stint" was keen after birds and reckless in his methods. One day he laid at a bunch of curlews and killed several;. then, forgetting the risks he ran, he sprang out of the boat, and tried to stump across the flat to retrieve them. He had not proceeded many steps before his wooden-leg disappeared up to the stump in ooze, throwing him off his balance, and placing him in an awkward predicament. There was nothing for it but to throw himself on his back in the mud, and yell at the top of his voice for help, which, fortunately, was not long in coming.

Jary grumbled about the way eels had fallen off in late years, thanks to the carbolic acid and sewage which polluted these lower waters. He had had some good hauls at times, but only at irregular intervals.

"My largest catch?" he queried. "Well, I got that at South Walsham a few years ago, on the 21st and 22nd of May, when the bream and other fresh-water fishes were 'rouding' (spawning). These first two nights of spawning fairly roused up the eels, which bit at anything. I made a rattling good haul. After that they were so full of ova that they went off feed so far as worms and babs was concerned. The bream crowded so into the reeds to spawn, that I got hold of three simply by dropping naked hooks in amongst them, and jerkin' 'em into them.

"How did I cook them? Well, I skinned 'em, flaked off each side, and fried 'em; and ripping tack they wor."

"Swans," Jary went on, "are awful fond of ova and gobble it up with gusto; so will tame ducks, which seem to know when spawning time comes on. My eel-pots and nets have been smothered with the slimy stuff, when I've laid up the rivers, and they took some getting clean.

"Swans are rum things, I can tell you. I know'd B—— get into a rare muddle with an old he-bird. B—— had taken a fancy to a fine cygnet in a brood of little 'uns—a nice duck-size little chap—thinking it would make him a decent dinner. He caught it, but the old 'un came at him like a steam-engine, and do what he would he couldn't beat it off. The swan actually started climbing up the stern of the boat, and certainly would have managed to get in if B—— hadn't thought it time to come to terms. So he hulled (threw) the cygnet overboard, and while the old 'un was assuring itself that it was all right, he rowed away as fast as his oars could take him. Swans are funny old nuts to crack, 'specially when they're in a bad temper."

"Hallo! you there!"

"What O!" said Jary, opening the door of the houseboat. "What's up, old Short'un?"

"Nothin' pertickler," said Short'un Page, hitching his painter to the ringle at the stern of the houseboat. "Only can you give us a match, for I've got my blessed pipe, and every bloomin' match gone. I hadn't only two in the box when I first lit up."

We got Short'un inside, and Jary poured out for him a cup of mahogany-coloured tea, which he drank almost at a draught.

"Not much doin'," went on Short'un, "fare as if there's nothin' stirrin'. What's come to the blessed eels goodness only knows."

"You've given up smelting?" I queried.

"Yes, bor, yes! I'm gettin' old and good-for-nothin'. I was obliged to give it up. I couldn't hold the net, it got too much for me; besides I got so giddy I was allers afeard of pitchin' in hid first. So I've hired this old boat (a veritable wash-trough it was!)

off 'Clamps', and I'm tryin' to do a bit of babbin':
I can't live on parish allowance."

"We were talking of swans," I remarked.

"Swans!" he jibed in—"I like swans' eggs, when
they're to be got easy. I once found no less than
five wind-eggs—lash-eggs, you know, without shells
on 'em—layin' in shallow water up the Norwich
river. I fished 'em out, sosh-ways, with the eel-pick,
and it took a bit of doin'. I afterwards eat 'em."

"Liked them ? "

"Liked 'em ? I should just say I did. Why, one
of 'em, and a bit of steak fried with it, filled the pan—
and me too!" And he chuckled over the recollection.
"I could jist do with one now this minnit!"

"Swans are fond of bream spawn, aren't they?" I
asked.

"Rather," replied the old man ; "so's eels, Lor'
bliss you, yes, you can't get them away from it. Old
Snicker 'an me have bin workin' up the rivers right
among the 'spawnin'' roach, and perch, and bream ;
all choose their own partic'lar places. I've seen the
spawn hangin' like curtains (festoons) on the reeds, and
heer'd the eels suckin' on it down. You could see
the reeds all a-work with eels. I once stuck in my
pick down below among the reeds, flat-ways, you
know, not upright, and I brought up at one stroke
thirteen eels as thick as your finger—six and seven to
the pound size. Eels die very quickly at that time,
if you cut 'em with the pick above the navel (vent);
spawn fare to spile 'em and reg'lar rot 'em.

"Big catches of eels? Well, bor, you've got to
go well up the rivers for 'em nowadays, and then it

ain't like what it wor. The best catch I ever know'd
of? Well, that was in May, 1896, when old 'Bugles'
and 'Sharper' got right in among 'em at South
Walsham Broad; they took seventeen stone of eels,
gettin' a £7 cheque from London for 'em.

"Bite! ah! It's a treat to feel 'em when they're
properly on the chuck; you feel it right up the
string through the stick, sorter electrifying you. Old
Crowther used ter say as how the biting of a nice eel
at a bab was a 'lovely sensation.' I liked the sensation of *seein'* it a scrigglin' in the boat; then I know'd
I'd got him!

"What's that? Who's shootin'?" he asked, whilst
refilling his pipe, preparatory to going.

"I expect that's Fred Clarke," said Jary, " killin'
rats over by his houseboat. He's been troubled a
bit with 'em lately. He baits 'em for a night or two,
and marks the spot; he can hear when they're
squakin', for they haggle for a bit of herrin'. He
killed four the 'tother night."

"Rats! ah, the varmin!" exclaimed Short'un.
" I 'member once layin' in my houseboat at Reedham, when I found I'd got a fam'ly of rats aboard.
They reg'lar run'd over me a-nights, and played the
dowst with my wittels. So I got a chap with a ferret
to see if he couldn't settle 'em. Blow my skin! if
they didn't skeddadle one arter the 'tother out
through the fore part of the boat, over the moorin'
rope and up the pilin's of the bridge. Every blessed
one of 'em escaped. But so long as they wor gone
I didn't care so much. I bunged up the hole so
they didn't get in ag'in, besides shifting my moorin's.

And when we comes to overhaulin' the boat I found in the lockers and under the floor-boards three bushels of mushel-shells clean and picked as if biled. They'd taken the mushels in when I laid on Breydon —picked 'em up off the flats at low-water. But I must be a-goin'. Good night, both on ye."

"Good night, Short'un !" "Good night . . . !"

Jary and I sat chatting long after tea, while he completed his task of float-making. We discussed various subjects interesting to both of us. Otters, rats, herons, eels, wildfowl, and man. At ten o'clock, when I took a last look out, the darkness shut out all the town-lights and the stars. The only sound to be heard was the mellow " *Smee-ou* " of a sentinel wigeon that was keeping watch while his companions dozed or fed.

"I don't like the feel of the air," said Jary, " there's a change comin'."

In the morning, at 5.45 a.m., I opened the house-boat door and looked out. The sun had risen with a glaring, watery eye, above a purple horizon.

"Look at those mock suns!" I said to Jary. Two circular spots, the parhelia of scientists, bore the sun company, one on either side of him. They looked like two magnificent glass marbles, with iridescent blotchings, for all the world like circular discs stamped out of a rainbow. The sun looked about as big as a large barrel-head ; the dogs were each about a fourth of that size.

"Lor', bor!" said he, "they're sun dogs, and a sure sign of weather a-comin'."

"Weather ?" I queried—" *what* weather ? "

RATS AND RINGED PLOVER

"There'll be some *weather* afore night," he replied sagely, "I've seen them afore."

He was not far out in his prophecy, for it blew pretty stiffly in the afternoon, and rained heavily at night.

AMONG THE SMELTS

"Snicker" Larn and his new smelting chum, "Buck" Smith, were carefully taking down their net from some spikes that for years had been stuck in the railway fencing at the entrance of the Bure. The prudent fisher was always careful of his nets; and just as the herring-fisher spreads his "fleet" upon the sand-dunes in order to dry out the salt sea water, so the smelter, when opportunity offers, expands his saturated net to the sun and wind.

"Ah, bor," said Snicker, "we get our livin' by our nets, and we'd need be kind to 'em. They ain't made for nothin', for the 'sheet' (the net proper) cost us £3 10s. athowt (without) the leads and ropes and that, though they ain't a great deal, becos we can use 'em for the next. We get the net part ready made; that come from Scotland. I hev a mould and cast my own leads; and we get plenty of floats, hulled or dropped from the herrin' luggers, what we can carve out for ours. We used ter braid our own nets in the old days, and we allers carry a needle to mend up a rent."

Whilst talking, the two smelters had been folding the net carefully on a wet sack on the stern sheets of the smelt-boat.

"It run off easier," volunteered Snicker, "and ain't so liable to chafe when payin' out."

"What's the depth of it?"

"Six-score mesh," he replied; "about seven feet."

There was very little to be stowed under the thwarts; for these hardy fellows work for hours without food, being quite content with a good supply of tobacco and a bottle of strong tea. Spirits they prefer to go without, as they do another favourite beverage, until a leisure hour comes round.

"You'd better jump in," said Larn, "we shall be back by about tea-time."

Less than an hour's steady pulling brought us to the end of Duffell's drain, where we made fast in order to await the first of the ebb, the intentions of the crew being to work down stream with the falling tide. The ebb tide is preferred by the smelters to the flood, for they believe that the smelts "come up" on the flood and work down into the deeper waters with the ebb. "Besides," they say, "the water ain't so sheer," a fact evident to any one; for the rush of water from the flats brings with it a good deal of ooze, which "thickens" the water.

"Smelts is that sharp-sighted," said Snicker, "they can see you in sheer water like a pound roach, and 'll reg'lar spring away from the sight o' you. They're wonderful nervous. Then a ebb-tide gives you more force to work the net along. My net is gettin' a bit tender; I've had it pritty nigh three year. Two years 'll spile a net on onkind ground."

While Snicker was imparting this information, he was fastening the trammel sticks to the ends of the net, the ends being only about half as deep as the rest of the net. Trammels are stoutish poles a yard in length, with a lump of lead on the lower ends. To them are attached bridle ropes, which, with the stick, make triangles. To the apex of each triangle the draught lines are fastened. Where the draught lines are attached, a flint stone is usually tied also to weight them. The net is a simple engine of destruction—a small edition of the well-known seine-net.

"We 'ont start yet," said Snicker, "the tide ha' hardly done. Lor, smeltin' ain't nothin' like what it wor, though I'll allow some on 'em light lucky even in these sorter wore-out times. But I get sick of grumblin'. Fare to me you may do nothin' else."

"What's the best time for 'em?" I asked.

" Why, in April and May we get our best catches ; we look to earn money by the middle of April. Then September agin ain't a bad season. Smelts go up-river to spawn the first part of April, and come back the latter part of May : that's when you get yer finest fish—real beauties, some on 'em. Small ones fare to hang about in and out from sea in August, though they don't fare to go up much above brackish waters. Then we get little titty ones like stanickles (though we only catch 'em like by accident, amon' the weeds) right down to November and December ; them I reckon are this year's brood. Eels 'll smoke into 'em ; so 'll pike. January's a rotten month for 'em.

" Last spring (1908) wor an awful one. Half a dozen smelts, offen only four, didn't pay for the slight of the net, let alone at dividin' up time. *Fifty year*, a'most to a day, I ha' follered smeltin' up here, and never know'd things wuss.[1]

"Smelts is pretty fish; and sharp as needles; they'll jump out arter whitebait, like hawks arter sparrows. I ha' had 'em land on the floor of the boat. They sune die; jist garp a time or two, and do a little floppin', and theer you are—dead, and scarce a scale awryed. Pretty they smell, too, don't they? jist like rale cucumbers. They'll gill theerselves in the meshes and drown'd afore you get the net out. Some'll drop out dead, afore you get the bight of the net in. I ha' seen crabs grabbin' hold of 'em as the net cum in. Seen theer tails bit off, and eyes grubbed out, and theer innerds out—all done by them beggarin' crabs in the fifteen minutes it take to draw the net round and ashore. I think we'll make the first draught."

"Buck" jumped out of the boat on to the mud— over which barely two inches of water trickled towards the "drain"—taking with him the shore-end of the draught rope, "Snicker" rowing across to the opposite side, and then down-stream, the net sliding off gently into the water, righting itself as the leads carried the under side of it downwards. The long line of small cork floats (each the size of a lunch biscuit, but much thicker) bobbed along on the surface. Down-stream for a full five hundred yards

[1] It is the amateur fisherman who revels in the narrative of his big catches; the professional never does more than " middlin'," if so well as that; but 1908 was the worst spring and summer on record.

Larn slowly rowed and then turned in. "Buck" meantime had been plodding along in the soft ooze. The net now made a half-circle, and Larn kept hauling it in, hand over hand, keeping the bottom on the mud and curved inward, so that no fish could escape.

"Look like gettin' a few," said "Snicker" cheerfully. We could see quite a score smelts enfolded in the meshes, as the fishermen dropped yard by yard of the net into an increasing pile. Shore crabs came in, kicking and entangled; now and then a flounder or a blenny could be seen enmeshed, not to mention whitebait (young herrings) that squirmed through the meshes, leaving behind them a few tiny bright scales, that hung to the cotton. A number of them were helplessly entangled in the weed that "cloyed" the net. Interest centred, however, in the last few yards drawn in—the "bight" of the net.

"What did I tell yer?" said Snicker. "We've made a nice draught—sixty, if theer's one. Two or three more draws like that'll do, perwidin' prices keep up to yesterday's. And I don't see as we've got many oppositioners up here to-day!"

"Hull that basket here," said Buck; and I threw to him a butter basket, a favourite receptacle with smelters, being light and handy.

The whole of the net was now gone over again, yard by yard, the smelts being gently unmeshed and thrown into the basket, while the crabs are unceremoniously dismembered. The catch was then rinsed in the tide, and carefully laid in rows in a box under the thwarts.

THE SMELTERS : LETTING OUT THE NET

M

"We treat them as we should a frind," laughed Snicker. "They're mighty tender," he added, as he replaced the lid of the box and covered it with a wet sack. "Nothin' go wrong quicker, 'cept, maybe, a mackerel. They 'ont stand no rough handlin'; and the suner they're up in Billin'sgate the better. They're in Breydon to-day, and in London and sold afore breakfast-time to-morrow."

The net was now replaced in the stern-sheets, yard by yard, the two smelters rinsing it of mud and weed in readiness for the next draught. The flat had run dry, and the refuse from the net—a small pile of "cabbage," and "raw" (weeds)—marked the spot where the haul had been made. In it glittered dead herring syle, like tiny bars of silver, and a few uninjured crabs which would soon scuttle back to the water.

Four more draughts bring us to the main channel; and, well content, our crew turn the boat's bows homewards. The captured smelts will be counted off in scores into shallow boxes, and sent off by the mail train to the city.

"It's a rum thing," said Snicker, as he rowed steadily behind his mate, "that lights will attrack smelts, ain't it? I ha' been fishin' at night up there at the Narrows, near Burgh, with a lantern stuck on the shore for guiding on us, and as we wor about to draw in the bight of the net, I've ackshilly seed smelts deliberately run ashore, jumpin' out and floppin' on the mud. And, bor, you may believe me, I've seed rats swim athort, probably attracted by the light—— "

"More likely," I suggested, "by the scent of the smelts blown across channel."

"That's very likely," he admitted, "but I ha' seed 'em ackshilly run up to the net and seize hold of a fish. I ha' stood and said to myself, 'Well, bor, you desarve one for yer pluck!' not as rats is favourites with us, not by no mander of means. An' if you ever see a rat have a chance to pick his meat, he'll pass over a butt,[1] or a pout, or anything, and nab a smelt afore he will any of the t'others.

"Fine smelts? Ah, bor, I've took them up to seven ounces, which wor the biggest I ever heer'd tell of; that measured a foot exactly.

"I once," he added, "set some eel-hooks up at the entrance of the Norwich river, baitin' on 'em with very small roach; and if I reckerlect right, I took *seven* smelts off in the mornin', all fine ones, only they was shotten (spent) ones. They must hev bin amazin' hungry."

"There! I worn't far out when I told you we'd git back afore tea-time. Well, if you 'on't hev no smelts, you 'on't; but why not take them butts? They're as fat as butter, them grass fed 'uns. Feel the thickness on 'em. Somehow, they fare to pack theerselves with them little winkle-sorter shells (*Hydrobia*) you see on the grass (*Zostera*), and grow tremenjuss fat in less 'an no time, and they eat as sweet as a nut."

[1] Flounder.

TURNSTONES

CHAPTER V

SHRIMPERS AND SHRIMPING

" I sing the natives of the boundless main,
  And tell what kinds the wat'ry depths contain.

　　　.　　　　.　　　　.　　　　.　　　　.

  And each cold secret of the fishers' toil,
  Intrepid souls ! who pleasing rest despise,
  To whirl in eddies, and on floods to rise ;
  Th' abyss they fathom, search the doubtful way,
  And through obscuring depths pursue the prey."

　　　　　　　　　　　　　　　　　OPPIAN.

AMONG THE SHRIMPS

IT matters not where you fall in with an east coast
shrimp-boat, whether moored by the quayside,
with its net drawn, poke-end first, up the mast to
dry, or sailing free in the roadstead with a favouring
wind, it at once impresses you as a neatly-rigged,

compact, sea-worthy little vessel. And if you watch it coming up-river from the shrimping-grounds, you will esteem the skipper a more than passable boat-man, as you see him tacking to and fro, dodging passing steam-tugs, and steadily gaining on every small board made.

Until the last year or so shrimping began in the early spring, and ended, as it does now, in October, when the inrush of herring drifters from Scotland, and the in-coming of our herring boats by their hundreds, make it dangerous for the smaller boats to navigate the river. The majority of our eighty shrimp-boats are then dismantled, and the hulls drawn up on to the ship-yards. There is one small yard, near the suspension bridge on the Bure, where quite a fleet of the " North-end " boats lie side by side through the earlier winter months. Christmas is hardly passed, however, ere their owners are at work with tar and "compo," preparing them for another season. During the slack time, they may have been repairing spars and gear, some of them braiding spare nets, and mending, tarring, or tanning old ones. There are busy days at the beginning of January, and long before the month is ended several of the boats are already at work.

All along the quays, from the lower part of the Bure to the Gorleston end of the Yare, these craft take up their berths, those above Breydon being known as the " North-enders " ; the others are the " South-enders." The men naturally moor as near to their homes as possible.

The shrimper is an industrious fellow ; often he

goes down to the sea before the day has dawned. He prefers the morning tide ; the shrimps are wanted by tea-time ; and they are wanted fresh—the fresher the better. He dislikes selling overdays, and for his credit's sake would rather lose on the sale of his catch than lose the confidence of the public. If stale shrimps come to the table you may be sure that they were brought to the door by some hawker who is not a legitimate shrimper.

Your shrimper has no special rig to distinguish himself; he dresses in canvas and broadcloth, his jumper often having been tanned in the cutch-vat in which his sail was dipped ; his nether garments are encased, when he is at work, in oily leggings. His home is a tidy one, and the "missus" is generally "pretty pertickler," for that snow-white cloth on the shrimp-board at the window appeals to her sense of tidiness ; and the rest of the front room must be in keeping, for customers sometimes step inside to purchase.

There must necessarily be a copper built up either in the kitchen or cellar, or the back shed where the boiling takes place: here, too, the whitewash brush is well plied.

Most of the sorting is done in the boats ; but long after the catch has been boiled, the shrimper's wife has a keen eye for foreign substances ; and even after a pint is measured out you may detect her snapping up a tiny piece of sea-fir (*Corallina officinalis*) or a small crustacean—more often than not, a "sawback" (*Amathilla homari*). Then there are young pogges, suckers, and gobies (boiled and quite fit to eat if you care for them), besides other fish fry, no larger than the shrimps themselves, which have hitherto escaped the eyes of both master and " missus."

I am rather sorry that there lives in the neighbourhood to-day no one who dabbles in amateur painting.   In my younger days there were two or three " artists " who, for a consideration (beer !) and a trifle in cash, would paint the shrimper's signboards [1] with brightly drawn shrimp-boats sailing under the tawniest of tanned sails on the bluest of water. Some of these efforts were, however, really works of art.   On either side the sea-piece was the legend that Dickens made a note of, and which told the passer-by how " Live and Boil'd Shrimps (were) Sold Here by the Catcher—R. Larn."   Larns, Liffens, and Edmonds are, and have been for generations, well-known names among the shrimping fraternity.   As with other Norfolk fishermen, the shrimpers have their well-established nicknames, which often descend from father to son.   Among them we have to-day : " Spring " Colby, " Scrump " Allen, " Darkey " Pillar, " Mouldy " Pillar, " Dodger " Thorpe, " Pekoe " Balls, " Garps " Chambers, " Dunny " Gedge, " Fancy " Edmonds, " Moker " Edmonds, " Pelham " Larn, " Rough " Hales, " Shah " Yaxley, " Ki " Harmer, " Lucky " Lodge, and others.

Our local shrimpers pride themselves upon their shrimps : "these ain't no Lynns, nor Harwiches, biled with saltpetre and muck—they're real Yarmith !"   Yet even among the local experts there

[1] Vide *Nature in Eastern Norfolk*, p. 103.

are those who excel, and *flavours*—slight indeed, I will admit—can be detected, differing in some degree.

A SHRIMPER'S YARN

The following is the gist of a yarn spun by my old shrimper friend Colby, when I visited him in January last. His youngest daughter sat near the window braiding a shrimp net. Six other daughters had been taught the same accomplishment before her ; and a more cunning maker of nets than Bob Colby cannot be found anywhere in East Anglia. Colby, himself, unable to walk,[1] sat propped up in bed, jovial in spite of his sufferings, and as chatty as if injured thighs and ribs were trivial things.

" Shrimp-boats," he said, " run from nineteen to twenty-two foot, with a beam of about eight foot five ; and are classed as two-tonners. A good boat (all English oak, mind you !) run at two pounds a foot (all copper fastened, you know), and that's only for the bare hull, but with care it'll last you a lifetime. I know chaps as sail shrimp-boats built years before by theer fathers afore 'em. With the sails and gear complete they'll run you to eighty pounds.

" The boats are cutter-rigged, mainsail, jib, and tops'l : and they can go, make you no error. What's prettier than a fleet of 'em beatin' up and down the roadstead in a nice off-shore wind ? They are fast sailers and well-handled, make you no error ! Theer ain't no prettier turn-out on the east coast.

[1] See p. 263.

" Now, then, you wanter to know about the nets. Well, we use, as you know, two sorts : the shrimp-trawl and the beam-net.   The trawl is pretty much like a ornery smack's trawl, only smaller, with a fifteen foot beam, with ground rope, and trawl-heads on the same scale.   In summer we fasten in pockets for soles and sich-like.   The net is about twenty-five foot long from beam to cod-end.   We fasten under-neath bits of old oil-skins and canvas—we call 'em linings—at the cod-end to save chafin' and tearin' it along the bottom."

" Did you ever put the trawl over without forget-ting to tie the cod-end ?" I asked, having myself had such an experience on one occasion.

" Yes, bor," he replied, " I was once workin' three nets at one time and hadn't tied the poke-ends up : I had a two hours' trawlin' for nothin'.   Everything went in at one end and comes out at the tother !

" When we're all ready to go, with tackle stowed, and a little refreshment aboard, we drop down on the first of the ebb, we South-enders gettin' an hour's start, because the water's still makin' up the North River strong while the ebb's already started on the lower river.

" I orter ha' told you that the beam-net, a sort of ornery dredge-net, hev a beam of thirteen foot, with a light bow top ; and is fastened with bridles so that, with the beam bein' weighted with iron, it is allers sure to alight right at the bottom.   We hev sixty fathom of rope for each net, but we don't allers pay that out."

Here he entered into details, as to the fixing of

the tow-ropes, which, although conversant with their manipulation, I cannot satisfactorily repeat.

"You see, we allers gets the tow-rope fixed afore the shrouds; suppose we get fast, say to a wreck, if we'd rigged it any other way, we might get broadside to the tide, and pulled right over. I've seen one or two chaps make a hash by heving the tow rope abaft the shrouds; but I hollered to 'em to cut the shrouds, and when they had done that they righted directly. If we cut or slip the guy rope, the boat 'll swing and hang bow on to the tide. If we get one net fast on a sunken wreck, the other 'll lift by the tide. The best thing to do then is to buoy your other warp, cut adrift, and work the remaining net, comin' back for the other when the tide turns.

"When we're a-fishing we keep the nets down three-quarters of an hour. We dodge the wrecks and anchors by havin' a number of land-marks; there's the morneymint (Nelson's monument), the church steeple, Gorleston steeple, tall chimbleys, and sich-like; so we generally know where to dodge in and out, first to escape a bit of wooden wreck, then an old iron hulk—they cut like a knife, and play old Harry up with you—and so on. We'd sooner get fast to forty wrecks than one anchor; you *can* mostly drift off a wreck at the turn of the tide, but not off *them*, bust 'em. Yet we like drawin' as close to a wreck as we can, becos the ground there's not so much worked, and theer's more feed—them there sea-flowers, sea-worams, and nobody knows what. Fish get round a wreck, too.

"Old 'Scrump' Allen's a clinker for gettin' close

to 'em. One day I see him fast; and I and the 'tothers holler as we go by—

"'Hallo! old Scrump! you've been shavin' too closely this time!'

"When we haul, if we've got too heavy a load to 'hand' in, we haul the net in by the jib halyards. We shoot the catch into a ped or box by untyin' the the cod-end. We sort them while we're drawin' along again. Of course we generally work two in a boat, and while one's sorting, the tother's mindin' the sails.

" We wear up a lot of nets ; most of 'em have four trawls and two bow-nets ready each spring. I allers make sure of havin' five trawls and three bow-nets. You see, it 'ud be awkward to lose one or two nets without havin' others to fall back on.

"Talkin' about gettin' fast : if you get both nets fast (supposin' you're usin' two), you have to hang there the rest of the tide, and if they 'on't come up by slackening, most likely you'll rend 'em or leave them there altogether.

" In foggy weather you lose your bearin's, and for a dafe man, like me, it worn't pertickler safe, becos you can't hear the bells goin on the ships.   Three of our shrimpers got fast one day on the North sand buoy, the warp goin' round the chain, and there they lay. They could hear me aboard my boat but couldn't see me.

"'Keep outside her, Bob!' they shouted (so they arterwards told me), but I didn't hear' em ; and presently I gets athort, and there we four had to hang till the tide slaked. Fortunately it was pretty calm or we'd had a jumble up.

"When we're agoin' out we tell the old woman what time to hev her copper hot—almost to a minute. Everything hev to be ready and waiting.

"Now to bile shrimps *scientifically* as you'd call it, you put a quarter peck of salt to two and a half pails of water; let that bile, then pop in your shrimps till the water's on the bile again, and then out with 'em. You've seen my old woman dydlin' them out with a hand-net. If you bile too long or too short they're limp or soft, or spiled anyway. After each lot you must add more water and more salt. Where 'll you find better lookin' or sweeter shrimps than Yarmouth? Them chaps at Harwich bile 'em aboard the boats ; they use saltpetre ; so they do at Lynn. What's the consequence? Why the 'browns' is about black, and the 'pinks' raw-red. They don't suit Yarmouth taste.

"We catch the pink shrimps (the Æsop's prawn *Pandalus annulicornis*) in deep water, two miles from the beach—near the *Cockle* (lightship) is a rare place for 'em—that's rough ground there (*Sabellæ*-covered)—and again down there in the Holm, off Corton. It's all ross-bottomed [1] and lumpy ; you can feel the nets jerk and bump along below, for you get the jar in the boat. In the old days we all used to go arter 'browns' first, seldom goin' after the 'pink' 'uns' afore the middle of June, now they're arter 'pink 'uns,' as you see 'em to day, here in January, when they're getting plenty of 'em—big 'uns, full of spawn. We used ter go right away to Winterton, Palling,

[1] See p. 184.

Hasbro', Bacton, and pretty nigh to Cromer.   They
want to fish at home nowadays.

"I've been a lucky man, though I say it myself, in
droppin' athort soles.   You know I'm an old smacksman, and got the deep-sea instinct.

"I remember one April I was fishing at Palling,
with three nets down in two fathoms of water.   When
I hauled the middle net, I got a lot of soles that
length" (spreading his hands nearly two feet apart),
"all full of spawn.   From the three nets I got a trunk
full.   You may know how quick soles spawn when I
tell you that by the time we got to harbour they'd
shed all their ova.   Yet we made £2 15s. of 'em.
This was at the end of the seventies.

"Thinks I 'I'll keep it dark.'   So I told my mate
to put in an extra trawl and off we started again—
three on us in all—to Palling; put down the nets
and trawled as far as Horsey, expectin', of course,
to get two or three trunks.   *We never took a blessed
sole!*   They'd spawned and gone!   The day afore,
had we been prepared, we might have done it
properly.   Another boat had fell in with 'em same
as we did.

"No, I never remember gettin' a mackerel or a
herrin' in the net, and only once a haddock, but I
have taken plenty of garnets, lots of brills, and chance
turbots, nice plaice, while we used ter take nice white
homers (skate) off Winterton.   They do that now
when they go a-long-lining from March to July—
catchin' all sorts.

"I remember once, twenty years ago, when I had
three nets down off Palling, getting six pecks of

shrimps—all clean ' browns '—in the middle bow-net, seven pecks in the stern bow-net, and fifteen pecks in the trawl. We had to hoist 'em in with the jib halyards. That was the biggest haul I ever made in my life. I had very big nets and a big boat."

"What is most marvellous to me," I said, "is this, that with so many nets being worked daily, month in and month out, the supply should still keep up."

"Ah," said Colby, "it's a rummen to me. They must breed tremenjuss, yet it fare a puzzler to me we don't clear them out."

CATCHING AND SORTING

A small black board fixed at right angles to the wall above a shrimper's window bears the announce-ment—

SHRIMPS SOLD

HERE.

painted in uneven white letters, probably by the proprietor of the establishment himself.

It was summer time, and the shrimper's clean-scrubbed board lay across the trestles, below the window, inside the green-painted palisades. In the middle of it a mass of sweet, wholesome "pink" shrimps invited purchase, while a dish of coarser "browns" stood on one side, and a small heap of "yellow" shrimps, selected from the bulk by patient sorting, lay on the other. These yellow shrimps are a smaller and sweeter kind than even the pinks, but they are not much in favour with those who like the latter. Two large peds, still wet and smelling of the sea, stand below; in their crevices between the canes are stuck many a tiny semi-transparent opossum shrimp, and here and there a sea-louse.

Mrs. Liffen was at the window.

"My old man's abed, sir," she warningly remarked. "He was up early this mornin', and have jist got outside his breakfast, and is havin' a rest. He says he'll take you in the mornin'—mind, at four o'clock, precise."

I am at the quayside punctually. The tide has fallen scarcely an inch before the boat pushes off, our provender and the skipper's big stone bottle having been safely stowed in the forepeak. Other guernsied skippers are pushing off quietly into the stream; and as there are two bridges to negotiate, halyards and shrouds have been unfastened or slackened, and the masts, with their raffle of sails and running gear, lie aslant, each shrimper *pushing* his boat along by means of a pair of big sculls, and downstream they glide. The oars click, not unmusically, on the silent river, and we move faster as we reach the down current that is coming from the channel, and faster still as we get into the main stream. Our skipper, directly we have shot the second bridge, tenderly lays the stump of his black pipe at the end of the thwarts, remarking—

"I don't want ter smash *that*—she's a good old frind of mine."

He now hands the tiller to me, and getting his brawny shoulder under the mast, hitches it into its vertical position, and makes all taut.

White-winged sea-gulls greet us noisily at the extreme end of Breydon, and fly to and fro over the river, snatching up flotsam that drifted harbourwards. As we glide downstream, we pass silent shipyards, grim old colliers lying broadside to the deserted quays, ketches awaiting cargoes, barges, and gaily-painted wherries; and so down to the sea we go before workmen and sailormen are awake.

" It's odd to me," says the skipper, "that with all this 'ere scrapin' of the sea bottom, day arter day, month arter month, we don't clear it of them shrimps. What millions untold there must be. If you'll allow that theer's two hundred and fifty shrimps to a pint measure, which theer are when they run only middlin' size (for my boy hev worked it out, bein' in the fifth standard) ; and if we gets only four pecks each for a tide, that cums to suffin like fower million and a half and some over. That boy (and he's a smart calcalator, though he's mine, as shouldn't say it) reckoned the catchin' at about two hundred days ; then he allowed only two pecks to a catch, and then agin he multiplied 'em by eighty, which is the number of boats, roughly told. He simply alarmed me by the terrific total.

"'Boy,' I says to him, 'you may reckon eighteen pecks sumtimes to a day's catch.'

"And you may believe me, he jist had to go over the other side of the slate figgerin' it up. His figgers fairly stemmed me. Life, as far as shrimps go, fare to be a very small thing, don't it? And I've heerd our little parson[1] say as Gord knows 'em all by number, same as he do the sparrers (sparrows). I dussent hardly think on it, it fare so tremenjuss!"

"Mornin', Ike!" "Mornin', 'Shah'!" "Nice mornin', 'Scrumps'!" Such are the laconic greetings of one shrimper to another, as we pick up the little fleet going onwards to the sea.

"Mornin', Pattson! so you've shipped as stowaway agin!"

"Ah, bor," I make reply; "goin' out to taache Liffen his bizness!"

"You on't be much *help!*" laughs another. "You'll be a-pawkin' in the net for curios!"

There is a gentle westerly breeze blowing, of which our skipper takes advantage when the town is left astern, and up go the sails, mainsail and tops'l, and the jib is sheeted home. Right merrily we dance over the bar, and the skipper soon drops the nets into the sea. . . .

It is time to haul. The sheet is let go; the boat steadies herself to the incoming nets; in a trice the poke-end of the nets have been untied, and their contents shot into the peds.

What a mass of kicking, jumping, flapping, squirming life! Brown shrimps flapping their tails (or *telsons*), as lobsters under similar conditions will do; tiny plaice kicking and opening their gill covers, as though trying to articulate their indignation; and crabs scuttling about on the top of their fellow-victims.

---

[1] The "parson" at the Shrimpers' Shelter, vide *Wild Life on a Norfolk Estuary*, pp. 70-71.

N

Patches of bright green and red seaweeds, and fronds of brown, with sea urchins, all prickles and passive resistance, help to make up the list of "common objects of the seashore."

"You can amuse yourselves sortin'," suggests the skipper, who has resumed the sheet and tiller. "Empty a big hatful or two into that riddle (sieve), hold it agin the gunnel, and hull out all the little fishes—soles, butts, whitin's, hummers (bullheads), hard-heads (pogges), and crabs. Mind them swimmers, they'll pinch yer like the dowst; and if you see a weaver, be *careful;* them nasty little beggars 'll turn on yer like the devil, and afore you know where you are, they'll stab yer finger with that black back fin—they're prickly and pizonous. You'll have a pain rite up yer arm till the next tide falls. *Mind 'em.* Jerk 'em out with this thole-pin, and stamp on 'em.

"Hull that sole—it ain't a bad 'un—into that box under the thwart. Soles ain't to be trifled with. Hull all the tongues (young soles) into the sea. We want 'em to grow for another day."

So overboard go small gobies, unctuous suckers, pipe-fishes, and a couple of spotted gunnels.

"What do you call them spotted things—gunnels? We call 'em nine-eyes," says Liffen; "look at the nine spots down that back fin. Gobies, aye? why, they're gobble-bellies. Look! Theer's a sawback agin your hand."

This sawback happens to be a fifteen-spined stickleback.

These are not all the fishes thrown back

into the sea, some to die, but most to recover. The next sieveful has its share of those already mentioned, varied, as are other hauls and sortings, by others just as curious and interesting. We notice a small lumpsucker, green as an emerald, a Montagu's sucker of mahogany hue, many a tiny herring —"whitebait" the skipper calls them—a sand-launce, a baby dab, a juvenile bib, and a viviparous blenny. There are small shells, too, dog-whelks, murex, top-shells, *Tellina, Mactra, Modolia,* and others ; here a sea anemone, there a sea-urchin, a strange "louse-like" crustacean, a spider crab, so small that its limbs are like hairs, sun stars, "five-fingered Jacks," a mass of whelk eggs, and many a little cephalopod.

"You talk about whelks," remarks Liffen, "we get more of 'em round by Bacton and Palling and that way nor'ard. But here we don't often get more 'an a few young ones ; we userally save 'em, for they're nice pickin', though they're foul feeders—bad as crabs for that, which on't bear hardly tellin' of. If you get a net fast where they are, and hev to lay the tide out, you'll see the poke-end of the net covered with 'em, when you do get it up. They're all busily feedin' on the shrimps inside, devourin' of 'em through the meshes ; and when you shoot the catch into the boat, you'll find handfuls of empty shells, like husks, where they've sucked out the bodies of the shrimps. They'll spile a catch, and eat the lot if you're fast long."

"What about the whelks ? "

"Well, when they serve us that trick it's no use talking to 'em, and wuss to throw 'em over. So we jist drops 'em into bilin' water and punish 'em that way. That's what you'd call a mild rewenge!"

There are many small creatures sifted through into the sea again whose identity we cannot stay to inquire into, and our bottles of spirits and tin boxes are already full. *Gammaridæ*, strange worms, tiny crustaceans of other sorts go through — banded shrimps, opossum shrimps, and hippolytes. Soldier crabs in winkle- and in whelk-shells are tossed back again, and many a bold-biting pugnacious swimming crab.

"Bust them fiddlers!" says Liffen; "they're the very devil's own for bitin'."

We find this out by experience, for their pincer claws come together like nippers; and as they persist in clinging, the quickest way to release one's fingers is to wrench off the offending claws—a rather cruel procedure, but have not our feelings as much right to be considered as theirs? We would fain compromise, "you let me alone and I'll let you," but they will have none of it, and come madly at tender flesh, made tenderer by salt water and the harsh prickly spines of hundreds of shrimps and prawns.

Haul succeeds haul, tack follows upon tack; and by the time the tide has turned and the flood has well made up, we have many a peck of fat pink beauties. Already many of the "pink 'uns" are dead, for unlike the "brown 'uns," they die soon after leaving the water. No wonder, then, that when "Home" is the word, the shrimper hastens thither with all despatch; for the summer heat soon affects his precious cargo.

SHRIMP AND CRAB GOSSIP

In an obscure back street lives one of my shrimper friends, a man of observation and some intelligence, who, differing from his fellows, whose chief end in life seems to be to secure full baskets and a quick sale for their catches, takes an interest in the various creatures which come to his net. A number of small bottles in his house contain quite a variety of strange specimens picked from his catches from time to time, and afford much interest to himself and his friends.

"My husband's got something funny this morning," said Mrs. Spanton, late in the month of February. "He says as he's not seen one like it before," she continued, holding forth a small scent-bottle, within which, in methylated spirits, was a very nice example of Sowerby's hippolyte (*Hippolyte spinus*). This was the first of the species I had ever seen ; indeed, I had not hitherto heard of its existence on the east coast ; and here, mixed with hundreds of thousands of distant relatives, the remarkable little stranger had been pounced upon and preserved. Among the millions of crustaceans I have seen since, I have met with only one other example.

I had found considerable difficulty in persuading the shrimpers to preserve for me any strange crustaceans and fishes they might meet with. They could not bother to bottle them—"bottles tumbled off the thwarts and broke, and they didn't want no bits of glass layin' about." But in March, 1906, I procured a number of paste-bottles with wide mouths and with broad bases ; these I cleaned, half filled with formalin at the proper strength, and fitted with sturdy bungs. Then I came to terms with Colby, the crippled shrimper, arranging that he should deliver the bottles to the shrimpers, and return them to me when they contained anything curious or rare. This arrangement worked very well, and 1906 proved to be a very profitable season, at least as far as I was concerned.

"Not a bad idea!" said Colby, popping his tobacco money into his pocket. "A'most as good as goin' yerself aboard a shrimper, specially in blowy weather."

Day by day interesting specimens "turned up." Now it was a Jago's Goldsinny,[1] or a megrim (*Arnoglossus laterna*), or some quaint, scarce crab or naked-gilled mollusc. One very remarkable "find" was a hermit crab that, for want of a more suitable shell to live in, had appropriated the empty house of a large garden snail that had drifted down to the sea from the country. It had been rolled about on the sea-floor until it became as polished and pretty as the shells often seen on fancy boxes. A sturdy and somewhat familiar crustacean I found to be well known to the shrimpers as the "sawback," and to science as *Amathilla homari*. The nickname is very appropriate, the overlapping segments of shell ending in long triangular points that, when the creature doubles itself up in its dying moments, remind one of a circular saw. There came also that tiny, but huge-clawed crab, *Porcellana longicornis*, and *Stenorhyncus tenuirostris*, one of the small spider crabs,

[1] Vide *Wild Life on a Norfolk Estuary*, p. 318.

with a body no larger than a horse-bean, but with legs of comparatively enormous length—a sea-spider on stilts, in fact.   Of pear crabs, *Hyas araneus* and *H. coarctatus*, I received a great number.

It was unfortunate for me that small shrimps are not only unsaleable, but are carefully riddled back into the sea ; for with them, undoubtedly, go many rare and interesting species of sessile and stalk-eyed crustaceans.   In overhauling the peds (baskets) of the shrimps after the catches had been turned out at home, however, I found several of the tinier species sticking in the interstices of the wicker-work.   Two species of opossum shrimps were discovered in that way—semi-transparent white things, for all the world like snips of fiddle-strings doubled together.   With these were specimens of *Gammaridæ*, known to the shrimpers as sea-lice.   A short list of other species of crustacea taken may not be out of place here.

SHRIMPS AND PRAWNS

Banded shrimp	*Crangon fasciatus*	Some numbers
Three-spined shrimp	*C. trispinosus*	ditto
Spinous shrimp	*C. spinosus*	Two or three
——	*Nika edulis*	Several
" Little shrimp "	*Hippolyte varians*	ditto
Cranch's hippolyte	*H. Cranchii*	Some numbers
Common prawn	*Palæmon serratus*	Several
Leach's prawn	*P. Leachii*	Three or four.

The last-named was discovered by Spanton, one of the shrimpers who have never before seen the species.   His example was taken in July, heavily berried ; and when he dropped it into his bottle, " the poor thing," according to his account, "gave a kick or two and shed all its spawn in a minute!"

The "pink shrimp" (Æsop's prawn) is often found with a curious parasite tenaciously attaching to its abdomen, between the edges of the first ring of its armour. This parasite grows to a somewhat remarkable size, as proportionate to that of the prawn as a rat to a terrier dog. It is always the female, and is an ugly, octopus-like creature; the male, which is a free swimmer, has much the appearance of an undersized earwig, and needs the assistance of a lens to be properly seen and examined. I noticed this year that prawns burdened with this unwelcome lodger were thin and out of condition.

"Did you ever see a ross crab?" asked Colby.

"No," I replied emphatically; "but I must have one. What is it like?"

"Ross crabs," he went on, "are crabs what we get among the ross."

"What's 'ross'?" I asked, pretending not to know.

"Well, ross," he answered, "is the name we give to the rough ground (sea-floor) what lies between Yarmouth and Lowestoft. We go there jinerally when we're workin' for pink shrimps; all on the bottom is millions of worams what build theerselves reg'lar sand-cottages, so to speak; you bring 'em up sometimes in big lumps like half-hardened cement or mortar, for all the world like what we used ter know as coral, what my uncle Parmenter used ter bring home from the South Seas, only you can crumble it in your hands. I suppose these worams suck down the sand and then spew it up, as it were, around 'em, and it hardens, possibly, with the spittle they hull up with it. But, theer you are, they reg'lar burrow in it—live in it, in fact; and if you was to put a lump in a bucket of cleer sea-water, and wait a little while, you'd see my lord pop out his hid, and a lot of little thin fingers, a'most like hairs, and feel about."

"You're speaking of sabella," I remarked, "a sea-worm that builds up a cell from particles of sand, and lives in it. The lumps you refer to are colonies——"

"Let 'em be what they like, I hold, and most shrimpers 'll tell you as how they're what the pink shrimps live on. Theer's all sorts of creatures get on this—what d'ye call it, Isabella?—ross-ground; and among 'em come these 'ere little ross crabs, some of 'em no bigger 'an hempseeds and none of 'em bigger nor a walnut."

"Colby!" said I.

"What?" he asked, turning sharply in his wheeled chair.

"Get me some ross crabs."

"Right you are, my boy, you *shell* have 'em."

I was not kept waiting long. Specimen after specimen came in, of a sturdy crab, with enormous pincer claws, brown-barred legs, and as hairy as Esau. It was Risso's crab (*Xantho rivulosa*), a species hitherto unknown to me, and not in the list of Norfolk species. I placed two or three in a tank, where they distinguished themselves as the clumsiest and laziest of crabs. It may be that the heavy pincer claws are somewhat of a hindrance to their free and certainly inelegant movements, although they may be of great use in cracking hard-shelled molluscs, or, as Colby wished me to believe, "in pullin' the ross to smuddereens to get at the worams."

"I suppose you know, sir," said a shrimper one day, "that a pin-prick 'll kill a crab? I'll show you how it's done," he added, taking up a large shore-crab from the bottom boards of the shrimp-boat, turning it over, and thrusting the sharp point of the end of one of its smaller claws into the centre of the body, at the apex of the closed tail. In an instant the crab's legs became limp, and one after another they fell off until there were only a few stumps left. The crab was dead. Intense pain or great fright will often cause crabs to shed their claws; and those who boil edible crabs and lobsters for sale are only too well aware of it.

Agnes Crane[1] says that "if one or more distant joints of a limb be torn off, the animal has the power of throwing off the remainder of the limb. This separation always takes place at the base of the first joint. The perfect restoration of the limb is not effected at once. After the first moult a new limb is produced of diminutive size. After a second, the new limb is very nearly twice as large as at the first, and at the third it advances nearly to its natural bulk and form."

Contrary to my belief, and the statement made above, Mr. A. H. Waters, B.A., wrote to the *Zoologist*[2] as follows: "Of the many specimens of *Carcinus*

[1] Vide *Cassell's Natural History*, vol. vi. p. 196.
[2] See February, 1906, p. 54.

mænas (the shore crab) I have had under my observation, I have never noticed a single instance of a new limb sprouting out and growing gradually . . . a lost limb has always been instantaneously, as it were, reproduced at the time of exuviation . . . yet sometimes we meet with crabs of the edible species having one large and one small pair of pincers and claws . . . it is, I think, analogous to the crippled wing of a moth."

I have seen—well, perhaps, hundredweights of crabs on Breydon, and have only rarely met with cases of mutilation, due more to rough usage in nets, I believe, than to the pugnacity so often ascribed to the species. It may be that there is so much carrion on Breydon, that cannibalism among the crabs is practically non-existent, while the fighting that goes on among them amounts to little more than a scrimmage. I once caught a crab in the Bure exhibiting the second stage of development in leg reproduction, one pincer claw being as large as my little finger, the other no stouter than a piece of pencil. In June, 1895, I saw a lobster with the *old* pincer claw at least an inch and a half across the widest part of it, the *new* claw (or leg) being no larger than an ordinary pen-nib, although perfect in shape and joints.

The malformations occurring among the larger crustaceans[1] have always greatly interested me. Some recent examples may be mentioned here. The most remarkable I have yet seen occurred in a Norwegian lobster (*Neprops norvegicus*) in August,

[1] Vide *Notes of an East Coast Naturalist*, pp. 283–284.

1905, at which time considerable numbers of this pretty, not to say delicious, crustacean were to be seen in the town. As the reader will know, the large pincer claws have on either of them a fixed *chelæ* on one side and a movable one on the other, and when the two extremities meet the animal is capable of giving one a very severe nip. In this case the lobster had a third *chelæ* growing between the two, of equal length, but which ended in a couple of points, making a complete V-shape—a supplementary ornament which must certainly have been useless for grasping or defence. The creature was fully adult, and had not recently cast its shell, as was apparent by the number of acorn barnacles on it.

On examining a number of these lobsters I found that the greatest tendency to abnormality was in the direction of growing the free *chelæ* shorter than the fixed one. In November, 1908, I overhauled a consignment, and found several with varying *chelæ*, one with a twisted claw and another with an extra point projecting at right angles to the *chelæ*.

"You can't account for these things, bor," said Colby; "they're like us: some's born crooked, others ha' grow'd so. I a'most wish *I* wor a crab, and could shoot my old claes; I'd sune hev some more toes to take the place of them what wor sliced off by the railway trucks—by gums! *That I would!*"

THE WOLDER AT HOME

For some years there was hauled up every October, on the boatyard within a few feet of my boat-shed, an ancient wolder, named the *Menai*. She was oak-built, half-decked, patched and cobbled by amateur carpentry, and a little bit leaky. Her skipper, one Tom, *alias* "Nobby," Skoyles, was as weather-beaten as his vessel ; he had thick sandy hair, a towzled beard, a merry laugh, and a resolute face. Year after year he spent the finer months at sea, going in and out of the harbour daily when the weather served, and spending few idle days during the winter, which for him lasted from September-end until the latter part of March. He spent the winter in braiding new nets, and in spending most of the money he had put by during the time of his " wolding."

Like most men who make no fuss over rough weather, and who appear to be as hard as nails, he lived, when at home, in an atmosphere like that of a baker's oven. Wherrymen and eel-babbers do just the same, and will go straight from their hot cabins to their work in the bitterest gales. . . .

"For thirty years,"[1] said " Nobby," "we had about fifteen wolders at work out of the harbour ; there's several—three or four, perhaps—now belongin' tu Yarmith and Gorleston, but they don't fare tu get fish like they used ter. I suppose they've worked 'em out. Us wolders worked within the three-mile limit, trawlin' from the fairway buoy of the Cockle, just off Caister, to Palling and Eccles, both outside an' inside the sands.

"The old *Menai* done me werry good service until she grow'd good for nothin', like me ; now she's broke up, and I'm well on that way. Howsoever,

[1] This was on December 1st, 1908.

I get jobs a-watchin' aboard the fishin' boats in harbour, and just keep the wolf from the door, while old 'Ikey' Dowsing, my chum, as has bin a foreign sailor and a coaster, live with me—two good-for-nothin' old bachelors. He draws a bit of Guvmint pension.

"Well, you wanter to know about woldin'. I reckon there's little as I can tell you you doan't know. Tonnage? Well, bor, wolders run from three and a half up to ten ton, larger ones bein' used nowadays.

"The trawl we use hev a twenty-four foot beam. Smacks, you know, hev 'em runnin' to forty feet. We use a seven-score net, that is, with seven-score meshes athort the head. Wolders drop out on the first of the ebb-tide, and drop down agin the Cockle ; the rest of the tide 'll carry us down to the wold.[1] Two of us hev to work a wolder, and one's jinerally on deck while the other is in the cuddy, dozin', perhaps, or fryin', becos a mess of dabs[2] is a favourite snack with us, and dabs is pretty cheap tackle. We hev the net down only once on a tide, and ag'in when we make the flood-tide back home.

"Oh yes, it's allers intrestin', and often an excitin' job letting a catch out of the cod-end into the well to sort 'em over. You never know your luck till you see it. I've trawled down a whole tide and hauled up—well, a—big hole in the cod-end where a big stone's gone through, and never a scale of a fish left in the net. I've hauled in the net after a westerly

---

[1] Off north-east Norfolk.
[2] Sand-dab.

wind, and had it ram-jam full a'most with red-reed,[1] and had to pick it out by hand till my fingers hev been right sore and raw, all because, perhaps, we've seen a few soles kickin' about here and there among it.   Sometimes I've cut the net at the side and dropt the weed out, mendin' it again with a bit of tarry twine. You see, rents and cuts run generally straight down, or athort the meshes.

"Fish! ah, bor, all sorts come tu the net.   Brill, turbot sometimes, dabs, butts,[2] codlin's—spriggs— that's half-grow'd cods, you know—roker,[3] homers,[4] —you don't often get blue skate—whitin's, sweet-Williams,[5] lemon soles,[6] and soles—beauties too. Sometimes I've made seven pound for two tides, of soles, and got a trunk and a half of 'em at a time.   Soles is very onreg'lar; sometimes you drop on 'em, sometimes you don't.   I can't say why—tides and that, perhaps, or grub bein' scarce or plenty.

"No, we don't get anything partic'lar among shellfish—three or four oysters sometimes, a few whelks, and crabs galore. We often got Cromer crabs, but they was generally in spawn.   I've found some odd things in the trawl.   Once we got a lot of hosses' nosebags, with oats still in 'em.   No doubt there'd been a wreck.   Timber gets drawed up, the nails being fast to the net, and if there's any copper bolts in it, all well and good; if not, the sooner that's heaved over the better, even if you have to cut the net to clear it.

[1] *Polysiphonia.*   [2] Flounders.
[3] Thornback ray.   [4] Spotted ray.
[5] Spotted dogfish.   [6] Smeared dabs.

" I once hauled up a case of wine. All the corks was sealed with wax, but they was half out the necks; I suppose it was the pressure of the water and the air in 'em. Anyway, what was inside was jist all right. Me and my mate had a reg'lar boze up, and got that tiddly we couldn't manage the boat, and didn't know where we wor. So I dropt anchor, and we turned in and slept it off. I've got other things what I shouldn't have took a exciseman into my confidence over.

" It's a risky life, of course. Steamboats 'll never trouble to get out of your way; they know very well a small craft 'on't du 'em no harm. My mate once hollered down to me, early one mornin'—

" ' Hi! Nobby! look'ee here!'

" I rushed on deck, and see a big steamer bearin' down on us. We'd got the net down, and so wus jist about helpless. We kept on hollerin' and screechin', but no one fared to notice us. The fact is they were either drunk or there worn't no watch set. We had our mast-head light still burning.

" ' Where the —— are you comin' tu ? ' I sung out; and when she was within ship's length of 'us two or three hids peered over the side.

" ' Cuss you for a lot of bloomin' scoundrels! ' I says, as loud as I could shout, for you ain't responsible for langwidge at sich times. ' What the—— ' Well, bor, I let 'em have it, hot and strong, as they managed jist to sheer off; but so close wus the shave they gave us, I wouldn't ha' put my fingers between our gunnel and the ship's side, unless I wanted 'em crushed off.

"Birds! Oh yes, we see thousands sometimes. Them old wil'-ducks (guillemots) and black ducks, deevers (divers), mollberries (skuas), what chase the old gulls about, and 'Tom Taylors' (storm petrels) chancetime afore a breeze. We used ter see no end of porpoises and scoulters (dolphins) down theer by the Wold; but there ain't so many nowadays, there ain't the feed for 'em, or else these 'ere steamers frighten' 'em away. Mackerel I've seen jumpin' about galore. They make a reg'lar breezy noise hustlin' along, with their fins cuttin' the water. One night my mate hears it, and hurries up and lowers the topsail, singin' out to me below as there wus a breeze of wind comin'. Then we discovers 'em close to the top of the water, and had a jolly good laugh over it. Herrings fare to make a similar noise; and though I never got any in the trawl, I've know'd 'em to jump aboard, as the bows pitched into the swell, and rose the herrin'.

"I remember once gettin' a brand new net fast to a wreck—this was within sight of the town. It was a Friday night, and most of the wolders run'd in on the Saturday mornin'. There we lay swettin', and tryin' our hardest to get clear, and for three nights and three days we stuck there and never a soul come nigh to help us. So at last we cut everything adrift and come home pritty nigh parched and starvin'.

"I had a near touch and go once in my time. There'd been a tempest, and the sky turned up ugly as the sun went down.

"'Look 'ere, mate,' I says, 'I don't like the look on't.' So we turned for home, when all in a few minutes a reg'lar gale sprung up with a southerly

o

wind ; it wor the middle of the ebb and we had to beat home. The seas broke over us suffin' terrible, and we was pretty soon half full of water. I pumped her out as we beat up, close reefed, for the harbour, and afore we got there the water was up to her bearers. I shouts to George—

" ' Now then, harbour under the lee ; we must run for it this time or we shall go down the cellar ! '

"Fortunately at that minute she rolled a bit to wind'ard and cleared the side-decks of water. The surf struck us as we raced in, and we wor safe, but it wor a near 'un. Another sea must have swamped us ! We'd passed another wolder burnin' a flare, but we was powerless to help her, hevvin' enough to do to save ourselves. She drawed in next mornin' with her mainsail split in halves.

" Thirty year even in a little offshore wolder ain't all beer and skittles ; and it ain't without its excitements. Now, here I am, at sixty-nine, pritty nigh wore out, and prayin' for next year when I hopes to nab hold of my old age pension—if I live so long."

HERON AND BLACK-HEADED GULLS

CHAPTER VI

WITH THE EEL FISHERS

" How mobile, fleet, and uncontrolled,
Glides life's uncertain day !
Who clings to it but grasps an eel,
That quicker slips away ! "

AN AFTERNOON'S ' LAMB-NETTING '

A LONG dreary heat-wave had made the marsh-lands parched and thirsty; for at least two weeks there had been no rain. It is rarely that the marshes cry out for moisture; but the grass had suffered and the ditches had done their work too well. On July 10th, Tom Brookes,[1] carpenter, bee-keeper, duck-breeder, and sportsman, had written to me to say that "owin' to the lowness of water in the

[1] Vide *Wild Life on a Norfolk Estuary*, p. 40.

deeks (ditches), Pettingill had let in water from the
river. The deek-eels might be stirred up a bit, and
if I'd come a-lambing with him, we might have a bit
of sport." I needed no second invitation, and on the
morrow joined Brookes and the village policeman
(who had an hour to spare), while a cunning native,
who "wor a bit gorn on eels," accompanied us. This
latter individual was a merry fellow—he was, I learnt,
Brookes' father—ready to laugh at anything and
everything, and who laughed none the less when,
slipping on a "ligger" (plank), he deposited a considerable part of his person in a ditch.

Berney Arms, Reedham, and St. Olaves are at the
corner of a triangle of waters, consisting of portions
of the rivers Yare and Waveney, with the New Cut
(canal) for its base; the apex of this triangle faces
Breydon, immediately opposite Burgh Castle. In it
lie numerous marshes known as the Toft Monks
levels, and intersecting them are many ditches, or
"deeks," all connected with the main cuts that end
near the pump-mills by the margin of the rivers.
These ditches are seldom disturbed by nets. Herons
drop down to them now and again to fish, and the
cattle draw down to them to drink. Reeds grow
densely by the margin of some of them ; pond-weeds
here and there grow in matted patches. Among
these weeds the three-spined sticklebacks manage to
exist ; but sturdy and somewhat stunted pike, from
their lairs in the reedy recesses of the overhanging
banks, keep a sharp eye on stragglers, and herons,
and often dabchicks, love the fat little fish. Numerous
fine eels contrive, somehow, to live comfortably above

and in the oozy bottoms, taking toll of both fish and ova ; they undoubtedly work in as elvers from the rivers, through the crevices at the sluice-gates.

Our ramble from Belton to the eeling quarters was not devoid of interest. We brushed through bracken and heather on the sandy upland, enjoying a wide view of the marshland, with wooded heights in the blue distance, and white-sailed mills dotting the rivers. We disturbed more than one lizard out fly-hunting, and not a few natterjack toads that were peering out of sandy hollows.

As we entered upon the marsh level, lapwings petulantly circled here and there, loudly protesting against our presence near the spots where their young lay crouching ; a few redshanks, too, were disturbed by our approaching the river banks ; and as we plodded along the top of the " walls," soaking our boots in the wet grasses, we saw moor-hens' nests stuck here and there in front of the reeds bordering a ditch.

One marsh we had to cross greatly interested me by the number of mole-casts with which it was speckled : quite half an acre had been so worked by these burrowing animals that it was difficult to step anywhere around without treading on hills of various sizes, whilst here and there were heaps that would have filled a wheelbarrow : these " wor the old 'uns castles and breeding quarters," said Brookes. As this was undoubtedly the case, there promised to be a plague of the sleek-coated creatures if their numbers were left unthinned. Brookes assured me he had seen herons, during a slight thaw following a frost, watching at these mole-heaps ; and he had known them to catch moles that came above-ground or within striking distance of the stiletto-like bill of the cunning bird.

.   .   .   .   .

I have been in more than one crazy boat, constructed by ingenious rustics, but this coffin-shaped trough, pointed at both ends like a trowel, with upright sides, and a fringing of long river-weed all around it, like a huge, green, unkempt beard, certainly was the strangest coracle ever launched since Noah built the ark.   In the gunnels were stuck a pair of rusted rowlocks, and for oars there were two queer pieces, adze and spokeshave carving, very much like bats : these groaned and squeaked as Brookes junior attempted the passage across the river.   Into this crazy craft were stowed the contingent of eelers, a net, and poles.   Brookes senior laughed loud and long at the suggestion of its having been Father Noah's dinghy.

My first impression of the Waveney marshes was of their utter loneliness.   One may row or walk miles without seeing a fellow creature, save on a passing yacht, or when the marshman is harvesting the litter on the ronds.   There is a great stillness, only broken occasionally by the wail of a wild bird, the rumble of a distant train, or the rustle of the reeds by the river. The creaking and screeching of the machinery of a marsh-mill seem quite companionable sounds after nightfall to the yachtsman anchored by the marshside, and the lonely eel-babber at his fishing. . . .

A lamb-net is a simple although ingenious machine.   Into a stout piece of fir some four feet long and three inches square, a sturdy hazel rod is planted, making in its curve an upright semi-circle. A second half-circle of hoop is fastened, with a swivel movement, at a right angle to the first, and a small-meshed net covers the lower hoop and the V-shaped space between it and the vertical bow. When the net is placed in position across a ditch, it reminds one of an enormous quarter of an orange in shape; the front, of course, is open save for a narrow apron of net some six inches high stretched across the beam and sloping inwards. A short stick with nicked ends deftly fixed between the hoops keeps the structure stiff and in position. A twelve-foot pole attached to the centre of the beam on a swivel serves the purposes of carrying the net, fixing it in position in the ditch, and holding it there. A very few minutes suffice to get this engine into working order, and then the fun begins. Two persons are neccessary to work a lamb-net, but as many as care to join in the sport can do so.

Brookes, as soon as we had everything in readiness, planted the net a few paces from the mill-sluice, while his father, armed with a twelve-foot "splouncing-pole" (a pole with a sort of knob on the end), commenced driving it smartly at every step into the mud. This process undoubtedly struck terror into the lurking or half-buried eels, for they dashed madly ahead of the pole, rustling the reeds as they squirmed through them, while rows of bubbles came to the surface as they "worked" in barer places. Our first "set" was a blank. A few yards further down the ditch we tried again, and before the "splouncer" had reached the net, Brookes remarked—

" There's the fust one in. I now felt him hit the net!"

And before the eel, which had immediately started exploring the net with a view to getting out again, had discovered that he must swim over the apron to do it, the net was drawn up with a jerk, and held mouth upwards, until I had opened my sack. The next twenty-yard "splounce" accounted for another eel; and with very few exceptions, each attempt was successful, although two eels at a time only twice rewarded our exertions. Lamb-netting is not so easy as it appears; to arms and muscles unaccustomed to lifting the net and thrusting with the "splouncer" it becomes exceeding tiring when continued for two or three hours.

We captured very few sticklebacks; and ditch-prawns (*Palæmon varians*) mostly jumped through the meshes back into the water. We found remark-ably little else—not a beetle, a roach, nor any pond-loving larvæ. I noticed that the ditch eels were curiously ruddy in hue, a fact due, in all probability, to their peculiar environment. They differ greatly from the silver-bellied, green-backed eels which spent their nomadic life in the neighbour-ing rivers, and in Breydon. Nor were those I took home with me nearly as good eating as a " fresh-run " eel; they were fat, " fulsome," and had that muddy flavour which distinguishes fresh-water fishes.

To a certain extent we were trespassing, although a certain amount of freedom of movement is permitted on the marshes, so long as no damage is done and the cattle are left undisturbed. In this instance, as we worked along one marsh, the cattle, far from being alarmed, were decidedly inquisitive, and capered towards us with tails up and nostrils dilating. They crowded so closely around us that I stroked the sleek nose of one plump steer. It happened, however, that the son of a marsh-farmer came to look at us, being himself a bit of a sportsman. Now Brookes had no desire that he should know we were doing fairly well, or the young man himself might bring into use his own lambing-net, and so spoil future "workings" in the neighbourhood. So while the young farmer was yet a long way off, Brookes deftly shot about seven pounds of eels from my sack into one he carried in his pocket, and pushed up his waistcoat! In my own bag their remained only three or four pounds of eels, which certainly did not appear to the new-comer an extraordinary catch when he peered into its depths and laughed at our labours. Brookes was by no means comfortable with his tightly-buttoned coat imprisoning the unhappy fishes; but our visitor, wishing us good luck, soon strode off on his round of cattle-watching.

Our total catch weighed in all about eighteen pounds and included a nice fat jack. The showers had passed long before evening; there was a freshness in the air that was delightful. The walk back by the river walls and marshes was enlivened by yarns of previous excursions, when bigger "bags" had rewarded an afternoon's "lambing," or when, overtaken by fog or night in the midst of the marshes, long wearisome wanderings had resulted in a failure to reach home before morning dawned.

A PROFESSIONAL LAMB-NETTER

George, *alias* "Toby," Blake is a small wiry fellow
about fifty years old, who for twenty years has
pursued, in their season, the eels inhabiting the East
Norfolk and North Suffolk marsh-ditches. His
brother, whom I knew as a successful eel-line fisherman, and who kept to the river, was also a "Toby," and
the family patronymic has descended to the present
holder's son he, too, being a born eel-fisher. George
is one of the most industrious workers I ever knew.
From early May until September he tramps many
miles nightly, starting out before dusk and returning
home by early breakfast-time, sometimes pushing a
hand-cart bearing his nets and poles and a trunk of
freshly-caught eels. As far as the borders of Horsey
Mere out in the broadlands, Acle farther west, and
Haddiscoe to the southward, all the marshland
ditches are in his beat and visited as circumstances
or instinct dictates to him.

"Don't you get wrong with the marsh-farmers
sometimes?" I asked him.

"No," he replied; "they've got to know me as
bein' harmless, and I ha' done 'em many a good turn
by getting sheep, cattle, and hosses out of the deeks
where they'd stuck in the mud and might ha' been
drowned."

"Where are you off to this evening?" This was
on Breydon walls, where I had met him in the course
of one of my rambles.

"Only as far as Burgh. I got a nice lot of eels
there last night."

"You never go lining?"

"No," he replied, "though my brother never catched eels any other way. He had an old boat, worked a line each side of her, with about fifteen hooks on 'em, layin' 'em right athort the river, and weightin' 'em with a lead at each end. I've know'd him take a stone and a half of eels in a night, mostly good 'uns; for little 'uns don't easily get outside of a bait. He baited with sliced herrin', shrimps, mushels and eel-pouts. He went bird-catchin' other times, and drove a coke barrow in winter.

"Me? Oh, you know, I spend the autumn in the fish-house, and make hassocks for shops all through the winter up till the time eels begin to run. Sleep? Oh, if I get four hours a night in summer-time I can manage."

Then Toby drifted into the technicalities of his profession.

"I start earlier than May if the weather's mild. I get eels sometimes up to three pounds; and I took one what lumped the scale at four pound. I don't want little 'uns, none less 'an quarter-pounders, and I always have a good-sized sheal in the net so they can pass through. We like thick water after rain, with the wind off the land, and the moon on the wane; and allers look for sport directly after a tempest. Eels are very uncertain; sometimes the noise of the net droppin' in the water 'll frighten 'em. The night afore a tempest they 'ont work at all, and you may try all night and not get one—they'll lay in the mud and 'ont budge. But only get the water freshened and thickened by a good tempest downpour, and *then you'll cop 'em.* My heaviest catch ? Why, one hot night I took thirty-two pounds —all fine eels—on the Burgh meshes.

"Cattle? Well, they don't often interfere with us ; the net slung athort our shoulders fare to set 'em wonderin' and keep 'em off. I once got set on by Long's bull. I know'd he wor on the mesh ; but I had never been interfered with by him afore. I happened to look round, and see him comin' for me. I skuted for the deek, and fortunately lights on the ligger [1] and run athort ; but it wor a near 'un ; I felt his hot breath on my hands as he nearly touched me. That wor the *nearest* I've had. I once set my basket down, half full of eels, while I plounced the deek—I wor workin' alone that night—and when I brought the net back to shoot out the eels I couldn't see it. I hunted all over the mesh and presently finds it without an eel missin'. Some bullock had bin pokin' around and caught his horn in the rope handle. No doubt he wor glad enough to lower it and get free. I certainly thought for a bit I'd been followed and the basket stole.

"On windy nights you get nothin', though east winds don't matter if they're gentle. Strong easterly blows are the worst of all.

"I've got water-rats in the net, and once a water-hen ; pike up to five pounds ; tench, too—I once got four weighing together a half-stone ; and once I caught a whoppin' great rudd. I once cut up a pike and found nearly a whole water-rat in it. I've found deek shrimps, water beetles and insects inside eels ;

[1] Plank bridge.

I've seen a hundred reed-shells (*Hydrobidæ*) in one's stomach, and in one I sent you, you found hundreds of stanickle's eggs.[1]

"How do eels get in these deeks? Well, that's a funny thing to say. I holds they get in from Breydon when the sluices are opened to freshen the deeks. I have thought they might breed in them, but shouldn't like to say. I know some of 'em run big. I got four eels one night last year [1907] what weighed half a stone. That was in the Bure meshes. I have a favourite deek there into which I know for certain eels get from the river through rat-holes. We call it 'Ebenezer' deek; for we give most of them names. We find several sorts of eels—there's white-belly, silver, dark silver, and yellow bellies; sometimes we get all of 'em in one deek. It's the nature—the difference of sile (soil); and they all keep to their own particular beat, if you'll call it such. I know what sort of eel I am likely to get in certain spots, and if a big 'un gets out of the net, I go to that place days after and perhaps catch him. When eels lay up they've two holes, one where they go in, the other where they head out. A good eel-picker'll know exactly where to strike to pin them by the middle.

"No, sir, nothin' scares me, weather nor nothin' else. I've been at it twenty year, and am gettin' used to it. If things got too far with a troublesome bull I should hull the net over his head, and while he wor investigatin' it I should shin out for the nearest stile. I've done twenty miles on a night and been at the Jetty next day selling the eels from my

[1] Vide *Wild Life on a Norfolk Estuary*, p. 172.

barrow. I allers guess the weight, and you can do it easy from long practice to the eighth of an ounce. I make ninepence a pound of 'em."

EELS AND EEL-CATCHERS

"Then softly drifting down the tide, a boat appears in sight ;
Good luck t'ye wily fishermen, this is a 'catching' night."
FOLKARD.

Jary, the Breydon watcher, slipped off home one night, on the last of the ebb-tide, with his stone bottles and an empty frail (basket) to replenish his larder. He came back in the early hours of the morning, on the top of the flood-tide, with provisions for two, and with a baker's tin three parts filled with mould and "black-headed" worms—a bluish-black species, tougher than lobs, and a greater favourite with the local race of eels, which, babbers will tell you, have their "fancies and fiddlesticks." Jary had dug these up in his garden long before dawn.

"I hadn't much sleep last night," he said. "I'm goin' to have an hour's doze of it now."

And with no more to do than flinging himself on the mattress and coiling himself up, he dropped off to sleep in an incredibly short time. His deep breathing told of a sleep dreamless and refreshing. His gold earings gleamed brightly against his deeply tanned skin. He had drawn off his big water-boots and thrown a dry sack across his feet ; another rolled up served him for a pillow.

. . . . .

"The rummest old eel-catcher I ever know'd," said

Jary, as we rowed up stream, "wor old 'Limpenny' King. He fared to know where big eels laid as if he'd got second sight. He used ter get 'em by flyin'——"

"Flying for eels!" I remarked.

"Yes; they used ter call it flyin'. George Sampson was another good hand at flyin'. I ha' seen him go along athort the flats as quiet, you'd scarce see the water part at the punt's bows, and all the while his eyes would be goin' this way and that like an old harnser's. Presently he'd spot an eel, but seldom afore it had spotted him. He'd see it a workin' and scrigglin' itself through the grass (*Zostera*); up goes his arm, and away goes the pick,[1] same as you've seen pictures of Zulus hullin' spears; and he'd fix the eel as neatly as want ter be, the pints of the tines stickin' in the mud and holdin' it there. Theer worn't many men as could do it neatly like that; but George was a rare big strong old feller."

I remembered George Sampson, a tall well-built fellow with long red hair, wiry as maram grass, and with a fringe of similar hue under his chin, looking like lichen on a stone wall. He had wild piercing eyes, and a wrinkled mouth that reminded me, when he was about to thrust into it the shank of a very short, dirty clay pipe, of the top of a spittoon. His crumpled-up sou'-wester was as weather-beaten as himself, and his "jumper," formed of coarse sacking, made a decided impression upon me as a small boy.

---

[1] The shaft, or handle, used does not exceed four feet in length, when spearing is done on the flats.

His prowess as an "eel-flier" still survives in the memory of some of the Breydoners, and his fame has been handed down to a generation that knew him not.

One of the queerest of the eel-men was House-mann, who was known as "The German." As I knew him, he was a fat, thick-set, erratic fellow, with big spectacles, and an accent which told at once that he was not an Englishman.

"Why did you come to this country?" I once asked him, when we were chatting together.

"Mein poy," he replied, "I didn't vant no soldiering. I vos drawn for ze Prussian army, but I vos not vanting to fight. I tells dem if ze king vants to fight, let him do his own for himself. So rader den fight I just comes to dis country. Ve opens an eel-pie shop, an' dat, in Londing; and I comes to here and puys up ze eels. See?"

He had a small amount of capital to start with, which he expended upon a Scotch fishing coble and a small dilapidated steam launch. The former was converted into a huge floating eel-trunk, a small portion only being used as a cabin for the owner. The wretched launch cost him £80, and an additional £20 for tinkering her up. She was named the *Fly*.

"Mein Gott!" exclaimed the astonished German, when the bills came in; "she haf ze name of *Fly*, but by mein crikey, she is von vasp, and haf stung me!"

For some months the launch plied up and down the rivers, coming back with cargoes of eels from the eel-sets and country catchers. For a time old Billy Sampson, one of my Breydon acquaintances, assisted

Housemann in his commercial transactions ; but they soon got to loggerheads, for the German was a bad paymaster.

The latter's next experiment was with a trawl-net, that was dragged along the river-bottom by the steam launch. Jary was employed as fisherman, the German undertaking the duties of engineer. Jary assures me that the first start scared him ; for as soon as the net was dropped overboard the erratic Housemann put the launch at full speed ahead. "She fairly jumped out of the water!" said Jary.

"Can't you start better than that?" he asked.

"Damme!" ejaculated the perspiring master, "I surely can do vat I likes mit mine own poat?"

There was a tube in the boiler which, being leaky, had been fitted with an iron plug. Matters went on all right until it was decided to haul the net. Not content to let Jary get it in, the German must leave the engine to itself and assist in the first hauling. The consequence was that from eighty pounds—which was even then a dangerous pressure for the boiler—it speedily jumped to a hundred and twenty. A loud report announced the departure of the plug from its proper place.

"Mein Gott!" shouted the excited man, "who ze devil haf shot me?"

The hauls made ran from a half to three-quarters of a stone of eels: a payable quantity.

Housemann's next venture was a huge cemented tank in the back kitchen of a little house he hired near the riverside. This receptacle would hold twenty stone of eels at a time. I have seen this filled with a mass of squirming fish, running water keeping them in fairly good health until despatching time came.

Eel-pots, of a pattern which originated in the German's distorted brain, were next tried, but as the bottoms were of iron and exceedingly heavy, they proved a failure by settling in the mud, where the baits soon became covered with silt.

Housemann's experiments, in the course of a year or two, brought the whole concern into the hands of the bailiffs, and Yarmouth saw no more of him.

. . . . .

"Peg-leg" Gates sat in meditative mood by his cosy fireside. I rapped at the door that opened into the Row.

"Come in!" said the cheery voice of the ever-merry Peg-leg.

"Things in the eel-line are slow," said I.

"They are, bor," he replied. "I ain't bin up Breydon for several weeks—ain't even seen it this side Christmas.",

I sat down in the proffered chair, and it was not long before he began to relate some of his early reminiscences. The upturned corners of his kindly mouth gave an optimistic look to the by no means characterless face. Something of his early Jack Tar joviality still lingered about him.

"My ship," he said, "was the old brig-rigged, paddle-sloop *Hydra*. I met with my accident when I was twenty. I fell from the main gaff off Deal: comes home invalided, and they sawed my leg off in Yarmouth horspital. I'd done six year aboard the *Hydra*; spent a long time off South America, and went up the Orinoco messin' arter the Venezeulans. We had a light draught—only sixteen feet astern—and got took in by a pilot. I didn't like the look of the bar.

" ' Think we'll do it?' I axes the bo's'n.

" ' *Do* it; in course!' says he, and we did.

" It fared a rum go—we left sharks one side the bar, and see alligators the tother. I shinned up aloft to see the country. Theer was no end of pillikins (pelicans) and ostriches (rheas) swarming the flat country. We got yellow fever at Greystown, and were shunted to Newfoundland to get over it. Some poor devils had to be lashed in their hammocks. We did a bit on the west coast of Africa, too."

" You water-folk," I said, " seem to have had a finger in many a pie!"

" Ah, bor," he replied, " some of us have been smacksmen, wherrymen, coasters, shrimpers, and the dowst know what, in turn. You see, it's pretty much all alike; there's a starvation livin' on the water, and plenty to do for it: and water is in our line, water bein' water all the world over.

" When I got back and fixed up I took to Breydon, where I'd been nussed afore I went cruising. I was the fust as started lookin' for eels in the deep water —in the channel. I've picked, lined, and babbed ever since. They've stopped lining up the rivers, these 'ere angler-people. Why, I used ter lay night-lines up the rivers afore they stopt lines with more 'an one hook. We used ter drop a line with a score hooks athort the river with a stone at each end, and we would creep 'em up next mornin'. Well, with seven or eight hundred hooks out, I've taken as many as seven or eight stone—all fine eels. We used small roach for bait. I've seen monstrous great eels in Hardley deek. The biggest eel I ever took was up the North River: I copt it on a butt-dart, one tine goin' through the tail: it coils itself around the shank of the pick, and I had it.

"Eels are very 'spotty'; you may work miles along a river and keep tryin' with your bab and not get none; then all on a sudden you drop in among a drove of 'em. I once copt a salmon that length" (measuring about a foot along his arm) "on the bab, up there against the Dickey Works (Breydon). I caught two real Cromer crabs (*Cancer pagurus*) when I was babbin' at the pier head once, agin the harbour mouth."

"Now, then, what do you think of eels coming up river from sea in the spring?" I queried.

"Bor, I fare sure they do," he replied; "look how you catch 'em even off the shore. Then look at Mutford lock, aginst Lowestoft. Sure-ly they can't get through the lock, and you can catch 'em, reg'lar sea eels, on the harbour side."

"You remember the eels dying by thousands in 1905?"

"Oh yes!" he replied; "that was through the heat and no fresh-water to liven up the river. They'd got 'red robins'!"

"Red—what?"

"Why, it came on like a disease, which it was. You see 'em all red, in patches, as if they'd got measles. I've seen 'em with it afore. They catch it when the deeks and rivers get drainage from the land dressed with artificial manures, and guano, and no rain to freshen the water.

"I never could get into the knack of gatherin' up my eels as some do with the fore finger bent; I allers use a knife to hold 'em with. It's a knack, and nothin' more. Did you get any eels when you was down in Lancashire?"

"No," I replied, "I was too busy; but we had big 'uns in the lake."

"Law!" said he, eager to hear more. Then I told him how we went "snig-fraeing" in spring in the Ribble,[1] and of a huge eel that came from the lake through an iron pipe into the seal-pond, where-upon the largest and most ferocious of my seals wobbled off his rocks towards it, seized it adroitly by the back of the head, and after shaking and breaking it vertebra from vertebra, bolted it whole.

"Law!" said he, "how I'd like to ha' seen it! I used ter watch the seals off the North American coast, but never see anything like that."

.   .   .   .   .

"Blue" Calver represents the third generation of a family of eel-catchers. It was his grandfather who once cut a little drain on Breydon in order to connect two larger ones, so that he could get his boat through without rowing a long way round.

---

[1] It was a common practice when I lived in Preston in 1884, for scores of mill-hands to go to the Ribble, armed with a small hand-net and a bucket. By making a miniature dam with the foot an eddy was caused. Along this eddy they ran their net (made of muslin), capturing hundreds of tiny eels, transparent in colour, with two tiny black dots of eyes. I understood that they made puddings of them.

That small " grup " became known as Calver's drain ;
it scoured and deepened until it is now wide enough
for a wherry to draw through, and I have failed
to reach the bottom of it with a very long pole.
At the corner of this drain, often for months together,
Calver's tarred houseboat, with its load of eel-boxes,
poles, and other gear upon the roof, lies moored.
"Blue" has raised a respectable family by the aid
of his eel-pots and small trawl-net. With the latter
he catches bushels of shrimps in the course of a
season, and with them he baits his eel-pots, which
he drops into the channel and " likely " drains.

The net also accounts for flounders and saleable
soles occasionally, not to mention a few " eel-pouts," or
viviparous blennies. Of the last-named he sometimes
gets fifty or sixty at a haul ; there was a time when
he might have brought up a thousand. They make
excellent bait, when cut up, for eel-pots or eel-lines.
Twenty-five years ago, he has assured me, he has
taken eight trunks of " butts " (flounders) by a night's
trawling.

Eels are his particular quest. He works a boat
with a jib and mainsail—a cut-down small boat
that once belonged to a fishing lugger.

"Eels, I allers say," said he, "come up, thousands
of 'em, from the sea in the spring time."

In this assertion I was at one with him, although
it was contrary to the belief of several of my
naturalist friends.

"I've heered old fellers say, years ago, as how
when theer wasn't much water on the bar—there's
sixteen fut there at low water nowadays, but in

them days a shrimp-boat couldn't draw over at low tide—they'd seen eels comin' in from sea in spring in thick droves. You know as well as I do how, down near the pier in April and May, eels may be caught when you can't catch 'em up river. The stickin' out of the North Pier fare to chuck fish off instead of drawin' up on the flood-tide[1] as they used ter.

"Oh yes, I've caught eels full of feed, some of 'em have been full of them smooth whitish shells you find on the beach sometimes (*Tellina balthica*), crabs, and nobody knows what else. I remember old 'Bugles' sittin' in the houseboat once, havin' a bit o' pork for dinner, and he hulled the rind overboard. Very sune after he caught an eel, and on openin' it to cook it, he found his own bit of pork rind inside it. A four and a half pound eel wor the heaviest I ever got in an eel pot."

.   .   .

"Morning, ' Short'un,' " I said.

"Mornin', Mr. Pattson," he replied.

"Will you go and tar my boat shed ? " I asked. " You're not very busy, I suppose ? "

"Busy! Aye? " he answered, his gold earrings undulating like small clock pendulums as he shook his funny little head, and pulled out his pipe. "Ain't got enough hardly to keep *that* a-going, let alone bein' busy."

It was a bleak January morning, and Breydon fretfully pushed its sullen waves against a bitter nor-wester. We could see its troubled waters from where we stood at the entrance of the Bure.

[1] See *Wild Life on a Norfolk Estuary*, p. 98.

"Looks like ernin' anything up there just now," he said.

" No picking ? "

" Pickin'! Aye? I couldn't do it now, even if I hadn't parted with my pick. I sold it a week ago to one of them young Ribbons's, who ha' started eel-catchin'. A nice trade to take up now Breydon's about done for. But young chaps don't know what to do with theerselves nowadays."

"Ah, that wor a good pick in its time," edged in Snicker, who had just drawn up for a gossip, " one of Bob Flaxman's make ; but a bit wore with use. They'll wear up in mud, let alone when you gets on a chingly¹ (shelly) bottom. Theer worn't any one as could touch Bob for makin' a pick ; he'd got a knack o' temperin' on 'em as no other man breethin' could touch him. He fared to take a wonderful pride in 'em ; he'd dingle (loiter) over 'em, right lovin'ly he would—I ha' helped him make many a one. His father afore him was a don hand at the bizness, and never let one go under fourteen shillin's, or thirteen and sixpence at the leasest. But Bob wor difrunt-natured ; and made a good many for nothin', bein' a bit wittery-natured (frail). I ha' seen him let a many go, and never got a fardin for all his trouble. Still, he'd got the master of his work, and you could open the tines apart with yer fingers and they'd spring back like high-classed table-knives ; and they were that reg'ler and neatly shaped, you wouldn't

¹ In the drains, usually where eddies are formed, deposits of empty brittle shells, relicta of dead *Hydrobidæ*, clams, and periwinkles occur.

GOING EEL-PICKING

find a weam in 'em big enuf for a micry-scupe to discover it.

"Now, what do you think they were made on?"

"Iron, of course."

"Well, they *worn't* iron. He made 'em out of old cart-springs, the best steel as ever cum out of a mind (mine). He used ter split 'em down in two; and I ha' swung the bout hammer many a time helpin' him cuttin' 'em down. The rivets wor made out of bolts from old Norraway and Swedish wrecks. The finest stuff in the world, they wor, as kind as a bit o' lead—they'd never fly, nor nothin'. When they broke up an old wreck they'd bring Bob the bolts; he gave 'em a shillin' for a skepful (hamperful). Bob ha' made hundreds of picks for Norwich, Lowestoft, Beccles, and all round. You could allers tell one of Bob's afore you looked for his name stamped on the shank. Poor Bob hev had imitators; one chap, Tom Read of Burgh, made a fairish pick; you might give the order for it one day and get it finished the next, and pay only three half-crowns for it. But, law! Bob's 'ud eat 'em up."

"And that monkey 'Jack' of his!" I suggested.

"Ah! bor, I a'most forgot that noint (rascal) of a monkey. They used ter say he wor a rheece (rhesus monkey), and had come over in a ship from India. Bein' used to a hot climate, I suppose, he never fared happier 'an when he wor perched among the cinders on the forge; and he used ter chatter and jabber to the flames as they sperrited up the chimbley as if he doted on 'em. He wor the very devil; and if you only made a face at him he'd fly in

a towerin' rage, and say, ' *O ah !* ' that natural, you'd
die a-larfin' a'most ; and he jump and turn round on
you, makin' the cinders fly under him, same as they
say a ostrich chucks stones when he's a-runnin'.
An' if you worn't careful he blind you with 'em, he
could shoot that straight.   And I ha' seen him watch
picks and other gear bein' made, with as knowin' a
look on him as if he could give you points in makin'
'em."

OTTER AND EEL

ON THE BURE

CHAPTER VII

ON QUIET WATERS

"And the wavy swell of soughing reeds,
  And the wave-worn horns of the echoing bank,
  And the silvery marsh flowers that throng
  The desolate creeks and pools among,
  Were flooded over with eddying song."

AN AUGUST RIVER TRIP

EARLY in 1894, the houseboat *Moorhen*, resplendent in her first coats of paint, was pushed by the designer and builder off the yard into the water. Her hull had been knocking about the North Sea for some years, as tender and ferrier to a fishing smack; but now, patched, renovated, and with a comfortable hut above her, the remainder of her days were to be spent on placid inland waters. For some years I spent my August holidays aboard her, living a Crusoe sort of life on the rivers and broads, drifting on the tides, her progress seldom exceeding four miles an hour, even when helped by a favouring breeze and a pair of large oars.[1] Those who know the Norfolk and Suffolk waterways are well aware how sinuous they are, and how annoyingly what you gain upon one "reach" you are safe to lose on the next. Looking across the marshlands from the river banks, a stranger is often amazed at the number of wherry and yacht-sails to the right and left, before and behind, the hulls unseen, because they are below the level of the "walls." They seem to be afloat on the marshlands!

To rip and tear along seems to be the delight of the yacht-sailer. I suppose it is the same lust for speed which makes a motor man always in a desperate hurry. No such desire must possess the voyager in a sail-less houseboat; he must be quite free from the spirit of unrest. With his house above him, and his lockers and water-bottles filled, the houseboater is the freest holiday-maker in the world. He can catch his tide, and go on his way for so long as it serves; he can drive his stakes into the bank, and moor wheresoever it pleases him; no crowded staithe nor rollicking yachting-crew need bother him, for he can "rond anchor" himself in the quietest reaches of the river, enjoy his meals in solitude, or, if so disposed, he can ramble to the nearest marshman's red-tiled house to "mardle" and barter for necessary provender. What matter it to him if he only covers a thirty-mile

1 Vide *Nature in Eastern Norfolk*, pp. 148-49.

"drift" in a week, and takes another week to drift back again?

Ah! I spent some jolly autumn holidays aboard the slow-moving *Moorhen*. As a rule, I got her under way at the end of July, and pushed her on as many miles as possible at a tide, when intending to spend some days of my vacation on the broads and rivers. Long in my memory will linger thoughts of idle days in Kendal Dyke, within a mile or so of the famous Hickling Broad; when the reeds were alive all night with starlings and martins, and the notes of the reed- and the sedge-warblers were heard at intervals above the rustling of the reeds. Moorhens clacked and coots clicked petulantly; bearded tits chinked their metallic chatter, and the wild ducks croaked a·deeper chorus. Even at dead o' night some migrating bird piped weirdly in the darkness overhead.

The jolliest of all my August trips was in 1896. I made a quick run to the broads, having obtained a tow behind a steam launch; the old *Moorhen* never travelled faster. Each day, while I loafed, fished, or read, brought new experiences. There was little need to go out of one's way for variety. Now a friend would sail by; another would bring rods and lines; there was, of course, the usual broadland anxiety about fresh water, which meant a row to a neighbouring farm for it; also about bread—you cannot always depend upon a supply, for sometimes yachting folk will empty the farmer's cupboard and, perhaps, the village baker's store. I have had to go asking from door to door for a supply of bread!

But a home-made country loaf, fresh from the quaint old oven, is worth all the trouble one has to get it!

As early as August 4th, the sand-martins had come to roost in the reed-beds. They were up before the sun had peered above the sandhills, and they raced to and fro under the nodding reeds, after insects that had innocently spent the night in close proximity to their relentless enemies. Thirty herons passed overhead, giving me the impression that they had determined to make a trip to Holland, for they went away seawards and passed beyond my ken.

That night I staked down some dead roach on the rond behind me, in order to settle the point whether water-voles ate fishes or not. And, sure enough, they came in the night and began their feast. I watched them, and they did not desist; it may be I was so still, they thought I was asleep. They left droppings behind them, and tiny munchings that slipped from between their teeth.[1]

No enthusiastic angler, however, need worry about the depredations of the water-vole, for he (the angler) often leaves to rot on the bank far more roach and bream than all the voles in the vicinity can clear off while fresh; indeed, rather than anathematise the innocent animal, he should feel indebted to it for clearing away what would otherwise become a nuisance. And I question if a water-vole, at home as it is beneath the surface, could overtake a roach in a fair chase. That it appropriates a dead fish is no evidence that it ever captures a live one. Then the bearded tits—whole families of young ones came

[1] Vide *Nature in Eastern Norfolk*, pp. 267-70.

ping-ping-ing at intervals as they dodged above and around the reeds in search of food, in that gregarious manner so apparent in the long-tailed and cole-tit species. Curlews passed overhead at a considerable height on several occasions; and green sandpipers sometimes showed themselves.

On the 13th I started leisurely on the homeward voyage, drifting down below Potter Heigham. On the 14th I reached Ant mouth, where I spent the morning in watching some beautiful butterflies, among them peacocks and the swallow-tails, fluttering around their favourite plants; I also caught some hungry little roach and rudd. A kingfisher, which must have mistaken me for a patient heron, attempted to alight upon the end of my fishing-rod; and later on I rescued a miserable toad, whose toes had been nibbled off, maybe by a water-vole. I suspected that the vole had been swimming with his victim and had failed to land it. I have since wondered whether I did that wretched toad a good turn by allowing it to live : anyway, I pitched it among the lash herbage beyond the bank, and gave it a chance.

The night of the 14th found me snugly moored in the entrance of Tunstall Dyke. Hard by, as I drifted downstream, I was entertained by three kestrel hawks and an enormous congregation of swallows. The latter had mistaken the intentions of the "mouse-hunters," and had started to bully them. The kestrels might have gone quickly away had they chosen to do so ; but it seemed to me that they had lost their tempers, and intended to make some of the smaller birds pay for their impertinence. How the scrimmage ended I did not see.

The 15th was a red letter day to me. A friend joined me; and poor old Billy Fransham, marsh-farmer, gamekeeper, and general dealer, also put in an appearance, accompanied by his dog and gun, and bringing with him a small hoop-net, with which he hoped to catch a few small rudd and roach for his ferrets at Tunstall.

Fransham ought to have been born fifty years before in some American backwoods settlement. He dared not touch hare or pheasant (openly, anyway!), for he held his little farm on sufferance; but he was a great hand at trapping stoats and weasels, and in his time had captured, in an ingenious home-made trap of some sort, four or five otters, which after-wards became pets of mine. He captured, in triangular hen-coops, the jackdaws and rooks that came to his marsh;[1] and moorhens, by the half-dozen, he managed to trap; indeed, he used to bring me for my aviaries numbers of the latter birds un-injured. He was a typical Broadlander, with clean-shaven face, and a towy fawn-coloured beard, that fringed his neck like a strip of Syrian bear-skin. He attended sales, buying ducks and hens for his wife to kill and prepare for the Saturday's market. His one cow he drove backwards and forwards between marsh and stable, his better and more industrious half milking it and churning the produce into butter. Apart from these light duties, and his spells of eel-picking, netting, and vermin-hunting, he did

[1] Vide *Notes of an East Coast Naturalist*, p. 72.

no more than he could possibly help. But not a better hunter of small game, nor a more observant rustic naturalist, did I ever meet with among men in his particular sphere of life.

"Hallo! yew there!" was his greeting; "if yow'll hurry up, an' cum to my mesh (marsh), I'll show yew some fun."

He had been expecting our coming, and early that morning had blocked up a "lobster" (stoat) in its burrow. He forthwith fetched his warren spade, also a roughly-made funnel of wire-netting, to the end of which he had tied a sack. Some little digging had to be done before we could start the poor little animal, which it was our intention to capture alive, to become one of my pets. Anyway, Fransham did not intend that it should escape, for if it did his hens and ducks would be by no means safe. Peter, the mongrel, keen as his master, dashed in as the animal bolted, and tenderly seized it behind the shoulders. Had he been ordered to kill it he would quickly have done so. But the stoat showed fight, and gave Peter a sharp bite on the nose, which caused him to drop it. I seized it by the tail, but I, too, was glad to let it go. However, after muddling the wretched animal about we got it safely into the sack, and, taking it into the cart-shed, we placed it in a cage. But while we were still looking at it the poor thing turned over and died, probably as much from terror as from ill-usage. He cut up the burrow from end to end, finding in it a dead long-tailed field mouse, which the stoat had recently killed.

Some rat hunting was the next entertainment

Q

provided for us, a diversion so well known that any description of it is unnecessary.

I should like to depict that quaint little homestead as it appeared, inside and out, on that bright August day. The ditch running hard by sparkled in the sunlight; fleabanes, willow-herbs, purple loose-strifes, and meadow vetchlings were mirrored in its cool waters.

"This is glorious—simply glorious!" said my friend, who was gathering a bunch of bright marsh-flowers. There was a rough bank near the house, where the hawthorns grew untrimmed. Nettles and brambles grew rankly among and below them; hemp agrimony and the toadflax added touches of colour; and tall marsh thistles looked quite in keeping with them. Around here, in spring, the brimstone butter-flies are abundant; and if the goldfinch haunts the neighbourhood in autumn, it is seen around here most plentifully. Fransham knew this, and many a cage full of goldfinches, larks, bramblings, chaffinches, siskins, and other birds did he bring to the market in late autumn. Once when he set a trap cage in this spot to catch a goldfinch he secured a great grey shrike that had hopped in hoping to secure the decoy-bird. That shrike became a famous pet of mine. The spot was alive with meadow-brown butterflies, bees, and bee-flies that beautiful day.

The old-fashioned cottage was gay with climbing nasturtiums; geraniums grew luxuriantly below the window-sills, together with many a commoner flower; a border of privet crept up to the edge of the little flower garden, and, with some hawthorns, trended down to the broken gate. Pumpkins trailed along below, and gay mallows bore them company. Beyond the privet hedge a prosy but useful kitchen garden smiled. Fattening hogs grunted complacently in their stys; rows of hutches held rabbits of all ages and colours; ferrets danced wonderingly behind their wires; and various pigeons peered out from their lockers. The fowl-yard, too, was alive with tenants.

The inside of the cottage was homely enough. There was the old Dutch clock on the wall, and Fransham's favourite gun slung upon a beam above-head: a bureau, which contained the household treasures; guns and bird nets stood up one corner; and rough chairs were drawn up at a table spread with Norfolk dumplings, meat, sausage rolls, boiled eggs, a rich cream cheese, and a huge steaming teapot. A tabby cat sat near the geraniums upon the window-sill, watching at intervals a goldfinch fluttering in a cage hard by.

After dinner we strolled to the little village, where we visited the decaying steeple of the roofless church. The owls had made it their habitation, and bushels of cast-up pellets were heaped upon the ground among the fallen flints. I took home a parcel of those pellets, and found in them the remains of many short-tailed field mice, long-tails, and shrews.

That night we slept in Mautby mill sluice. Alas! since that pleasant day poor old Fransham has passed over to the great majority. Peace be to his ashes ![1]

[1] Fransham, under the name of Jim Trett, the fenman, was

MY CHUM DYE

In the seventies I first made the acquaintance of Ben, my baker friend. I met him in one of my rambles near the Charity Gardens, on the outskirts of the town, which he then frequented in the intervals of bread-making. He was seeking fieldfares and missel-thrushes, which in those days were abundant in that neighbourhood, where hawthorns flourished and trees were numerous. As a small boy, when he should have been at school, he had worked for a sportive baker, whom he followed like a spaniel, from whom he learned to wish for a gun, and by whom he was shown how to use one. Snipe and woodcocks lured both of them abroad in the wintry days, and thrushes and starlings filled their game-bag when the fruit-bushes were laden in summer-time.

Ben's first gun was his idol. He loafed around the manure heaps with it in search of rare wagtails ; and hard by the gardens he shot his first kingfisher. One day he wandered to the beach with a chum, and a man asked them to lend him the gun, saying he had seen a rare bird behind a sand-hill. They let him have it and heard him fire it off. He did not return with it, so they peered over the sand-hill, and saw the man lying dead. He had nearly blown his head off!

At a very irresponsible age Ben began to manage his widowed aunt's little bakehouse ; and his spare hours with his gun became a delight to him. Rabbits,

one of my favourite characters in my *Man and Nature on the Broads*, 1895.

turtle-doves, and wood-pigeons lured him to the Denes, and so wild then was the vicinity of the little bakehouse that a shot could now and again be taken from its very door. There were gardens near by, and in his own small one gold-crested wrens visited the gooseberry bushes, while siskins would peep in at the window where one of their kind was encaged.

Many of our adventures together are already narrated in one of my books.[1] Ben was the worst fellow in the world to get up in the early morning, for he used to sit up late into the night bird-stuffing. I was an early bird then, and when I called him at three o'clock in the morning, it was like trying to wake the dead. I used a linen prop to rattle on his window, and used it persistently, or he would not have risen at all. It was equally difficult to get him home when we had once started.

One autumn—it was in 1881, I think—we shot several kingfishers ; they were exceedingly numerous that year. I should not have killed my seven, only Ben had killed his, and we never liked being beaten by each other. We then became so sick of this senseless slaughter, that we never molested this pretty species again.

In January, 1881, Ben fell in with a lot of shore-larks on the sand-dunes and shingle patches. There were twenty-five in all, and they attracted his attention by their three-syllable cry. He shot two, afterwards seeing many more—some sixty in all. That morning he secured in all fourteen birds. In 1883 he watched two nests of the ringed plover, from the day when the

[1] Vide *Nature in Eastern Norfolk*, p. 5.

first egg was laid until the young hatched out.[1]   In
May, 1882, he noticed two birds on the beach, which
he at first mistook for ringed plovers ; but he was
curious to know why their black collars did not join
across their throats.   He shot both, and discovered
that they were Kentish plovers.   In one he found an
egg the size of a large pea.

A little later he became the proud possessor of a
small, amateur-made gun-punt, not quite fifteen feet in
length.   It was made of galvanized iron, and rattled
when rowed like a big tin saucepan, but more particularly when mischievous urchins, finding out what
it was made of, pelted it with stones as it lay by
the riverside.   In this fragile craft he made many
excursions to Breydon, securing godwits, knots, and
rarer birds.   It was, perhaps, fortunate for him that
one day his painters broke, and the *Iron Duke*—
for so his punt was named—slid into the river, having
previously been filled by a big tide.   She was not
fished out again until the river was dredged some
years after.   She then came to the surface a bundle
of scrap-iron, punctured with a hundred holes made
by the sharp iron toe of the wherryman's quant-
pole.

Ben had a collecting hobby.   For several years he
stuffed his own birds ; but before his collection had
grown to any size his eyesight failed him, and by
degrees he became almost totally blind.   Like the
owl, he now finds his way about best at dusk ; but he
meets with many unpleasant mishaps through stumb-
ling against pedestrians, ladders, and kerb-stones.

[1] Vide *Notes of an East Coast Naturalist*, pp. 30–33.

KENTISH PLOVER, KNOT, AND TURNSTONE

The merest glimmer of sight remains to him : just enough to distinguish between light and darkness.

Before his affliction for ever ended his bird-hunting rambles, he learnt a great deal of bird-lore, and to this day he is constantly adding to his knowledge of it. He was keenly observant, and had, in his prime, remarkably acute sight. He could "tell" a bird flying or resting far beyond my powers of vision ; but I beat him out and out in keenness of hearing ; I could often distinguish a bird by its note long before he could hear it, or before it came within range of his sight. He secured a fine spoonbill, an avocet, a grey phalarope, a white-winged black tern, a Richardson's skua, ruffs, and several other good birds ; and he has added to his collection since, although latterly he has been sadly handicapped, not only by the loss of his sight, but by a falling off in his business. Little shopkeepers fare badly in these days of large firms and limited companies.

To-day Ben will identify many a bird by handling it, aided, of course, by his memory. Some time ago, I took him for a ramble down to the harbour's mouth ; there had been a strong wind from the eastward, and I felt sure that guillemots and razor-bills must have been driven in by the sea. Nor was I disappointed. Presently I picked up a bird, and placed it in his hands.

"If you tell me what it is you can have it," I said.

Ben started at the feet, felt the length of the wings, the shape of the head, and finally let his fingers travel down to the tip of the thin curved beak.

"By Jove!" he said, "it's a Manx shear-water!"
He was quite right. The bird is a very rare visitor
to this part of the coast.

To this day he venerates his "Yarrell," and in
the long winter nights he will listen to his wife reading aloud page after page of its contents. His
eagerness to hear me read my *Zoologist* and *British
Birds* evidences the delight he still takes in his
favourite birds; and although he lives to a great
extent out of the world, no new warbler is shot at
Cley or Blakeney, nor any other rare species comes
to this hostile land, but he somehow gets to know of
it, and comes to discuss its points and peculiarities
with me. Were it left to Ben, no new species would
be placed on the British list unless all evidence was
in favour of its having a legitimate claim to be there.

.   .   .   .   .

THIRTY YEARS AFTER

Thirty years ago, and perhaps a little earlier, Ben
and I took our first trip together up the river Bure.
He shot two wild ducks that night on a marsh not
two miles above the town; also, I believe, a couple of
reeves, at a pool in the rond beside the river.

What changes have come about since then!
Many of our old gunning friends have passed away,
and Time has not dealt kindly with my poor old
chum. As for myself, those days are pleasant to
dream of, when the heart was young and eager, and
there was romance attaching to even the commonest
objects; the very ditch weeds charmed me, and the

cry of every bird was music. Time has been more friendly towards me; and the recording of my re- collections and observations has afforded me as much pleasure as my experiences gave me in earlier days.

"Ben," said I, on August 28th, 1907, "I'm going over some of the old scenes this afternoon, up the Bure. What say you to a trip with me?"

"I'm game," replied Ben, thumping into his batch of dough with redoubled vigour in order to get his work done early enough to permit him to indulge in a few hours' pleasure. I say pleasure, for it is his delight to listen to the calls of the birds and to my descriptions of things as I see them.

Soon after noon I launched the punt and entered the Bure on a flowing tide, a south-easterly wind filling the little sail so that she bowled along merrily. The ripple of the water was music to both of us. I stepped ashore several times in order to peer over the walls, into favourite marshy corners where in years gone by we had put up snipe and green sand- pipers, watched for lapwings, and piped with evil intent to the redshanks which nested there.

On a post near the walls sat a black-headed gull, somnolent and careless: I suspected he was there as sentry. I quickly pushed under the cover of the " wall " and cautiously peered over. There was a low part to the marsh which the water had left soft and miry, and the cattle stood there cooling their hoofs by scores. Among and around them were quite two hundred gulls of different species, digesting the food they had captured in the morning. Gulls and cattle were on the best of terms; and if a bullock strolled a few yards in any direction it carefully avoided the slumbering birds. All this I had to describe to Ben, who waited in the boat, holding it fast to the shore by clutching the rank grasses by the riverside.

"Now for the mill corner!" I said; and we lowered the sail and rowed further upstream. Cautiously raising my head above the bank, for I had heard the calling of a redshank, I was delighted with the nature picture I saw. There was a puddle, a "low" not thirty yards distant on the marsh. It was no larger than a table-cloth; but a huge farm horse was standing in it, his fore-quarters lower than his hind, his fore feet being fetlock deep in the water. It stood with eyes closed and head hanging—dozing. Around him were eight redshanks, one greenshank, one green sandpiper, three lapwings, three black-headed gulls, and three ringed plovers, the farthest being not more than six feet away from his hoofs. The redshanks were at their toilet, the "pewits" gossiping, the gulls nodding, and the ringed plovers pretending to find something to eat. The others were looking on.

"Like old times, Ben," said I.

"Good God!" said poor Ben; "would but I could see 'em."

MUSSEL-DREDGING

CHAPTER VIII

SOME LOST INDUSTRIES

"O thou vast ocean! ever sounding sea!
Thou symbol of a drear immensity!

. . . . .

On thy heavily laden breast
Fleets come and go. . . ."

BARRY CORNWALL.

MUSSEL-DREDGING

THE struggles of the poor to make a bare living
are often pathetic. Of more than ordinary
interest are the toils, the shifts, the strange ways of
some of the waterside folk. True, there are callings
that are still at times remunerative—those of the
smelter, the shrimper, and the eel-catcher are among
these; while the wherryman looks upon his work as
being almost a profession. Many of the Breydoners
have followed all of these occupations in turns.

Little "Short'un" Page, "Pintail" Thomas, and others living and dead, alternately, or as the vicissitudes of the times compelled them, went shrimping, smelting, wild-fowling, wherrying, trawling in deep seas, and drifting, nearer home, for herrings.

There was one pursuit which, not so many years ago, was eagerly undertaken by many a waterside *habitué*, especially when things were dull, and that was musseling. Any man who did not object to mud, cold water, and real hard work, and who was able to provide himself with a dredge or two, could always fall back upon musseling to provide himself with his rent and the bare necessities of life.

All over the muddy bottoms of the channels of Breydon, the river Bure from the entrance at Breydon to the yachting station, and the Yare from Breydon to the harbour mouth, up till within the last ten years or so, myriads of mussels were to be found. Thirty years ago they were healthy molluscs, and highly esteemed as an article of food; then the abomination of sewage disposal by means of the tidal waters came into municipal favour, and soon polluted the local waters to such an extent that the tides could not wash all the filth out to sea.

To-day, although one sees, at very low ebb, many mussels clinging to the buttresses of the haven bridge, and patches are to be found in the channels and drains of Breydon, the mussel has become much scarcer; even on the piles of the breakwaters at Gorleston, where there were myriads of young mussels a few years ago, comparatively few are now to be found. I think it more than likely that the sewage,

the carbolic acid and other disinfectants, together
with the various pollutions mingled with the waters,
have killed the spat.   When I was a lad a vessel had
but to lie in the river a few months and thousands of
mussels would settle on her bottom and rapidly grow
to maturity.

There was a time, well within my own recollection, when Breydon might have been converted into
a very remunerative mussel-farm : there was a
sufficient rise and fall of tides over a great acreage
of the estuary, and the alternation of salt and fresh
water was just what was necessary for the successful
culture of the mussel.   The number of piles in the
channel might have been indefinitely added to, and
the *bouchet* system, so advantageously pursued in the
Bay of Aiguillon, might have been successfully
adopted.   But the growing up of the flats,[1] and the
constant presence of offensive matter, have made this
quite impossible.   Under proper conditions nothing
is more simple than mussel culture.   The seedling
mussels to be transplanted are placed in a roll of net
and tied to the stakes on which they are to grow.
In a few days they have attached themselves firmly to
the stakes, and in course of time the net rots, leaving
them in position. . . .

To enter into the mussel trade required a comparatively small outlay of capital.   An old boat
discarded by some fishing lugger was purchased
for a few shillings ; a couple of " streaks," or strakes,
were cut off and a new gunnel was added.   At the

[1] Vide *Wild Life on a Norfolk Estuary*, pp. 96, 97, where
this process of " growing up " is explained.

OYSTER-CATCHER : A LOVER OF SHELLFISH

bow of the boat a couple of iron uprights were affixed to carry the spindles of a horizontal winch, in which three or four holes were drilled to receive short staves. A long rope was wound round the winch, and there only remained to add a dredge—an apparatus much like those used on oyster beds, consisting of a frame with a scraping blade below, and a net attached behind it. The process of musseling was simple enough. The end of the winch-rope was attached to a stake, or to some vessel moored to the quayside, and the boat was allowed to drift the length of it. When the rope was all unwound, the dredge was thrown over and a hand-over-hand turning of the winch by means of the pegs slowly dragged the net over the bottom. When it was hauled up, after a preliminary rinsing to clear away the mud, its contents were shot into the boat, and a mixed gathering it was! Bones, coal, stones, crabs, mussels, pieces of scrap iron, and even flounders and pogges were turned out of the dredge. Subsequently the "catch" was shovelled into baskets, taken ashore, and shot on to a board supported by trestles, where it was sorted over, perhaps by the musseler's wife and children.

"Ah! bor," said "Short'un" Page, "I've done my whack at musselin'. In the winter months, when other work was scarce, theer'd be as many as a dozen or more boats at it, musselin' in the river, or up Breydon. I once worked for *old* Ben Bessey, gettin' a guinea a week and all my beer. That was in the seventies and eighties, afore this muck came and spiled the rivers. We used ter get thirty and forty bushels of mushels in a tide. We'd send bags of 'em to Nottin'gim, Birming-gim, and Cambridge, and got back from two to five shillin's a bag ; if we got only half a crown, that paid us. And I ha' hawked 'em about the town at a penny and tuppence a quarter. Folks used ter buy 'em as fast as you like."

"Were no other jobs spoiled by the sewage ?" I queried.

"Not so much," he replied, "although smeltin' and eel-catchin' ain't bin improved. Yet it's werry funny as how eels 'll draw round sewer outlets for garbage, and yet if you shet 'em up in a eel-trunk and float it in tarnted (tainted) water, they'll die in less 'an no time.

"The butt-nettin', in course, was spiled by the flats a-growin up so. Theer's plenty of 'em in the drains ginerally, but you can't do much nettin' theer. Several men had nets in the old days and done a pritty good thing catchin' butts for shops, and to send away for crab-bait.[1] But that's all done with.

"Then theer was mulletin'.[2] You know, we done pretty well with that in the old days ; and allers had a ready sale both in town and up in London. Some people say as they can't do with mullet, and turn up their noses at 'em. But, of course, they don't cook 'em quick enough. You want tu get 'em into the fish-kettle straight out of the water, and then eat 'em with a little vinegar, parsley, and melted butter. We

---

[1] Vide " Flounder-catching," *Wild Life on a Norfolk Estuary*, pp. 120-127.

[2] *Ibid.* pp. 98 and 182.

R

sometimes get an odd mullet in the smelt-nets and toss up to see who's to have it; but as for goin' arter 'em special, well, we don't think on it nowadays."

A WORD ABOUT WOODEN SHIPS

Ship-building for a great many years found employment for a large number of men in Yarmouth. An enormous quantity of oak was brought to the local shipyards from the surrounding country, being conveyed here in keels and wherries.

When shipbuilding was first introduced into Yarmouth I am unable to ascertain; Palmer, a local historian, states that—"The first ship-building yard in Southtown was that of Mr. Isaac Preston, who, in 1782, obtained a lease for eighty years of ground which he converted to that purpose. . . . Here in the course of forty years Mr. Preston built one hundred and fifty-three vessels," and from 1823 to 1841, a descendant built one hundred and two ships; "one of them, the *Maria Somes*, being the largest ever launched in Yarmouth, having brought from China upwards of nine hundred tons of tea."

But on going farther back into history, we find that "the port of Yarmouth attained its greatest relative importance in the reign of Edward III., when it furnished the king with 43 ships and 1083 mariners, being a much larger number than could be obtained from any other port in the kingdom." At that period Bristol supplied 23 ships and 608 men; Newcastle, 17 ships and 314 men; Hull, 16 ships and 283 men.

In 1818 the ship-building trade was so flourishing

that nearly 100 vessels were on the stocks at the same time, among them being H.M. gun-brig *Havoc*. Sloops and other small government vessels were constantly being launched from the yards.

The following short entries from Crisp's *Chronological History of Yarmouth*, deal with several succeeding years :—

1832, May 10th. " The following vessels [for the week] had been launched : the big *Sarah*, 190 tons (from Messrs. Tuck's yard) and the brig *Sarepta*, 160 tons (from Mr. Lubbock's yard)."

1833, Feb. 7th. A fine vessel of 216 tons had been launched from Mr. Preston's yard, and it was stated that "It is now allowed by merchants from all parts of the world that the finest and handsomest vessels are now built at this port."

1833, Oct. 18th. There had been a strong wind from the N.N.W. and from 150 to 200 vessels had sustained damage. It is contemplated that there were between 2000 and 3000 ships at anchor within sight of the Jetty.

It can easily be imagined what this gale, and others like it, meant for hundreds of the local shipwrights, sailmakers, caulkers, ropemakers, beachmen, provision dealers, etc.

For some years after 1833, new vessels were launched from the yards of Preston, Fellows, Palmer, Chapman, Rand, Bessey and others : all these shipyards have been built over in late years or used for timber storage, with the exception of Fellows, where a few iron lighters are occasionally constructed. The last two-masted vessel was built and launched in the eighties. Until recently wooden fishing smacks and herring luggers were built in some numbers on Beechings', Crittens', and other yards; but they, too, have become obsolete, the only similar industry remaining being the building of iron drifters, and this too, in 1908, has been at a very low ebb.

One other "entry," dated October 17th, 1845, refers to the trade in Dutch cattle (once a very flourishing business), which was carried on between this country and Holland, many beasts being sent through to Norwich. This entry is of tragic interest, and conjures us an appalling picture in a few words: "The *Enterprise* had encountered bad weather, and had to throw half her cargo of sheep and bullocks overboard." This traffic ceased within my own recollection, and a high-sided gangway, in which we lads used to play, stood on the Quay near the Haven bridge until a few years ago.

The seaman's calling has likewise deteriorated, and only a few crazy old vessels now belong to the port, the advent of the tramp steamer and the more general conveyance of goods by railways having all but ousted them.

In the early '50's we still numbered among our townsmen hundreds of sturdy sailors, who were a power in local politics. Early in February, 1851, a Seamen's Union had been formed, numbering 450 members. The new Mercantile Marine Act had excited much dissatisfaction, and the sailors were out on strike. Subsequently they mustered up to the number of 1000 and paraded the town with flags and bands. Again on the 22nd there was a muster of

1500 with bands, flags, rosettes, emblematical garb, shoulder-borne models of quaint vessels, and floral decorations. These demonstrations did not end without disorder and stone throwing ; nor was the excitement lessened by the reading of the Riot Act, the swearing in of special constables, and the arrival of armed coastguard's-men and a troop of the 11th Hussars from Norwich, not to mention a couple of warships which entered the harbour. Eventually there was a cessation of hostilities, and a mutual agreement was arrived at, followed by the inevitable prosecution of the leading offenders, with whom the townsfolk generally greatly sympathised.

There is not likely to be another similar riot, for to-day only a few nondescripts, more land-lubbers than sailor-men, man the few small coasters that creep as far as the coaling-ports and back again. I can well remember the time when, as a lad, I walked the length of the Quay under the bowsprits of a long array of ships that lay bow-on to the Quay side. There come, of course, the worn-out Indiamen, with Russian and Scandinavian names adorning their more or less ornamental sterns, and occasionally having a striking figure-head ; small rakish schooners drop in with slates and other goods from the western sea-ports ; and ungainly steam ships, like huge iron pots, lean up against the quays, laden with timber, stone, or salt. But the Yarmouth seaman hardly counts : the quaint old skipper, with his tall hat, has almost vanished, or he coughs asthmatically in his humble tenement in some obscure row, or lives forgotten in the workhouse, waiting for the end. Never again will such a sight, as the following note conjures up visions of, be witnessed off Yarmouth :—

1833. Nov. 1st. "There had been from 1500 to 2000 vessels windbound and at anchor in the Roads; these had got under sail on Sunday, and were immediately followed by about 1000 vessels from beyond Lowestoft, and it was contemplated that more than 3000 vessels had passed through the Roads in five hours, in so close procession that the sea could not be discerned beyond them."

The day of the sailing vessel has nearly passed; the iron ship, numbering her tons by as many thousands as these old coasters numbered hundreds, have taken their place. The romance of our shipping, too, is a thing of the past. Old seamen will tell you that "steam is the very devil!"

THE WHALE FISHERY

Almost entirely forgotten is the fact that Yarmouth once had a considerable share in the Greenland whale fishery. Fragmentary allusions are made to it in Manship's *History of Great Yarmouth*,[1] and by a still later historian, Palmer, in his *Perlustration of Great Yarmouth*[2]; but it remained for Mr. T. Southwell, F.Z.S., to piece together the very scanty and scattered references, in a paper entitled "Notes on the Arctic Whale Fishery from Yarmouth and Lynn."[3]

[1] Published 1619.
[2] Published 1872.
[3] Printed in the *Transactions of the Norfolk and Norwich Naturalists' Society*, 1906.

It appears that the local merchants first directed their attention to the whale fishery early in the seventeenth century, when one Thomas Hoarth fitted out some ships for the purpose. In 1627 competition seems to have been rife, for the " Fellowship of English Merchants " made complaint to the Privy Council that Nathaniel Wright, previously one of the directors, had joined Hoarth, had cajoled one Sampson, their chief harpooner, into their service, and were fitting out ships at Yarmouth for the fishery. Litigation followed, and Hoarth was compelled "to give bail not to engage in any such fishing." He appealed, but in vain, after having suffered to the tune of £2000. This prohibition refers to a monopoly granted to the Muscovy Company by James I. in 1613. In the early part of the next century Parliament granted a bounty on all whalers over two hundred tons, and the fishing was pursued with renewed vigour. The *Elizabeth and Mary* arrived in port in 1746 with a cargo of four whales, and reported having been in a fearful gale among the ice, when thirty Dutch and three English whaling ships were destroyed. Mr. Southwell quotes from the *Gentleman's Magazine* of July 23rd, 1753, a notice of the arrival of a ship in that year with one whale, and from the same journal, for July 10th, 1754, an announcement of the arrival in Yarmouth Roads of the *Alexander* with three, and the *Charming Polly* with five whales. In 1758 the *Three Brothers*, of Yarmouth, returning with one whale, was captured by the French ; who, however, the year previous, had not been so fortunate ; for the Yarmouth

Greenlander, *Prince William*, assisted by the *Hope*, of London, captured a French privateer with forty-seven men and three "ransomers" on board, and sailed her into Shields harbour.

Seven ships were fitted out from Yarmouth in 1764; these only returned with one whale apiece. Palmer says that, in 1801, twenty ships were employed in this fishery, and returned from Greenland with big catches; but heavy losses subsequently occurred, and early in the seventeenth century the fishery was abandoned, the vessels, which I believe were nearly all built on our own shipyards, being sold or used for other purposes. One vessel, the *Yarmouth*, traded out of this port until 1853, when she was sent to Australia, and beached at St. Kilda, near Melbourne, having been purchased for conversion into a bathing hut; a space in front of her was fenced in to keep out the sharks. My informant (a Yarmouth gentleman), who had been some years in Australia, informed me that he had frequently bathed from the old hulk.

The "oil houses," once used for boiling the blubber and refining the oil, were situated just to the south of the present Trinity wharf; indeed they still remain, although somewhat altered in internal structural arrangements, being used in connection with the Trinity Service. A few ancient lamp-brackets are still to be seen in the strong iron palisadings remaining in front of certain houses on the quays. In these, lamps containing train-oil did their best to enlighten a far less progressive age.

For a number of years whales' jawbones of various dimensions were still standing in divers parts of the town ; but most of them have now disappeared. Arches made of the lower jaws were to be seen in the neighbouring villages, having undoubtedly been brought thither from Yarmouth.

Southey, writing to his wife from Ormesby on May 29th, 1798, says, " Another peculiarity about Yarmouth is the number of arches formed by the jawbones of a Whale ; they trade much with Greenland there."

The finest pair of jaws still standing is to be seen on the premises of the Great Yarmouth gasworks. It formerly stood on the South Denes, and it was a common practice for young couples and their elders to stroll thither ; there appears to have been a lovers' seat at the base of one of the bones. I have chatted with old folks, who assured me that they had walked under it in their younger days.

When an old fishhouse, that stood near the old north-west tower, was demolished some twenty years ago, I saw some labourers unearth a section of what must have been an enormous whale's jaw-bone. If my recollection serves me rightly, it was some ten feet in length and fifteen inches in diameter ; the entire length of the jaw must have been at least twenty feet.

THE TRAWL FISHERY

A long chapter might be devoted to the once flourishing trawling industry. When I was a small boy, this fishery was also comparatively in its infancy in this port. The first smacks I can remember were not larger than the fishing luggers, indeed, the same hulls were used, with a difference of mast and rig to suit the fishery. No sooner was the herring harvest over, than the shorter foremast was replaced by one sporting a topmast; new suits of sails were bent on, and the drift-net was exchanged for the trawl.

At the beginning of the nineteenth century trawling was hardly known locally; in 1853 sixty-five vessels were engaged; in the middle sixties a hundred and twenty boats were sailing out of the port. The common practice was to sail in fleets, under the common flag of a favourite skipper or "admiral." It was the practice in later years to be provisioned for an eight weeks' voyage.

The trawling smack of my younger days was a cutter-rigged sixty tonner; in time the smacks became much larger, until, in recent years, they were magnificent seaworthy vessels. It was no rare thing to see a smack hauled up on to a ship-yard, cut in twain, the two ends separated, and an additional amidship built between. The Silver Pits, Sole Pit, and Haddock Bank were favourite trawling grounds in the old days; but when the supply of fish failed the smacks were obliged to go further and further afield —to the Texel and nor'ard of the far-famed Dogger. Smacks now sailing out of other ports go as far as Iceland, and even further into Arctic waters—a sorry outlook for the near future.

The great fleet of smacks, when at home at Christmas-time and fair-time, made an imposing array in the harbour. The men, after the wild life on the

North Sea, proved a rough lot ashore, and drunkenness, debauchery, and profanity were rife. Tales in the
police courts of drunkenness and disaster at sea ; of
copers with their floating grog-bars ; of nets lost and
fish bartered for drink, made very sorry reading.
Then the beneficent work of the Deep Sea Mission
brought about brighter days. But even then smacksmen ashore were all too easily drawn into bad ways.

A short history of Yarmouth[1] records the
following :—

"August, 1871. The new smack *Zephyr* was
launched ; and on the 7th, the dandy smack *Coral*.
Since last August, thirty smacks and fishing boats
have been launched from the various shipyards. "

Another note, dated 1882, shows the number of
herring luggers and smacks fishing out of the port at
that time—

"In Yarmouth there are 621 fishing boats, 333
being smacks, and the remainder [herring] luggers·
. . . Trawl fish caught in 1877, 11,863 packages ;
1878, 39,508 ; 1879, 31,072 ; 1880, 28,400 ; 1881,
24,003."

The number of smacks increased until, in 1889, we
had some four hundred vessels. After that year the
trawl fishery went all to pieces. Companies that had
devoured little owners themselves experienced disaster ; and the number of craft employed dwindled
down to only a few smacks. Various causes tended
to this decay ; but especially the handicapping of the
town by the railway companies, Yarmouth being
sacrificed for the benefit of Lowestoft, where the

[1] Crisp's *Chronological History of Yarmouth*, 1885.

railway company has great interests at stake. That port at present possesses a fine fleet of trawlers; and thither migrated many smacksmen's families, others going to Grimsby and Shields. A smacksman in Yarmouth is a *rara avis* to-day,[1] and what deep sea fish the town requires have to be carted over from Lowestoft. Prime fish was never to be had here; and we have now, as in times of yore, to be content with what is known to the trade as "offal."

SWIPING FOR ANCHORS

There is still carried on, in a desultory fashion, a curious pursuit known by the inelegant name of "swiping." Never at any time, as far as I can gather, were more than three or four craft engaged in this "swiping," or creeping for lost anchors, in the roadstead; at the present time there appears to be only one company of beachmen who occasionally launch their yawl and go in search of these awkward, cumbersome prizes. Anchors are not often lost in these steamship days; but only a few years ago it was no rare occurrence for sailing vessels to part with their anchors during a gale, in some cases losing a goodly part of a chain cable as well. It was then time for the seamen to exert themselves to save their vessels and their own lives; also for the beachmen to hasten afloat in quest of salvage. Among the latter there was sure to be some one who carefully marked the positions of these chains and anchors,

[1] Vide *Nature in Eastern Norfolk*, p. 97.

unless the accident occurred at night; and in due
course they would venture out to recover them.

A broken man, prematurely aged by the hard
life and wearing toil of the sea, for some years
pursued this occupation, which is carried on only
during the finer months. His fleet consisted of a
condemned Scotch fishing boat and a ship's boat:
his mates and he made up a crew of eight all told.
They worked together and shared alike. The more
anchors they recovered the better it was for them.
To make a boat into a "swiper" is no great task: a
pair of cheeks for running gear are fitted on to either
side of the bows; a capstan is set up for haulage;
sundry ropes and chains are procured; and a small
boat follows astern.

Arrived at a given spot, or taking a drag at
a venture, the small boat is rowed out, taking with
it a heavy rope, one end of which remains attached
to the larger craft. As they drift with the tide the
curved bight of the rope drags along the bottom of
the sea.

"How do you know when you 'foul' an anchor?"
I asked him.

"Well," he replied, "the bight catches; and the
two craft driftin' along come together. If it's a
wreck they 'on't.' Besides, on an anchor the rope
will 'render,' or run easy, while a wreck fare always
to hold it fast."

When the two parts of the rope are drawn together,
a "shackle" or "lock" is run down them, with a
small rope attached. A wire rope follows, which is
also "locked." This rope is then made fast to the

winch, and the crew commence to haul by means of the capstan bars. When an anchor is brought to the surface, a "boarding chain" is attached to it, and it is slowly hauled on board. Six years ago, my informant and his crew brought in no less than fourteen anchors, big and small, with much chain.

"Some of 'em," said he, "had plenty of rotten stuff around 'em; but it's all weighed in at two and tuppence a hundredweight at the Custom's House."

He had known an anchor to "chip away," *i.e.* to be cleared of rust and "sea-growths," and leave the iron "as thin a'most as a teaspune." This extraneous matter consists of corroded iron, to which stones and sand cling, cemented and reddened by oxidisation. Fine oysters sometimes come up adhering to the anchors; also many sea-anemones, *Serpula*, *Sabella*, and mussels. "He'd eaten 'em—him and his mates —them oysters, when they'd got the anchor aboard." Much fishing net also gets fast to these anchors in some localities, including trawl, drift, and shrimp-nets. The shrimper looks upon the "swiper" as a friend in need.

One year—scarcely a decade since—this swiper crew fished out of Corton Roads no fewer than thirty-seven anchors, four from Yarmouth Roads, and several from the Wold. Ship's winches, engine work, gudgeons, and other parts of sunken wrecks also become attached to the swiping-ropes. These men sometimes went out for a week together.

"'Tain't bad work, perwidin' you can fall in with

anchors ; if you don't, well——— " He gave a signifi-
cant shrug of the shoulders, and a wry expression
crossed his shaven face, accentuating the grotesque
tuft of reddish hair left at the point of his chin.

OLD ANCHORS

MACKEREL

CHAPTER IX

DEAD LOW WATER

"Next morn they rose and set up every sail ;
The wind was fair, but blew a mackerel gale."
DRYDEN.

AN OBSOLETE MACKEREL FISHERY

THE late Frank Buckland, in his Report on the
Fisheries of Norfolk (1875), remarked in writing of the mackerel fishery, that "the mackerel voyage
on the east coast, even in its best days, was rarely
remunerative either to owners or men ; more frequently the amount realised barely paid charges for
provisions, leaving nothing for wages, or wear and

tear of boats and nets. The owners never expected much, and it was more to keep their men in employment than in anticipation of profit, that this voyage was carried on for many years."

This state of things certainly obtained at the time when Buckland wrote ; but I am inclined to believe that in " the best days," which had passed in 1874, things were not quite so bad. The mackerel is known to be remarkably capricious, continuing to visit certain localities year after year fairly regularly, and then suddenly, for no obvious reason, it fails to put in an appearance. I am strongly of opinion that its appearance and non-appearance coincides with the movements of its favourite prey, which in local waters consists largely of herring-syle. I have taken from its stomach numerous sand-launces.

After a very long absence, mackerel turned up in unprecedented numbers in the neighbourhood of Wells-next-the-Sea, and considerable numbers were taken during the month of August, 1908. Herring-syle appear to have been unusually abundant there at that time, whilst Breydon, which swarmed with these young herrings the year previous, was singularly free of them. It was, undoubtedly, from this circumstance that the terns, which nest in one or two localities in the Wells neighbourhood, were also absent from Breydon, where, in other years, they appeared simultaneously with the herring-syle.

A few notes, chronologically arranged, will give a fair idea of the uncertain movements of this species, and the consequent risks undertaken by those who fish for it.

S

The *Gentleman's Magazine* for October 1st, 1758, records as follows: " The herring fishery at Yarmouth, Norfolk, has taken but 1200 barrels of herrings ; whereas they usually by this time took about 20,000. Instead of herrings they have caught mackrell, which were sold just out of the boats for 3*s.* per 1000, and large mackrell at 12 and 14 a penny."

1807. The most extravagant price for early supplies of mackerel was paid in May, 1807, when the first boat-load (from Brighton) sold at Billingsgate for forty guineas per hundred (or six score), or about seven shillings each. The next boat realised only thirteen guineas per hundred. At Dover the following year they were so plentiful that they were sold at sixty a shilling.

1821. The mackerel fishery for this year was unprecedented. On June 30th, the Lowestoft boats alone, numbering sixteen, made a catch valued at £5252, the huge sum of £14,000 being realised for the total catches taken off this coast on that date !

1823. During this season 142 lasts were taken off Yarmouth, a last, roundly speaking, being 10,000 fish (really 12,000).

1825. The total catch realised £17,000. At or about this period some hundred boats fished out of Yarmouth, thirty of them going south of the port, the others distributing themselves northward and eastward. They kept at sea, lighter vessels known as cutters going off to the several companies, relieving them of their catches, and hastening with all speed to the London or the local markets. An attempt was made to salt some of the mackerel, as many as 150 barrels being cured in 1824; but this process did not seem to meet with general favour. No fish deteriorates so quickly, hence the scramble and haste which has always characterised this particular fishing. The farther the boats were compelled to fish, the more difficult was it to get their mackerel fresh to market: the cutters carried ice for their better preservation. This ice was taken on the broads and rivers and stored in ice-houses,[1] three of which are still standing, two adjoining the Haven bridge (now used as corn stores), and one by the side of Vauxhall Station (now used as a beer store).

In 1863, the mackerel fishery was much hampered through lack of ice, due to the exceptionally mild winter of 1862–63, when Norway ice seems first to have been imported, the price jumping up from ten shillings to one pound per ton. Ice continued to be imported in shiploads yearly, until the decline of the trawling industry in the early nineties.

Mackerel were allowed to be sold publicly on Sundays, an enactment, dating from 1698, allowing them to be cried in the streets of London:

> " Law ordered that the Sunday should have rest,
> And that no nymph her noisy food should sell
> Except it were ' new milk ' or mackerel."

Rough and breezy weather is the most favourable to the capture of mackerel; for they then come to the surface from the deeper waters, their behaviour in this respect being just the reverse to that of the herrings. I have noticed that mackerel are most

---

[1] Vide Chapter I., p. 28.

plentiful in breezy weather, even during the autumnal herring fishing. Dryden's "mackerel gale," Johnson, in his Dictionary, describes as "a strong breeze, such as is desired to bring mackerel fresh to market." Fishermen desire "a bit of a breeze" in order to expedite their capture.

1832. "The firstfruits of the fishing season" had been landed on May 10th from boat "No. 3," the night's hauling resulting in the capture of forty-eight mackerel, which were sold at one shilling and sixpence each. By May 24th the fishery had been going so badly that "there was great distress in the town, as thousands depended on that industry for a living."

1845. The mackerel fishery was estimated at £35,000; in 1854 £30,000; and in 1855 £27,994.

For several seasons preceding 1862, the fishery was a disastrous failure, thoroughly disheartening the fishermen; in that year they were abundant, although at a very unusual distance from land; indeed, they were caught within sight of the Dutch coast. The year 1863, however, proved more remunerative, when "200 lasts were taken, weighing 1200 tons, and averaging £1 per hundred of six score."

When I was a lad the mackerel fishery was still in full swing; commencing early in May, it lasted for some eight weeks. The numbers of men and boats employed at that time I am unable to ascertain. As many as eighty-five boats were engaged in it in 1855. Buckland speaks of twenty mackerel boats fishing out of Lowestoft in 1854; in 1863 the number had decreased to three. He makes reference to 1874, when "Yarmouth and Gorleston had a few boats engaged . . . for a short time in the autumn, *i.e.* four months later than the mackerel voyage of former years commenced."

For several years the local fishery was in a very bad way, the early summer voyage being entirely abandoned, and mackerel nets only being hurriedly brought into use during the autumnal fishing when this fish happened to appear in more than usual numbers. In the late eighties and early nineties they appeared in great numbers off the Cornish coast,[1] and away went some over-venturesome boats, which for a time were fairly successful; but the 1904 and 1905 seasons were failures. Then the erratic fish turned up, in 1906, in their old Norfolk haunts, and the fisher folk, with praiseworthy promptness and energy, went in pursuit of them, finding the chase profitable. During May and June 140 lasts were taken, numbering in all some million and three-quarter fishes. One boat earned as much as £250.

1908. In November the herring boats fell in with big shoals of mackerel at Lowestoft; they were never before so plentiful, and several boat owners hastened to change their herring-nets for mackerel-nets. One craft, the *Nugget*, had a record catch; it was estimated that she landed just over four lasts, or 50,000 fish, causing no little excitement as she lay near the "dump-head" discharging her cargo of iridescent beauties. So full of fish were the nets that not half of them could be stowed in the net room, and the remainder, gleaming with fish still

[1] See *Wild Life on a Norfolk Estuary*, pp. 295-96.

"gilled," lay in a huge heap piled on deck. With such numbers, prices in this case unfortunately ruled very low, only five shillings and sixpence per hundred (of 120) being realised. Other boats, with fishes ready for market made ten shillings and sixpence. One boat is reckoned to have earned £400 in four nights. In some cases the mackerel were "struck" so thickly, that sections of the net were "grounded," or sank to the bottom.

Yarmouth also shared in this great catch. The largest mackerel of which I have any record was taken on October 21st, 1898; its length was $21\frac{1}{4}$ inches; girth 12 inches; weight 3 lbs. 7 ozs.

The landing of mackerel on the beach was an interesting and stirring sight to me in my boyhood. The pushing-off of the huge ferriers, called bullock-boats, laden with swills into which the carriers shot the fish, to be hurried ashore, and sold by auction on the sands, to the clash of bells and clamour of hoarse voices, was an unique spectacle, and the old Jetty would be crowded with onlookers. Large keelers, or tubs, were rolled into position and filled with sea-water; and quaint fish wives, aproned and pocketed, set to work to wash and pack the beautiful *Scomber*, carefully laying aside the largest specimens, with which to "top" the smaller ones in the hampers, in which they were despatched to various inland towns and cities. They placed sixty mackerel in a "ped" (hamper), at least ten of which would be magnificent fish; then the lids were smartly corded down, labels were attached, and ped after ped would be deposited on the convenient troll-carts, which could be loaded

up to a remarkable height, and away up the impro-
vised roadway, made of tan thrown upon the sand,
went horse and man and fish to the railway stations,
where the trucks were in waiting.

MACKEREL FISHING REMINISCENCES

"Bob" Colby[1] had followed the mackerel voyage
year after year, having gone through all the proba-
tionary periods of "boy," capstan-man, etc., up to
mate. There stood in a case on a chest of drawers in
his room a neat model of one of the boats he had
sailed in, a mackerel cutter named the *Saucy Jack*.
The model was made, he told me, by a man aboard
the light-ship.

"Part with it?" he asked. "Tain't so likely! It
was the only thing he'd got as reminded him of those
stirrin' old times." He then went on to describe the
fishing craft, which we re three-mast luggers—"reg'lar
sashmarees," he said, with foremast, mainmast, and

---

[1] This most interesting character, to whom I have made
frequent reference, followed the sea during the greater part of
his life, as mackerel fisherman, herring-drifter, smacksman, and,
in later years, shrimper. Incidentally he has been a wherryman and waterman, like many others of this restless class. At
the time when these mackerel notes were being jotted down
(December, 1908), he was sitting up in bed, having a few days previously been sent home from hospital, where he had been taken
suffering from a broken thigh and smashed ribs. Six weeks
previously he had been ridden over by a runaway horse and
cart, his invalid chair being broken up in the accident. Some
five years before he had had the toes of both feet cut off by
being run over by a railway truck. He is even now as merry as
a cricket, and full of reminiscences. Colby is 61 years of age.

mizenmast, the sails belonging to each being known by similar names ; "they had a main topsail which was hoisted on the other side to the mainsail, so that one was a-pullin' which ever way they tacked. If they went on a long board then, of course, they'd shift the tops'l." Within my own recollection all these boats, of which there were scores, have vanished, models in the Tólhouse Museum, and a painting here and there, yellowing with age and bad varnish, being all that remain to remind one of them.

"The boats lay on the ship-yards all winter," resumed Colby, "and they got to work on 'em with paint brush and caulkin' tools, so as to get 'em fit to launch by the first of May, the voyage beginnin' within the week after. A lugger carried eleven hands ; they was skipper, mate, net-hauler, net-stower, cast-off-seizeman (the man who looked after 'seizing on' the buoys), four capstan-men, and a boy.

"What did the boy do ? Well, all sorts of jobs, from helpin' at a pinch, to makin' the plum-duff in the foc's'l. The net-hauler and the net-stower shot the nets—twelve score of 'em ; in twenty minutes they *could* do it, though it took some doin' : the mate and the hauler got 'em in. They carried twelve score nets, each fourteen yards long ; they was two fathoms deep. You could shove a crown-piece through the meshes, diamond-wise, that 'ud hold the biggest mackerel livin', if he poked his nose in fair and square ; but they let th' little 'uns go through.

"The boats went out in tow of the tugs, or if the wind suited 'em and the tide as well, they would drop out theerselves. Some on 'em went single boating, and others formed into companies. They'd go away for eight weeks right off; sometimes they'd never make the shore the whole voyage. Cutters would go out to 'em to fetch the fish, for they sometimes had to travel to find up the mackerel. I remember one voyage when we laid in sight of the Dutch coast nearly all the time. We'd bring up on long hempen cables and the cutters 'ud take off our catches, relievin' us in turn. It wor rough work, I can tell you, in a stiff breeze, though we made light on it.

"Mackerel allers fared to me to reg'lar enjoy a breeze of wind; it made 'em as frisky as a cat with a gale in her tail, as you've heerd speak of, no doubt. And there wor several little ditties, as I suppose you'd call 'em, about mackerel. I remember one what said—

> " ' Mackerel's scales and mare's tails,
>   Make lofty ships carry low sails.'

And you've seen a mackerel sky, of course. I've heerd say—

> " ' A mackerel sky—'tain't long wet
>   and 'tain't long dry,'

and that's pretty true."

"Colby," said I, "have you *heerd* this?

> " ' Up jumped the mackerel
>   With his strip'd back,
> Says he, " Reef the main ! " and " Haul in the tack ! "
>   For it's windy weather,
>   It's stormy weather ;
> And when the wind blows, pipe all hands together,
> For, upon my word, it's stormy weather.' "

"Who writ that?" asked Colby.

"Tom Hood," said I.

"Didn't know him," responded Colby, and went on—

"You may believe it, or you may not, but we know'd by the very look of the water (there wor a sort of greasiness about it)[1] where the mackerel wor." (He here described the particular appearance by a very inelegant term used by fishermen.) "It was sorter greeny-white; it was full of 'syle,' little titty fishes like stanickles (sticklebacks), only long and thin. I've found the mackerel what we've cleaned for breakfast chuck-full of 'em. They used ter play the deuce with them little herrin'-like things.

"The boats kept out, no matter how hard it blowed, givin' out cable, and lowerin' the foremast on to the mitch, and they'd ride it out as comfortable as you like. If we *had* to make for home, we'd get this side Scroby and lay-to in the Roads.

"Oh yes! you can *hear* the mackerel as plain as you like: they swim in great frisky shoals, their tails and fins often out of the water, goin' like anything, the sea lookin' right black with 'em, and soundin' for all the world like a rain-squall. You never catch 'em *then*. I've heer'd herrin's make a similar to-do; and heer'd 'em sorter squake, in a faint tiny sorter way, when shook out of the net. You jist look at a mackerel in May, you'll see him as bright-eyed as can be; in June theer's a film comin' at the corner

---

[1] I have observed this over a shoal of herrings, and a porpoise presently come tumbling about in it, preying on them.

of his eyes; and in July you'll see it right over, till he's blind, and unfit to eat.

"In them days we had a rare bit of fun with long tret-lines, when the lugger was hangin' to her cable. We've shoved on from fifty to a hundred hooks, and havin' baited 'em with bits of mackerel or herrin', dropt 'em over on slake water. We copt splendid skate, cod, and ling; they was the skipper's perks, same as wor the herrin's we catched, and he'd make more of his extras than some skippers earn nowadays for the voyage. We got all sorts of things in the nets with the mackerel. Sometimes a half-score red mullet[1] would get gilled in a night; at another, perhaps, we'd take a score nice salmon-trout, and now and agin no end of guard-fish (garfish). Eat 'em? You trust us when we got the skipper in the mind to let us. Guard-fish was best biled like eels, to take the grease out. I ha' known a score wil' ducks (guillemots) to get fast in the net in a night. And then we often got crabs—them swimmin' crabs—and didn't them little devils lay hold on your fingers if you wasn't careful. We once got a bottle-nose shark,[2] with six or seven rows of teeth, what a bloke from Norwich bought off us and showed in a tent all round Norfolk.[3] That fellow 'ud talk your head off!

---

[1] *Mullus surmulletus.* Pagets, in 1834, wrote of this species : "In some mackerel seasons abundant, in others scarcely seen ; in May, 1831, 10,000 were sent in one week to the London markets."

[2] Probably a basking shark (*Selache maxima*), or more likely a Porbeagle (*Lamna cornubica*), our commonest of the larger sharks.

[3] Ben Sexton, a notorious fish-hawker hailing from Norwich,

"We shot the nets afore dusk. As I told you, we fished with fourteen score nets, two lints deep. As we cast 'em off, the seize-man and his pal seized on (tied) the warp ropes and fastened on the bowls with short seizings to the warp ropes ; a bowl was attached to every seventh net. These bowls, which are still used in the herring fishing, are about the size of a bucket, tub-shaped, and preferred as floats by Yarmouth fishermen to the round canvas buoys of the Scotch. And you need have 'em too, for a thousand or two, perhaps more, fat mackerel, running to an average of a pound each, require a little holdin' up. The sixteen warp ropes were each 125 fathoms long.

"When the nets were out, we took our spells of watchin' and turnin' in. We hauled afore sunrise— anyway, afore it was properly light—for the blessed dogs (dogfish) would be pretty sure to be early on the job, bitin' great pieces out of the finest mackerel, while the larger ones—sharks, I suppose you naturalists 'ud call 'em—would reg'lar whip 'em out of the nets, and bolt 'em whole. We wor reg'lar pestered by 'sweet Williams'[1] and them flat-heads,[2] they was nasty warmin ; you'd see 'em alongside the boat ; and them common dogs reg'lar cleaned out th' nets

who varied his business by spells of exhibiting, for which he had a remarkable liking. He would do "good business " with a shark, dolphin, or any other marine monster, and once took hundreds of pennies one day by exhibiting a common monk-fish !

[1] In all probability smooth-hounds (*Mustelus vulgaris*).
[2] Topes (*Galeus vulgaris*).

if we wasn't pretty smart. It wor a sort of scramble of men aginst dogs.

"We sometimes fished in the Wold, and if the wind wasn't fair enough, we'd run in and lay off Palling, Winterton, and Newport (California next Scratby), get the mackerel ashore, and hurry 'em off to Yarmouth by carriers' carts.

"Cock mackerel? Oh, they take them a mid-summerin'; they'd be about as big as herrin's, and they often take quite as many of the one as the tother.

"'Twasn't a bad life, take it all round. It was ginerally pretty decent weather, but the grubbin' in them days wasn't up to much. We didn't often see a bit of meat, though we got a bit of salt junk, or pig, now and again—reg'lar gran'mother pig, you know—and the everlastin' duff for dinner, with mackerel for breakfast and the same for tea. The capstan-men and younker berthed in the fo'c's'l; but they mostly got the best pickin's as far as grub went, exceptin' of course, the skipper.

"Now about the pay? Well, we went by the share. The master got what we called a 16-dole; the mate, 10-dole; net-hauler, 8; net-stower, 7; cast off-seizin's man, 6; capstan-men, 5; boy, 4. Them were the proportions on the takin's.

"Then the fishin' went down, and old 'Shady' Bennyfield set the fashion—inwented it, if you like—of autumn mackerel fishin'. Then they revived it a bit by steamboats; but it fell off and didn't pay, though this last autumn or two things have looked up a bit, and several on 'em have done very well. I

know one chap as took £30 for his share—not a bad
'un for the voyage, what do you say? "

HADDOCKING

Lining for haddocks, cods, plaice, and such-like is,
in this neighbourhood, a thing of the past.   Chance
time a few beachmen will push off the beach, anchor
a "dan" or float, and attach a line with a few score
hooks on it ; but like the visits of the deep-sea fishes,
their attempts at lining are more or less sporadic.

It was a customary thing, a few years since, to
send out a few boats "hand-lining" in Botany gat,
near the Dogger.   An old friend of mine went in a
45-tonner, "fore and after," with a well in the centre
with perforated bottom, through which entered the
sea-water by means of which the catches were kept
alive.   Hewett's, the great fish-factors of that day,
sent out as many as eight boats, which were really
worn-out smacks: the *Renown*, the *Diligence*, and
Mercer were well-known craft in this little fleet.
The bait used was Lynn mussels : these were opened
and the hooks baited while the tide ran strongest ;
they fished at slack water.   The ten men fished with
a line of two hooks each : this particular mode was
termed "crooking."   A "dan" was fixed at a suitable
"spot," generally in the neighbourhood of a herring
spawning ground.   The smack would sail to this
spot, ease off the jib, slack the mainsail, and drift
away, the men fishing meanwhile ; when all but out
of sight of the buoy, they sailed back to it, and
drifted again.

Directly a bite was felt the fish was jerked into

the boat, giving it no time to swallow the bait. If the hook got too far down, the fish was much less likely to live; the stomach must not be injured. Thirty and forty score cods would be caught on a tide, sometimes a hundred and twenty score on two tides. The smacks sailed up into the roads with their living cargoes, moored there, and a certain number of fish per day, according to the demand, were sent ashore for the markets. The haddocks were packed alive so as to arrive fresh in London.

Hake, coalfish, pollack, and halibut varied the catches. Halibut often came to the surface. When caught they were hung in the wells by means of a rope fastened to their tails. Occasionally the small boat was sent out from the smack with a hundred-hook line. Red-looking water was sought for, the spawning grounds of the herrings assuming that colour.

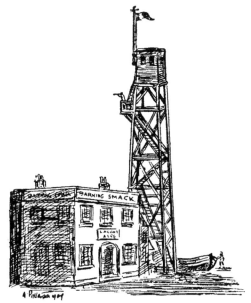

BEACHMEN'S LOOK-OUT

ANCIENT FISHING LUGGER
(*From a* 16*th Century Dutch tile*)

CHAPTER X

A HARVEST OF THE SEA

" For now in our trim boats . . .
   We must dance on the waves with the porpoise and seal ;
   The breeze it shall pipe, so it pipe not too high,
   And the gull be our songstress whene'er she flits by."
                                        NORSE DITTY.

ON THE HERRING

AS the hurly-burly of the Big City passes to a great extent unheeded by the dweller in the midst of it, so the turmoil and vastness of the great herring harvest fail to make much impression on the native of far-famed Herringopolis. We of King Herring's stronghold see, smell, and handle the silvery hosts of the North Sea, holding out both hands for the gains they bring, and there our interest in the matter ceases. But the stranger within our gates, when the harvest of the sea is in full swing, is filled with astonishment.

Since the remote days, when the sand on which Yarmouth stands was a bare island at the entrance of the *Garienis ostium*, and a few wandering Saxons came there to dry their nets, remarkable changes have come about. The rude vessels and nets of those early days were probably not improved upon for several centuries, for the herring luggers that were in use in my early days, with their awkward rig and ancient gear, seemed to me to differ but little from the old Norseman's ships. The masts had increased in number from one, planted amidship, to three. The sails, too, had been altered in shape to allow the vessel to go on either tack without their being lowered ; but, as in the case of the yawls, their manipulation was almost as primitive as the methods of the Middle Ages.

With Mr. de Caux,[1] I should be exceedingly interested "to know when fishes were first used as human food, whether they were first caught by hook or by net, and when hooks and when nets were invented." Both processes of capture undoubtedly had a very remote origin. Certainly "drawing" (from the shore) for fishes was a much earlier method than " drifting " with suspended nets, which are used in deep waters. And as the herring rarely looks at a hook,[2] and is not taken in any number by draw-nets,

[1] *The Herring and the Herring Fishery*, by J. W. de Caux, 1881.

[2] It is a rare circumstance to hook an adult herring in East

it is more than likely that the drift-net was in use many centuries ago.

We have, however, a tradition in regard to the introduction of the herring-cure for which Yarmouth has long been famous. It is said that one day a fisherman returned to his ill-ventilated hut, hung up a "warp" (four) of fresh herrings he had brought home for his family, and somehow managed to forget them for a day or two. When he remembered them he found them red and golden in hue, having been changed by the smoke of his cabin into mummies, that not only appealed to him by their hue, but also by their tempting odour. For a novelty he ate them. He was delighted with their flavour, and putting his wits together, he came to the conclusion that the smoke had brought about this wonderful change. From that time smoked herrings became a recognised article of food, eventually gaining a world-wide repu-tation.

The herring is too well known to need describing in these pages. Some writers have thought that there are more than one species, but the balance of evidence is against this theory ; varieties there may be, their difference, in all probability, being due to age, habitat, and environment. Men who come in contact with successive shoals of herrings, immedi-ately recognise differences which, to them, are well marked, and there are also distinct differences in flavour. Of them all, the "longshorer" is by far the

Coast waters, yet in Lowestoft harbour it is a common thing in summer to capture, on a tiny hook baited with a fragment of shrimp, small herrings of three or four inches in length.

best eating. A longshore herring caught immediately off shore, ranges from ten to eleven inches in length, whereas the huge and hard-boned " Norway" herring is always coarse and tasteless. Of the millions " gutted " in the fishing season, very few are found with food in their stomachs ; yet I have seen small examples under six inches in length crammed with their favourite prey—the *Gammaridæ* and allied forms, and opossum shrimps. Just before and after spawning, herrings appear to feed very little ; anyway, I have examined many during the height of the fishery, when the spawning season is at its height, and have found little else but mucous matter, which may be the "residuum" of minute creatures, *Medusæ* and microscopic forms, and which seem almost to justify the fishermen's crude idea that they "live by suction."

There still exists a belief that sprats are the young of the herring, notwithstanding the differences in shape, belly serrations, etc. Sprats may be distinguished from young herrings of their own length by their flavour if by no other dissimilarity.[1] The ova of the sprat (which spawns in February and March) is proportionately larger than that of *Clupea harengus*. Herrings are known when captured as full (ova nearly ripe), mazy (in process of spawning), and shotten (empty). I have collected small herrings many months in the year,[2] all of similar length ; this would point to the frequent spawning of successive shoals.

[1] Vide *Notes of an East Coast Naturalist*, pp. 243-44.
[2] Vide *Wild Life on a Norfolk Estuary*, pp. 294-95.

The herring is exceedingly prolific; it is estimated that its "roe" or "cob" (ova) contains some thirty-three thousand eggs. I have found a very miniature specimen, not seven inches in length, packed with roe. It had need be extraordinary fecund in order to hold its own against the vast army of enemies, from man to rorqual whales and porpoises, and from hordes of hungry cods and dog-fishes to hosts of gannets, guillemots, and cormorants, which follow it from day to day and from year to year. As to the delicacy of the herring as an article of food, too much cannot be said in its praise. Fresh out of the boat, daintily fried, pickled in vinegar, lightly smoked as a bloater, or specially cured as a kipper, it is delicious; it is also very nutritious. The poor in Herringopolis almost live upon it in the days of the fishing, and at other times they can always fall back upon a plump rich "red" when more expensive dishes are unobtainable.

As Mr. de Caux remarks, "the history of the herring fishery is interwoven inextricably with the history of Great Yarmouth." The contemporary growth of the town and this stupendous fishery; the accounts of the herring fairs, charters, bounties, ordinances, litigations, and fights between rival ports, make entrancing reading that is more like romance than matter-of-fact history.[1] Statistics are largely given of the fishery down to 1866[2]; and in Mr. de

---

[1] I must refer the reader for these interesting details to Nall's *Great Yarmouth and Lowestoft*, chap. "The Herring Fishery," pp. 258–405.

[2] *Ibid.*

Caux's book they are brought down to the year 1881, since which date it has increased by leaps and bounds, more especially since steam has ousted a fleet of sailers that were at the mercy of wind and tides. To-day we have an enormous fleet of Scotch and English vessels, iron-hulled and steam propelled, that has turned a once easy-going, romantic industry into a restless, shrieking, scrambling, greedy rush for fish—and dividends. The romance of the thing has departed as irrecoverably as that which clung to the wooden walls of Old England in the days when Nelson flew his pennant from the *Bellerophon*.

When I first knew the autumnal herring fishery it begun, as now, at the end of September and ended just before Christmas. The boats were then merging from the ancient three-mast luggers into the more yacht-like cutter-rigged vessels. Nets were braided by the women at home and in *beetstering* chambers : the fraternity locally were slow in accepting the produce of the net-weaving loom of James Paterson, an old Waterloo soldier who settled at Musselburgh in the earlier half of last century. To-day the nets are made of cotton, but in the old days they were made of hemp-twine when spinning was a flourishing industry, and ropeworks were to be seen in many parts of the town. Twine spinning with the ship-builders' craft have almost entirely disappeared ; and the fisherman goes to sea in a vessel turned out by a mechanic in iron and steel.

Fifty years ago the herring-nets were smaller ; they were then thirteen yards long, whereas to-day they are twenty. A " fleet " of nets (joined end to end) consisted of some sixty or eighty nets; to-day it consists of from a hundred to a hundred and eighty, extending to a length of from a mile and a quarter to two full miles. To-day many hundreds of miles of nets are in the sea at one time. Formerly the boats could not be depended on to return to port at any given time, contrary winds making the trip subject to much delay; now the steam drifter can time its home-coming almost to an hour. The landing of the catches was carried on much after the fashion of the old mackerel days;[1] but some of the boats came up the river, and landed their catches on the quays.

LANDING THE FISH

For many years—centuries, in fact—the Yarmouth sea-beach was the great herring-mart of East Norfolk: it was not until February, 1869, that the fish-wharf on the east side of the river was completed, and greater facilities, in the shape of deep-water berths, offices and shelter, were provided for landing, selling, and packing the fish. With the construction of the fish-wharf and the decay of the mackerel fishery began the breaking up of a community known as the Yarmouth beachmen. One writer enthusiastically describes these men as " of Danish origin, and exhibiting all the qualities of the sea kings, of gigantic stature, noble bearing, and of great courage; at a moment's notice ready to man their enormous yawls and put to sea in the worst weather, to assist the vessels which

[1] See page 262.

so frequently come to grief on the Scroby Sands;
and as gaining enormous sums and spending their
lives in perpetual vicissitude of violent exertions and
luxurious idleness." Others frequently characterised
them as "sharks," an epithet not esteemed inappro-
priate by those who had interests at stake on the sea;
but in justice to the beachmen one must describe
them as being at that period a hardy, useful, and
adventurous class of men. They formed themselves
into Companies, *e.g.* the Holkham, Standard, Star
Companies, and others; they were recruited princi-
pally from the ranks of the herring-fishers; and they
were very exclusive. Their boats were held in shares:
they included ferry boats for carrying fish, anchors,
and heavy stores, large and graceful yawls for salvage
purposes, long gigs that were used in fine weather
and they usually possessed pleasure boats for use
during the visiting season. A yawl, fully equipped
with sails, oars, etc., cost from £250 upwards; a
ferry boat £40. They also had "look-outs"—cabin-
like structures placed on four enormously long legs,
and reached by stair-like ladders ziz-zagging to the
top, as in a church spire. Telescopes, stores, and
warehouses were part and parcel of their paraphernalia. They ferried ashore the "peds" and boxes
of trawl fish from the cutters that daily moored in the
roadstead, and in the old days of wooden ships and
frequent shipwrecks they provided lawyers with
many cases for arbitration.

Then came the evil days. The fishing boats
entered the harbour instead of unloading their fish on
to the beach, and steam-tugs came out of the harbour

to tow in smacks and drifters and assist the lame ducks in trouble among the sandbanks. The beach-men, of whom there were two hundred in Yarmouth alone, found their work being taken from them, and had to seek other employment ; those who now claim the title of beachmen are mere degenerates, who cater for the nautical inclinations of visitors in the season, do a little draw-netting at other times, and in winter prowl along with drooping shoulders and hands in pockets—" pawking," *i.e.* looking for pence and trifles lost by summer idlers on the sands.[1] The smartest of them form the lifeboat crews.

To-day not a solitary look-out is standing, every ferry boat has vanished, and only one small yawl, a recent *present* to the little fraternity, is to be seen upon the sands. The troll carts are reduced to two —now in the local museum ; and not a solitary fish-basket is seen on the shore, save an occasional one cast up by the sea.

HERRING CATCHING : THEN

When conversing recently with an old skipper who took part in the herring voyage some thirty years ago, he very vividly brought to mind those early days. He remembered the advent of the first dandy-rigged, yacht-hulled drifter, *Osprey*. There had been transitions attempted from the old three-mast lugger, resulting until then in a mongrel

[1] Vide Nall's *Great Yarmouth and Lowestoft*, pp. 417-421.

vessel. He remembered well the ancient capstan with its three long poles "shoved through to make six bars for the hands to turn it with," and how the noisy tramp round above head, as he lay in his berth, sounded like thunder! Then came the crank-handle capstan, and finally the steam-driven one. The crew were rated very much after the fashion of the mackerel-drifters': master, mate, hawseman, walesman, net-ropeman, net-stower, younker (of all work), four capstan men, and the boy. They were paid by the last; the master got 16 shillings on the last; the mate 10 shillings; the next two 8 shillings each; the net-ropeman 6 shillings; the stower 5 shillings; younker, 4 shillings and 6 pence; capstan men, 4 shillings each; and boy half a crown. A mate sometimes took £75 for the voyage; the cabin boy £20 for his share; and the others sums in proportion. When herring fetched as high as £40 a last so much the better for the owner—"it makes no differs to the men"; and by a smaller price they fared no worse. It was to the fisherman's advantage then to fish for all they were worth. There were many "small owners" in those days, who owned from one to half a dozen vessels; nowadays a company may exploit forty, and there is not a verse of poetry left in the fisherman's calling. The lottery (as it ever was) of to-day is only a sordid business, though the carrying on of the fishery is still interesting from an outsider's point of view.

A wooden drifter costs £2000 when completely equipped for sea; the life of a vessel was longer than that of the present iron craft. The herrings, my friend informed me, are not improved by the *heat* of "these ere tin-kittle-biler sort of ships." The tonnage of the boats then, as now, ranged from 25 to 45 tons. "An iron steam drifter isn't so nice a boat as a wooden craft. She's hotter all round, and the engine-gear takes up a lot of room. I'll allow you," he said, "she's more independenter of wind and weather, and can catch the markets much more to a certainty."

To quote from the old man's gossip: "The first thing, after you got the fresh-painted vessel afloat, was to get in eight ton or so of rough salt. The nets was taken aboard and 'bent' (put into fishing trim). Sails, of course, had already been bent; bowls fixed, coals got aboard, and provisions, not forgettin' water. Then off we started for the Dogger Bank. With a slant of wind we got there in two days; if it was bad it took us a week; the same back again. We shot the net about 4 or 5 o'clock. Sometimes we got enough in a night to run back with; mostly we got only two or three last. When we'd got about twelve we'd run home. It took us a week sometimes to fill; I've been a fortnight, and run'd short of grub in the meantime, when we'd run into Grimbsy to re-victual. We used to fish in fleets, and if things was slow several would put our catches aboard one boat, and send her home—we called it 'makin' up a boat!'

"When the nets was shot, we'd set a watch, and turn in. We'd heave up a portion of the net about 8 o'clock to see how things looked, for we might, if we wasn't careful, strike a shoal of herrin's, and

ground 'em (sink them).   I was aboard a boat once
where they did that, and we was twelve hours haulin'
up the torn nets, with herrin's meshed in bunches, like
bananas—spoiled, of course, and so was the nets.   It's
allers a pretty sight, when the weather is fine, haulin'
in the nets ; the herrin's hangin' like silver bars, all
a-glistering and sparklin' ; we'd get gurnets, whitins,
meshed in the nets, and dog-fish, weavers, grey-
mullet, and sometimes red mullet.   Salmon-trout too,
and shrads (shads) and hoss-mackerel (scads).   Then
we got great dollops of jelly fishes—in soapy strings
a danglin' in the nets,—they'd sting too ; and little
warmins of swimmin' crabs, what bit your fingers till
you'd jump again.   And now and again a porpoise,
and sharks : law ! how *they'd* roll up in the nets and
you'd reg'lar to onscrew 'em, specially their tails.
We had a spare man with a dydle (handnet) at the
side to scoop in the fish as dropped from the net—
always the biggest fishes ; and the dogs (dogfish)
always bit the best herrin's when they come on the
scene."

My informant, with that dogmatism characteristic
of elderly men, praised the old times and anathema-
tized the new.   He had much to say about how the nets
had to be tended, dried, and stowed ; he'd "seen 'em
reek with steam when laid long enough to heat, which
they will do if stowed damp."   He described how
the Dutchmen and the " Frenchies " " put in in small
fleets when the weather came on bad."   The boys
used to go down to the harbour in shoals, pestering
" Johnnie " for brown bread and a bit of tobacco,
many boats from Rye, Ramsgate, and other ports

also put into harbour. "Then the Scotties mustered up," he said, "comin' thicker and thicker, like hail, till nowadays you might as well be in Aberdeen or Buckie as in Yarmouth."

HERRING CATCHING : NOW

The herring fishery of to-day is a gigantic industry: for some years past the number of boats engaged in it has been steadily increasing, so that the catching power is now enormous. In 1907—the record year for herrings—there fished out of Yarmouth over 900 boats, 220 of which belonged to the port, and 720 to Scotch and other ports. From Lowestoft there fished 251 local vessels, and 413 Scotch and other craft. The modern fishing-boat is a shapely vessel, screw propelled, from sixty to seventy tons measurement, eighty feet long, with a beam of eighteen feet. Steam is not without its drawbacks; the engine-room and appurtenances take up much room, and it is a far more expensive propelling power than sails. The compensations are that the boat is not subject to the caprices of the wind, port is reached early, "the first of the market" prices are often obtained, and in bad weather it is generally easy to make a sheltering harbour.

The number of "lasts" of herrings (of 13,200 fish to the last) landed in Yarmouth and Lowestoft during the year totalled 91,319. An analysis of that year's enormous catches may not be uninteresting :—

HERRINGS LANDED AT YARMOUTH IN 1907.

Month.	Lasts.	Month.	Lasts.
		Brought forward 257	
January ...	—	July ...	133
February ...	—	August ...	989
March ...	2	September	1,330
April	40	October ...	22,541
May	58	November	23,404
June ...	157	December	3,468
Carried forward 257		Total	52,122

HERRINGS LANDED AT LOWESTOFT IN 1907.

Month.	Lasts.	Month.	Lasts.
		Brought forward 1,277	
January ...	—	July ...	37
February ...	—	August ...	28
March ...	34	September	75
April	979	October ...	15,602
May .	100	November	18,579
June ...	164	December	3,599
Carried forward 1,277		Total	39,197

The above figures do not include the considerable quantities of herrings taken and landed without coming under the pencil of the wharfage man and the hammer of the auctioneer. Nor must it be forgotten that thousands upon thousands of barrels of salted herrings are rolled into the steam-ships for conveyance to the Russian markets.

I need not enlarge upon the processes of capture: they differ very little from those of the old time fishing already described. The tramp-tramp of the capstan men has been succeeded by the clank and jerk of the steam-driven capstan ; the flap of the

sails by the snort and spit of the engines. Seaman-
ship has deteriorated; the fisherman is the creature
and slave of the capitalist and shareholder; only the
skipper, and maybe his mate, look upon themselves
as seamen. It is only a matter of time, and the last
sailing-boat will have been replaced by a steam-
drifter.

The only romantic side of the fishery is the actual
fishing. The sea changes but little, and the habits of
the herring and its many foes remain the same.
The passage of the great shoals of fish is marked by
day by the tumbling of the sleek-hided porpoise, the
onslaughts of the white-beaked dolphin and "blow
fishes," and the circling hordes of gulls, the dash of
the gannet and the dodging of the guillemots. By
night the presence of the swimming legions is
betrayed by the phosphorescent gleaming of the
troubled waters. The keen eye of the skipper detects
"sign" of the herring in these omens, and at word of
command the long procession of nets "shoots" forth
over the rollers, the vessel keeping enough way on her
to have them straightening out behind her. With the
shooting of the last net he brings her to, and she
drifts with the tide. As night comes on the lights of
the vast fleet gleam out of the gloom, flickering and
changing with the rolling of the sea waves.

In the cabin below the stalwart fishermen,
begrimed and weary, have thrown themselves into
their bunks to sleep, ready at a hail to scramble on
deck again and to do the skipper's bidding. Sometimes the herrings only strike "spottily;" at other
times the dancing buoys that support the nets

indicate a good "strike." Then it is that, even before the morning sometimes, they set to work to haul in the nets. Every man jumps to his station and the engines are set going. Up come the nets, gliding in hand over hand, some of the herrings wriggling in a final protest, but most of them dead, and flashing in the fitful glare of the swinging lamp. Every man works his hardest in shaking out the enmeshed fishes until they, too, splashed and sprinkled with glittering scales, glisten from rugged beard to heavy thigh boots as though clad in armour.

What puzzles me most is, not the vastness of the fishing, when hundreds of boats are driving with their miles of netting, but how it is that so few get "foul" of each other's "shoot." That mishaps do occur, and that men's passions are sometimes aroused, is proved by the litigation that so frequently follows. At times the lawyers reap as fat a harvest as do those who gather in the harvest of the sea.

The scenes within sight of port are by no means uninteresting. To watch from the grim old break-water the incoming of the laden boats, and the outgoing of the freshly washed-down steamers bound for the herring grounds, is most entertaining. Turn-ing to the roadstead one sees the sailing-boats forging ahead, with their dark tanned sails bellying to the breeze ; and the smart rakish steamboats racing past them, with the wave curling up on either side the sharp prow. A few years ago the prettiest sight of all was to be witnessed early on Monday mornings, when the tide was favourable; for then the Scotch boats, after their Sunday's rest, put out to sea in a seemingly never-ending fleet.   To-day this moving picture is less impressive.   Fifteen years ago there were hardly any steam-drifters; to-day by far the greater number of the boats are steamers, independent of tides and winds.   The Scotchman, conservative and careful, finding himself handicapped in the scramble, has been steadily, if reluctantly, parting with his picturesque but unwieldy sailing craft, and replacing it by the more reliable if less beautiful steamboat.   There was bustle and haste only a decade since, when the Scotchman plied his long narrow "sweep" to help the boat seaward while the brown sail was hauled up to catch the fitful wind that now and then blew down the river: and when the smoking tugs laid hold of batches of empty or laden boats and hurried them out to sea or to the fish-wharf.   But of late years the scenes have been still livelier, as the steam-drifters rushed to and fro, to the hideous accompaniment of discordant syrens and clamorous hooters.

The scene at the fish-wharf on a busy day, from sunrise to sunset, and after, is an animated one.   Out at sea the waves may be flinging up weeds amid the foam, but in the harbour this is forgotten as the high-funnelled, rust-speckled vessels push their way up to their berths at the quayside.   The fish-market is full of bustle and excitement.   Brawny and begrimed fishermen shovel the glistening heaps of herrings into handy "maunds," scale-speckled fishermen haul at the derricks, and pass on the maunds to oily-clad fishermen ashore; and rows upon rows of "swills" down the whole length of the wharf and quays are filled up with the harvest of the sea. Only a few years ago hosts of "tellers" lined the quaysides, ready to jump aboard each incoming boat to count the herrings warp by warp, until the full tale of every last on board was "told." This work was a boon to hordes of unskilled labourers. But the evil day came when the Scotch method of "cranning," or judging fish by measure instead of by numbering, superseded the slower and more *expensive* method. As a writer once said, " The Scotchman saves time by averaging his fish. He also saves money." It was inevitable that sooner or later his English rival, more speculative and enterprising in the matter of using steam power, should follow suit.

When the fish have been landed there is heard the clangour of bells and the babble of many voices. "Buy! buy! buy!" shout the auctioneers. "Hurry up!" bawl the fish-buyers to their carters and fisher-girls. All day long on busy days the rattle and rumble of carts goes on as they hasten away with their loads of ten swills or twenty crans—a full half-last of salt or fresh or overday herrings, as the case may be.

What a glut of herrings means one cannot fully describe to the reader. I shall never forget the record catch, which occurred on the eve of October 21st, 1907. On the 22nd the boats raced in, laden to excess; there had never been such a miraculous "strike" of herrings. The oldest herring folk described it tersely as a "staggerer." There was piled up along two and a half miles of quays a solid bank of herrings—from the Haven bridge right down

U

to the mouth of the river, the air was laden all day, and for days after, with the odour of herrings. The boats brought them in by the million, from early dawn till the close of day, and when night came on the boats were still crowding in. Those that were fortunate enough to get a berth, lay moored end-on to the quays; while boat after boat, deeply laden, tried to force their way in between them or took up places in the rear, waiting for the opening of the slightest gap in the solid phalanx of craft. The nets had been so heavily struck that they filled almost at once with fish : the top catch reported was two hundred and thirty crans. Fish salesmen could only dispose of such catches as were landed on the quays. Prices naturally ruled low, and from twelve shillings per cran in the morning, they speedily fell to six, and then to three. There were no idlers that day ; every man that could lift a swill, every horse that could pull a cart was requisitioned, and proper meals were unthought of.

It was unfortunate that the weather was very fine, a bright sun and clear sky being bad for a glut of herrings, which do best under opposite conditions, and are the better for a keen air. Of salt there was soon a dearth, for such an invasion had been undreamt of. I well remember pushing my way through the reeking mass of fish and humanity, squeezing between the piled up "swills" (baskets), and slipping and slopping amid the ooze that besmeared the stones. Men and horses were at it until they nearly dropped with exhaustion ; the men worked day and night ; their poor beasts dozed in the shafts while the carts were loaded at the wharf and quays or unloaded at the fish houses. The wretched animals hung their heads as they ran ; they shambled for want of rest. The strangest of vehicles were requisitioned to remove the fish from the wharves ; and even then the carrying power was utterly unable to cope with the catch. Train loads of salt were frantically wired for. It was the fish-buyers' opportunity ; the previous year they had done badly, whilst the fishermen had made big sums. The sight at night on the denes between the river and the sea, was a striking one, as it is on any busy night or ordinary day. Highland lasses, bare headed and bare armed, stood around their troughs on the pickling plots in the glare of flaring naptha lamps, working their hardest, and lightening their by no means easy toil by singing quaint songs and hymns. Many of the boats failed in landing their catches at all—they could not even get into harbour with them. and many loads of fish were thrown back into the sea.

Much more might be written about the great herring harvest, and those who labour in it. Some of the changes that have taken place have already been noted. The superseding of the wooden sailers by the iron steamers, resulted in the shipyards, that found employment to hundreds of men, becoming idle, while engineering sheds have arisen like gigantic mushrooms. The artificer in iron and steel has ousted the shipwright, the spinner of ropes, and the rigger. The lofts of the sail-makers are forsaken. The beachmen disappeared ; and last of all the teller—the last hanger-on to the old methods.

The clear skies that smiled down on the fleet at home are now obscured by coal smoke; and the smoke-cure, although still largely pursued, is a small affair compared with the barreling of salted herrings. The cooper, who twenty years ago was an obscure worker, is now a busy man.

A striking feature of the herring season are the Scotch lassies, who every year come in train loads from Aberdeen, Wick, and even far away Shetlands and other Scottish Isles; they come in their thousands. The old steady typical Scotch fisherman, whose good behaviour moralists used to enlarge upon to our east coast fisherman's disadvantage, comes no longer alone, for the steamboats ship engineers, stokers, and others, whose training may have been in the Glasgow slums. The coopers generally are not a blameless race. All too many of them love their whisky, and indulge too freely in the vile liquors provided especially for their use during the herring fishing.

The great majority of the men and lasses, however, behave well; their services on the wharf and in the local chapels are hearty and decorous; their conduct when the boats are kept in by rough weather, or late unlading, is beyond reproach. On Saturday nights the lasses, bare headed, but wearing their best skirts, perambulate the streets in their companies, while the stolid-faced men, with hands deep in pockets, stroll idly up and down, talking in Gaelic or some northern dialect understood only by themselves. On other idle nights and workless afternoons, the lasses roam about with their knitting needles busy and their tongues busier still.

SCOTCH GIRLS "GUTTING" HERRINGS

THE CURING OF THE HERRINGS

A "fresh" herring, newly captured and landed, should be stiff, well scaled, and without the slightest tinge of red between the eyes and the gill-covers. The uninitiated may be misled by this infusion of blood which follows on "death by suffocation," from which the creature really expires; but this does not really obtain until some hours after decease. Than a plump herring, fresh from the sea, packed firmly with roe, and fat with its native juices, no sweeter morsel can be placed in a fry-pan and fried to a rich brown; not even the mackerel can beat it. To add to its appearance, and to improve its cooking, the sides should be slightly "scored" (cut), and the beef dripping should be of the very best.

But there are few people outside a fishing town by whom the luxury can be enjoyed; for the herring is frail, although lending itself to several methods of smoke and pickle-curing.

Real Yarmouth Bloaters have a world-wide fame, and are unsurpassed by any imitations which may be cured outside the herring metropolis.

The following methods of herring cure are pursued; and herring-curing forms a not inconsiderable item in the economy of a huge industry. A considerable acreage of the outskirts of Yarmouth consists of fish-yards, curing-sheds and smoke-houses, and a fish-house, in full going order, is a hive of industry. In many of the narrow "Rows" ancient curing-houses, where long past generations of

Yarmouthians conjured with the herring, still exist ; horses and barrow-carts rattle up and down them now, as did horses and troll-carts in the days of Queen Elizabeth. In the fishing season the south part of the town lies under a fog of wood smoke, reeking with the aroma of smoking fish in every stage of their cure.

Not long ago, a fish-curer named Jerrard sat in an armchair by my fireside. Quite a " character " is this merry, hard-working fellow, who, in the days when the fish-houses are comparatively idle, earns a scanty livelihood by perambulating the streets with a barrow of trawl fish.[1]

"Now then, Jerrard," I said, " chop your sentences short, and modulate your voice. Gesticulate as much as you like, but keep away from those vases."

"Very well," said he, "tell us how to begin and what you really want to know."

"Well, first of all tell me how you help to turn a fresh herring into a bloater," I replied.

" Very good," he remarked, with a sort of Parisian flourish of both hands, " I'll tell you. As soon as we get the fresh herrin's, say a last of 'em—that's two loads of ten swills each—ten crans, as they'd say to-day—we shoot them out of the swills on to the floor (of brick or concrete). For bloaters, we slightly salt 'em, sprinklin' and mixin' about a quarter ton of bay salt. (Sea salt). We let 'em remain there about thirty hours. You don't need to turn the fish about durin' that time for bloaters. We then pump the 'vat,'

[1] Jerrard has been one of my most devoted and industrious " fish-curio " collectors.

a very large half-shaped tub, full of fresh well-water. One man stands at the vat with a 'maund' (a round basket of rather open vertical wicker work), and another shovels (with a great wooden shovel) the herrin's into it. Then they are well rinsed, after which they are shot into a trow——"

"Trough?" I said.

"Yes! a trow—t-r-o-w," said Jerrard, spelling it. "But that is near enough. Six women we call 'rivers' (the accent on the 'i') then 'rive' the herrin's on ash sticks—'speets' we call 'em—what hold from twenty-five to thirty. They shove the sharp end of the 'spect' (spit) through under the right gill (gill cover) bringing it out at the mouth; you see, they hold the herrin' with the back to the hand. You may see fifty million of herrin's smoked and not one 'rove' wrong. Directly a 'speet' is filled it is hung on a 'hoss,' a stand with arms projecting, to drain, and as sune as it is filled, the first one hung on is handed by women to the chaps in the 'loves.' The 'loves,' you know, are the cross-beams in the smoke-house, what reach from about eight feet from the floor to the roof. Three men generally stand straddle-leg athort from 'love' to 'love' handin' 'em up; the top man is the 'hanger.' Some 'rooms' will hold a last and a quarter (pritty nigh seventeen thousand herrin's); and some fish-houses have three smoke-rooms, or even more. There they hang twelve hours, only oak billets bein' used; you may say they're hung in the evenin' and 'struck' (taken down) in the mornin'. These are packed into boxes for London, Antwerp, and country orders.

"These boxes hold fifty herrin's. We mostly make 'em in slack times, gettin' from ninepence to a shillin' a hundred boxes."

"That's the *bloater*," said I.; "now the——"

"Well, the next," snapped Jerrard, in a pert sort of way, "is Light Reds. If we handle fresh herrin's for 'em, we let 'em lay in salt three or four days. If already salted, say four days salted, we get on with 'em at once; and then smoke 'em from ten to twelve days. As 'selected milds' we pack 'em in boxes of fifty and send 'em to London for home use or for exportation.

"Now you come to Salted Reds. These are October herrin's and hang for long keepin'. They lay three weeks in salt, and hang for two or three months. They are packed in barrels of 250 to 500, pressed in a screw press, headed down, and sold for London or country orders. These herrin's 'll keep good for a couple of years if kept dry.

"Let me see," said Jerrard, scratching his half-bald pate, "exports next. These are rough, cheap fish. Perhaps we get in six, or even a half score, lasts; we hull 'em on the floor together, makin' one big 'cob'; and there they lay for a month or six weeks. Then they're washed, and hung for two or three days, packed in barrels, and sent abroad. Next to them we have the pickle-cured. These are bought fresh, put into vats (huge cemented storage vats sunk in the floors of certain of the houses); salt is thrown over 'em, and they lay and make their own pickle, lyin' there three or four weeks. They are then taken out and barrelled; some bein' gutted, and some not, accordin' to order.

"Gutted herrin's," went on my pedagogue, "go through the hands of the Scotch gals and the women generally. They are thrown into troughs, slightly salted, and picked up one by one and the gills and entrails jerked out—well, like the wink of yer eye, in a manner of speakin'. The gutted herrin's are then packed with plenty of salt in barrels, holdin' roughly, from 500 to 1000 fish. Coopers head them down, and Scotch gals fill 'em up with liquid brine, pourin' it out of a can through a funnel into a hole bored in the lid. The hole is plugged—'spiked down' we call it—and the barrels are put aboard-ship and sent to Russia and all over Europe. I've heerd say they turn the herrin's out solid, like cheese, and sell 'em in junks, and people eat 'em raw."

"Now tell me about the kippers," I said.

"Well, we use fresh herrin's; women split' em down the backs, take all the innerds out, put 'em in brine for twenty minutes, and hang 'em, tail downwards, on narrow 'baulks' on tenter hooks. They're then hung on the 'hoss' to drain for about twenty minutes, passed up into the 'loves' and smoked for about ten hours over oak-dust and shruff, or anything that make plenty of smoke, but has no resin in it. Packed in boxes of from thirty to forty pairs, they are sent to Billingsgate and big inland towns.

"You'd like to know about haddocks?"

"Of course."

"Well, haddocks are bought fresh on the wharf or at Lowestoft—pity we don't get more smacks in here without havin' to send over there for 'em. The heads are wrung off, and the fish split down the belly. After bein' in brine a few minutes they're washed, hung on thin iron 'speets,' run through the fin-flaps, if I may call 'em so, and then smoked for five or six hours, accordin' to whether it's 'pale' or 'dark' brands you want.

"Mackerel we usurelly ice in boxes and send away fresh ; but a little smokin's done occasionally. To cure 'em, we split 'em behind, like kippers, pickle 'em a few minutes, smoke 'em with oak all night and strike 'em in the mornin'. You pack as many in a box as 'll go in and send 'em to town or country."

"Thank you."

"Oh! I ain't quite done. I must just mention sprats. These we buy on the market, wash 'em in small 'maunds,' speet 'em, as you do herrin's for bloaters, but on smaller speets, dip 'em in brine for 'reds' or 'bloaters'; for the one smoke 'em two days, for the 'tother, say a hour or a little over. We pack 'em in small 'kids'—them little wee tub-kind of things —and away they go."

Jerrard being small and nimble, is a handy man in the fish-house, assisting in various departments, more particularly in the smoke-houses, where he is master of the bellows. Before he had left me, he told me all the art of building a fire from three and four feet lengths of billet, which, when ready for lighting, he compared to a great wooden starfish, one end of each laying to, or overlapping the others, according to the "krinks" of the wood. Smaller pieces were interpersed to "catch hold" as he termed it, which they soon did when the wind from the big bellows roared into the ignited pile.

"You mustn't blaze too much," he added emphatically, "or you fire your fish; they'll cook instead of smoke, and turn soft, and the bodies are apt to fall, leaving only the heads on the speets."

THREE-MAST SAILING LUGGER

(*In use early part of* 19*th century*)

LAPWINGS

CHAPTER XI

FLOTSAM

" It blew great guns, when gallant Tom
    Was taking in a sail ;
    And squalls came on in sight of home,
    That strengthened to a gale."

                                    DIBDIN.

A FAMOUS LIFEBOATMAN

BRAVE as a lion, modest to a degree, gentle, resourceful, daring, and with a voice at once masterful and yet kindly, old "Laddie" Woods, at sixty-eight, is resting on his oars. "Laddie" is

Gorleston's hero, and his name has been a household word on our eastern coast for many a year.

I met him not long ago at Colby's. He had dropped in for a " mardle " with my crippled shrimper friend, " just to chip the old chap up " as is his wont ; and we yarned full two hours of the sea and things stormy, wild and daring.

The big round-bodied, great-hearted fellow, in bright blue guernsey and pilot coat, chatted freely on his adventures, telling, in terse sentences, graphic stories of gales and wrecks, and mentioning dates and names as readily as if they were deeply graven on his mind. I could not mention a gale or incident, but he at once gave me date and detail.

" Now what do you want fust ? " he asked, as I edged him into a yarn.

" I remember most vividly," said I, " a big barque going ashore in the Ham (at Gorleston) and seeing her go to pieces. I was then a lad, and had raced beachward from Sunday school to see that smart vessel drifting at her anchors."

" That was in 1870," he replied promptly ; " the ship was the *Victoria* of North Shields. The date was the fust of December. It was blowin' a whole gale from the east'ard, and there was icicles hangin' on Gorleston pier as long as your arm, and growin' bigger and longer with every burst of sea water as broke on 'em. Ah, bor, we was handicapped that afternoon. We couldn't launch, and the rockets wouldn't reach her."

" Yes," said I, " I saw her break in halves, the bow half swinging one way as the other swung the other; I saw the masts fall one after the other, bringing death to more than one of the crew as the raffle of the gear held them down to the wreck. One by one they were drowned, some of them being washed into the boiling seas before our eyes."

"I went in," he went on, "through the breakers, and seft (saved) one poor fellow as was stark naked, the sea throwin' him right into my arms. We rubbed and chafed him back to life. There was only four others out of a big crew saved, and they come ashore on spars. We'd been out that mornin' and seft the crew of an Austrian brig what struck on the Scroby sands.

"The fishin' boat *Chosen*, of Yarmouth, comes ashore on the north sand (near the harbour mouth). It was blowin' a gale from the east'ard. Snow was thick on the ground. We couldn't get the boat out, it bein' so rough; so we rowed athort the river to the Yarmouth side. Then I just swims off to the fishin' boat, clambers aboard, and drifted a line ashore tied to a cork fender, and sent the crew after it.

"On the 13th of January, 1866—it was a Saturday —we see signals of distress, and put off in the lifeboat *Rescuer*. The wind was off shore, and we didn't feel much of it while we was going along under the lee of the pier; in fact, it fared right calm at the pier end. It was ebb tide. We'd got the mainsail up, but hadn't yet got the jib up, when the wind struck her, filled the sail and hove her down, the sea breakin' into her, and capsized her. None of us had got our lifebelts on; and in the rough seas each had to look after hisself. There was twelve on us strugglin' in the sea, and eight was drowned. The wurst on it was, there wor eight widows left, and thirty youngsters with 'em ; and one of us as was seft lived only forty hours, and then pegged out.

"On the 12th of November, 1891, it came on to blow a heavy gale from the south'ard. We heerd there was a vessel on the Scroby Sands, and we soon saw her burnin' flares for assistance. Two boats was launched—the *Mark Lane* (my boat) and the *Elizabeth Simpson*. We went on to the pier, and the seas was breakin' clean over, smotherin' the light-house on the end of it.

"Two pilots come to me, and one says—

" ' I believe the wind's westerin' a bit, and fancy we can get to sea.' But the wind wasn't, not a bit of it.

" ' I'll try it,' I says. ' Now then, lads, it's *off!* '

"So we shot out for the harbour under reefed canvas, and must have had at least a hundred Scotchmen towin' the boat towards the sea ; you see, they was holdin' us off, so we didn't go athort the harbour, for the sea what was runnin' would have smashed us to matchwood if we'd drifted to le'ward. When we'd got her under command, several heavy seas broke over us, and buried us. But thank Gord we just cleared the north sands.[1] We went and found the ketch *Aid* of Portsmouth (Captain Newman) ridin'—draggin' her anchors abreast of the jetty. We at once dropped our anchor and wore down to her by the cable, takin' off the crew.

[1] A sand bank running northward from the north pier and at right angles to it.

Then we got a large cable from the ketch to stop her from drivin', and got it fast to the lifeboat. That and her two anchors stayed her till the weather 'bated. Our boat had got a hundred and twenty fathoms of cable out. When the weather cleared enough, we fetched vessel and crew into the harbour.

"What is the most valuable bit of salvage I've had a share in? Why, when we got the *Agabar*, worth seventy or eighty thousand pounds. She'd got part of a cargo of jute aboard; she'd been on Winterton Ridge, losin' stern-post and rudder, and playin' the dowst up with herself.

"I remember goin' out to the *Livadia* (fourteen hundred tons), of South Shields, on the East Cross Sands. She was an iron vessel, and had broke up into three parts afore we got to her, only the middle part bein' out of the water. All the crew of twenty-six hands was lost, except two, when we got to her; and even while we were drawin' up, one of 'em went mad and jumped into the sea afore our eyes. The only one we brought in was Tom Sewell, a Yarmouth man. That wasn't the finish of this awful job, for in the second week in March, the *Livadia's* lifeboat was picked up with three poor dead fellows in it.

"One of the worst—in fact, the worst gale I was ever in, was on that awful Sunday, the 24th March, 1895. You remember what a lot of trees was blowed down for miles around, and half Yarmouth fared stripped of tilin's. The rate of the wind was eighty-six miles. Well, a barquentine came into Yarmouth Roads and let go her two anchors. It was blowin' from the west-sou'-west. She parted from both, and the crew at once run'd up the red ensign, union jack reversed, in the riggin'. We mustered and launched, and as we was goin' out of the harbour, we meets the steam tug *Meteor*, and hailed 'em. They shouted back as they couldn't take us in tow, for they'd got their work cut out to look after theerselves : she'd been layin' outside when the storm broke, and it was all she could do to get in. However, we managed to get out, and finds the ship—she was the *Isabella* of Swansea—outside the bell buoy. We drew up to her close reefed, ranged up alongside, and took nine hands off her. Lor'! how it blew! We braced her up and tacked back to Gorleston.

"We had a rare Gord-send once. A steamboat got on Winterton Ness and broke up, and no end of sacks of flour fell into our hands ; in fact, folks all along the coast got well in amongst 'em. They'd took water in less than half an inch, the flour under that rind, as you might call it, being dry and uninjured. At the same time, a vessel loaded with dead meat from a Baltic port comes to grief, and sheep floated about everywhere. People lived like fighting cocks that hard winter: it was some thirty-eight yeer ago.

"A Scotch fishin' boat, some eight year ago, got aground on Scroby. When we went out we found the Yarmouth and the Caister lifeboats makin' towards her, but the *Mark Lane* (our boat) got alongside her first. The wessel got off and bumped on again. The crew was drunk, and one fool was tearin' around with a big hatchet, theatenin' to cut down the first man as come aboard. As it was he chopt through the fore halyards and let the foresail down all on top the crew. They were all more like madmen than anything else. When one of our chaps clambered aboard the Scottie comes for him ; but he was too quick for him, seized his wrist, snatched away the hatchet, and hulled it overboard. After a bit of argerin' we got 'em to come into the lifeboat.

"The longest spell I ever had," continued Laddie, "was in November, 1881. We went out at eleven o'clock on Sunday night (it was the 14th), and went in search of a ship as had shown signals of distress. We sailed as far as the *Hasbro'* lightship, and from there to the *Leman and Ower.* From the *Leman* we went to the *Dudgeon*, spoke her, and directly found ourselves abreast of the Humber. We'd got one spell of towin' behind a steamboat ; but we sighted no craft in distress. It comes on a gale on the Monday night from the south-east, so we run'd up the Humber to Grimsby."

"What had you been living on?" I asked.

"Well," said he, "from the Sunday night until the Tuesday mornin' we been livin' on the wind, and a few sea-biscuits we happened to have on board. We'd been sittin', too, all them hours.

"Some of us once went out in a yawl of our own to a full-rigged ship grounded on Corton sands ; but the wind from the south-east proved too much for us, and we run'd home again, and went out to her in the lifeboat *Rescue.* We took twenty-eight hands out of the raffle—riggin' and everything bein' mixed up— and when we'd got 'em aboard there was another craft—a brig—burnin' a tar bucket. We found her water-logged, laden with coal, and we took nine hands off her. What with them thirty-seven poor fellows and our own crew of sixteen, we looked a fair Noah's ark, you may reckon, when we made the harbour early next mornin'.

"Is there anything more I can tell you?" he asked; "for I could jaw on for a fortnight, if I didn't tire you. I ain't been a lifeboat man for forty-two years (I've been retired eight) without goin' through suffin: bruises, broken limbs, hunger, cold, and perils enough to satisfy a glutton."

"How many lives have you helped to save?"

"How many? why suffin' like a thousand, roughly told. And I didn't get these 'ere for nothin' (holding out for my inspection some bronze and silver medals he had been carrying in his pocket). If you go into the lifeboat shed at Gorleston, you'll see any amount of vessels named and the crews rescued, chalked up on the notice boards ; and you can see how many of 'em figure durin' my two score years' service. I'm sixty-eight; so I didn't lose much time, you see, afore I jined the crew."

THE LAST OF THE EBB TIDE

" The wind was high and the clouds were dark,
And the boat returned no more."
T. MOORE.

There is a knock at the door, impetuous and commanding. It is a raw, windy December night; the gas-jets flicker fitfully in the dripping street-lamps, threatening, at the street corners, to go out altogether.   Another sharp rap follows before I reach the door.

"Excuse me, master," says the kindly voice of old "Snicker" Larn, "but old Billy's wussened since nune-time, and for aught I know it's jest about all up with him.   He keep sorter wanderin' at times, talkin' about Breydon, an' the tides, and that; an' he's bin axing for you, sir.   I know'd you was kinder an old pal, in a way, sir, of his, and I thowt he'd feel aisier in his mind if I come—an' I did.   I've jest took him sum warm eel-stew as he kep' cravin' for; my neyber biled a eel as I got off young 'Stork'; but law, I didn't think as he'd take more 'an a spuneful, an' he ain't; but it kinder chipt him up. . . ."

This is the half-row, and here is the "snack" of the door; a glimmer of lamplight through the worn keyhole guides us to it.   We step down from the draughty alley into the sparingly furnished room and turn to the left.   Here lies the poor old fellow whose life is fast ebbing away.

By the bedside, on a backless chair, sits the little parson[1] of the Shrimpers' Shelter, with an open Testament on his knee.

"Hallo! Pattson, my lad. . . . I'm glad you've come.   So Snicker told you I've bin axin' for you.   Well, I thought you jest like to give me one more call afore I cross the bar.   You fare suffin' like one on us.   I'm a poor old hulk, an' driftin' out on the ebb: it's allers the ebb afore the tide makes up agin. . . . There's the old house-boat—my niece'll see to that, and the gear.   There'll be enough to bury me

[1] Vide *Wild Life on a Norfolk Estuary*, pp. 70-71.

decent, without callin' on the parish. . . . I allers dreaded *that*.   Flaxman, go on with Peter, what you wor a readin'."

"——*But the ship was now in the midst of the sea, tossed with the waves*," the little parson reads slowly and distinctly, while the old man lies with closed eyes, "*for the wind was contrary*."

"Why didn't they tack a bit?" soliloquises the dying man.   "Never mind, go on."

"*And in the fourth watch of the night——*"

"That 'ud be about *now*, Pattson, wouldn't it?"

"——*The fourth watch of the night. . . . Jesus went unto them, walking on the sea. And when the disciples saw Him walking on the sea, they were troubled . . . and they cried out for fear. But straightway Jesus spake unto them, saying: Be of good cheer; it is I; be not afraid. And Peter answered Him, and said, Lord, if it be Thou, bid me come unto Thee on the water. And He said, come. And when Peter was come down out of the ship, he walked on the water, to go to Jesus. But when he saw the wind boisterous, he was afraid; and beginning to sink, he cried, saying, Lord save me——*"

"They hadn't no lifebuoy——" murmurs the old fellow.   "Poor . . . old . . . Peter! and no rope . . . neither!"

"*And immediately Jesus stretched forth His hand——*"

"*That* done it!"

"*And caught him . . . and . . . the wind ceased.*"

The old man lies still and peaceful, his breast heaving, his eyes closed, making no further comment

" It's about low water with him," says the kindly little parson, a tear standing in the corner of each eye. My own throat feels lumpy.

Suddenly the old man's eyes open, and he lifts his hand feebly, as if bidding us adieu.

" *And Jesus caught hold of Peter's hand!* " whispers the little parson.

" Ah!" pants the dying man, " Peter . . . caught him.—Let go . . . the painter . . . the flood-tide's . . . makin'! —— "

The old Breydoner has gone out alone on to the Great Silent Sea, on the last of the ebb tide.

FLOTSAM

INDEX

311

PRINTED BY
WILLIAM CLOWES AND SONS, LIMITED,
LONDON AND BECCLES

A SELECTION OF BOOKS PUBLISHED BY METHUEN AND CO. LTD., LONDON 36 ESSEX STREET W.C.

CONTENTS

JULY 1912

A SELECTION OF
MESSRS. METHUEN'S
PUBLICATIONS

In this Catalogue the order is according to authors. An asterisk denotes that the book is in the press.

Colonial Editions are published of all Messrs. METHUEN'S Novels issued at a price above 2s. 6d., and similar editions are published of some works of General Literature. Colonial editions are only for circulation in the British Colonies and India.

All books marked net are not subject to discount, and cannot be bought at less than the published price. Books not marked net are subject to the discount which the bookseller allows.

Messrs. METHUEN'S books are kept in stock by all good booksellers. If there is any difficulty in seeing copies, Messrs. Methuen will be very glad to have early information, and specimen copies of any books will be sent on receipt of the published price plus postage for net books, and of the published price for ordinary books.

This Catalogue contains only a selection of the more important books published by Messrs. Methuen. A complete and illustrated catalogue of their publications may be obtained on application.

Andrewes (Lancelot). PRECES PRIVATAE. Translated and edited, with Notes, by F. E. BRIGHTMAN. Cr. 8vo. 6s.

Aristotle. THE ETHICS. Edited, with an Introduction and Notes, by JOHN BURNET. Demy 8vo. 10s. 6d. net.

Atkinson (C. T.). A HISTORY OF GERMANY, 1715-1815. Demy 8vo. 12s. 6d. net.

Atkinson (T. D.). ENGLISH ARCHITECTURE. Illustrated. Fcap. 8vo. 3s. 6d. net.

A GLOSSARY OF TERMS USED IN ENGLISH ARCHITECTURE. Illustrated. Second Edition. Fcap. 8vo. 3s. 6d. net.

ENGLISH AND WELSH CATHEDRALS. Illustrated. Demy 8vo. 10s. 6d. net.

Bain (F. W.). A DIGIT OF THE MOON: A HINDOO LOVE STORY. Ninth Edition. Fcap. 8vo. 3s. 6d. net.

THE DESCENT OF THE SUN: A CYCLE OF BIRTH. Fifth Edition. Fcap. 8vo. 3s. 6d. net.

A HEIFER OF THE DAWN. Seventh Edition. Fcap. 8vo. 2s. 6d. net.

IN THE GREAT GOD'S HAIR. Fifth Edition. Fcap. 8vo. 2s. 6d. net.

A DRAUGHT OF THE BLUE. Fourth Edition. Fcap. 8vo. 2s. 6d. net.

AN ESSENCE OF THE DUSK. Third Edition. Fcap. 8vo. 2s. 6d. net.

AN INCARNATION OF THE SNOW. Second Edition. Fcap. 8vo. 3s. 6d. net.

A MINE OF FAULTS. Second Edition. Fcap. 8vo. 3s. 6d. net.

THE ASHES OF A GOD. Fcap. 8vo. 3s. 6d. net.

*BUBBLES OF THE FOAM. Fcap 4to. 5s. net. Also Fcap. 8vo. 3s. 6d. net.

Balfour (Graham). THE LIFE OF ROBERT LOUIS STEVENSON. Illustrated. Fifth Edition in one Volume. Cr. 8vo. Buckram, 6s. Also Fcap. 8vo. 1s. net.

Baring (Hon. Maurice). A YEAR IN RUSSIA. Second Edition. Demy 8vo. 10s. 6d. net.

LANDMARKS IN RUSSIAN LITERATURE. Second Edition. Crown 8vo. 6s. net.

RUSSIAN ESSAYS AND STORIES. Second Edition. Crown 8vo. 5s. net.

THE RUSSIAN PEOPLE. Demy 8vo. 15s. net.

Baring-Gould (S.). THE LIFE OF NAPOLEON BONAPARTE. Illustrated. Second Edition. Royal 8vo. 10s. 6d. net.

THE TRAGEDY OF THE CÆSARS: A STUDY OF THE CHARACTERS OF THE CÆSARS OF THE JULIAN AND CLAUDIAN HOUSES. Illustrated. *Seventh Edition. Royal 8vo.* 10s. 6d. net.
THE VICAR OF MORWENSTOW. With a Portrait. *Third Edition. Cr. 8vo.* 3s. 6d. *Also Fcap. 8vo.* 1s. net.
OLD COUNTRY LIFE. Illustrated. *Fifth Edition. Large Cr. 8vo.* 6s.
A BOOK OF CORNWALL. Illustrated. *Third Edition. Cr. 8vo.* 6s.
A BOOK OF DARTMOOR. Illustrated. *Second Edition. Cr. 8vo.* 6s.
A BOOK OF DEVON. Illustrated. *Third Edition. Cr. 8vo.* 6s.

Baring-Gould (S.) and **Sheppard (H. Fleetwood).** A GARLAND OF COUNTRY SONG. English Folk Songs with their Traditional Melodies. *Demy 4to.* 6s.
SONGS OF THE WEST: Folk Songs of Devon and Cornwall. Collected from the Mouths of the People. New and Revised Edition, under the musical editorship of CECIL J. SHARP. *Large Imperial 8vo.* 5s. net.

Barker (E.). THE POLITICAL THOUGHT OF PLATO AND ARISTOTLE. *Demy 8vo.* 10s. 6d. net.

Bastable (C. F.). THE COMMERCE OF NATIONS. *Fifth Edition. Cr. 8vo.* 2s. 6d.

Beckford (Peter). THOUGHTS ON HUNTING. Edited by J. OTHO PAGET. Illustrated. *Third Edition. Demy 8vo.* 6s.

Belloc (H.). PARIS. Illustrated. *Second Edition, Revised. Cr. 8vo.* 6s.
HILLS AND THE SEA. *Fourth Edition. Fcap. 8vo.* 5s.
ON NOTHING AND KINDRED SUBJECTS. *Third Edition. Fcap. 8vo.* 5s.
ON EVERYTHING. *Third Edition. Fcap. 8vo.* 5s.
ON SOMETHING. *Second Edition. Fcap. 8vo.* 5s.
FIRST AND LAST. *Second Edition. Fcap. 8vo.* 5s.
MARIE ANTOINETTE. Illustrated. *Third Edition. Demy 8vo.* 15s. net.
THE PYRENEES. Illustrated. *Second Edition. Demy 8vo.* 7s. 6d. net.

Bennett (W. H.). A PRIMER OF THE BIBLE. *Fifth Edition. Cr. 8vo.* 2s. 6d.

Bennett (W. H.) and **Adeney (W. F.).** A BIBLICAL INTRODUCTION. With a concise Bibliography. *Sixth Edition. Cr. 8vo.* 7s. 6d. *Also in Two Volumes. Cr. 8vo.* Each 3s. 6d. net.

Benson (Archbishop). GOD'S BOARD. Communion Addresses. *Second Edition. Fcap. 8vo.* 3s. 6d. net.

Bicknell (Ethel E.). PARIS AND HER TREASURES. Illustrated. *Fcap. 8vo.* Round corners. 5s. net.

Blake (William). ILLUSTRATIONS OF THE BOOK OF JOB. With a General Introduction by LAURENCE BINYON. Illustrated. *Quarto.* 21s. net.

Bloemfontein (Bishop of). ARA CŒLI: AN ESSAY IN MYSTICAL THEOLOGY. *Fifth Edition. Cr. 8vo.* 3s. 6d. net.
FAITH AND EXPERIENCE. *Second Edition. Cr. 8vo.* 3s. 6d. net.

Bowden (E. M.). THE IMITATION OF BUDDHA: Quotations from Buddhist Literature for each Day in the Year. *Sixth Edition. Cr. 16mo.* 2s. 6d.

Brabant (F. G.). RAMBLES IN SUSSEX. Illustrated. *Cr. 8vo.* 6s.

Bradley (A. G.). ROUND ABOUT WILTSHIRE. Illustrated. *Second Edition. Cr. 8vo.* 6s.
THE ROMANCE OF NORTHUMBERLAND. Illustrated. *Second Edition. Demy 8vo.* 7s. 6d. net.

Braid (James). ADVANCED GOLF. Illustrated. *Seventh Edition. Demy 8vo.* 10s. 6d. net.

Brodrick (Mary) and **Morton (A. Anderson).** A CONCISE DICTIONARY OF EGYPTIAN ARCHÆOLOGY. A Handbook for Students and Travellers. Illustrated. *Cr. 8vo.* 3s. 6d.

Browning (Robert). PARACELSUS. Edited with an Introduction, Notes, and Bibliography by MARGARET L. LEE and KATHARINE B. LOCOCK. *Fcap. 8vo.* 3s. 6d. net.

Buckton (A. M.). EAGER HEART: A Christmas Mystery-Play. *Tenth Edition. Cr. 8vo.* 1s. net.

Bull (Paul). GOD AND OUR SOLDIERS. *Second Edition. Cr. 8vo.* 6s.

Burns (Robert). THE POEMS AND SONGS. Edited by ANDREW LANG and W. A. CRAIGIE. With Portrait. *Third Edition. Wide Demy 8vo.* 6s.

Calman (W. T.). THE LIFE OF CRUSTACEA. Illustrated. *Cr. 8vo.* 6s.

Carlyle (Thomas). THE FRENCH REVOLUTION. Edited by C. R. L. FLETCHER. *Three Volumes. Cr. 8vo.* 18s.
THE LETTERS AND SPEECHES OF OLIVER CROMWELL. With an Introduction by C. H. FIRTH, and Notes and Appendices by S. C. LOMAS. *Three Volumes. Demy 8vo.* 18s. net.

4   METHUEN AND COMPANY LIMITED

Celano (Brother Thomas of). THE LIVES OF S. FRANCIS OF ASSISI. Translated by A. G. FERRERS HOWELL. With a Frontispiece. *Cr. 8vo. 5s. net.*

Chambers (Mrs. Lambert). LAWN TENNIS FOR LADIES. Illustrated. *Cr. 8vo. 2s. 6d. net.*

*Chesser, (Elizabeth Sloan). PERFECT HEALTH FOR WOMEN AND CHILDREN. *Cr. 8vo. 3s. 6d. net.*

Chesterfield (Lord). THE LETTERS OF THE EARL OF CHESTERFIELD TO HIS SON. Edited, with an Introduction by C. STRACHEY, and Notes by A. CALTHROP. *Two Volumes. Cr. 8vo. 12s.*

Chesterton (G. K.). CHARLES DICKENS. With two Portraits in Photogravure. *Seventh Edition. Cr. 8vo. 6s.*
ALL THINGS CONSIDERED. *Sixth Edition. Fcap. 8vo. 5s.*
TREMENDOUS TRIFLES. *Fourth Edition. Fcap. 8vo. 5s.*
ALARMS AND DISCURSIONS. *Second Edition. Fcap. 8vo. 5s.*
THE BALLAD OF THE WHITE HORSE. *Third Edition. Fcap. 8vo. 5s.*
*TYPES OF MEN. *Fcap. 8vo. 5s.*

Clausen (George). SIX LECTURES ON PAINTING. Illustrated. *Third Edition. Large Post 8vo. 3s. 6d. net.*
AIMS AND IDEALS IN ART. Eight Lectures delivered to the Students of the Royal Academy of Arts. Illustrated. *Second Edition. Large Post 8vo. 5s. net.*

Clutton-Brock (A.) SHELLEY: THE MAN AND THE POET. Illustrated. *Demy 8vo. 7s. 6d. net.*

Cobb (W. F.). THE BOOK OF PSALMS. With an Introduction and Notes. *Demy 8vo. 10s. 6d. net.*

Conrad (Joseph). THE MIRROR OF THE SEA: Memories and Impressions. *Third Edition. Cr. 8vo. 6s.*

Coolidge (W. A. B.). THE ALPS: IN NATURE AND HISTORY. Illustrated. *Demy 8vo. 7s. 6d. net.*

*Correvon (H.). ALPINE FLORA. Translated and enlarged by E.␣W. CLAYFORTH. Illustrated. *Square Demy 8vo. 16s. net.*

Coulton (G. G.). CHAUCER AND HIS ENGLAND. Illustrated. *Second Edition. Demy 8vo. 10s. 6d. net.*

Cowper (William). THE POEMS. Edited with an Introduction and Notes by J. C. BAILEY. Illustrated. *Demy 8vo. 10s. 6d. net.*

Cox (J. C.). RAMBLES IN SURREY. *Second Edition. Cr. 8vo. 6s.*

Crowley (Ralph H.). THE HYGIENE OF SCHOOL LIFE. Illustrated. *Cr. 8vo. 3s. 6d. net.*

Davis (H. W. C.). ENGLAND UNDER THE NORMANS AND ANGEVINS: 1066–1272. *Third Edition. Demy 8vo. 10s. 6d. net.*

Dawbarn (Charles). FRANCE AND THE FRENCH. Illustrated. *Demy 8vo. 10s. 6d. net.*

Dearmer (Mabel). A CHILD'S LIFE OF CHRIST. Illustrated. *Large Cr. 8vo. 6s.*

Deffand (Madame du). LETTRES DE MADAME DU DEFFAND À HORACE WALPOLE. Edited, with Introduction, Notes, and Index, by Mrs PAGET TOYNBEE. *In Three Volumes. Demy 8vo. £3 3s. net.*

Dickinson (G. L.). THE GREEK VIEW OF LIFE. *Seventh Edition. Crown 8vo. 2s. 6d. net.*

Ditchfield (P. H.). THE PARISH CLERK. Illustrated. *Third Edition. Demy 8vo. 7s. 6d. net.*
THE OLD-TIME PARSON. Illustrated. *Second Edition. Demy 8vo. 7s. 6d. net.*
*THE OLD ENGLISH COUNTRY SQUIRE. Illustrated. *Demy 8vo. 10s. 6d. net.*

Ditchfield (P. H.) and Roe (Fred). VANISHING ENGLAND. The Book by P. H. Ditchfield. Illustrated by FRED ROE. *Second Edition. Wide Demy 8vo. 15s. net.*

Douglas (Hugh A.). VENICE ON FOOT. With the Itinerary of the Grand Canal. Illustrated *Second Edition. Round corners. Fcap. 8vo. 5s. net.*
VENICE AND HER TREASURES. Illustrated. *Round corners. Fcap. 8vo. 5s. net.*

Dowden (J.). FURTHER STUDIES IN THE PRAYER BOOK. *Cr. 8vo. 6s.*

Driver (S. R.). SERMONS ON SUBJECTS CONNECTED WITH THE OLD TESTAMENT. *Cr. 8vo. 6s.*

Dumas (Alexandre). THE CRIMES OF THE BORGIAS AND OTHERS. With an Introduction by R. S. GARNETT. Illustrated. *Second Edition. Cr. 8vo. 6s.*
THE CRIMES OF URBAIN GRANDIER AND OTHERS. Illustrated. *Cr. 8vo. 6s.*
THE CRIMES OF THE MARQUISE DE BRINVILLIERS AND OTHERS. Illustrated. *Cr. 8vo. 6s.*
THE CRIMES OF ALI PACHA AND OTHERS. Illustrated. *Cr. 8vo. 6s.*

MY MEMOIRS. Translated by E. M WALLER. With an Introduction by ANDREW LANG. With Frontispieces in Photogravure. In six Volumes. *Cr. 8vo. 6s. each volume.*
VOL. I. 1802-1821. VOL. IV. 1830-1831.
VOL. II. 1822-1825. VOL. V. 1831-1832.
VOL. III 1826-1830. VOL. VI. 1832-1833
MY PETS. Newly translated by A. R. ALLINSON. Illustrated. *Cr. 8vo. 6s.*

Duncan (F. M.). OUR INSECT FRIENDS AND FOES. Illustrated. *Cr. 8vo. 6s.*

Dunn-Pattison (R. P.). NAPOLEON'S MARSHALS. Illustrated. *Demy 8vo. Second Edition.* 12s 6d net.
THE BLACK PRINCE. Illustrated. *Second Edition. Demy 8vo. 7s. 6d. net.*

Durham (The Earl of). THE REPORT ON CANADA. With an Introductory Note. *Demy 8vo. 4s. 6d. net.*

Dutt (W. A.). THE NORFOLK BROADS. Illustrated. *Second Edition. Cr. 8vo. 6s.*

Egerton (H. E). A SHORT HISTORY OF BRITISH COLONIAL POLICY. *Third Edition. Demy 8vo. 7s. 6d. net.*

Evans (Herbert A.). CASTLES OF ENGLAND AND WALES. Illustrated. *Demy 8vo. 12s. 6d. net*

Exeter (Bishop of). REGNUM DEI. (The Bampton Lectures of 1901.) *A Cheaper Edition. Demy 8vo. 7s. 6d. net.*

Ewald (Carl). MY LITTLE BOY. Translated by ALEXANDER TEIXEIRA DE MATTOS. Illustrated. *Fcap. 8vo. 5s.*

Fairbrother (W. H.). THE PHILO-SOPHY OF T. H. GREEN. *Second Edition. Cr. 8vo. 3s. 6d.*

*ffoulkes (Charles). THE ARMOURER AND HIS CRAFT. Illustrated. *Royal 4to. £2 2s. net.*

Firth (C. H.). CROMWELL'S ARMY: A History of the English Soldier during the Civil Wars, the Commonwealth, and the Protectorate. Illustrated. *Second Edition. Cr. 8vo. 6s.*

Fisher (H. A. L.). THE REPUBLICAN TRADITION IN EUROPE. *Cr. 8vo. 6s. net.*

FitzGerald (Edward). THE RUBA'IYAT OF OMAR KHAYYÁM. Printed from the Fifth and last Edition. With a Commentary by H. M. BATSON, and a Biographical Introduction by E. D. ROSS. *Cr. 8vo. 6s.*

Flux (A. W.). ECONOMIC PRINCIPLES. *Demy 8vo. 7s. 6d. net.*

Fraser (J. F). ROUND THE WORLD ON A WHEEL. Illustrated. *Fifth Edition. Cr. 8vo. 6s.*

Galton (Sir Francis). MEMORIES OF MY LIFE. Illustrated. *Third Edition. Demy 8vo. 10s. 6d. net.*

Gibbins (H. de B). INDUSTRY IN ENGLAND: HISTORICAL OUT-LINES. With Maps and Plans. *Seventh Edition, Revised. Demy 8vo. 10s 6d.*
THE INDUSTRIAL HISTORY OF ENGLAND. With 5 Maps and a Plan. *Eighteenth and Revised Edition. Cr. 8vo. 3s.*
ENGLISH SOCIAL REFORMERS. *Second Edition. Cr. 8vo. 2s. 6d.*

Gibbon (Edward). THE MEMOIRS OF THE LIFE OF EDWARD GIBBON. Edited by G. BIRKBECK HILL. *Cr. 8vo. 6s.*
THE DECLINE AND FALL OF THE ROMAN EMPIRE. Edited, with Notes, Appendices, and Maps, by J. B. BURY. Illustrated. *In Seven Volumes. Demy 8vo. Each 10s. 6d. net. Also in Seven Volumes. Cr. 8vo. 6s. each.*

Glover (T. R.). THE CONFLICT OF RELIGIONS IN THE EARLY ROMAN EMPIRE. *Fourth Edition. Demy 8vo. 7s. 6d. net.*

Godley (A. D.). LYRA FRIVOLA. *Fourth Edition. Fcap. 8vo. 2s. 6d.*
VERSES TO ORDER. *Second Edition. Fcap. 8vo. 2s. 6d.*
SECOND STRINGS. *Fcap. 8vo. 2s. 6d.*

Gostling (Frances M.). THE BRETONS AT HOME. Illustrated. *Third Edition. Cr. 8vo. 6s.*
AUVERGNE AND ITS PEOPLE. Illustrated. *Demy 8vo. 10s. 6d. net.*

*Gray (Arthur). CAMBRIDGE AND ITS STORY. Illustrated. *Demy 8vo. 7s. 6d. net.*

Grahame (Kenneth). THE WIND IN THE WILLOWS. Illustrated. *Sixth Edition. Cr. 8vo. 6s.*

Granger (Frank). HISTORICAL SOCI-OLOGY : A TEXT-BOOK OF POLITICS. *Cr. 8vo. 3s. 6d. net.*

Grew (Edwin Sharpe). THE GROWTH OF A PLANET. Illustrated. *Cr. 8vo. 6s.*

Griffin (W. Hall) and Minchin (H. C.). THE LIFE OF ROBERT BROWNING. Illustrated. *Second Edition. Demy 8vo. 12s. 6d. net.*

Hale (J. R.). FAMOUS SEA-FIGHTS: FROM SALAMIS TO TSU-SHIMA. Illustrated. *Cr. 8vo. 6s. net.*

*Hall (H. R.). THE ANCIENT HISTORY OF THE NEAR EAST FROM THE EARLIEST PERIOD TO THE PERSIAN INVASION OF GREECE. Illustrated. *Demy 8vo.* 15s. *net.*

Hannay (D.). A SHORT HISTORY OF THE ROYAL NAVY. Vol. I., 1217-1688. Vol. II., 1689-1815. *Demy 8vo. Each* 7s. 6d. *net.*

Harper (Charles G.). THE AUTOCAR ROAD-BOOK. With Maps. *In Four Volumes. Cr. 8vo. Each* 7s. 6d. *net.*
  Vol. I.—SOUTH OF THE THAMES.
  Vol. II.—NORTH AND SOUTH WALES AND WEST MIDLANDS.
  Vol. III.—EAST ANGLIA AND EAST MIDLANDS.
  * Vol. IV.—THE NORTH OF ENGLAND AND SOUTH OF SCOTLAND.

Harris (Frank). THE WOMEN OF SHAKESPEARE. *Demy 8vo.* 7s. 6d. *net.*

Hassall (Arthur). THE LIFE OF NAPOLEON. Illustrated. *Demy 8vo.* 7s. 6d. *net.*

Headley (F. W.). DARWINISM AND MODERN SOCIALISM. *Second Edition. Cr. 8vo.* 5s. *net.*

Henderson (M. Sturge). GEORGE MEREDITH: NOVELIST, POET, REFORMER. With a Portrait. *Second Edition. Cr. 8vo.* 6s.

Henley (W. E.). ENGLISH LYRICS: CHAUCER TO POE. *Second Edition. Cr. 8vo.* 2s. 6d. *net.*

Hill (George Francis). ONE HUNDRED MASTERPIECES OF SCULPTURE. Illustrated. *Demy 8vo.* 10s. 6d. *net.*

Hind (C. Lewis). DAYS IN CORNWALL. Illustrated. *Third Edition. Cr. 8vo.* 6s.

Hobhouse (L. T.). THE THEORY OF KNOWLEDGE. *Demy 8vo.* 10s. 6d. *net.*

Hobson (J. A.). INTERNATIONAL TRADE: AN APPLICATION OF ECONOMIC THEORY. *Cr. 8vo.* 2s. 6d. *net.*
PROBLEMS OF POVERTY: AN INQUIRY INTO THE INDUSTRIAL CONDITION OF THE POOR. *Seventh Edition. Cr. 8vo.* 2s. 6d.
THE PROBLEM OF THE UNEMPLOYED: AN ENQUIRY AND AN ECONOMIC POLICY. *Fifth Edition. Cr. 8vo.* 2s. 6d.

Hodgson (Mrs W.). HOW TO IDENTIFY OLD CHINESE PORCELAIN. Illustrated. *Third Edition. Post 8vo.* 6s

Holdich (Sir T. H.). THE INDIAN BORDERLAND, 1880-1900. Illustrated. *Second Edition. Demy 8vo.* 10s. 6d. *net*

Holdsworth (W. S.). A HISTORY OF ENGLISH LAW. *In Four Volumes. Vols. I., II., III. Demy 8vo. Each* 10s. 6d. *net.*

Holland (Clive). TYROL AND ITS PEOPLE. Illustrated. *Demy 8vo.* 10s. 6d. *net.*
THE BELGIANS AT HOME. Illustrated. *Demy 8vo.* 10s. 6d. *net.*

Horsburgh (E. L. S.). LORENZO THE MAGNIFICENT: AND FLORENCE IN HER GOLDEN AGE. Illustrated. *Second Edition. Demy 8vo.* 15s. *net.*
WATERLOO: A NARRATIVE AND A CRITICISM. With Plans. *Second Edition. Cr. 8vo.* 5s.
THE LIFE OF SAVONAROLA. Illustrated. *Cr. 8vo.* 5s. *net.*

Hosie (Alexander). MANCHURIA. Illustrated. *Second Edition. Demy 8vo.* 7s. 6d. *net.*

Hudson (W. H.). A SHEPHERD'S LIFE: IMPRESSIONS OF THE SOUTH WILTSHIRE DOWNS. Illustrated. *Third Edition. Demy 8vo.* 7s. 6d. *net.*

Humphreys (John H.). PROPORTIONAL REPRESENTATION. *Cr. 8vo.* 5s. *net.*

Hutchinson (Horace G.). THE NEW FOREST. Illustrated. *Fourth Edition. Cr. 8vo* 6s.

Hutton (Edward). THE CITIES OF SPAIN. Illustrated. *Fourth Edition. Cr. 8vo.* 6s.
THE CITIES OF UMBRIA. Illustrated. *Fourth Edition. Cr. 8vo.* 6s.
* THE CITIES OF LOMBARDY. Illustrated. *Cr. 8vo.* 6s.
FLORENCE AND NORTHERN TUSCANY WITH GENOA. Illustrated. *Second Edition. Cr. 8vo.* 6s.
SIENA AND SOUTHERN TUSCANY. Illustrated. *Second Edition. Cr. 8vo.* 6s.
VENICE AND VENETIA. Illustrated. *Cr. 8vo.* 6s.
ROME. Illustrated. *Third Edition. Cr. 8vo.* 6s.
COUNTRY WALKS ABOUT FLORENCE. Illustrated. *Second Edition. Fcap. 8vo.* 5s. *net.*
IN UNKNOWN TUSCANY. With Notes by WILLIAM HEYWOOD. Illustrated. *Second Edition. Demy 8vo.* 7s. 6d. *net.*
A BOOK OF THE WYE. Illustrated. *Demy 8vo.* 7s. 6d. *net.*

Ibsen (Henrik). BRAND. A Dramatic Poem, Translated by WILLIAM WILSON. *Fourth Edition. Cr. 8vo.* 3s. 6d.

Inge (W. R.). CHRISTIAN MYSTICISM. (The Bampton Lectures of 1899.) *Second and Cheaper Edition. Cr. 8vo.* 5s. *net.*

Innes (A. D.). A HISTORY OF THE BRITISH IN INDIA. With Maps and Plans. *Cr. 8vo.* 6s.
ENGLAND UNDER THE TUDORS. With Maps. *Third Edition. Demy 8vo.* 10s. 6d. net.

Innes (Mary). SCHOOLS OF PAINT-ING. Illustrated. *Second Edition. Cr. 8vo.* 5s. net.

Jenks (E.). AN OUTLINE OF ENG-LISH LOCAL GOVERNMENT. *Second Edition.* Revised by R. C. K. ENSOR, *Cr. 8vo.* 2s. 6d. net.
A SHORT HISTORY OF ENGLISH LAW: FROM THE EARLIEST TIMES TO THE END OF THE YEAR 1911. *Demy 8vo.* 10s. 6d. net.

Jerningham (Charles Edward). THE MAXIMS OF MARMADUKE. *Second Edition. Cr. 8vo.* 5s.

Johnston (Sir H. H.). BRITISH CEN-TRAL AFRICA. Illustrated. *Third Edition. Cr. 4to.* 18s. net.
THE NEGRO IN THE NEW WORLD. Illustrated. *Demy 8vo.* 21s. net.

Julian (Lady) of Norwich. REVELA-TIONS OF DIVINE LOVE. Edited by GRACE WARRACK. *Fourth Edition. Cr. 8vo.* 3s. 6d.

Keats (John). THE POEMS. Edited with Introduction and Notes by E. de SÉLINCOURT. With a Frontispiece in Photogravure. *Third Edition. Demy 8vo.* 7s. 6d. net.

Keble (John). THE CHRISTIAN YEAR. With an Introduction and Notes by W. LOCK. Illustrated. *Third Edition. Fcap. 8vo.* 3s. 6d.

Kempis (Thomas à). THE IMITATION OF CHRIST. From the Latin, with an Introduction by DEAN FARRAR. Illustrated. *Third Edition. Fcap. 8vo.* 3s. 6d.

Kingston (Edward). A GUIDE TO THE BRITISH PICTURES IN THE NATIONAL GALLERY. Illustrated. *Fcap. 8vo.* 3s. 6d. net.

Kipling (Rudyard). BARRACK-ROOM BALLADS. 108th Thousand. *Thirty-first Edition. Cr. 8vo.* 6s. Also *Fcap. 8vo, Leather.* 5s. net.
THE SEVEN SEAS. 89th Thousand. *Nineteenth Edition. Cr. 8vo.* 6s. Also *Fcap. 8vo, Leather.* 5s. net.
THE FIVE NATIONS. 72nd Thousand. *Eighth Edition. Cr. 8vo.* 6s. Also *Fcap. 8vo, Leather.* 5s. net.
DEPARTMENTAL DITTIES. *Twentieth Edition. Cr. 8vo.* 6s. Also *Fcap. 8vo, Leather.* 5s. net.

Lamb (Charles and Mary). THE COMPLETE WORKS. Edited with an Introduction and Notes by E. V. LUCAS. *A New and Revised Edition in Six Volumes.* With Frontispiece. *Fcap 8vo.* 5s. each. The volumes are:—
I. MISCELLANEOUS PROSE. II. ELIA AND THE LAST ESSAYS OF ELIA. III. BOOKS FOR CHILDREN. IV. PLAYS AND POEMS. V. and VI. LETTERS.

Lankester (Sir Ray). SCIENCE FROM AN EASY CHAIR. Illustrated. *Fifth Edition. Cr. 8vo.* 6s.

Le Braz (Anatole). THE LAND OF PARDONS. Translated by FRANCES M. GOSTLING. Illustrated. *Third Edition. Cr. 8vo.* 6s.

Lock (Walter). ST. PAUL, THE MASTER-BUILDER. *Third Edition. Cr. 8vo.* 3s. 6d.
THE BIBLE AND CHRISTIAN LIFE. *Cr. 8vo.* 6s.

Lodge (Sir Oliver). THE SUBSTANCE OF FAITH, ALLIED WITH SCIENCE: A Catechism for Parents and Teachers. *Eleventh Edition. Cr. 8vo.* 2s. net.
MAN AND THE UNIVERSE: A STUDY OF THE INFLUENCE OF THE ADVANCE IN SCIENTIFIC KNOWLEDGE UPON OUR UNDERSTANDING OF CHRISTIANITY. *Ninth Edition. Demy 8vo.* 5s. net. Also *Fcap. 8vo.* 1s. net.
THE SURVIVAL OF MAN. A STUDY IN UNRECOGNISED HUMAN FACULTY. *Fifth Edition. Wide Crown 8vo.* 5s. net.
REASON AND BELIEF. *Fifth Edition. Cr. 8vo.* 3s. 6d. net
*MODERN PROBLEMS. *Cr. 8vo.* 5s. net.

Lorimer (George Horace). LETTERS FROM A SELF-MADE MERCHANT TO HIS SON. Illustrated. *Twenty-second Edition. Cr. 8vo.* 3s. 6d. Also *Fcap. 8vo.* 1s. net.
OLD GORGON GRAHAM. Illustrated. *Second Edition. Cr. 8vo.* 6s.

Lucas (E. V.). THE LIFE OF CHARLES LAMB. Illustrated. *Fifth Edition. Demy 8vo.* 7s. 6d. net.
A WANDERER IN HOLLAND. Illustrated *Thirteenth Edition. Cr. 8vo.* 6s.
A WANDERER IN LONDON. Illustrated. *Twelfth Edition. Cr. 8vo.* 6s.
A WANDERER IN PARIS. Illustrated. *Ninth Edition. Cr. 8vo.* 6s. Also *Fcap. 8vo.* 5s.
*A WANDERER IN FLORENCE. Illustrated. *Cr. 8vo.* 6s.
THE OPEN ROAD: A Little Book for Wayfarers. *Eighteenth Edition. Fcap. 8vo.* 5s.; *India Paper,* 7s. 6d.
*Also Illustrated in colour. *Cr. 4to* 15s. net.

THE FRIENDLY TOWN : A Little Book for the Urbane. *Sixth Edition. Fcap. 8vo.* 5s. ; *India Paper,* 7s. 6d.
FIRESIDE AND SUNSHINE. *Sixth Edition. Fcap. 8vo.* 5s.
CHARACTER AND COMEDY. *Sixth Edition. Fcap. 8vo.* 5s.
THE GENTLEST ART. A Choice of Letters by Entertaining Hands. *Seventh Edition. Fcap 8vo.* 5s.
THE SECOND POST. *Third Edition. Fcap. 8vo.* 5s.
HER INFINITE VARIETY : A FEMININE PORTRAIT GALLERY. *Sixth Edition. Fcap. 8vo.* 5s.
GOOD COMPANY : A RALLY OF MEN. *Second Edition. Fcap. 8vo.* 5s.
ONE DAY AND ANOTHER. *Fifth Edition Fcap. 8vo.* 5s.
OLD LAMPS FOR NEW. *Fourth Edition. Fcap. 8vo.* 5s.
LISTENER'S LURE : AN OBLIQUE NARRATION. *Ninth Edition. Fcap. 8vo.* 5s.
OVER BEMERTON'S : AN EASY-GOING CHRONICLE. *Ninth Edition. Fcap. 8vo.* 5s.
MR. INGLESIDE. *Ninth Edition. Fcap. 8vo.* 5s.
See also Lamb (Charles).

Lydekker (R. and Others). REPTILES, AMPHIBIA, FISHES, AND LOWER CHORDATA. Edited by J. C. CUNNINGHAM. Illustrated. *Demy 8vo.* 10s. 6d *net.*

Lydekker (R.). THE OX AND ITS KINDRED. Illustrated. *Cr. 8vo.* 6s.

Macaulay (Lord). CRITICAL AND HISTORICAL ESSAYS. Edited by F. C. MONTAGUE. *Three Volumes. Cr. 8vo.* 18s.

McCabe (Joseph). THE DECAY OF THE CHURCH OF ROME. *Third Edition. Demy 8vo.* 7s. 6d. *net.*
THE EMPRESSES OF ROME. Illustrated. *Demy 8vo.* 12s. 6d. *net.*

MacCarthy (Desmond) and Russell (Agatha). LADY JOHN RUSSELL: A MEMOIR. Illustrated. *Fourth Edition. Demy 8vo.* 10s 6d. *net.*

McCullagh (Francis): THE FALL OF ABD-UL-HAMID. Illustrated. *Demy 8vo.* 10s. 6d. *net.*

McDougall (William). AN INTRODUCTION TO SOCIAL PSYCHOLOGY. *Fourth Edition. Cr. 8vo.* 5s. *net.*
BODY AND MIND : A HISTORY AND A DEFENCE OF ANIMISM. *Demy 8vo.* 10s. 6d. *net.*

*Mdlle. Merl'(Author of). ST. CATHERINE OF SIENA AND HER TIMES. Illustrated. *Second Edition. Demy 8vo.* 7s. 6d. *net.*

Maeterlinck (Maurice). THE BLUE BIRD : A FAIRY PLAY IN SIX ACTS. Translated by ALEXANDER TEIXEIRA DE MATTOS. *Fcap. 8vo. Deckle Edges.* 3s. 6d. net. *Also Fcap. 8vo. Cloth,* 1s. net. An Edition, illustrated in colour by F. CAYLEY ROBINSON, is also published. *Cr. 4to. Gilt top.* 21s. *net.* Of the above book Twenty-nine Editions in all have been issued.
MARY MAGDALENE : A PLAY IN THREE ACTS. Translated by ALEXANDER TEIXEIRA DE MATTOS. *Third Edition. Fcap. 8vo. Deckle Edges.* 3s. 6d. net. *Also Fcap. 8vo.* 1s. *net.*
DEATH. Translated by ALEXANDER TEIXEIRA DE MATTOS. *Fourth Edition. Fcap. 8vo.* 3s. 6d. *net.*

Mahaffy (J. P.). A HISTORY OF EGYPT UNDER THE PTOLEMAIC DYNASTY. Illustrated. *Cr. 8vo.* 6s.

Maitland (F. W.). ROMAN CANON LAW IN THE CHURCH OF ENGLAND. *Royal 8vo.* 7s. 6d.

Marett (R. R.). THE THRESHOLD OF RELIGION. *Cr. 8vo.* 3s. 6d. *net.*

Marriott (Charles). A SPANISH HOLIDAY. Illustrated. *Demy 8vo.* 7s. 6d. *net.*
THE ROMANCE OF THE RHINE. Illustrated. *Demy 8vo.* 10s. 6d. *net.*

Marriott (J. A. R.). THE LIFE AND TIMES OF LUCIUS CARY, VISCOUNT FALKLAND. Illustrated. *Second Edition. Demy 8vo.* 7s. 6d. *net.*

Masefield (John). SEA LIFE IN NELSON'S TIME. Illustrated. *Cr. 8vo.* 3s. 6d. *net.*
A SAILOR'S GARLAND. Selected and Edited. *Second Edition. Cr. 8vo.* 3s. 6d. *net.*

Masterman (C. F. G.). TENNYSON AS A RELIGIOUS TEACHER. *Second Edition. Cr. 8vo.* 6s.
THE CONDITION OF ENGLAND. *Fourth Edition. Cr. 8vo.* 6s. *Also Fcap. 8vo.* 1s. *net.*

*Mayne (Ethel Colburn). BYRON. Illustrated. *In two volumes. Demy 8vo.* 21s. *net.*

Medley (D. J.). ORIGINAL ILLUSTRATIONS OF ENGLISH CONSTITUTIONAL HISTORY. *Cr. 8vo.* 7s. 6d. *net.*

Methuen (A. M. S.). ENGLAND'S RUIN : DISCUSSED IN FOURTEEN LETTERS TO A PROTECTIONIST. *Ninth Edition. Cr. 8vo.* 3d. *net.*

Miles (Eustace). LIFE AFTER LIFE: OR, THE THEORY OF REINCARNATION. *Cr. 8vo* 2s. 6d. *net.*
THE POWER OF CONCENTRATION : HOW TO ACQUIRE IT. *Fourth Edition. Cr. 8vo.* 3s. 6d. *net.*

Millais (J. G.). THE LIFE AND LET-TERS OF SIR JOHN EVERETT MILLAIS. - Illustrated. - *New Edition. Demy 8vo.* 7s. 6d. net.

Milne (J. G.). A HISTORY OF EGYPT UNDER ROMAN RULE. Illustrated. *Cr. 8vo.* 6s.

Moffat (Mary M.). QUEEN LOUISA OF PRUSSIA. Illustrated *Fourth Edition. Cr. 8vo.* 6s.
MARIA THERESA. Illustrated. *Demy 8vo.* 10s. 6d. net.

Money (L. G. Chiozza). RICHES AND POVERTY, 1910. *Tenth and Revised Edition. Demy 8vo.* 5s. net.
MONEY'S FISCAL DICTIONARY, 1910. *Second Edition. Demy 8vo.* 5s. net.
INSURANCE VERSUS POVERTY. *Cr. 8vo.* 5s. net.
THINGS THAT MATTER: PAPERS ON SUBJECTS WHICH ARE, OR OUGHT TO BE, UNDER DISCUSSION. *Demy 8vo.* 5s. net.

Montague (C. E.). DRAMATIC VALUES. *Second Edition. Fcap. 8vo.* 5s.

Moorhouse (E. Hallam). NELSON'S LADY HAMILTON. Illustrated. *Third Edition. Demy 8vo.* 7s. 6d. net.

*****Morgan (C. Lloyd).** INSTINCT AND EXPERIENCE. *Cr. 8vo.* 5s. net.

*****Nevill (Lady Dorothy).** MY OWN TIMES. Edited by her son. *Demy 8vo.* 15s. net.

Norway (A. H.). NAPLES: PAST AND PRESENT. Illustrated. *Fourth Edition. Cr. 8vo.* 6s.

*****O'Donnell (Elliott).** WEREWOLVES *Cr. 8vo.* 5s. net.

Oman (C. W. C.), A HISTORY OF THE ART OF WAR IN THE MIDDLE AGES. Illustrated. *Demy 8vo.* 10s. 6d. net.
ENGLAND BEFORE THE NORMAN CONQUEST. With Maps. *Second Edition. Demy 8vo.* 10s. 6d. net.

Oxford (M. N.). A HANDBOOK OF NURSING. *Sixth Edition, Revised. Cr. 8vo.* 3s. 6d. net.

Pakes (W. C. C.). THE SCIENCE OF HYGIENE. Illustrated. *Second and Cheaper Edition.* Revised by A. T. NANKIVELL. *Cr. 8vo.* 5s. net.

Parker (Eric). THE BOOK OF THE ZOO. Illustrated. *Second Edition. Cr. 8vo.* 6s.

Pears (Sir Edwin). TURKEY AND ITS PEOPLE. *Second Edition. Demy 8vo.* 12s. 6d. net.

Petrie (W. M. Flinders). A HISTORY OF EGYPT. Illustrated. *In Six Volumes. Cr. 8vo.* 6s. each.
VOL. I. FROM THE 1ST TO THE XVITH DYNASTY. *Seventh Edition.*
VOL. II. THE XVIITH AND XVIIITH DYNASTIES *Fourth Edition.*
VOL. III. XIXTH TO XXXTH DYNASTIES.
VOL. IV. EGYPT UNDER THE PTOLEMAIC DYNASTY. J. P. MAHAFFY.
VOL. V. EGYPT UNDER ROMAN RULE. J. G. MILNE.
VOL. VI. EGYPT IN THE MIDDLE AGES. STANLEY LANE-POOLE.
RELIGION AND CONSCIENCE IN ANCIENT EGYPT. Illustrated. *Cr. 8vo.* 2s. 6d.
SYRIA AND EGYPT, FROM THE TELL EL AMARNA LETTERS. *Cr. 8vo.* 2s. 6d.
EGYPTIAN TALES. Translated from the Papyri. First Series, ivth to xiith Dynasty. Illustrated. *Second Edition. Cr. 8vo.* 3s. 6d.
EGYPTIAN TALES. Translated from the Papyri. Second Series, xviiith to xixth Dynasty. Illustrated. *Cr. 8vo.* 3s. 6d.
EGYPTIAN DECORATIVE ART. Illustrated. *Cr. 8vo.* 3s. 6d.

Phelps (Ruth S.). SKIES ITALIAN: A LITTLE BREVIARY FOR TRAVELLERS IN ITALY. *Fcap. 8vo. Leather.* 5s. net.

Pollard (Alfred W.). SHAKESPEARE FOLIOS AND QUARTOS. A Study in the Bibliography of Shakespeare's Plays, 1594-1685. Illustrated. *Folio.* 21s. net.

Porter (G. R.). THE PROGRESS OF THE NATION. A New Edition. Edited by F. W. HIRST. *Demy 8vo.* 21s. net.

Power (J. O'Connor). THE MAKING OF AN ORATOR. *Cr. 8vo.* 6s.

Price (Eleanor C.). CARDINAL DE RICHELIEU. Illustrated. *Second Edition. Demy 8vo.* 10s. 6d. net.

Price (L. L.), A SHORT HISTORY OF POLITICAL ECONOMY IN ENGLAND FROM ADAM SMITH TO ARNOLD TOYNBEE. *Seventh Edition. Cr. 8vo.* 2s. 6d.

Pycraft (W. P.). A HISTORY OF BIRDS. Illustrated. *Demy 8vo.* 10s. 6d. net.

Rawlings (Gertrude B.). COINS AND HOW TO KNOW THEM. Illustrated. *Third Edition. Cr. 8vo.* 6s.

Regan (C. Tate). THE FRESHWATER FISHES OF THE BRITISH ISLES. Illustrated. *Cr. 8vo.* 6s.

Reid (Archdall). THE LAWS OF HERE-DITY. *Second Edition. Demy 8vo.* 21s. net.

Robertson (C. Grant). SELECT STAT-
UTES, CASES, AND DOCUMENTS,
1660–1894. *Demy 8vo.* 10s. 6d *net.*
ENGLAND UNDER THE HANOVER-
IANS. Illustrated. *Second Edition. Demy
8vo.* 10s. 6d. *net.*

Roe (Fred). OLD OAK FURNITURE.
Illustrated. *Second Edition. Demy 8vo.*
10s 6d. *net.*

*Ryan (P. F. W.). STUART LIFE AND
MANNERS; A SOCIAL HISTORY. Illustrated. *Demy 8vo.* 10s. 6d. *net.*

St. Francis of Assisi. THE LITTLE
FLOWERS OF THE GLORIOUS
MESSER, AND OF HIS FRIARS.
Done into English, with Notes by WILLIAM
HEYWOOD. Illustrated. *Demy 8vo.* 5s. *net.*

'Saki' (H. H. Munro). REGINALD.
Third Edition. Fcap. 8vo. 2s. 6d *net.*
REGINALD IN RUSSIA. *Fcap. 8vo.*
2s. 6d. *net.*

Sandeman (G. A. C.). METTERNICH.
Illustrated. *Demy 8vo.* 10s. 6d. *net.*

Schidrowitz (Philip). RUBBER. Illustrated. *Demy 8vo.* 10s. 6d. *net.*

Selous (Edmund). TOMMY SMITH'S
ANIMALS. Illustrated. *Eleventh Edi-
tion. Fcap. 8vo.* 2s. 6d.
TOMMY SMITH'S OTHER ANIMALS.
Illustrated. *Fifth Edition. Fcap. 8vo.*
2s. 6d.
JACK'S INSECTS. Illustrated. *Cr. 8vo.* 6s.

Shakespeare (William).
THE FOUR FOLIOS. 1623; 1632; 1664;
1685. Each £4 4s. *net,* or a complete set,
£12 12s. *net.*
THE POEMS OF WILLIAM SHAKE-
SPEARE. With an Introduction and Notes
by GEORGE WYNDHAM. *Demy 8vo. Buckram.* 10s. 6d.

Shelley (Percy Bysshe). THE POEMS
OF PERCY BYSSHE SHELLEY. With
an Introduction by A. CLUTTON-BROCK and
notes by C. D. LOCOCK. *Two Volumes.
Demy 8vo.* 21s. *net.*

Sladen (Douglas). SICILY: The New
Winter Resort. Illustrated. *Second Edition.
Cr. 8vo.* 5s. *net.*

Smith (Adam). THE WEALTH OF
NATIONS. Edited by EDWIN CANNAN.
Two Volumes. Demy 8vo. 21s. *net.*

Smith (G. Herbert). GEM-STONES
AND THEIR DISTINCTIVE CHARAC-
TERS. Illustrated. *Cr. 8vo.* 6s. *net.*

Snell (F. J). A BOOK OF EXMOOR.
Illustrated. *Cr. 8vo.* 6s.
THE CUSTOMS OF OLD ENGLAND.
Illustrated. *Cr. 8vo.* 6s.

'Stancliffe.' GOLF DO'S AND DONT'
Fourth Edition. Fcap. 8vo. 1s. *net.*

Stevenson (R. L.). THE LETTERS C
ROBERT LOUIS STEVENSON. Edit
by Sir SIDNEY COLVIN. A New and E
larged Edition in four volumes. The
Edition. *Fcap. 8vo.* Each 5s. Leathe
each 5s. *net.*

Stevenson (M. L.). FROM SARAN
TO THE MARQUESAS AND BEYON
Being Letters written by Mrs. M. I. STEVE
SON during 1887–88. Illustrated. *Cr. 8:*
6s. *net.*
LETTERS FROM SAMOA, 1891-95. Edit
and arranged by M. C. BALFOUR. Ill
trated. *Second Edition. Cr. 8vo.* 6s. *n*

Storr (Vernon F.). DEVELOPMEN
AND DIVINE PURPOSE. *Cr. 8vo.*
net

Streatfeild (R A.). MODERN MUS
AND MUSICIANS. Illustrated. *Seco
Edition. Demy 8vo.* 7s. 6d. *net.*

Swanton (E. W.). FUNGI AND HO
TO KNOW THEM. Illustrated. *Cr. 8:*
6s *net.*

Symes (J E.). THE FRENCH REV
LUTION. *Second Edition. Cr. 8vo.* 2s.

Tabor (Margaret E.) THE SAINTS I
ART. Illustrated. *Fcap. 8vo.* 3s. 6d. *r*

Taylor (A E). ELEMENTS OF MET
PHYSICS. *Second Edition. Demy 8
10s 6d. *net.*

Taylor (Mrs. Basil) (Harriet Osgoo
JAPANESE GARDENS. Illustra
Cr. 4to. 21s. *net.*

Thibaudeau (A. C.). BONAPARTE AI
THE CONSULATE. Translated a
Edited by G. K. FORTESCUE. Illustrat
Demy 8vo. 10s. 6d. *net.*

Thomas (Edward). MAURICE MA
TERLINCK. Illustrated. *Second Editi
Cr. 8vo.* 5s. *net.*

Thompson (Francis). SELECTF
POEMS OF FRANCIS THOMPSO
With a Biographical Note by WILF
MEYNELL. With a Portrait in Photogravu
Seventh Edition. Fcap. 8vo. 5s. *net.*

Tileston (Mary W.). DAILY STRENG
FOR DAILY NEEDS Nineteenth E
tion. Medium 16mo. 2s. 6d net. La
skin 3s. 6d. net. Also an edition in super
binding, 6s.
THE STRONGHOLD OF HOP
Medium 16mo. 2s. 6d. *net.*

Toynbee (Paget). DANTE ALIGHIE
His LIFE AND WORKS. With 16 Illust
tions. *Fourth and Enlarged Edition.
8vo.* 5s. *net.*

Trevelyan (G M.). ENGLAND UNDER THE STUARTS. With Maps and Plans. *Fifth Edition. Demy 8vo.* 10s. 6d. *net.*

Triggs (H. Inigo). TOWN PLANNING: PAST, PRESENT, AND POSSIBLE. Illustrated. *Second Edition. Wide Royal 8vo.* 15s. *net.*

*Turner (Sir Alfred E.).** SIXTY YEARS OF A SOLDIER'S LIFE. *Demy 8vo.* 12s. 6d. *net.*

Underhill (Evelyn). MYSTICISM. A Study in the Nature and Development of Man's Spiritual Consciousness. *Fourth Edition. Demy 8vo.* 15s. *net.*

*Underwood (F. M.).** UNITED ITALY. *Demy 8vo.* 10s. 6d. *net.*

Urwick (E. J.). A PHILOSOPHY OF SOCIAL PROGRESS. *Cr. 8vo.* 6s.

Vaughan (Herbert M.). THE NAPLES RIVIERA. Illustrated. *Second Edition. Cr. 8vo.* 6s.
FLORENCE AND HER TREASURES. Illustrated. *Fcap. 8vo. Round corners.* 5s. *net.*

Vernon (Hon. W. Warren). READINGS ON THE INFERNO OF DANTE. With an Introduction by the REV. DR. MOORE. *Two Volumes. Second Edition. Cr. 8vo.* 15s. *net.*
READINGS ON THE PURGATORIO OF DANTE. With an Introduction by the late DEAN CHURCH. *Two Volumes. Third Edition. Cr. 8vo.* 15s. *net.*
READINGS ON THE PARADISO OF DANTE. With an Introduction by the BISHOP OF RIPON. *Two Volumes. Second Edition. Cr. 8vo.* 15s. *net.*

Wade (G. W.), and Wade (J. H.). RAMBLES IN SOMERSET. Illustrated. *Cr. 8vo.* 6s.

Waddell (L. A.). LHASA AND ITS MYSTERIES. With a Record of the Expedition of 1903-1904. Illustrated. *Third and Cheaper Edition. Medium 8vo.* 7s. 6d. *net.*

Wagner (Richard). RICHARD WAGNER'S MUSIC DRAMAS: Interpretations, embodying Wagner's own explanations. By ALICE LEIGHTON CLEATHER and BASIL CRUMP. *Fcap. 8vo.* 2s. 6d. *each.*
THE RING OF THE NIBELUNG.
Fifth Edition.
PARSIFAL, LOHENGRIN, AND THE HOLY GRAIL.
TRISTAN AND ISOLDE.
TANNHAUSER AND THE MASTERSINGERS OF NUREMBERG.

Waterhouse (Elizabeth). WITH THE SIMPLE-HEARTED: Little Homilies to Women in Country Places. *Third Edition. Small Pott 8vo.* 2s. *net.*
THE HOUSE BY THE CHERRY TREE. A Second Series of Little Homilies to Women in Country Places. *Small Pott 8vo.* 2s. *net.*
COMPANIONS OF THE WAY. Being Selections for Morning and Evening Reading. Chosen and arranged by ELIZABETH WATERHOUSE. *Large Cr. 8vo.* 5s. *net.*
THOUGHTS OF A TERTIARY. *Small Pott 8vo.* 1s. *net.*

Waters (W. G.). ITALIAN SCULPTORS AND SMITHS. Illustrated. *Cr. 8vo.* 7s. 6d. *net.*

Watt (Francis). EDINBURGH AND THE LOTHIANS. Illustrated. *Second Edition. Cr. 8vo.* 10s. 6d. *net.*

*Wedmore (Sir Frederick).** MEMORIES. *Demy 8vo.* 7s. 6d. *net.*

Weigall (Arthur E. P.). A GUIDE TO THE ANTIQUITIES OF UPPER EGYPT: From Abydos to the Sudan Frontier. Illustrated. *Cr. 8vo.* 7s. 6d. *net.*

Welch (Catharine). THE LITTLE DAUPHIN. Illustrated. *Cr. 8vo.* 6s.

Wells (J.). OXFORD AND OXFORD LIFE. *Third Edition. Cr. 8vo.* 3s. 6d.
A SHORT HISTORY OF ROME. *Eleventh Edition.* With 3 Maps. *Cr. 8vo.* 3s. 6d.

Wilde (Oscar). THE WORKS OF OSCAR WILDE. *In Twelve Volumes. Fcap. 8vo.* 5s. *net each volume.*
I. LORD ARTHUR SAVILE'S CRIME AND THE PORTRAIT OF MR. W. H. II. THE DUCHESS OF PADUA. III. POEMS. IV. LADY WINDERMERE'S FAN. V. A WOMAN OF NO IMPORTANCE. VI. AN IDEAL HUSBAND. VII. THE IMPORTANCE OF BEING EARNEST. VIII. A HOUSE OF POMEGRANATES. IX. INTENTIONS. X. DE PROFUNDIS AND PRISON LETTERS. XI. ESSAYS. XII. SALOMÉ, A FLORENTINE TRAGEDY, and LA SAINTE COURTISANE.

Williams (H. Noel). THE WOMEN BONAPARTES. The Mother and three Sisters of Napoleon. Illustrated. *Two Volumes. Demy 8vo.* 24s. *net.*
A ROSE OF SAVOY: MARIE ADÉLAÏDE OF SAVOY, DUCHESSE DE BOURGOGNE, MOTHER OF LOUIS XV. Illustrated. *Second Edition. Demy 8vo.* 15s. *net.*
THE FASCINATING DUC DE RICHELIEU: LOUIS FRANÇOIS ARMAND DU PLESSIS (1696-1788). Illustrated. *Demy 8vo.* 15s. *net.*
A PRINCESS OF ADVENTURE: MARIE CAROLINE, DUCHESSE DE BERRY (1798-1870). Illustrated. *Demy 8vo.* 15s. *net.*

Wood (Sir Evelyn). FROM MIDSHIP-MAN TO FIELD-MARSHAL. 'Illustrated. *Fifth Edition. Demy 8vo.* 7s. 6d. net. *Also Fcap. 8vo.* 1s. net.
THE REVOLT IN HINDUSTAN (1857-59). Illustrated. *Second Edition. Cr. 8vo.* 6s.

Wood (W. Birkbeck), and Edmonds (Col. J. E.). A HISTORY OF THE CIVIL WAR IN THE UNITED STATES (1861-5). With an Introduction by SPENSER WILKINSON. With 24 Maps and Plans. *Third Edition. Demy 8vo.* 12s. 6d. net.

Wordsworth (W.). THE POEMS. Wi an Introduction and Notes by Nowe C. SMITH. *In Three Volumes. Demy 8* 15s. net.

Yeats (W. B.). A BOOK OF IRIS VERSE. *Third Edition. Cr. 8vo.* 3s. 6

PART II.—A SELECTION OF SERIES.

Ancient Cities.

General Editor, B. C. A. WINDLE.

Cr. 8vo. 4s. 6d. *net each volume.*

With Illustrations by E. H. NEW, and other Artists.

BRISTOL. Alfred Harvey.
CANTERBURY. J. C. Cox.
CHESTER. B. C. A. Windle.
DUBLIN. S. A. O. Fitzpatrick.

EDINBURGH. M. G. Williamson.
LINCOLN. E. Mansel Sympson.
SHREWSBURY. T. Auden.
WELLS and GLASTONBURY. T. S. Holmes.

The Antiquary's Books.

General Editor, J. CHARLES COX

Demy 8vo. 7s. 6d. *net each volume.*

With Numerous Illustrations.

ARCHÆOLOGY AND FALSE ANTIQUITIES. R. Munro.
BELLS OF ENGLAND, THE. Canon J. J. Raven. *Second Edition.*
BRASSES OF ENGLAND, THE. Herbert W. Macklin. *Second Edition.*
CELTIC ART IN PAGAN AND CHRISTIAN TIMES. J. Romilly Allen. *Second Edition.*
CASTLES AND WALLED TOWNS OF ENGLAND, THE. A. Harvey.
DOMESDAY INQUEST, THE. Adolphus Ballard.
ENGLISH CHURCH FURNITURE. J. C. Cox and A. Harvey. *Second Edition.*
ENGLISH COSTUME. From Prehistoric Times to the End of the Eighteenth Century. George Clinch.
ENGLISH MONASTIC LIFE. Abbot Gasquet. *Fourth Edition.*
ENGLISH SEALS. J. Harvey Bloom.
FOLK-LORE AS AN HISTORICAL SCIENCE. Sir G. L. Gomme.
GILDS AND COMPANIES OF LONDON, THE. George Unwin.

MANOR AND MANORIAL RECORDS, TH Nathaniel J. Hone. *Second Edition.*
MEDIÆVAL HOSPITALS OF ENGLAND, TH Rotha Mary Clay.
OLD ENGLISH INSTRUMENTS OF MUS F. W. Galpin. *Second Edition.*
OLD ENGLISH LIBRARIES. James Hutt.
OLD SERVICE BOOKS OF THE ENGLI CHURCH. Christopher Wordsworth, a Henry Littlehales. *Second Edition.*
PARISH LIFE IN MEDIÆVAL ENGLAN Abbot Gasquet. *Third Edition.*
PARISH REGISTERS OF ENGLAND, TH J. C. Cox.
REMAINS OF THE PREHISTORIC AGE ENGLAND. B. C. A. Windle. *Seco Edition.*
ROMAN ERA IN BRITAIN, THE. J. Ward.
ROMANO-BRITISH BUILDINGS AND EART WORKS. J. Ward.
ROYAL FORESTS OF ENGLAND, THE. J. Cox.
SHRINES OF BRITISH SAINTS. J. C. Wall.

The Arden Shakespeare.

Demy 8vo. 2s. 6d. net each volume.

An edition of Shakespeare in single Plays; each edited with a full Introduction, Textual Notes, and a Commentary at the foot of the page.

ALL'S WELL THAT ENDS WELL.
ANTONY AND CLEOPATRA.
CYMBELINE.
COMEDY OF ERRORS, THE.
HAMLET. *Third Edition.*
JULIUS CAESAR.
*KING HENRY IV. PT. I.
KING HENRY V.
KING HENRY VI. PT. I.
KING HENRY VI. PT. II.
KING HENRY VI. PT. III.
KING LEAR.
*KING RICHARD II.
KING RICHARD III.
LIFE AND DEATH OF KING JOHN, THE.
LOVE'S LABOUR'S LOST.
MACBETH.

MEASURE FOR MEASURE.
MERCHANT OF VENICE, THE.
MERRY WIVES OF WINDSOR, THE.
MIDSUMMER NIGHT'S DREAM, A.
OTHELLO.
PERICLES.
ROMEO AND JULIET.
TAMING OF THE SHREW, THE.
TEMPEST, THE.
TIMON OF ATHENS.
TITUS ANDRONICUS.
TROILUS AND CRESSIDA.
TWO GENTLEMEN OF VERONA, THE.
TWELFTH NIGHT.
VENUS AND ADONIS.
*WINTER'S TALE, THE.

Classics of Art.

Edited by DR. J. H. W. LAING.

With numerous Illustrations. Wide Royal 8vo.

THE ART OF THE GREEKS. H. B. Walters. 12s. 6d. net.
THE ART OF THE ROMANS. H. B. Walters. 15s. net.
CHARDIN. H. E. A. Furst. 12s. 6d. net.
DONATELLO. Maud Cruttwell. 15s. net.
FLORENTINE SCULPTORS OF THE RENAISSANCE. Wilhelm Bode. Translated by Jessie Haynes. 12s. 6d. net.
GEORGE ROMNEY. Arthur B. Chamberlain. 12s. 6d. net.
GHIRLANDAIO. Gerald S. Davies. *Second Edition.* 10s. 6d.

MICHELANGELO. Gerald S. Davies. 12s. 6d. net.
RUBENS. Edward Dillon, 25s. net.
RAPHAEL. A. P. Oppé. 12s. 6d. net.
REMBRANDT'S ETCHINGS. A. M. Hind.
*SIR THOMAS LAWRENCE. Sir Walter Armstrong. 21s. net.
TITIAN. Charles Ricketts. 15s. net.
TINTORETTO. Evelyn March Phillipps. 15s. net.
TURNER'S SKETCHES AND DRAWINGS. A. J. Finberg. 12s. 6d. net. *Second Edition.*
VELAZQUEZ. A. de Beruete. 10s. 6d. net.

The "Complete" Series.

Fully Illustrated. Demy 8vo.

THE COMPLETE BILLIARD PLAYER. Charles Roberts. 10s. 6d. net.
THE COMPLETE COOK. Lilian Whitling. 7s. 6d. net.
THE COMPLETE CRICKETER. Albert E. Knight. 7s. 6d. net. *Second Edition.*
THE COMPLETE FOXHUNTER. Charles Richardson. 12s. 6d. net. *Second Edition.*
THE COMPLETE GOLFER. Harry Vardon. 10s. 6d. net. *Twelfth Edition.*
THE COMPLETE HOCKEY-PLAYER. Eustace E. White. 5s. net. *Second Edition.*
THE COMPLETE LAWN TENNIS PLAYER. A. Wallis Myers. 10s. 6d. net. *Third Edition, Revised.*
THE COMPLETE MOTORIST. Filson Young. 12s. 6d. net. *New Edition (Seventh).*

THE COMPLETE MOUNTAINEER. G. D. Abraham. 15s. net. *Second Edition.*
THE COMPLETE OARSMAN. R. C. Lehmann. 10s. 6d. net.
THE COMPLETE PHOTOGRAPHER. R. Child Bayley. 10s. 6d. net. *Fourth Edition.*
THE COMPLETE RUGBY FOOTBALLER, ON THE NEW ZEALAND SYSTEM. D. Gallaher and W. J. Stead. 10s. 6d. net. *Second Edition.*
THE COMPLETE SHOT. G. T. Teasdale-Buckell. 12s. 6d. net. *Third Edition.*
THE COMPLETE SWIMMER. F. Sachs. 7s. 6d. net.
*THE COMPLETE YACHTSMAN. B. Heckstall-Smith and E. du Boulay. 15s. net.

The Connoisseur's Library.

With numerous Illustrations.   Wide Royal 8vo.   25s. net each volume.

ENGLISH FURNITURE. F. S. Robinson.

ENGLISH COLOURED BOOKS. Martin Hardie.

ETCHINGS. Sir F. Wedmore. *Second Edition.*

EUROPEAN ENAMELS. Henry H. Cunyng-
hame.

GLASS. Edward Dillon.

GOLDSMITHS' AND SILVERSMITHS' WORK.
Nelson Dawson. *Second Edition.*

ILLUMINATED MANUSCRIPTS. J. A. Herbert.
Second Edition.

IVORIES. Alfred Maskell.

JEWELLERY.   H. Clifford Smith.   *Secon*
Edition.

MEZZOTINTS. Cyril Davenport.

MINIATURES. Dudley Heath.

PORCELAIN. Edward Dillon.

*FINE BOOKS. A. W. Pollard.

SEALS. Walter de Gray Birch.

WOOD SCULPTURE. Alfred Maskell. *Secon*
Edition.

Handbooks of English Church History.

Edited by J. H. BURN.   Crown 8vo.   2s. 6d. net each volume.

THE FOUNDATIONS OF THE ENGLISH CHURCH.
J. H. Maude.

THE SAXON CHURCH AND THE NORMAN CON-
QUEST. C. T. Cruttwell.

THE MEDIÆVAL CHURCH AND THE PAPACY.
A. C. Jennings.

THE REFORMATION PERIOD. Henry Gee.

THE STRUGGLE WITH PURITANISM. Bru
Blaxland.

THE CHURCH OF ENGLAND IN THE EIG
TEENTH CENTURY. Alfred Plummer.

Handbooks of Theology.

THE DOCTRINE OF THE INCARNATION. R. L.
Ottley. *Fifth Edition, Revised. Demy*
8vo. 12s. 6d.

A HISTORY OF EARLY CHRISTIAN DOCTRINE.
J. F. Bethune-Baker. *Demy 8vo. 10s 6d.*

AN INTRODUCTION TO THE HISTORY OF
RELIGION. F. B. Jevons. *Fifth Edition.*
Demy 8vo. 10s. 6d.

AN INTRODUCTION TO THE HISTORY OF TH
CREEDS. A. E. Burn. *Demy 8vo. 10s 6*

THE PHILOSOPHY OF RELIGION IN ENGLAN
AND AMERICA. Alfred Caldecott. *Demy 8v*
10s. 6d.

THE XXXIX ARTICLES OF THE CHURCH O
ENGLAND. Edited by E. C. S. Gibso
Seventh Edition. Demy 8vo. 12s. 6d.

The "Home Life" Series.

Illustrated.   Demy 8vo.   6s. to 10s. 6d. net.

HOME LIFE IN AMERICA.   Katherine G.
Busbey. *Second Edition.*

HOME LIFE IN FRANCE.   Miss Betham-
Edwards. *Fifth Edition.*

HOME LIFE IN GERMANY. Mrs. A. Sidgwick.
Second Edition.

HOME LIFE IN HOLLAND. D. S. Meldrum.
Second Edition.

HOME LIFE IN ITALY. Lina Duff Gordo
Second Edition.

HOME LIFE IN NORWAY.   H. K. Daniel

HOME LIFE IN RUSSIA. Dr. A. S. Rappopor

HOME LIFE IN SPAIN.   S. L. Bensusa
Second Edition.

The Illustrated Pocket Library of Plain and Coloured Books.

Fcap. 8vo. `3s. 6d. net each volume.*

WITH COLOURED ILLUSTRATIONS.

OLD COLOURED BOOKS. George Paston. 2s. net.

THE LIFE AND DEATH OF JOHN MYTTON, ESQ. Nimrod. *Fifth Edition.*

THE LIFE OF A SPORTSMAN. Nimrod.

HANDLEY CROSS. R. S. Surtees. *Fourth Edition.*

MR. SPONGE'S SPORTING TOUR. R. S. Surtees. *Second Edition.*

JORROCKS'S JAUNTS AND JOLLITIES. R. S. Surtees. *Third Edition.*

ASK MAMMA. R. S. Surtees.

THE ANALYSIS OF THE HUNTING FIELD. R. S. Surtees.

THE TOUR OF DR. SYNTAX IN SEARCH OF THE PICTURESQUE. William Combe

THE TOUR OF DR. SYNTAX IN SEARCH OF CONSOLATION. William Combe.

THE THIRD TOUR OF DR. SYNTAX IN SEARCH OF A WIFE. William Combe.

THE HISTORY OF JOHNNY QUAE GENUS. The Author of 'The Three Tours.'

THE ENGLISH DANCE OF DEATH, from the Designs of T. Rowlandson, with Metrical Illustrations by the Author of 'Doctor Syntax.' *Two Volumes.*

THE DANCE OF LIFE: A Poem. The Author of 'Dr. Syntax.'

LIFE IN LONDON. Pierce Egan.

REAL LIFE IN LONDON. An Amateur (Pierce Egan). *Two Volumes.*

THE LIFE OF AN ACTOR. Pierce Egan.

THE VICAR OF WAKEFIELD. Oliver Goldsmith.

THE MILITARY ADVENTURES OF JOHNNY NEWCOME. An Officer.

THE NATIONAL SPORTS OF GREAT BRITAIN. With Descriptions and 50 Coloured Plates by Henry Alken.

THE ADVENTURES OF A POST CAPTAIN. A Naval Officer.

GAMONIA. Lawrence Rawstorne.

AN ACADEMY FOR GROWN HORSEMEN. Geoffrey Gambado.

REAL LIFE IN IRELAND. A Real Paddy.

THE ADVENTURES OF JOHNNY NEWCOME IN THE NAVY. Alfred Burton.

THE OLD ENGLISH SQUIRE. John Careless.

THE ENGLISH SPY. Bernard Blackmantle. *Two Volumes. 7s. net.*

WITH PLAIN ILLUSTRATIONS.

THE GRAVE: A Poem. Robert Blair.

ILLUSTRATIONS OF THE BOOK OF JOB. Invented and engraved by William Blake.

WINDSOR CASTLE. W. Harrison Ainsworth.

THE TOWER OF LONDON. W. Harrison Ainsworth

FRANK FAIRLEGH. F. E. Smedley.

THE COMPLEAT ANGLER. Izaak Walton and Charles Cotton.

THE PICKWICK PAPERS. Charles Dickens.

Leaders of Religion.

Edited by H. C. BEECHING. *With Portraits.*

Crown 8vo. 2s. net each volume.

CARDINAL NEWMAN. R. H. Hutton.

JOHN WESLEY. J. H. Overton.

BISHOP WILBERFORCE. G. W. Daniell.

CARDINAL MANNING. A. W. Hutton.

CHARLES SIMEON. H. C. G. Moule.

JOHN KNOX. F. MacCunn. *Second Edition.*

JOHN HOWE. R. F. Horton.

THOMAS KEN. F. A. Clarke.

GEORGE FOX, THE QUAKER. T. Hodgkin. *Third Edition.*

JOHN KEBLE. Walter Lock.

THOMAS CHALMERS. Mrs. Oliphant. *Second Edition.*

LANCELOT ANDREWES. R. L. Ottley. *Second Edition.*

AUGUSTINE OF CANTERBURY. E. L. Cutts.

WILLIAM LAUD. W. H. Hutton. *Third Ed.*

JOHN DONNE. Augustus Jessop.

THOMAS CRANMER. A. J. Mason.

LATIMER. R. M. Carlyle and A. J. Carlyle.

BISHOP BUTLER. W. A. Spooner.

The Library of Devotion.

With Introductions and (where necessary) Notes.
Small Pott 8vo, cloth, 2s.; leather, 2s. 6d. net each volume.

THE CONFESSIONS OF ST. AUGUSTINE. *Seventh Edition.*

THE IMITATION OF CHRIST. *Sixth Edition.*

THE CHRISTIAN YEAR. *Fifth Edition.*

LYRA INNOCENTIUM. *Third Edition.*

THE TEMPLE. *Second Edition.*

A BOOK OF DEVOTIONS. *Second Edition.*

A SERIOUS CALL TO A DEVOUT AND HOLY LIFE. *Fourth Edition.*

A GUIDE TO ETERNITY.

THE INNER WAY. *Second Edition.*

ON THE LOVE OF GOD.

THE PSALMS OF DAVID.

LYRA APOSTOLICA.

THE SONG OF SONGS.

THE THOUGHTS OF PASCAL. *Second Edition.*

A MANUAL OF CONSOLATION FROM THE SAINTS AND FATHERS.

DEVOTIONS FROM THE APOCRYPHA.

THE SPIRITUAL COMBAT.

THE DEVOTIONS OF ST. ANSELM.

BISHOP WILSON'S SACRA PRIVATA.

GRACE ABOUNDING TO THE CHIEF OF SINNERS.

LYRA SACRA: A Book of Sacred Verse. *Second Edition.*

A DAY BOOK FROM THE SAINTS AND FATHERS.

A LITTLE BOOK OF HEAVENLY WISDOM. Selection from the English Mystics.

LIGHT, LIFE, and LOVE. A Selection from the German Mystics.

AN INTRODUCTION TO THE DEVOUT LIFE.

THE LITTLE FLOWERS OF THE GLORIOUS MESSER ST. FRANCIS AND OF HIS FRIARS.

DEATH AND IMMORTALITY.

THE SPIRITUAL GUIDE. *Second Edition.*

DEVOTIONS FOR EVERY DAY IN THE WEEK AND THE GREAT FESTIVALS.

PRECES PRIVATAE.

HORAE MYSTICAE: A Day Book from the Writings of Mystics of Many Nations.

Little Books on Art.

With many Illustrations. Demy 16mo. 2s. 6d. net each volume.

Each volume consists of about 200 pages, and contains from 30 to 40 Illustrations including a Frontispiece in Photogravure.

ALBRECHT DÜRER. L. J. Allen.

ARTS OF JAPAN, THE. E. Dillon. *Third Edition.*

BOOKPLATES. E. Almack.

BOTTICELLI. Mary L. Bonnor.

BURNE-JONES. F. de Lisle.

CELLINI. R. H. H. Cust.

CHRISTIAN SYMBOLISM. Mrs. H. Jenner.

CHRIST IN ART. Mrs. H. Jenner.

CLAUDE. E. Dillon.

CONSTABLE. H. W. Tompkins. *Second Edition.*

COROT. A. Pollard and E. Birnstingl.

ENAMELS. Mrs. N. Dawson. *Second Edition.*

FREDERIC LEIGHTON. A. Corkran.

GEORGE ROMNEY. G. Paston.

GREEK ART. H. B. Walters. *Fourth Edition.*

GREUZE AND BOUCHER. E. F. Pollard.

HOLBEIN. Mrs. G. Fortescue.

ILLUMINATED MANUSCRIPTS. J. W. Bradley.

JEWELLERY. C. Davenport.

JOHN HOPPNER. H. P. K. Skipton.

SIR JOSHUA REYNOLDS. J. Sime. *Second Edition.*

MILLET. N. Peacock.

MINIATURES. C. Davenport.

OUR LADY IN ART. Mrs. H. Jenner.

RAPHAEL. A. R. Dryhurst.

REMBRANDT. Mrs. E. A. Sharp.

*RODIN. Muriel Ciolkowska.

TURNER. F. Tyrrell-Gill.

VANDYCK. M. G. Smallwood.

VELAZQUEZ. W. Wilberforce and A. Gilbert.

WATTS. R. E. D. Sketchley. *Second Edition.*

GENERAL LITERATURE

The Little Galleries.

Demy 16mo. 2s. 6d. net each volume.

Each volume contains 20 plates in Photogravure, together with a short outline o
the life and work of the master to whom the book is devoted.

A LITTLE GALLERY OF REYNOLDS.
A LITTLE GALLERY OF ROMNEY.
A LITTLE GALLERY OF HOPPNER.

A LITTLE GALLERY OF MILLAIS.
A LITTLE GALLERY OF ENGLISH POETS.

The Little Guides.

With many Illustrations by E. H. NEW and other artists, and from photographs.

Small Pott 8vo, cloth, 2s. 6d. net; leather, 3s. 6d. net, each volume.

The main features of these Guides are (1) a handy and charming form ; (2) illus
trations from photographs and by well-known artists ; (3) good plans and maps ; (4)
an adequate but compact presentation of everything that is interesting in the
natural features, history, archæology, and architecture of the town or district treated.

CAMBRIDGE AND ITS COLLEGES. A. H.
Thompson. *Third Edition, Revised.*

CHANNEL ISLANDS, THE. E. E. Bicknell.

ENGLISH LAKES, THE. F. G. Brabant.

ISLE OF WIGHT, THE. G. Clinch.

LONDON. G. Clinch.

MALVERN COUNTRY, THE. B. C. A. Windle.

NORTH WALES. A. T. Story.

OXFORD AND ITS COLLEGES. J. Wells.
Ninth Edition.

SHAKESPEARE'S COUNTRY. B. C. A. Windle.
Fourth Edition.

ST. PAUL'S CATHEDRAL. G. Clinch.

WESTMINSTER ABBEY. G. E. Troutbeck.
Second Edition.

BERKSHIRE. F. G. Brabant.

BUCKINGHAMSHIRE. E. S. Roscoe.

CHESHIRE. W. M. Gallichan.

CORNWALL. A. L. Salmon.

DERBYSHIRE. J. C. Cox.

DEVON. S. Baring-Gould. *Second Edition.*

DORSET. F. R. Heath. *Second Edition.*

ESSEX. J. C. Cox.

HAMPSHIRE. J. C. Cox.

HERTFORDSHIRE. H. W. Tompkins.

KENT. G. Clinch.

KERRY. C. P. Crane.

LEICESTERSHIRE AND RUTLAND. A Harvey
and V. B. Crowther-Beynon.

MIDDLESEX. J. B. Firth.

MONMOUTHSHIRE. G. W. Wade and J. H.
Wade.

NORFOLK. W. A. Dutt. *Second Edition,
Revised.*

NORTHAMPTONSHIRE. W. Dry. *Second Ed.*

NORTHUMBERLAND. J. E. Morris.

NOTTINGHAMSHIRE. L. Guilford.

OXFORDSHIRE. F. G. Brabant.

SHROPSHIRE. J. E. Auden.

SOMERSET. G. W. and J. H. Wade. *Second
Edition.*

STAFFORDSHIRE. C. Masefield.

SUFFOLK. W. A. Dutt.

SURREY. J. C. Cox.

SUSSEX. F. G. Brabant. *Third Edition.*

WILTSHIRE. F. R. Heath.

YORKSHIRE, THE EAST RIDING. J. E.
Morris.

YORKSHIRE, THE NORTH RIDING. J. E.
Morris.

YORKSHIRE, THE WEST RIDING. J. E.
Morris. *Cloth, 3s. 6d. net; leather, 4s. 6d.
net.*

BRITTANY. S. Baring-Gould.

NORMANDY. C. Scudamore.

ROME. C. G. Ellaby.

SICILY. F. H. Jackson.

The Little Library.

With Introductions, Notes, and Photogravure Frontispieces.

Small Pott 8vo. Each Volume, cloth, 1s. 6d. net.

Anon. A LITTLE BOOK OF ENGLISH LYRICS. *Second Edition.*

Austen (Jane). PRIDE AND PREJUDICE. *Two Volumes.*
NORTHANGER ABBEY.

Bacon (Francis). THE ESSAYS OF LORD BACON.

Barham (R. H.). THE INGOLDSBY LEGENDS. *Two Volumes.*

Barnett (Annie). A LITTLE BOOK OF ENGLISH PROSE.

Beckford (William). THE HISTORY OF THE CALIPH VATHEK.

Blake (William). SELECTIONS FROM THE WORKS OF WILLIAM BLAKE.

Borrow (George). LAVENGRO. *Two Volumes.*
THE ROMANY RYE.

Browning (Robert). SELECTIONS FROM THE EARLY POEMS OF ROBERT BROWNING.

Canning (George). SELECTIONS FROM THE ANTI-JACOBIN : with some later Poems by GEORGE CANNING.

Cowley (Abraham). THE ESSAYS OF ABRAHAM COWLEY.

Crabbe (George). SELECTIONS FROM THE POEMS OF GEORGE CRABBE.

Craik (Mrs.). JOHN HALIFAX, GENTLEMAN. *Two Volumes.*

Crashaw (Richard). THE ENGLISH POEMS OF RICHARD CRASHAW.

Dante Alighieri. THE INFERNO OF DANTE. Translated by H. F. CARY.
THE PURGATORIO OF DANTE. Translated by H. F. CARY.
THE PARADISO OF DANTE. Translated by H. F. CARY.

Darley (George). SELECTIONS FROM THE POEMS OF GEORGE DARLEY.

Deane (A. C.). A LITTLE BOOK OF LIGHT VERSE.

Dickens (Charles). CHRISTMAS BOOKS. *Two Volumes.*

Ferrier (Susan). MARRIAGE. *Two Volumes.*
THE INHERITANCE. *Two Volumes.*

Gaskell (Mrs.). CRANFORD. *Second E.*

Hawthorne (Nathaniel). THE SCARLE LETTER.

Henderson (T. F.). A LITTLE BOO OF SCOTTISH VERSE.

Kinglake (A. W.). EOTHEN. *Seco Edition.*

Lamb (Charles). ELIA, AND THE LA ESSAYS OF ELIA.

Locker (F.). LONDON LYRICS.

Marvell (Andrew). THE POEMS ANDREW MARVELL.

Milton (John). THE MINOR POEMS JOHN MILTON.

Moir (D. M.). MANSIE WAUCH.

Nichols (Bowyer). A LITTLE BOO OF ENGLISH SONNETS.

Smith (Horace and James). REJECTE ADDRESSES.

Sterne (Laurence). A SENTIMENT/ JOURNEY.

Tennyson (Alfred, Lord). THE EAR POEMS OF ALFRED, LORD TENN SON.
IN MEMORIAM.
THE PRINCESS.
MAUD.

Thackeray (W. M.). VANITY FAI *Three Volumes.*
PENDENNIS. *Three Volumes.*
HENRY ESMOND.
CHRISTMAS BOOKS.

Vaughan (Henry). THE POEMS C HENRY VAUGHAN.

Waterhouse (Elizabeth). A LITTL BOOK OF LIFE AND DEAT *Thirteenth Edition.*

Wordsworth (W.). SELECTIONS FRO THE POEMS OF WILLIAM WORD WORTH.

Wordsworth (W.) and Coleridge (S. T. LYRICAL BALLADS. *Second Edition.*

The Little Quarto Shakespeare.

Edited by W. J. CRAIG. With Introductions and Notes.
Pott 16*mo. In* 40 *Volumes. Leather, price* 1*s. net each volume.*
Mahogany Revolving Book Case. 10*s. net.*

Miniature Library.

Demy 32*mo. Leather,* 1*s. net each volume.*

EUPHRANOR : A Dialogue on Youth. Edward FitzGerald.

THE LIFE OF EDWARD, LORD HERBERT OF CHERBURY. Written by himself.

POLONIUS: or Wise Saws and Modern Instances. Edward FitzGerald.

THE RUBÁIYÁT OF OMAR KHAYYÁM. Edward FitzGerald. *Fourth Edition.*

The New Library of Medicine.

Edited by C. W. SALEEBY. *Demy* 8*vo.*

CARE OF THE BODY, THE. F. Cavanagh. *Second Edition.* 7*s.* 6*d. net.*

CHILDREN OF THE NATION, THE. The Right Hon. Sir John Gorst. *Second Edition.* 7*s.* 6*d. net.*

CONTROL OF A SCOURGE ; or, How Cancer is Curable, The. Chas. P. Childe. 7*s.* 6*d. net.*

DISEASES OF OCCUPATION. Sir Thomas Oliver. 10*s.* 6*d. net. Second Edition.*

DRINK PROBLEM, in its Medico-Sociological Aspects, The. Edited by T. N. Kelynack. 7*s.* 6*d. net.*

DRUGS AND THE DRUG HABIT. H. Sainsbury.

FUNCTIONAL NERVE DISEASES. A. T. Schofield. 7*s.* 6*d. net.*

HYGIENE OF MIND, THE. T. S. Clouston. *Fifth Edition.* 7*s.* 6*d. net.*

INFANT MORTALITY. Sir George Newman. 7*s.* 6*d. net.*

PREVENTION OF TUBERCULOSIS (CONSUMPTION), THE. Arthur Newsholme. 10*s.* 6*d. net. Second Edition.*

AIR AND HEALTH. Ronald C. Macfie. 7*s.* 6*d. net. Second Edition.*

The New Library of Music.

Edited by ERNEST NEWMAN. *Illustrated. Demy* 8*vo.* 7*s.* 6*d. net.*

BRAHMS. J. A. Fuller-Maitland. *Second Edition.*

HANDEL. R. A. Streatfeild. *Second Edition.*
HUGO WOLF. Ernest Newman.

Oxford Biographies.

Illustrated. Fcap. 8*vo. Each volume, cloth,* 2*s.* 6*d. net ; leather,* 3*s.* 6*d. net.*

DANTE ALIGHIERI. Paget Toynbee. *Third Edition.*

GIROLAMO SAVONAROLA. E. L. S. Horsburgh. *Fourth Edition.*

JOHN HOWARD. E. C. S Gibson.

ALFRED TENNYSON. A. C. Benson. *Second Edition.*

SIR WALTER RALEIGH. I. A. Taylor.

ERASMUS. E. F. H. Capey.

THE YOUNG PRETENDER. C. S. Terry.
ROBERT BURNS. T. F. Henderson.
CHATHAM. A. S. McDowall.
FRANCIS OF ASSISI. Anna M. Stoddart.
CANNING. W. Alison Phillips.
BEACONSFIELD. Walter Sichel.
JOHANN WOLFGANG GOETHE. H. G. Atkins.
FRANÇOIS DE FÉNELON. Viscount St. Cyres.

Three Plays.

Fcap. 8vo. 2s. net.

THE HONEYMOON. A Comedy in Three Acts. | MILESTONES. Arnold Bennett and Edwar
Arnold Bennett. *Second Edition.* | Knoblauch. *Second Edition.*
KISMET. Edward Knoblauch.

The States of Italy.

Edited by E ARMSTRONG and R. LANGTON DOUGLAS.

Illustrated. Demy 8vo.

A HISTORY OF MILAN UNDER THE SFORZA. | A HISTORY OF VERONA. A. M. Allen. 12s. 6
Cecilia M. Ady. 10s. 6d. *net.* | *net.*
A HISTORY OF PERUGIA. W. Heywood. 12s. 6d. *net.*

The Westminster Commentaries.

General Editor, WALTER LOCK.

Demy 8vo.

THE ACTS OF THE APOSTLES. Edited by R. B. Rackham. *Sixth Edition.* 10s. 6d.

THE FIRST EPISTLE OF PAUL THE APOSTLE TO THE CORINTHIANS. Edited by H. L Goudge. *Third Edition.* 6s.

THE BOOK OF EXODUS Edited by A. H. M'Neile. With a Map and 3 Plans. 10s. 6d.

THE BOOK OF EZEKIEL. Edited by H. A. Redpath. 10s. 6d.

THE BOOK OF GENESIS. Edited with Introduction and Notes by S. R. Driver. *Eighth Edition.* 10s. 6d.

THE BOOK OF THE PROPHET ISAIAH. Edit by G. W. Wade. 10s. 6d.

ADDITIONS AND CORRECTIONS IN THE SEVEN AND EIGHTH EDITIONS OF THE BOOK GENESIS. S. R. Driver. 1s.

THE BOOK OF JOB. Edited by E. C. S. Gibsc *Second Edition.* 6s.

THE EPISTLE OF ST. JAMES. Edited with I troduction and Notes by R. J. Knowlir *Second Edition.* 6s.

The "Young" Series.

Illustrated. Crown 8vo.

THE YOUNG BOTANIST. W. P. Westell and C. S. Cooper. 3s. 6d. *net.*

THE YOUNG CARPENTER. Cyril Hall. 5s.

THE YOUNG ELECTRICIAN. Hammond Hall. 5s.

THE YOUNG ENGINEER. Hammond H. *Third Edition.* 5s.

THE YOUNG NATURALIST. W. P. West *Second Edition.* 6s.

THE YOUNG ORNITHOLOGIST. W. P. West 5s.

Methuen's Shilling Library.

Fcap. 8vo. 1s. net.

CONDITION OF ENGLAND, THE. G. F. G. Masterman.

DE PROFUNDIS. Oscar Wilde.

FROM MIDSHIPMAN TO FIELD-MARSHAL. Sir Evelyn Wood, F.M., V.C.

*IDEAL HUSBAND, AN. Oscar Wilde.

*JIMMY GLOVER, HIS - BOOK. James M. Glover.

*JOHN BOYES, KING OF THE WA-KIKUYU. John Boyes.

LADY WINDERMERE'S FAN. Oscar Wilde.

LETTERS FROM A SELF-MADE - MERCHANT TO HIS SON. George Horace Lorimer.

LIFE OF JOHN RUSKIN, THE. W. G. Collingwood.

LIFE OF ROBERT LOUIS STEVENSON, THE. Graham Balfour.

*LIFE OF TENNYSON, THE. A. C. Benson.

*LITTLE OF EVERYTHING, A. E. V. Lucas.

LORD ARTHUR SAVILE'S CRIME. Oscar Wilde.

LORE OF THE HONEY-BEE, THE. Tickner Edwardes.

MAN AND THE UNIVERSE. Sir Oliver Lodge.

MARY MAGDALENE. Maurice Maeterlinck.

SELECTED POEMS. Oscar Wilde.

SEVASTOPOL, AND OTHER STORIES. Leo Tolstoy.

THE BLUE BIRD. Maurice Maeterlinck.

UNDER FIVE REIGNS. Lady Dorothy Nevill.

*VAILIMA LETTERS. Robert Louis Stevenson.

*VICAR OF MORWENSTOW, THE. S. Baring-Gould.

Books for Travellers.

Crown 8vo. 6s. each.

Each volume contains a number of Illustrations in Colour.

*A WANDERER IN FLORENCE. E. V. Lucas.

A WANDERER IN PARIS. E. V. Lucas.

A WANDERER IN HOLLAND. E. V. Lucas.

A WANDERER IN LONDON. E. V. Lucas.

THE NORFOLK BROADS. W. A. Dutt.

THE NEW FOREST. Horace G. Hutchinson.

NAPLES. Arthur H. Norway.

THE CITIES OF UMBRIA. Edward Hutton.

THE CITIES OF SPAIN. Edward Hutton.

*THE CITIES OF LOMBARDY. Edward Hutton.

FLORENCE AND NORTHERN TUSCANY, WITH GENOA. Edward Hutton.

SIENA AND SOUTHERN TUSCANY. Edward Hutton.

ROME. Edward Hutton.

VENICE AND VENETIA. Edward Hutton.

THE BRETONS AT HOME. F. M. Gostling.

THE LAND OF PARDONS (Brittany). Anatole Le Braz.

A BOOK OF THE RHINE. S. Baring-Gould.

THE NAPLES RIVIERA. H. M. Vaughan.

DAYS IN CORNWALL. C. Lewis Hind.

THROUGH EAST ANGLIA IN A MOTOR CAR. J. E. Vincent.

THE SKIRTS OF THE GREAT CITY. Mrs. A. G. Bell.

ROUND ABOUT WILTSHIRE. A. G. Bradley.

SCOTLAND OF TO-DAY. T. F. Henderson and Francis Watt.

NORWAY AND ITS FJORDS. M. A. Wyllie.

Some Books on Art.

ART AND LIFE. T. Sturge Moore. Illustrated. *Cr. 8vo. 5s. net.*

AIMS AND IDEALS IN ART. George Clausen. Illustrated. *Second Edition. Large Post 8vo. 5s. net.*

SIX LECTURES ON PAINTING. George Clausen. Illustrated. *Third Edition. Large Post 8vo. 3s. 6d. net.*

FRANCESCO GUARDI, 1712-1793. G. A. Simonson. Illustrated. *Imperial 4to. £2 2s. net.*

ILLUSTRATIONS OF THE BOOK OF JOB. William Blake. *Quarto. £1 1s. net.*

JOHN LUCAS, PORTRAIT PAINTER, 1828-1874. Arthur Lucas. Illustrated. *Imperial 4to. £3 3s. net.*

ONE HUNDRED MASTERPIECES OF PAINTING. With an Introduction by R. C. Witt. Illustrated. *Second Edition. Demy 8vo. 10s. 6d. net.*

A GUIDE TO THE BRITISH PICTURES IN THE NATIONAL GALLERY. Edward Kingston. Illustrated. *Fcap. 8vo. 3s. 6d. net.*

ONE HUNDRED MASTERPIECES OF SCULPTURE. With an Introduction by G. F. Hill. Illustrated. *Demy 8vo.* 10s. 6d. net.

A ROMNEY FOLIO. With an Essay by A. B. Chamberlain. *Imperial Folio.* £15 15s. net.

THE SAINTS IN ART. Margaret E. Tabor. Illustrated. *Fcap. 8vo.* 3s. 6d. net.

SCHOOLS OF PAINTING. Mary Innes. Illustrated. *Cr. 8vo.* 5s. net.

THE POST IMPRESSIONISTS. C. Lewis Hind. Illustrated. *Royal 8vo.* 7s. 6d. net.

CELTIC ART IN PAGAN AND CHRISTIAN TIMES. J. R. Allen. Illustrated. *Second Edition.* *Demy 8vo.* 7s. 6d. net.

"CLASSICS OF ART." See page 13.

"THE CONNOISSEUR'S LIBRARY." See page 14.

"LITTLE BOOKS ON ART." See page 16.

"THE LITTLE GALLERIES." See page 17.

Some Books on Italy.

A HISTORY OF MILAN UNDER THE SFORZA. Cecilia M. Ady. Illustrated. *Demy 8vo.* 10s. 6d. net.

A HISTORY OF VERONA. A. M. Allen. Illustrated. *Demy 8vo.* 12s. 6d. net.

A HISTORY OF PERUGIA. William Heywood. Illustrated. *Demy 8vo.* 12s. 6d. net.

THE LAKES OF NORTHERN ITALY. Richard Bagot. Illustrated. *Fcap. 8vo.* 5s. net.

WOMAN IN ITALY. W. Boulting. Illustrated. *Demy 8vo.* 10s. 6d. net.

OLD ETRURIA AND MODERN TUSCANY. Mary L. Cameron. Illustrated. *Second Edition.* *Cr. 8vo.* 6s. net.

FLORENCE AND THE CITIES OF NORTHERN TUSCANY, WITH GENOA. Edward Hutton. Illustrated. *Second Edition. Cr. 8vo.* 6s.

SIENA AND SOUTHERN TUSCANY. Edward Hutton. Illustrated. *Second Edition.* *Cr. 8vo.* 6s.

IN UNKNOWN TUSCANY. Edward Hutton. Illustrated. *Second Edition. Demy 8vo.* 7s. 6d. net.

VENICE AND VENETIA. Edward Hutton. Illustrated. *Cr. 8vo.* 6s.

VENICE ON FOOT. H. A. Douglas. Illustrated. *Fcap. 8vo.* 5s. net.

VENICE AND HER TREASURES. H. A. Douglas. Illustrated. *Fcap. 8vo.* 5s. net.

*THE DOGES OF VENICE. Mrs. Aubrey Richardson. Illustrated. *Demy 8vo.* 10s. 6d. net.

FLORENCE: Her History and Art to the Fall of the Republic. F. A. Hyett. *Demy 8vo.* 7s. 6d. net.

FLORENCE AND HER TREASURES. H. M. Vaughan. Illustrated. *Fcap. 8vo.* 5s. net.

COUNTRY WALKS ABOUT FLORENCE. Edward Hutton. Illustrated. *Fcap. 8vo.* 5s. net.

NAPLES: Past and Present. A. H. Norway. Illustrated. *Third Edition. Cr. 8vo.* 6s.

THE NAPLES RIVIERA. H. M. Vaughan. Illustrated. *Second Edition. Cr. 8vo.* 6s.

SICILY: The New Winter Resort. Douglas Sladen. Illustrated. *Second Edition. Cr. 8vo.* 5s. net.

SICILY. F. H. Jackson. Illustrated. *Small Pott 8vo. Cloth,* 2s. 6d. net, *leather,* 3s. 6d. net.

ROME. Edward Hutton. Illustrated. *Second Edition. Cr. 8vo.* 6s.

A ROMAN PILGRIMAGE. R. E. Roberts. Illustrated. *Demy 8vo.* 10s. 6d. net.

ROME. C. G. Ellaby. Illustrated. *Small Pott 8vo. Cloth,* 2s. 6d. net; *leather,* 3s. 6d. net.

THE CITIES OF UMBRIA. Edward Hutton. Illustrated. *Fourth Edition. Cr. 8vo.* 6s.

*THE CITIES OF LOMBARDY. Edward Hutton. Illustrated. *Cr. 8vo.* 6s.

THE LIVES OF S. FRANCIS OF ASSISI. Brother Thomas of Celano. *Cr. 8vo.* 5s. net.

LORENZO THE MAGNIFICENT. E. L. S. Horsburgh. Illustrated. *Second Edition. Demy 8vo.* 15s. net.

GIROLAMO SAVONAROLA. E. L. S. Horsburgh. Illustrated. *Cr. 8vo.* 5s. net.

ST. CATHERINE OF SIENA AND HER TIMES. By the Author of "Mdlle Mori." Illustrated. *Second Edition. Demy 8vo.* 7s. 6d. net.

DANTE AND HIS ITALY. Lonsdale Ragg. Illustrated. *Demy 8vo.* 12s. 6d. net.

DANTE ALIGHIERI: His Life and Works. Paget Toynbee. Illustrated. *Cr. 8vo.* 5s. net.

THE MEDICI POPES. H. M. Vaughan. Illustrated. *Demy 8vo.* 15s. net.

SHELLEY AND HIS FRIENDS IN ITALY. Helen R. Angeli. Illustrated. *Demy 8vo.* 10s. 6d. net.

HOME LIFE IN ITALY. Lina Duff Gordon. Illustrated. *Second Edition. Demy 8vo.* 10s. 6d. net.

SKIES ITALIAN: A Little Breviary for Travellers in Italy. Ruth S. Phelps. *Fcap. 8vo.* 5s. net.

*A WANDERER IN FLORENCE. E. V. Lucas. Illustrated. *Cr. 8vo.* 6s.

*UNITED ITALY. F. M. Underwood. *Demy 8vo.* 10s. 6d. net.

PART III.—A SELECTION OF WORKS OF FICTION

Albanesi (E Maria). SUSANNAH AND ONE OTHER. *Fourth Edition.* Cr. 8vo. 6s.
LOVE AND LOUISA. *Second Edition.* Cr. 8vo. 6s.
THE BROWN EYES OF MARY. *Third Edition.* Cr. 8vo. 6s.
I KNOW A MAIDEN. *Third Edition.* Cr. 8vo. 6s.
THE INVINCIBLE AMELIA; OR, THE POLITE ADVENTURESS. *Third Edition.* Cr. 8vo. 3s. 6d.
THE GLAD HEART. *Fifth Edition.* Cr. 8vo. 6s.
*OLIVIA MARY. Cr. 8vo. 6s.

Bagot (Richard). A ROMAN MYSTERY. *Third Edition.* Cr. 8vo. 6s.
THE PASSPORT. *Fourth Edition.* Cr. 8vo. 6s.
ANTHONY CUTHBERT. *Fourth Edition.* Cr 8vo. 6s.
LOVE'S PROXY. Cr. 8vo. 6s.
DONNA DIANA. *Second Edition.* Cr. 8vo. 6s.
CASTING OF NETS. *Twelfth Edition.* Cr. 8vo. 6s.
THE HOUSE OF SERRAVALLE. *Third Edition.* Cr. 8vo. 6s.

Bailey (H. C.). STORM AND TREASURE. *Third Edition.* Cr. 8vo. 6s.
THE LONELY QUEEN. *Third Edition.* Cr. 8vo. 6s.

Baring-Gould (S.). IN THE ROAR OF THE SEA. *Eighth Edition.* Cr. 8vo. 6s.
MARGERY OF QUETHER. *Second Edition.* Cr. 8vo. 6s.
THE QUEEN OF LOVE. *Fifth Edition.* Cr. 8vo. 6s.
JACQUETTA. *Third Edition.* Cr. 8vo. 6s.
KITTY ALONE. *Fifth Edition.* Cr. 8vo. 6s.
NOÉMI. Illustrated. *Fourth Edition.* Cr. 8vo. 6s.
THE BROOM - SQUIRE. Illustrated. *Fifth Edition.* Cr. 8vo. 6s.
DARTMOOR IDYLLS. Cr. 8vo. 6s.
GUAVAS THE TINNER. Illustrated. *Second Edition.* Cr. 8vo. 6s.
BLADYS OF THE STEWPONEY. Illustrated. *Second Edition.* Cr. 8vo. 6s.
PABO THE PRIEST. Cr. 8vo. 6s.
WINEFRED. Illustrated. *Second Edition.* Cr. 8vo. 6s.
ROYAL GEORGIE. Illustrated. Cr. 8vo. 6s.
CHRIS OF ALL SORTS. Cr. 8vo. 6s.
IN DEWISLAND. *Second Edition.* Cr. 8vo. 6s.
MRS. CURGENVEN OF CURGENVEN. *Fifth Edition.* Cr. 8vo. 6s.

Barr (Robert). IN THE MIDST OF ALARMS. *Third Edition.* Cr. 8vo. 6s.
THE COUNTESS TEKLA. *Fifth Edition.* Cr. 8vo. 6s.
THE MUTABLE MANY. *Third Edition.* Cr. 8vo. 6s.

Begbie (Harold). THE CURIOUS AND DIVERTING ADVENTURES OF SIR JOHN SPARROW, BART.; OR, THE PROGRESS OF AN OPEN MIND. *Second Edition.* Cr. 8vo. 6s.

Belloc (H). EMMANUEL BURDEN, MERCHANT. Illustrated. *Second Edition.* Cr. 8vo. 6s.
A CHANGE IN THE CABINET. *Third Edition.* Cr. 8vo. 6s.

Belloc-Lowndes (Mrs.). THE CHINK IN THE ARMOUR. *Fourth Edition.* Cr. 8vo. 6s.
*MARY PECHELL. Cr. 8vo. 6s.

Bennett (Arnold). CLAYHANGER. *Tenth Edition.* Cr. 8vo. 6s.
THE CARD. *Sixth Edition.* Cr. 8vo. 6s.
HILDA LESSWAYS. *Seventh Edition.* Cr. 8vo. 6s.
* BURIED ALIVE. *A New Edition.* Cr. 8vo. 6s.
A MAN FROM THE NORTH. *A New Edition.* Cr. 8vo. 6s.
THE MATADOR OF THE FIVE TOWNS. *Second Edition.* Cr. 8vo. 6s.

Benson (E. F.). DODO: A DETAIL OF THE DAY. *Sixteenth Edition.* Cr. 8vo. 6s.

Birmingham (George A.). SPANISH GOLD. *Sixth Edition.* Cr. 8vo. 6s
THE SEARCH PARTY. *Fifth Edition.* Cr. 8vo. 6s.
LALAGE'S LOVERS. *Third Edition.* Cr. 8vo. 6s.

Bowen (Marjorie). I WILL MAINTAIN. *Seventh Edition.* Cr. 8vo. 6s.
DEFENDER OF THE FAITH. *Fifth Edition.* Cr. 8vo. 6s.
*A KNIGHT OF SPAIN. Cr. 8vo. 6s.
THE QUEST OF GLORY. *Third Edition.* Cr. 8vo. 6s.
GOD AND THE KING. *Fourth Edition.* Cr. 8vo. 6s.

Clifford (Mrs. W. K.). THE GETTING WELL OF DOROTHY. Illustrated. *Second Edition.* Cr. 8vo. 3s. 6d.

Conrad (Joseph). THE SECRET AGENT: A Simple Tale. *Fourth Ed.* Cr. 8vo. 6s.
A SET OF SIX. *Fourth Edition.* Cr. 8vo. 6s.
UNDER WESTERN EYES. *Second Ed.* Cr. 8vo. 6s.

*Conyers (Dorothea.). THE LONELY MAN. *Cr. 8vo. 6s.*

Corelli (Marie). A ROMANCE OF TWO WORLDS. *Thirty-first Ed. Cr 8vo. 6s.*
VENDETTA; OR, THE STORY OF ONE FORGOTTEN. *Twenty-ninth Edition. Cr. 8vo. 6s.*
THELMA : A NORWEGIAN PRINCESS. *Forty-second Edition. Cr. 8vo. 6s.*
ARDATH: THE STORY OF A DEAD SELF. *Twentieth Edition. Cr. 8vo. 6s.*
THE SOUL OF LILITH. *Seventeenth Edition. Cr. 8vo. 6s.*
WORMWOOD : A DRAMA OF PARIS. *Eighteenth Edition. Cr. 8vo. 6s.*
BARABBAS : A DREAM OF THE WORLD'S TRAGEDY. *Forty-sixth Edition. Cr. 8vo. 6s.*
THE SORROWS OF SATAN. *Fifty-seventh Edition. Cr. 8vo. 6s.*
THE MASTER-CHRISTIAN. *Thirteenth Edition.* 179th Thousand. *Cr. 8vo. 6s.*
TEMPORAL POWER : A STUDY IN SUPREMACY. *Second Edition.* 150th Thousand. *Cr. 8vo. 6s.*
GOD'S GOOD MAN : A SIMPLE LOVE STORY. *Fifteenth Edition.* 154th Thousand. *Cr. 8vo. 6s.*
HOLY ORDERS: THE TRAGEDY OF A QUIET LIFE. *Second Edition.* 120th Thousand. *Crown 8vo. 6s.*
THE MIGHTY ATOM. *Twenty-ninth Edition. Cr. 8vo. 6s.*
BOY: a Sketch. *Twelfth Edition. Cr. 8vo. 6s.*
CAMEOS. *Fourteenth Edition. Cr. 8vo. 6s.*
THE LIFE EVERLASTING. *Fifth Ed. Cr. 8vo. 6s.*

Crockett (S. R). LOCHINVAR. Illustrated. *Third Edition. Cr. 8vo. 6s.*
THE STANDARD BEARER. *Second Edition. Cr. 8vo. 6s.*

Croker (B. M.). THE OLD CANTONMENT. *Second Edition. Cr. 8vo. 6s.*
JOHANNA. *Second Edition. Cr. 8vo. 6s.*
THE HAPPY VALLEY. *Fourth Edition. Cr. 8vo. 6s.*
A NINE DAYS' WONDER. *Fourth Edition. Cr. 8vo. 6s.*
PEGGY OF THE BARTONS. *Seventh Edition. Cr. 8vo. 6s.*
ANGEL. *Fifth Edition. Cr. 8vo. 6s.*
KATHERINE THE ARROGANT. *Sixth Edition. Cr. 8vo. 6s.*
BABES IN THE WOOD. *Fourth Edition. Cr. 8vo. 6s.*

Danby (Frank.). JOSEPH IN JEOPARDY. *Third Edition. Cr. 8vo. 6s.*

Doyle (Sir A. Conan). ROUND THE RED LAMP. *Twelfth Edition. Cr. 8vo. 6s.*

Fenn (G. Manville). SYD BELTON: THE BOY WHO WOULD NOT GO TO SEA. Illustrated. *Second Ed. Cr. 8vo. 3s. 6d.*

Findlater (J. H.). THE GREEN GRAVE OF BALGOWRIE. *Fifth Edition. C 8vo. 6s.*
THE LADDER TO THE STARS. *Second Edition. Cr. 8vo. 6s.*

Findlater (Mary). A NARROW WA *Third Edition. Cr. 8vo. 6s.*
OVER THE HILLS. *Second Edition. C 8vo. 6s.*
THE ROSE OF JOY. *Third Editio Cr. 8vo. 6s.*
A BLIND BIRD'S NEST. Illustrate *Second Edition. Cr. 8vo. 6s.*

Fry (B. and C. B). A MOTHER'S SO. *Fifth Edition. Cr. 8vo. 6s.*

Harraden (Beatrice). IN VARYIN MOODS. *Fourteenth Edition. Cr. 8vo. t*
HILDA STRAFFORD and THE REMI TANCE MAN. *Twelfth Ed. Cr. 8vo.*
INTERPLAY. *Fifth Edition. Cr. 8vo. 6*

Hichens (Robert). THE PROPHET O BERKELEY SQUARE. *Second Editio Cr. 8vo. 6s.*
TONGUES OF CONSCIENCE. *Thi Edition. Cr. 8vo. 6s.*
THE WOMAN WITH THE FAN. *Eigh Edition. Cr. 8vo. 6s.*
BYEWAYS. *Cr. 8vo. 6s.*
THE GARDEN OF ALLAH. *Twent first Edition. Cr. 8vo. 6s.*
THE BLACK SPANIEL. *Cr. 8vo. 6s.*
THE CALL OF THE BLOOD. *Seven Edition. Cr. 8vo. 6s.*
BARBARY SHEEP. *Second Edition. C 8vo. 3s. 6d.*
THE DWELLER ON THE THRE HOLD. *Cr. 8vo. 6s.*

Hope (Anthony). THE GOD IN TH CAR. *Eleventh Edition. Cr. 8vo. 6s.*
A CHANGE OF AIR. *Sixth Edition. C 8vo. 6s.*
A MAN OF MARK. *Seventh Ed. Cr. 8vo. 6*
THE CHRONICLES OF COUNT AI TONIO. *Sixth Edition. Cr. 8vo. 6s.*
PHROSO. Illustrated. *Eighth Editio Cr. 8vo. 6s.*
SIMON DALE. Illustrated. *Eighth Editio Cr. 8vo. 6s.*
THE KING'S MIRROR. *Fifth Editio Cr. 8vo. 6s.*
QUISANTÉ. *Fourth Edition. Cr. 8vo. THE DOLLY DIALOGUES. Cr. 8vo.*
TALES OF TWO PEOPLE. *Third E tion. Cr. 8vo. 6s.*
THE GREAT MISS DRIVER. *Four Edition. Cr. 8vo. 6s.*
MRS. MAXON PROTESTS. *Third E tion. Cr. 8vo. 6s.*

Hutten (Baroness von). THE HAL *Fifth Edition. Cr. 8vo. 6s.*

'Inner Shrine' (Author of the). THE WILD OLIVE. *Third Edition. Cr. 8vo.* 6s.

Jacobs (W. W.). MANY CARGOES. *Thirty-second Edition. Cr. 8vo. 3s. 6d.* *Also Illustrated in colour. *Demy 8vo. 7s. 6d. net.*
SEA URCHINS. *Sixteenth Edition. Cr. 8vo. 3s. 6d.*
A MASTER OF CRAFT. Illustrated. *Ninth Edition. Cr. 8vo. 3s. 6d.*
LIGHT FREIGHTS. Illustrated. *Eighth Edition. Cr. 8vo. 3s. 6d.*
THE SKIPPER'S WOOING. *Eleventh Edition. Cr. 8vo. 3s. 6d.*
AT SUNWICH PORT. Illustrated. *Tenth Edition. Cr. 8vo. 3s. 6d.*
DIALSTONE LANE. Illustrated. *Eighth Edition. Cr. 8vo. 3s. 6d.*
ODD CRAFT. Illustrated. *Fifth Edition. Cr. 8vo. 3s. 6d.*
THE LADY OF THE BARGE. Illustrated. *Ninth Edition. Cr. 8vo. 3s. 6d.*
SAILORS' KNOTS. Illustrated. *Fifth Edition. Cr. 8vo. 3s. 6d.*
SHORT CRUISES. *Third Edition. Cr. 8vo. 3s. 6d.*

James (Henry). THE GOLDEN BOWL. *Third Edition. Cr. 8vo.* 6s

Le Queux (William). THE HUNCHBACK OF WESTMINSTER. *Third Edition. Cr. 8vo.* 6s.
THE CLOSED BOOK. *Third Edition. Cr. 8vo.* 6s.
THE VALLEY OF THE SHADOW. Illustrated. *Third Edition. Cr. 8vo.* 6s.
BEHIND THE THRONE. *Third Edition. Cr. 8vo.* 6s.

London (Jack). WHITE FANG. *Eighth Edition. Cr. 8vo.* 6s.

Lucas (E. V.). LISTENER'S LURE: AN OBLIQUE NARRATION. *Eighth Edition. Fcap. 8vo.* 5s.
OVER BEMERTON'S: AN EASY-GOING CHRONICLE. *Ninth Edition. Fcap 8vo.* 5s.
MR. INGLESIDE. *Eighth Edition. Fcap. 8vo.* 5s.
LONDON LAVENDER. *Cr. 8vo.* 6s.

Lyall (Edna). DERRICK VAUGHAN, NOVELIST. *44th Thousand. Cr. 8vo.* 3s. 6d.

Macnaughtan (S.). THE FORTUNE OF CHRISTINA M'NAB. *Fifth Edition. Cr. 8vo.* 6s.
PETER AND JANE. *Fourth Edition. Cr. 8vo.* 6s.

Malet (Lucas). A COUNSEL OF PERFECTION. *Second Edition. Cr. 8vo.* 6s.

THE WAGES OF SIN. *Sixteenth Edition. Cr. 8vo.* 6s.
THE CARISSIMA. *Fifth Ed. Cr. 8vo.* 6s.
THE GATELESS BARRIER. *Fifth Edition. Cr. 8vo.* 6s.

Maxwell (W. B.). THE RAGGED MESSENGER. *Third Edition. Cr. 8vo.* 6s.
THE GUARDED FLAME. *Seventh Edition. Cr. 8vo.* 6s.
ODD LENGTHS. *Second Ed. Cr. 8vo.* 6s.
HILL RISE. *Fourth Edition. Cr. 8vo.* 6s.
THE COUNTESS OF MAYBURY: BETWEEN YOU AND I. *Fourth Edition. Cr. 8vo.* 6s.
THE REST CURE. *Fourth Edition. Cr. 8vo.* 6s.

Milne (A. A.). THE DAY'S PLAY. *Third Edition. Cr. 8vo.* 6s.
*THE HOLIDAY ROUND. *Cr. 8vo.* 6s.

Montague (C. E.). A HIND LET LOOSE. *Third Edition. Cr. 8vo.* 6s.

Morrison (Arthur). TALES OF MEAN STREETS. *Seventh Edition. Cr. 8vo.* 6s.
A CHILD OF THE JAGO. *Sixth Edition. Cr. 8vo.* 6s.
THE HOLE IN THE WALL. *Fourth Edition. Cr. 8vo.* 6s.
DIVERS VANITIES. *Cr. 8vo.* 6s.

Ollivant (Alfred). OWD BOB, THE GREY DOG OF KENMUIR. With a Frontispiece. *Eleventh Ed. Cr. 8vo.* 6s.
THE TAMING OF JOHN BLUNT. *Second Edition. Cr. 8vo.* 6s.
*THE ROYAL ROAD. *Cr. 8vo.* 6s.

Onions (Oliver). GOOD BOY SELDOM: A ROMANCE OF ADVERTISEMENT. *Second Edition. Cr. 8vo.* 6s.

Oppenheim (E. Phillips). MASTER OF MEN. *Fifth Edition. Cr. 8vo.* 6s.
THE MISSING DELORA. Illustrated. *Fourth Edition. Cr. 8vo.* 6s.

Orczy (Baroness). FIRE IN STUBBLE. *Fifth Edition. Cr. 8vo.* 6s.

Oxenham (John). A WEAVER OF WEBS. Illustrated. *Fifth Ed. Cr. 8vo.* 6s.
PROFIT AND LOSS. *Fourth Edition. Cr. 8vo.* 6s.
THE LONG ROAD. *Fourth Edition. Cr. 8vo.* 6s.
THE SONG OF HYACINTH, AND OTHER STORIES. *Second Edition. Cr. 8vo.* 6s.
MY LADY OF SHADOWS. *Fourth Edition. Cr. 8vo.* 6s.
LAURISTONS. *Fourth Edition. Cr. 8vo.* 6s.
THE COIL OF CARNE. *Sixth Edition. Cr. 8vo.* 6s.
*THE QUEST OF THE GOLDEN ROSE. *Cr. 8vo.* 6s.

Parker (Gilbert). PIERRE AND HIS PEOPLE. *Seventh Edition. Cr. 8vo* 6s.
MRS. FALCHION. *Fifth Edition. Cr. 8vo.* 6s.
THE TRANSLATION OF A SAVAGE. *Fourth Edition. Cr. 8vo.* 6s.
THE TRAIL OF THE SWORD. Illustrated. *Tenth Edition. Cr. 8vo.* 6s.
WHEN VALMOND CAME TO PONTIAC: The Story of a Lost Napoleon. *Seventh Edition. Cr. 8vo.* 6s.
AN ADVENTURER OF THE NORTH. The Last Adventures of ' Pretty Pierre.' *Fifth Edition. Cr. 8vo.* 6s.
THE BATTLE OF THE STRONG: a Romance of Two Kingdoms. Illustrated. *Seventh Edition. Cr. 8vo.* 6s.
THE POMP OF THE LAVILETTES. *Third Edition. Cr. 8vo.* 3s. 6d.
NORTHERN LIGHTS. *Fourth Edition. Cr. 8vo.* 6s.

Pasture (Mrs. Henry de la). THE TYRANT. *Fourth Edition. Cr. 8vo.* 6s.

Pemberton (Max). THE FOOTSTEPS OF A THRONE. Illustrated. *Fourth Edition. Cr. 8vo.* 6s.
I CROWN THEE KING. Illustrated. *Cr. 8vo.* 6s.
LOVE THE HARVESTER: A STORY OF THE SHIRES. Illustrated. *Third Edition. Cr. 8vo.* 3s. 6d.
THE MYSTERY OF THE GREEN HEART. *Third Edition. Cr. 8vo.* 6s.

Perrin (Alice). THE CHARM. *Fifth Edition. Cr. 8vo.* 6s.
*THE ANGLO-INDIANS. *Cr. 8vo.* 6s.

Phillpotts (Eden). LYING PROPHETS. *Third Edition. Cr. 8vo.* 6s.
CHILDREN OF THE MIST. *Sixth Edition. Cr. 8vo.* 6s.
THE HUMAN BOY. With a Frontispiece. *Seventh Edition. Cr. 8vo* 6s.
SONS OF THE MORNING. *Second Edition. Cr. 8vo.* 6s.
THE RIVER. *Fourth Edition. Cr. 8vo.* 6s.
THE AMERICAN PRISONER. *Fourth Edition. Cr. 8vo.* 6s.
KNOCK AT A VENTURE. *Third Edition. Cr. 8vo.* 6s.
THE PORTREEVE. *Fourth Edition. Cr. 8vo* 6s.
THE POACHER'S WIFE. *Second Edition. Cr. 8vo.* 6s.
THE STRIKING HOURS. *Second Edition. Cr. 8vo.* 6s.
DEMETER'S DAUGHTER. *Third Edition. Cr. 8vo.* 6s.

Pickthall (Marmaduke). SAÏD THE FISHERMAN. *Eighth Edition. Cr. 8vo.* 6s.

'Q' (A. T. Quiller Couch). THE WHITE WOLF. *Second Edition. Cr. 8vo.* 6s.

THE MAYOR OF TROY. *Fourth Edition Cr. 8vo.* 6s.
MERRY-GARDEN AND OTHER STORIE *Cr. 8vo.* 6s
MAJOR VIGOUREUX. *Third Edition Cr. 8vo.* 6s.

Ridge (W. Pett). ERB. *Second Edition Cr. 8vo.* 6s.
A SON OF THE STATE. *Third Edition Cr. 8vo.* 3s. 6d.
A BREAKER OF LAWS. *Cr. 8vo.* 3s. 6
MRS. GALER'S BUSINESS. Illustrate *Second Edition. Cr. 8vo.* 6s.
THE WICKHAMSES. *Fourth Edition Cr. 8vo.* 6s
NAME OF GARLAND. *Third Edition Cr. 8vo.* 6s.
SPLENDID BROTHER. *Fourth Edition Cr. 8vo.* 6s.
NINE TO SIX-THIRTY. *Third Edition Cr. 8vo.* 6s.
THANKS TO SANDERSON. *Second Edition. Cr. 8vo.* 6s.
*DEVOTED SPARKES. *Cr. 8vo.* 6s.

Russell (W. Clark). MASTER ROCK. FELLAR'S VOYAGE. Illustrate *Fourth Edition. Cr. 8vo.* 3s. 6d.

Sidgwick (Mrs. Alfred). THE KIN MAN. Illustrated. *Third Edition. C 8vo.* 6s.
THE LANTERN-BEARERS. *Thi Edition. Cr. 8vo.* 6s.
ANTHEA'S GUEST. *Fifth Edition. 8vo.* 6s.
*LAMORNA. *Cr. 8vo.* 6s.

Somerville (E. Œ.) and Ross (Martin DAN RUSSEL THE FOX. Illustrate *Fourth Edition. Cr. 8vo.* 6s.

Thurston (E. Temple). MIRAGE. *Four Edition. Cr. 8vo.* 6s.

Watson (H. B. Marriott). THE HIG TOBY. *Third Edition. Cr. 8vo.* 6s.
THE PRIVATEERS. Illustrated. *Secon Edition. Cr. 8vo.* 6s.
ALISE OF ASTRA. *Third Edition. C 8vo.* 6s
THE BIG FISH. *Second Edition. Cr. 8 6s.

Webling (Peggy). THE STORY VIRGINIA PERFECT. *Third Edition Cr. 8vo.* 6s.
THE SPIRIT OF MIRTH. *Fifth Edition Cr. 8vo.* 6s.
FELIX CHRISTIE. *Second Edition. C 8vo.* 6s.

Weyman (Stanley). UNDER THE RE ROBE. Illustrated. *Twenty-third Editio Cr. 8vo.* 6s.

Whitby (Beatrice). ROSAMUND. *Secon Edition. Cr. 8vo.* 6s.

Williamson (C. N. and A. M.). THE LIGHTNING CONDUCTOR: The Strange Adventures of a Motor Car. Illustrated. *Seventeenth Edition. Cr. 8vo. 6s.* Also *Cr. 8vo. 1s. net.*

THE PRINCESS PASSES: A Romance of a Motor. Illustrated. *Ninth Edition. Cr. 8vo. 6s.*

LADY BETTY ACROSS THE WATER. *Eleventh Edition. Cr. 8vo. 6s.*

SCARLET RUNNER. Illustrated. *Third Edition. Cr. 8vo. 6s.*

SET IN SILVER. Illustrated. *Fourth Edition. Cr. 8vo. 6s.*

LORD LOVELAND DISCOVERS AMERICA. *Second Edition. Cr. 8vo. 6s.*

THE GOLDEN SILENCE. *Sixth Edition. Cr. 8vo. 6s.*

THE GUESTS OF HERCULES. *Third Edition. Cr. 8vo. 6s.*

*THE HEATHER MOON. *Cr. 8vo. 6s.*

Wyllarde (Dolf). THE PATHWAY OF THE PIONEER (Nous Autres). *Sixth Edition. Cr. 8vo. 6s.*

THE UNOFFICIAL HONEYMOON. *Seventh Edition. Cr. 8vo. 6s.*

THE CAREER OF BEAUTY DARLING. *Cr. 8vo. 6s.*

Methuen's Two-Shilling Novels.

Crown 8vo. 2s. net.

*BOTOR CHAPERON, THE. C. N. and A. M. Williamson.

*CALL OF THE BLOOD, THE. Robert Hichens.

CAR OF DESTINY AND ITS ERRAND IN SPAIN, THE. C. N. and A. M. Williamson.

CLEMENTINA. A. E. W. Mason.

COLONEL ENDERBY'S WIFE. Lucas Malet.

FELIX. Robert Hichens.

GATE OF THE DESERT, THE. John Oxenham.

MY FRIEND THE CHAUFFEUR. C. N. and A. M. Williamson.

PRINCESS VIRGINIA, THE. C. N. and A. M. Williamson.

SEATS OF THE MIGHTY, THE. Sir Gilbert Parker.

SERVANT OF THE PUBLIC, A. Anthony Hope.

*SET IN SILVER. C. N. and A. M. Williamson.

SEVERINS, THE. Mrs. Alfred Sidgwick.

SIR RICHARD CALMADY. Lucas Malet.

*VIVIEN. W. B. Maxwell.

Books for Boys and Girls.

Illustrated. Crown 8vo. 3s. 6d.

CROSS AND DAGGER. The Crusade of the Children, 1212. W. Scott Durrant.

GETTING WELL OF DOROTHY, THE. Mrs. W. K. Clifford.

GIRL OF THE PEOPLE, A. L. T. Meade.

HEPSY GIPSY. L. T. Meade. *2s. 6d.*

HONOURABLE MISS, THE. L. T. Meade.

MASTER ROCKAFELLAR'S VOYAGE. W. Clark Russell.

ONLY A GUARD-ROOM DOG. Edith E. Cuthell.

RED GRANGE, THE. Mrs. Molesworth.

SYD BELTON: The Boy who would not go to Sea. G. Manville Fenn.

THERE WAS ONCE A PRINCE. Mrs. M. E. Mann.

Methuen's Shilling Novels.

*ANNA OF THE FIVE TOWNS. Arnold Bennett.
BARBARY SHEEP. Robert Hichens.
CHARM, THE. Alice Perrin.
*DEMON, THE. C. N. and A. M. Williamson.
GUARDED FLAME, THE. W. B. Maxwell.
JANE. Marie Corelli.
LADY BETTY ACROSS THE WATER. C. N. & A. M. Williamson.
*LONG ROAD, THE. John Oxenham.
MIGHTY ATOM, THE. Marie Corelli.
MIRAGE. E. Temple Thurston.
MISSING DELORA, THE. E Phillips Oppenheim.

ROUND THE RED LAMP. Sir A. Conan Doyl
*SECRET WOMAN, THE. Eden Phillpotts.
*SEVERINS, THE. Mrs. Alfred Sidgwick.
SPANISH GOLD. G. A. Birmingham.
TALES OF MEAN STREETS. Arthur Morriso
THE HALO. The Baroness von Hutten.
*TYRANT, THE. Mrs. Henry de la Pasture
UNDER THE RED ROBE. Stanley J. Weym
VIRGINIA PERFECT. Peggy Webling.
WOMAN WITH THE FAN, THE. Rob Hichens.

The Novels of Alexandre Dumas.

Medium 8vo.　Price 6d.　Double Volumes, 1s.

ACTÉ.
ADVENTURES OF CAPTAIN PAMPHILE, THE.
AMAURY.
BIRD OF FATE, THE.
BLACK TULIP, THE.
BLACK : the Story of a Dog.
CASTLE OF EPPSTEIN, THE.
CATHERINE BLUM.
CÉCILE.
CHÂTELET, THE.
CHEVALIER D'HARMENTAL, THE. (Double volume.)
CHICOT THE JESTER.
CHICOT REDIVIVUS.
COMTE DE MONTGOMMERY, THE.
CONSCIENCE.
CONVICT'S SON, THE.
CORSICAN BROTHERS, THE ; and OTHO THE ARCHER.
CROP-EARED JACQUOT.
DOM GORENFLOT.
DUC D'ANJOU, THE.
FATAL COMBAT, THE.
FENCING MASTER, THE.
FERNANDE.
GABRIEL LAMBERT.
GEORGES.
GREAT MASSACRE, THE.
HENRI DE NAVARRE.
HÉLÈNE DE CHAVERNY.

HOROSCOPE, THE.
LEONE-LEONA.
LOUISE DE LA VALLIÈRE. (Double volum
MAN IN THE IRON MASK, THE. (Dou volume.)
MAÎTRE ADAM.
MOUTH OF HELL, THE.
NAHON. (Double volume.)
OLYMPIA.
PAULINE ; PASCAL BRUNO ; and BONTEKO
PÈRE LA RUINE.
PORTE SAINT-ANTOINE, THE.
PRINCE OF THIEVES, THE.
REMINISCENCES OF ANTONY, THE.
ST. QUENTIN.
ROBIN HOOD.
SAMUEL GELB.
SNOWBALL AND THE SULTANETTA, THE.
SYLVANDIRE.
TAKING OF CALAIS, THE.
TALES OF THE SUPERNATURAL.
TALES OF STRANGE ADVENTURE.
TALES OF TERROR.
THREE MUSKETEERS, THE. (Double volum
TOURNEY OF THE RUE ST. ANTOINE
TRAGEDY OF NANTES, THE.
TWENTY YEARS AFTER. (Double volum
WILD-DUCK SHOOTER, THE.
WOLF-LEADER, THE.

Methuen's Sixpenny Books.

Medium 8vo.

Albanesi (E Maria). LOVE AND LOUISA.
I KNOW A MAIDEN.
THE BLUNDER OF AN INNOCENT.
PETER A PARASITE.
*THE INVINCIBLE AMELIA.

Anstey (F.). A BAYARD OF BENGAL.

Austen (J.). PRIDE AND PREJUDICE.

Bagot (Richard). A ROMAN MYSTERY.
CASTING OF NETS.
DONNA DIANA.

Balfour (Andrew). BY STROKE OF SWORD.

Baring-Gould (S.). FURZE BLOOM.
CHEAP JACK ZITA.
KITTY ALONE.
URITH.
THE BROOM SQUIRE.
IN THE ROAR OF THE SEA.
NOÉMI.
A BOOK OF FAIRY TALES. Illustrated.
LITTLE TU'PENNY.
WINEFRED.
THE FROBISHERS.
THE QUEEN OF LOVE.
ARMINELL.
BLADYS OF THE STEWPONEY.
CHRIS OF ALL SORTS.

Barr (Robert). JENNIE BAXTER.
IN THE MIDST OF ALARMS.
THE COUNTESS TEKLA.
THE MUTABLE MANY.

Benson (E. F.). DODO.
THE VINTAGE.

Brontë (Charlotte). SHIRLEY.

Brownell (C. L.). THE HEART OF JAPAN.

Burton (J. Bloundelle). ACROSS THE SALT SEAS.

Caffyn (Mrs.). ANNE MAULEVERER.

Capes (Bernard). THE GREAT SKENE MYSTERY.

Clifford (Mrs. W. K.). A FLASH OF SUMMER.
MRS. KEITH'S CRIME.

Corbett (Julian). A BUSINESS I GREAT WATERS.

Croker (Mrs. B. M.). ANGEL.
A STATE SECRET.
PEGGY OF THE BARTONS.
JOHANNA.

Dante (Alighieri). THE DIVIN COMEDY (Cary).

Doyle (Sir A. Conan). ROUND TH RED LAMP.

Duncan (Sara Jeannette). THO DELIGHTFUL AMERICANS.

Eliot (George). THE MILL ON TH FLOSS.

Findlater (Jane H). THE GREE GRAVES OF BALGOWRIE.

Gallon (Tom). RICKERBY'S FOLLY.

Gaskell (Mrs.). CRANFORD.
MARY BARTON.
NORTH AND SOUTH.

Gerard (Dorothea). HOLY MATR MONY.
THE CONQUEST OF LONDON.
MADE OF MONEY.

Gissing (G.). THE TOWN TRAVELLE.
THE CROWN OF LIFE.

Glanville (Ernest). THE INCA' TREASURE.
THE KLOOF BRIDE.

Gleig (Charles). BUNTER'S CRUISE.

Grimm (The Brothers). GRIMM FAIRY TALES.

Hope (Anthony). A MAN OF MARK.
A CHANGE OF AIR.
THE CHRONICLES OF COUN ANTONIO.
PHROSO.
THE DOLLY DIALOGUES.

Hornung (E. W.). DEAD MEN TEL NO TALES.

Hyne (C. J. C.). PRINCE RUPERT TH BUCCANEER.

Ingraham (J. H.). THE THRONE C DAVID.

Le Queux (W.). THE HUNCHBACK OF WESTMINSTER.
THE CROOKED WAY.
THE VALLEY OF THE SHADOW.

Levett-Yeats (S. K.). THE TRAITOR'S WAY.
ORRAIN.

Linton (E. Lynn). THE TRUE HISTORY OF JOSHUA DAVIDSON.

Lyall (Edna). DERRICK VAUGHAN.

Malet (Lucas). THE CARISSIMA.
A COUNSEL OF PERFECTION.

Mann (Mrs. M. E.). MRS. PETER HOWARD.
A LOST ESTATE.
THE CEDAR STAR.
THE PATTEN EXPERIMENT.
A WINTER'S TALE.

Marchmont (A. W.). MISER HOADLEY'S SECRET.
A MOMENT'S ERROR.

Marryat (Captain). PETER SIMPLE.
JACOB FAITHFUL.

March (Richard). A METAMORPHOSIS.
THE TWICKENHAM PEERAGE.
THE GODDESS.
THE JOSS.

Mason (A. E. W.). CLEMENTINA.

Mathers (Helen). HONEY.
GRIFF OF GRIFFITHSCOURT
SAM'S SWEETHEART.
THE FERRYMAN.

Meade (Mrs. L. T.). DRIFT.

Miller (Esther). LIVING LIES.

Mitford (Bertram). THE SIGN OF THE SPIDER.

Montrésor (F. F.). THE ALIEN.

Morrison (Arthur). THE HOLE IN THE WALL.

Nesbit (E.). THE RED HOUSE.

Norris (W. E.). HIS GRACE.
GILES INGILBY.
THE CREDIT OF THE COUNTY.
LORD LEONARD THE LUCKLESS.
MATTHEW AUSTEN.
CLARISSA FURIOSA.

Oliphant (Mrs.). THE LADY'S WALK.
SIR ROBERT'S FORTUNE.

THE PRODIGALS.
THE TWO MARYS.

Oppenheim (E. P.). MASTER OF MEN

Parker (Sir Gilbert). THE POMP C
THE LAVILETTES.
WHEN VALMOND CAME TO PONTIA
THE TRAIL OF THE SWORD.

Pemberton (Max). THE FOOTSTE OF A THRONE.
I CROWN THEE KING.

Phillpotts (Eden). THE HUMAN BO
CHILDREN OF THE MIST.
THE POACHER'S WIFE.
THE RIVER.

'Q' (A. T. Quiller Couch). T H WHITE WOLF.

Ridge (W. Pett). A SON OF THE STAT
LOST PROPERTY.
GEORGE and THE GENERAL.
A BREAKER OF LAWS.
ERB.

Russell (W. Clark). ABANDONED.
A MARRIAGE AT SEA.
MY DANISH SWEETHEART.
HIS ISLAND PRINCESS.

Sergeant (Adeline). THE MASTER BEECHWOOD.
BALBARA'S MONEY.
THE YELLOW DIAMOND.
THE LOVE THAT OVERCAME.

Sidgwick (Mrs. Alfred). THE KIN MAN.

Surtees (R. S.). HANDLEY CROSS.
MR. SPONGE'S SPORTING TOUR.
ASK MAMMA.

Walford (Mrs. L. B.). MR. SMITH.
COUSINS.
THE BABY'S GRANDMOTHER.
TROUBLESOME DAUGHTERS.

Wallace (General Lew). BEN-HUR.
THE FAIR GOD.

Watson (H. B. Marriott). THE ADVE TURERS.
CAPTAIN FORTUNE.

Weekes (A. B.). PRISONERS OF WA

Wells (H. G.). THE SEA LADY.

Whitby (Beatrice). THE RESULT AN ACCIDENT.

White (Percy). A PASSIONATE PI GRIM.

Williamson (Mrs. C. N.). PAPA.

PRINTED BY
UNWIN BROTHERS, LIMITED,
LONDON AND WOKING.